RECENT BORZOI FICTION

DEFY THE FOUL FIEND
by John Collier

PRAYER FOR THE LIVING
by Bruce Marshall

ANOTHER CAESAR
by Alfred Neumann

THE PROUD AND THE MEEK
by Jules Romains

AND QUIET FLOWS THE DON
by Mikhail Sholokhov

PUBLISHED BY ALFRED A. KNOPF

HARVEST IN THE NORTH

Harvest
in the
NORTH

<small>BY</small>

James Lansdale Hodson

19 34

NEW YORK · ALFRED · A · KNOPF

To
A. M.
for the help of
constant criticism

BOOK I

Chapter One

THERE ARE OCCASIONS in the story of mankind when enormous groups of people have behaved with, as is plain afterwards, an insanity that is well-nigh complete, and have remained unaware that they were acting strangely. A no-more-war man would assert, no doubt, that every war in history is a manifestation of that sort; but before (or after) coming to that conclusion you may well ponder on whether man is able to shape his course, and whether Napoleon actually won his battles or had victory bestowed on him by a succession or assembly of minor acts and circumstances over which he had no control; whether, therefore, he was anything more than a figure who suited Destiny or God or whatever you will to take a leading part in an event to be performed at a certain time in the world's history, designed to achieve a certain end. If that is what he was and Lenin was, and what Mussolini is and Hitler is and Gandhi is, we may observe them as museum pieces or stage figures and reflect on how seldom it is that the tragic-comedians holding the centre of the stage are chosen from the aristocracy; but as for praise or abuse, worship or blame—they are entitled neither to the one nor the other. And so you may, perhaps, believe that, as the plankton on which the herring feeds rises to the surface of the sea at its appointed time, and as the billions of micro-organisms in a teaspoonful of garden

3

soil vary according to the hour of day, as, in short, the earth moves to its set rhythm whether in the sun and stars or in the land and the waters, so peoples rise and decline, so men speak the words put into their mouths, so they build up or break down, so they murder or they bring salvation; and temporary madness (as it afterwards seems) you may hold to be but one of the stock devices used for accomplishing the Divine purpose, or the purpose of whoever or whatever holds this world in thrall.

.   .   .   .

You may walk from Burnham Town Hall to Saddlebridge Town Hall in twenty minutes, but in that brief space of time you will have made a prodigious journey in spirit and out-look; you will have travelled from the gentlemen who merchant to the men who manufacture; from streets of massive cotton and velvet warehouses, insurance offices, banks, and emporiums, to streets of ironworks and mills and corner shops; from speech that may or may not be coloured and flavoured with the abruptness and salt humour of Lancashire to speech that leaves you in no sort of doubt that you are not only in the North and in Lancashire, but in Saddlebridge and nowhere but Saddlebridge. For Saddle-bridge talk is not so slow nor so pure as that of Burnley or Preston or Bolton. Saddlebridge has the crisp, biting wit of the city mixed with the slang of the gutter and the American film, and its Lancashire speech has the additional defilement of cutting off almost all the middle "t" in such a phrase as "Got it?"—a trick which speaks of the slums—and of using the word "us" instead of "our." "It is time for us to 'ave us tea," a Saddlebridge man will say, and his friend from Burnley will think: "By the mon, why corn't 'e talk proper and say *'eawr* tay'?" But let it be put on record that Saddlebridge supports a Rugby football club whereas Burnham goes in its scores of thousands to watch Soccer (a game which Saddlebridge regards as a mongrel, mincing, and comparatively girlish pastime), that Saddlebridge makes the stuff that Burnham sells, that Saddlebridge boasts a fairground and something of the Elizabethan atmosphere in its boxing-booths, steam swing-boats, and gondolas, and that Burnham and more remote parts of Lancashire are glad to consume Saddlebridge's cow-heels and tripe and black puddings and to keep themselves warm with its aromatic and penetrating cough-drops and sports tablets.

. . . .

I have said you may walk from Burnham Town Hall to Saddlebridge Town Hall in twenty minutes. It seemed a good deal longer than that to Mrs. Harriet Renshaw who had put on a pair of boots that cold afternoon in early March 1920; for Mrs. Renshaw thought nothing of boots. She had done her washing in clogs and gone to church in clogs and all her children had worn clogs also. Her faith in clogs had made life a little harder to bear—for neighbours had begun to say she was both stuck-up and stubborn in not wearing the shoes she could afford—but Harriet Renshaw could stand that. She had been compelled to bear a great deal, had Harriet. For too long the gift of children had been withheld from her and now the gift had been bestowed far too abundantly. Harriet was forty-five, and she had now five children, the eldest of whom was nine years old; and he, George, seemed to have less sense than any of the others. Why *was* the eldest so often a bit "doolally" compared with the rest, wondered Harriet, limping slightly. Sam, when he was a bit tiddly the other night, had said he reckoned God did it to make sure you had some more childer—since nobody would

be satisfied with one that had "broken threads." Sam had
laughed about it, as he did about most things. No relying on
him; no knowing what *he* would do, she was thinking. Sam
was a "masher," as they said in Chesterford; too good-looking, too fond of his gill, too expert at putting his arm round a
girl's shoulder; there was not a ginnel in Chesterford where
he hadn't courted a girl at one time or another, they said. And
Harriet knew well enough what was said when he started
courting *her;* but it made no difference. When he first came to
her with his jaunty walk, his fine grey eyes that twinkled so,
his brown, long moustache over red, finely curved lips, and
asked her to let him take her for a walk on the moor, her
knees had trembled; and when he had put his arms round her
and kissed her, her blood might have turned to water, she
had felt so weak. He could have done what he wanted with
her. It was still very much the same to-day, fifteen years afterwards. Whatever he wanted he could have. She might listen
with wildly beating heart to the gossip of how he had been
drinking with that fly-by-night who sang in the Black Bull,
she knew too well how he threw money away on football
coupons and horses, but it made no difference—not when he
came near to her. He had only to approach her and take
hold of her arm, or put his lips behind her ear, or his arm
round her waist so that his fingers touched her breast; and
she knew she loved him as intensely and utterly as when he
first took her.

If Sam had been less of a scamp she wouldn't have been
trapesing down John Porter Street this afternoon, she was
thinking. "Here I am," she thought, "gettin' forms to apply
for Corporation Bonds as if I was a millionaire—all because
Sam had a bit o' luck wi' his fifty pounds in t' mill—gettin'
fifteen pound ten for every quid he had. An' if I'm not sharp
it'll all be gone. Sam'll put it into summat as'll go bang. An'
this seven hundred an' seventy-five pounds must be saved for

the childer. There'll never be another chance." So she had put
her boots on—a great concession that, to wealth and style;
but she remembered, too, how the corridors at Burnham
Town Hall rasped to your clogs and threatened to slide your
feet from under you. And, anyhow, it would attract less attention, she thought, if a woman in shoes asked for forms.
The whole affair had required a good deal of arrangement;
persuading Mrs. Edmunds next door to take young Sam
and Bessie, the two youngest, making sure Aunt Alice
wouldn't mind the other three going for tea after school.
Sam had nearly wrecked the conspiracy too by announcing
after his dinner that he didn't feel very well and he thought
an afternoon off wouldn't hurt him, but luckily Tom Edmunds—Tom who mixed weaving and barbering—had
shouted over the back-yard wall that he knew something to
put your vest on for the three-thirty, by gow, and he and Sam
had hurried off to make a little more "money for nowt," as
Tom called it. She had had to hurry after that—to wash
herself, to take out her Sunday clothes, do her hair so that
she could pin on the blue velvet hat that wasn't quite big
enough, but which Sam liked better than any other, and get
her boots on. The boots, glacé kid with patent-leather toes,
had been 10s. 11d. at the Co-operative Stores, and she had
begrudged the money. She was never quite sure that the discomfort they inflicted on her wasn't deserved for pandering
to fashion like that, but this was a "do," she thought. The
tram conductor, who knew her, had joked about the "March
Wakes" being on, and asked her— "Can anybody come?"
but she was in no mood for banter—least of all, Harry Sharp-
les's banter. "Nay," she had said, "it upsets me even to have
my ticket punched by *thee*." And, saying it with her sallow
face as impassive as a stone image and her eyes void of either
anger or amusement, looking not at him but past him, he had
been silenced; not an easy thing to do in Chesterford, where

you and your husband and your children and your family
were known as intimately as All Saints' Church clock. She
had got off the tram at Burnham and walked, a tall woman
with a touch of hauteur in her carriage, down Cardigan
Street. Trams clanged past her, mighty saloon cars rolled
arrogantly by, boys whisked close to her, yelling early edi-
tions of the evening papers, salesmen and yarn agents and
brokers lounged along, smoking cigars and looking podgy
and complacent. She was feeling far less self-contained than
she looked; Burnham was an ordeal. She might be a power in
Lavender Street, Chesterford, but Burnham was different.
She thought: "If a tram knocked me down in Chesterford,
it 'ud make a stir, but here . . . I doubt if they'd pick me
up." Having made that admission, and knowing it was rather
overstating it, she felt better. She pushed open the heavy door
of the Town Hall, walked past Mr. Gladstone in marble
and past another stone gentleman in flowing dressing-gown
whom she did not recognise but who was taking his ease half
reclined and examining in perpetuity something that seemed
to her to be a cross between an hourglass and the works of a
clock. She walked to and fro in the dim pillared corridors.
She found almost every department in the Town Hall—
Police, Water Board, Gas Department, Town Clerk—before she lighted on the City Treasurer's office, and when she
did find the door she could not believe it was the right one.
For it was solid and merely said: "City Treasurer," in black
on painted oak. And she could not believe it was on that door
she must knock. She didn't want the Treasurer; nothing but
a form. She stared at the door and walked past, hoping to
find something less forbidding, returned, and stared once
more. A doorkeeper in a tall hat, braided with dirty gold,
passed, looked at her, cocking his head and wiping his mouth,
while she pretended she was admiring a heavily leaded

stained-glass window. She sat down and nursed her feet, leaning her back against the black Portland stone of the window corner and thinking what a coward she was. Finally, as if almost without control over herself, she rose quite rapidly, walked to the door, knocked and waited. Nothing happened. She gently turned the knob of the door, pushed it slowly, for it was heavy, and sidled through the space, making sure not to open more than was needful. There was a breast-high counter and she walked to it and looked over. Nobody there. But there was a bell with a sort of trigger and a notice printed on a small card which said: "Ring for attention." That seemed a bit cheeky, she thought. She didn't like ringing, as if it were a shop. She carefully looked all round and tentatively pressed the trigger down—so softly that it just flicked the metal and emitted a sharp click. She waited, lifting her right foot off the tiled floor to ease it. She tried the bell again, this time with some firmness and the bell rang and rang so that she put her finger on to stop it. A benevolent man with a beard and frock coat who looked at her over gold-rimmed spectacles came and said kindly and interrogatively: "Yes?"

"I want a form to put some money into t' Corporation, please," she said.

"Your own, madam, or on behalf of a minor?"

"My husband's." She flushed a little, wondering what a miner had to do with it.

He pursed his lips so that the bottom of his beard moved forward a little and he took a form from beneath the counter, and handed it delicately to her. He spoke no more. She took the form which she wanted to begin to read but didn't dare to, and she folded it up precisely, thinking it was akin to folding a sheet or a handkerchief on washing-day—and put it in her bosom. When she got outside she found her eyes and her hands slightly moist through nervousness and was ashamed; but the feeling soon passed. She had the form; that was what mattered.

And now she was walking down John Porter Street to Saddlebridge because, although Burnham Corporation might be safe enough, she had no intention of putting all her eggs into one basket. Her head was beginning to ache. The blue hat was pressing too tightly on her forehead and she pushed it back a little but when she caught sight of herself in a darkly curtained window she saw that she looked a little drunk and she pulled the hat down again. The afternoon was growing colder. A wind was blowing dirt along the footpath, picking up chaff and bits of sharp straw from between the cobbles and hurtling them at her face. It occurred to her that she ought to have taken a tram but she had wanted to be quiet and less part of a community than a tram makes you, and she had unconsciously, too, been saving the fare—a stupid act she knew, considering how Sam threw money away. But she and Sam were different. One spendthrift was enough in a house. And she wouldn't take a tram now because she was half-way there and the money would be wasted. She walked on, watching a lorry-wheel that had a bright iron chain slipped through the spokes to prevent it revolving so that it might be turned into a brake. The wheel was sliding over the cobbles and throwing the lorry slightly askew and the horse shook its head, wondering, no doubt, what was amiss. Electric trams went by, their drivers stamping impatiently on their gongs to keep the lorries laden with packing-cases off the lines. Over the river bridge which was Saddlebridge boundary she caught a glimpse of some young men in dirty cotton shorts and sweaters stooping to put a rowing skiff in the murky water flowing sluggishly, the colour of an unleaded kitchen grate, among fat barges. She hurried on, past a pipe hospital and two public-houses both so flamboyant with coloured tiles and brass rods guarding doors and windows that she wondered how they could both pay their way at the end of this dingy street, and what drew men into the red-tiled Lord Nelson rather than the blue-tiled Angel or *vice versa*. Into the Angel cellar a drayman and his mate were lowering a barrel on ropes through a street trap-door. The drayman with his billycock on the back of his head was braced backwards stiffly at an angle, singing in grunts—"She—was a—sweet lick-le—dicky—bird—cheep—cheep-cheep—she went"—as the barrel descended in small jerks. She had to wait a moment to get past and he walked to the edge of the opening and winked envelopingly at her, saying: "Aye, she was an' all, missis. Mind the rope, lady, don't want no accidents 'ere, as the 'angman said, askin' 'im if 'e'd have a drop." She couldn't help smiling and he lifted his billycock and gave her another wink, smaller this time—no more than a confidential twitch of the muscle. She walked past and felt his small brown eyes following her, and wondered—but quickly discarded the thought again as unworthy —what would become of *her* if anything happened to Sam and whether anybody would offer for her. She felt the blood suffusing her face and her back tingling in her confusion and discomfort as a vision of the stout drayman flashed through her mind. The roar of a train over the overhead bridge helped to drown her thoughts and when she had rounded Deanhouse Lane and paused to look in the piano shop with its array of violins, flageolets, mouth-organs, kettle-drums and tin whistles, she had forgotten the drayman and was reflecting whether she oughtn't to persuade Sam to buy a piano. "Our George," she was thinking, "may be a numbyed at sums but he might be a bobby-dazzler at a piano—you never know. Geniuses are a bit daft, they say." But if they bought a piano it must be paid for—she couldn't abide having anything on tick; she had had a rare fight with Sam to stop him furnishing the second bedroom immediately they got married. She could hear him now, saying jocosely as he put his arm round her: "You want to make sure I don't go and sleep somewhere else, eh?" and then his kissing her and saying he was sorry, when tears had started to her eyes. Sam was quick to know when he had hurt her; she thanked God for that. He could see as far through her as she could through him; they didn't need to tell one another much. She had heard it said you grew to be like the folk you lived with; she supposed there was a lot in it. Past tripe shops she went, past Oldroyd, the jeweller, sitting in his window with a magnifying glass screwed, an aluminium cylinder, in his eye; past the art-metal works, past the religious shop, full of Virgins and the Child, that exuded from its door a faint smell of incense; past three more public-houses and an off-licence, past the corn-chandler's, a social menace to-day the way it filled your eyes and nose with grain dust; past two solicitors who occupied former sweets shops and had hung their windows with faded green-baize curtains which made a fine looking-glass for all the passers-by; past the "Twenty-five-shillings tailors" and the dentist who had placed a set of false teeth with big red gums over his fanlight; past old Mitcham, bald as Mr. Punch and twice as lively, still putting up a fight, in his tiny grocer's shop, against the Home and Colonial; past Vickers's pawnshop with windows crammed with watches, binoculars, clarinets, old silver, chains, lockets, shooting rifles, boots, brooches, flutes, violoncellos, rings, bracelets, cutlery, all marked in indelible figures that had run so thick that it was a morning's work to take your fill of all the treasures and note their prices; past the midwife's and the surgery of Dr. Bentley who refused to give up his dog-cart and wore a stiff white cravat like a horse-dealer; and then, rather unexpectedly, to the Town Hall; for Saddlebridge Town Hall was modest to the point of retirement. It had retired as far as it could among cottage property and stood, aged, faded and Victorian, a cross between a chapel of ease and a masonic hall, at the back of Montgomery Square. You could hire it for a dance for five pounds or you could, at week-ends, play hopscotch over its front steps with impunity. Nevertheless it *was* the Town Hall and to Harriet it presented a homely and altogether admirable sight. She had no feeling of awe when she looked on it and she pushed open its glass door—much easier to push than the one at Burnham—and walked in almost as if she belonged there. And when she saw, surprisingly, a footman in knee-breeches and a gold-braided coat, wearing a stiff shirt and white tie, she announced almost truculently: "I want to see t' Treasurer," as if seeing the Treasurer was what she was in the habit of doing every afternoon at ten minutes past four. For that was now the time.

"Madam," he said, "the Treasurer has gone 'ome."

But she was not to be dismayed. "Happen," she said, "somebody else'll do. Where do I go?" He walked to the second pair of glass doors and drew one back. She had never seen anybody move like him; it was as if his body and head were immovable, almost like a doll running on wheels. She thought: "We ought to have one o' these in Chesterford." Her levity was beginning to surprise her.

"Second on the right, madam." But he was looking straight ahead like a soldier on parade. She felt he disowned her, took no responsibility for her. She wanted to say: "I'll bet *tha* weren't born i' Saddlebridge," but she didn't. She gave him a curt nod which made the blue hat move unsteadily on her head and strode over the immense mat ten yards wide. The door that was indicated admitted her to a large room crowded with men stooping under green lamps on high long desks surmounted with brass rails bearing ledgers. Near the door was an enamel sign—"Enquiries," but nobody was sitting near it. She waited a long time there and presently

walked farther down to a young man with a sharp nose and
jet black hair that was parted in the middle and fell in slight
disarray over his forehead. She noticed he had a pen over
each ear—one red ink, one black—and a blue pencil hori-
zontal in his mouth. He took no notice of her whatever. She
said: "Hem!" but he never even heard it. She might have
been invisible, for all the attention she attracted.

Harriet stood there a while longer, growing hot with in-
dignation. Suddenly, containing herself no longer, she said:
"Here! what do you think y'are? A post-office?" The young
man raised his head, lifting his chin so that he looked down
his face at her, and pointed with his pencil to the end of the
desk where the enamel plate was. But Harriet's blood was
up. "Are you deaf and dumb, or is it only daft?" she said.
"*I* don't live i' Saddlebridge, nor I don't want to. *I*'ve come
fro' Chesterford, and I want a form to put some brass into
your owd Corporation, and I'm stoppin' here till I get it."
Half a dozen clerks lifted their heads and gazed at her—
one or two incredulously; one or two smiled. Somebody said:
"Go on, Jackson, attend to her." But all Jackson said was,
plaintively: "You know *you* can't come here talking like
this." "Oh?" she said, "why can't I?"; but he was going on
wearily: "Why don't you find out the right *place*? This is the
gas-bill department—and besides, we're reely *closed*—just
making up accounts. And *you* want the stock and bond office."

"Wheer is it?"

"It's across the corridor—a wide door—the name's
written on it. But *they* shut at four o'clock, anyhow."

"If you'd wakened up sooner I might ha' been in time."
This wasn't true, as Harriet was well aware, but she couldn't
help saying it. She was so angry she could have cried.

"Nay, reely," he said, "you know you can't go on like
this. Why didn't you *write* for a form—so easy—just a post-
card—a ha'penny stamp. You know people come *long* dis-

tances when a ha'penny stamp . . ."

Oh, what a fool the man was—thinking she could sit down like a sixpenny lawyer and send letters and postcards. "I wonder you don't ask me to ring on my telephone," she said with fine scorn, tossing her head and dislodging the blue hat slightly again. "I do believe this office is full o' forms," she said, staring so hard at him that he flinched.

"Nay, reelly . . ."

"And as for shutting up at four o'clock—did you ever hear tell o' the bank clerk who went to lock the front door at three o'clock when t' day were finished and who found he had forgotten to *unlock* it in t' morning? He must ha' served his apprenticeship i' this place."

She turned and went. Nobody laughed at the story. Jackson thought: "Well, reelly, people are awful," and bent over his figures again. Harriet walked back over the enormous mat. The flunkey was still there gazing at but not perceiving the fat pigeons hopping about the front steps. He turned and glanced towards her and she said: "Well, it won't be *my* money as'll pay your wages," but she might have been talking Hindustani for all the sign of enlightenment he gave. Outside in Montgomery Square she felt the wind biting into her legs and breast and with the cold a sense of failure swept over her. No Saddlebridge form—probably the children had had no tea—perhaps young Sam and Bessie were crying for her—and Sam himself might be home before her and wonder what she had been up to and disbelieve her tale; after all, why *had* she been secretive? It was all plain as daylight to her but Sam wouldn't see it. And oh, her head ached so and she wished to God she was back home in Lavender Street where folk took notice of what she said and asked her advice even if she *was* pronounced "stuck up." She must hurry, but it was difficult because she was sure her feet had swollen. Had she time to go into a shop and have a cup of tea and unlace her boots? She hadn't wanted a cup of tea so much since young Sam was born. She looked longingly into a confectioner's, but she didn't stop. No, she would go home, and she must go back into Burnham by tram, too. Where did they stop? She glanced up and down Deanhouse Lane, but it was growing dusk and the standards with STOP on them were in the centre of the road and difficult to see. A tram came jangling by and pulled up with grinding brakes fifteen yards ahead. She waved, the conductor saw her, and she began a stumbling run. She was two yards off when he stood with his hand on the bell-push, a man with tilted nose, false teeth grinning and a waxed moustache, and as her right foot reached the bottom step he grinned more widely, and pressed the bell. With a terrific jerk the car started, and she realised with a horrid certainty that she was not on it. She was swung round, her right arm was drawn sickeningly taut as she clung to the brass rail, there was a furious bang in the middle of her back as if someone had kicked her and . . . and then she heard somebody saying (it was Dr. Bentley, but she didn't know): "She'd better be taken home in a cab. Winded, that's all, and bruised, and knocked about." She shut her eyes again, thinking, "Knocked about—aye! One o' the monuments Cromwell knocked about a bit." The music-hall line ran through her head. She had a curious, child-like desire to hear what else they would say about her. She felt her face puckering stiffly into a foolish smile, and then hot tears were running down her cheeks and she began to sob. She sobbed uncontrollably as she had done as a little girl, sobbed as though the world were in pieces and her heart broken. She was crying on behalf of Sam and of her children, who would all be wanting her, and because she hadn't obtained a form for Saddlebridge Corporation Stock, and hadn't had her tea, and because her boots had hurt her so and her hat had tortured her, and because that conductor with the grin and waxed moustache had been cruel.

But she didn't know these things. She only knew she hadn't cried like that for thirty-five years, and that she couldn't believe she would ever stop, and that, as she cried, her misery and bitter distress were being, somehow, slowly washed away.

•   •   •   •   •   •   •   •

It was half-past six when Harriet's taxi-cab pulled up with a squeak at 23 Lavender Street. She pushed herself up from the seat where the cab's swinging round corners had thrown her in a half-reclining position and picked up the bent and soiled blue velvet hat that had been jerked off the seat on to the floor. Her hands were stiff and brittle with dirt (they had washed her face and overlooked her hands) and she found them crooked as if with rheumatism when she laboriously fumbled with the door catch. The driver all at once snatched the door viciously open and she well-nigh fell on him. " 'Ere, 'ere," he said, "take it easy now, take it easy. That's a daisy" —helping her to stand steady.

"How much is it?" she asked. But the anticipation of his reply didn't frighten her. She was beyond being frightened of anything. If he had said, "Five pounds," she wouldn't have wondered. She was living in a sort of Arabian Night when anything might happen. But he said: "Nine an' six," and she walked a little giddily across the pavement to where her door with its scrupulously stoned step and pavement glinted ghostly grey in the dusk and the pot-grey and gold spaniel sat in the fanlight over the door looking across the street with the tip of his red tongue showing. The door was open but nobody was in—she could hear the clatter of small feet and tinkle of children's laughter next door in Mrs. Edmunds's. That was where they were, then. Nobody was bothering, it seemed. She fumbled in the second shelf of the cupboard behind the tea-caddy for the old china teapot, lifted it down, and took from it the ten-shilling note she had put away towards the gas bill, and stared for a moment at the fire which leapt up and down warmly, cosily, making her feel safe and at home. Tears sprang into her eyes and she wiped them away with the back of her harsh, dirty hand, smearing her nose and cheeks. After she had paid the man and before she had lit the gas the lobby was suddenly filled with a tornado of children, yelling, scampering, bursting into the kitchen and hurling themselves on her. "Mum! Where've you bin, mum? . . . What 'ave you brought me back, mum? . . . Mum, I'd five slices o' bread for tea, mum. . . . Mum, daddy's not bin 'ome yet . . . Mum, our George got t' cane for readin' a boy's paper durin' sums. . . . Didn't . . . Yes, you told us . . . What's up, mum, you look funny . . . Mum, your face is dirty . . . Mum . . . mum . . . mum, what . . . what . . . what . . ."

She thought the children would never be got off to bed. She thought Mrs. Edmunds would never go and leave her alone. She thought Sam would never come home. But those things duly happened; and Sam came home. It was half-past eight. He stood about a yard and a half away from her. His cap was pushed back and his cheeks were flushed and his grey eyes were radiant with excitement and drink. He waved his right hand in a magniloquent gesture. " 'Arriet, mi lass," he said, "I've done a . . . done a deal, mi lass. I'm a dam' share-broker, lass. What dost think o' that, eh? A pro-proceshional —profeshional chap now, mi lass. We'll show 'em. We'll show 'em who's who. An' I've done a deal, too . . . I have an' all . . . Some on 'em think I'm a dam' numbyed but I'll bloody-well . . . Sorry, lass. Didn't mean to swear. Aye, I've done a deal . . . A thousand shares at fifteen bob. . . . Two fifty Wigtan . . . two fifty Sandiway . . . two e, sir. Does 'e know 'e's for the 'igh jump?"

ere's to be no high jump. The war's over. Though I

mes think it's finished a bit too soon." The long slender

of his left hand gripped the black, figured wheel till

uckles shone white through the pale skin. "These

es at the mill who're getting six pounds a week and

ng it should be ten—and who were on velvet while we

Well, what the devil were we?" He turned and looked

otter's sharp nose under his peaked cap. Trotter with

in wide mouth screwed up, his eyes creased shrewdly till

were surrounded by crow's-feet, and his head cocked a

was staring disapprovingly at a coal-pit they were pass-

from which there was issuing a spasmodic stream of

-looking, grimy-faced men, wearing old, dirty, decrepit

ts dangling open in the keen wind, and black-grey shirts

hed over the tops of their belted trousers—trousers

ed and grown short with crouching and kneeling till

frayed ends barely reached the tops of their heavy

l-pointed clogs. Trotter felt Houghton's eyes on him

turned and grinned.

What was we, sir? The lousiest troops in France." After

ment he went on: "When I see them blokes comin' aht

at coal dug-out lookin' 'arf dead I'm glad my ole man

a barrer dahn Lime'ouse. The war's still on 'ere, it looks

e. No wonder they was good diggers. The trenches must

bin like a day out on the allotment arter this. Wouldn't

that job, sir, fer a pension—pickin' and shovellin' in a

e 'ole, 'arf undressed."

There's some I know would be glad enough," Houghton

drily.

n the valley on their right the mills were springing into

t. Beyond them the scarred grey-green slopes were losing

at colour had been theirs, and the sky was turning a darker

sh of grey. At their foot the square, dark shapes of

fifty Derrick . . . an' two fifty Polar. Best bargain to-neet I'm tellin' thee. . . ."

She watched him, fascinated, and the small strength that was left in her was drained out of her. A thousand shares at fifteen shillings. Seven hundred and fifty pounds. Seven hundred and fifty pounds. Seven hundred and fifty . . .

Sam was going on. He was too drunk to notice anything wrong with her.

"Aye, lass, we'st make a bloody fortune . . . Sorry, 'Arriet, didn't mean to swear. Make a fortune, I'm tellin' thee . . ."

She got up and took the kettle which had boiled itself nearly dry and fumbled her way off to the scullery tap to fill it. Sam lurched half a pace back to let her go by.

"Tha doesn't seem so dam' pleased, neither," he said.

Chapter Two

IF MRS. HARRIET RENSHAW, walking down John Porter Street, had closely observed the traffic that went by, she would have seen a dark-red saloon car with a long metal bonnet impatiently threading its way round tramway-cars and lorries, and shooting forward, as if released from a spring, every time a clear stretch of forty or fifty yards occurred. And if Harriet had noticed it, she would undoubtedly have thought, "Hullo! There goes t' fire engine!" For this car was known in Chesterford and often received that greeting. It was not ill-deserved. None moved quite so fast, none had a similar musical horn of four ascending and three descending notes. You might have pronounced the horn triumphant or mocking or merely a damned nuisance. Chesterford by turns pronounced it all three, though in more decorative and decisive language. Chesterford also asserted in its four-ale bars and wine vaults, when the car was heard to go by, that if anybody but Philip Houghton had owned it, he would have been locked up long since. "It's losin' his arm, as has done it," they said. Or, "He thinks he's a bloomin' Nelson wi' his sleeve pinned across him." Or, "He cares for nowt but horse-racin', and when he does gie us a tip, it's a loser." Or, "Let him be. He's never had an accident yet, has he?" "No, but if th'art not quick, th'art dead aw reet."

At the corner of Deanhouse Lane the car turned right,

raced past the triangular plot o[...]
the organ of a lonely set of gond[...]
You Were the Only Girl in the W[...]
road past the black Gothic mass o[...]
and began to climb the hill on to t[...]
six miles between Linthorpe and [...]
County Borough of Chesterford s[...]
land—the well-to-do live, appropr[...]
Chesterford Edge, and the worki[...]
known broadly as Paradise Meado[...]
eighty cotton mills are littered higg[...]
town, here in clusters, there along [...]
regular intervals, yonder hugging th[...]
comparative isolation alongside wa[...]
puddles and hen-cotes. But wherever [...]
the neighbourhood—stiff, square, red[...]
seventy or eighty feet high, with inn[...]
every side, and the chimneys thrustin[...]
lar or hexagonal forms (on which t[...]
blazoned in white tiles) another hund[...]
endeavour to carry the contaminating[...]
stead of to Chesterford. (Vain attempt[...]
ford's women spend a fourth of their w[...]
ing that smoke and cleansing themselv[...]
and their houses from it. But they sel[...]
think about it, and if they did they woul[...]
as being inevitable—as the price that m[...]
ton, in like manner as death and mutila[...]
price to be paid for coal.)

As the car climbed the rise to Linthorp[...]
to his chauffeur, who was sitting beside hin[...]
Henderson's coming round to-night, Tro[...]

"Him you threatened wiv' a revolver[...]
sir?" Trotter whistled like a shell that is [...]

factories, with a window here and there, had been catching
a momentary gleam of light from the setting sun and flashing
half-gold, half-ruby.

"Like Gawd A'mighty doin' a bit o' heliographin' ain't
it?" Trotter had remarked the first night he witnessed it.
Now he said: "I'd like to press the button wot lights up
them mills. Magic, eh? I used to follow the lamplighter
rahnd when I was a kid, watchin' 'im workin' the oricle.
My first ambition that was—lamp lightin'. I used ter think
when I grew up an' I 'ad the job I'd light 'em up specially
early-like, to give everybody a treat."

Houghton didn't hear him. He was back at Martinpuich
the night the shell had got him and he had felt himself rising
into the air with heavily ringing bells in his ears. Often on a
winter's night such as this, when the light was leaving the
earth and the ground grew cold and the chill brought a sharp
tickling cough to his throat he lived over again the hour or
two before it happened; the going out to fix the first listening-
post with Trotter waddling over the mud behind him. But
memory went further back than that, too. Madam Bourdain
in his billet had been curiously sad when he was saying *au re-
voir* that morning—had besought him to kneel with her before her tiny draped crucifix that stood before the Virgin; and
he had done it to please her. She had stood as he rode out of
the farmyard, her right hand raised aloft and her lips moving
in her broad pale face framed in a black neckerchief. Over
tea in the dug-out Templeman had been saying aloud in
his vibrant barytone, ranting to hide his love of it, Mere-
dith's—

> "Pitch here the tent, while the old horse grazes;
>   By the old hedge-side we'll halt a stage.
> It's nigh my last above the daisies:
>   My next leaf'll be man's blank page.

Yes, my old girl! and it's no use crying:
Juggler, constable, king, must bow.
One that outjuggles all's been spying
Long to have me, and he has me now."

The mud was slime on the top when he (Houghton) wriggled out on his stomach, Trotter and the corporal and two men strung out behind him like the tail of a brontosaurus. The damp mist linking day with night was rising and the sweet fœtid smell of death was in his nostrils. "Pitch here the tent . . ." How foul the soil was. The shell had dropped close, he knew, and they all waited, faces in the ground. Then followed the erupting earth and a roaring in his head and the terrible jangle of bells and himself rising. "One that outjuggles all . . ." the words galloping like thunder. Nothing more till the dressing-station and the sickly smell of chloroform and the retching and wanting to lean on his arm and the half-numbed, nightmarish knowing that his arm wasn't there; and then delirium again, and after the delirium agony, till, even now, driving to Chesterford over three years later, he could have permitted his head, were he not firm with himself, to swim with the thought of it. Sometimes he looked at himself in the glass to see what marks had been laid on his face, but beyond a ridge on his brow caused by his frowning and a pallidity of cheek—a cheek that flushed too readily and pinkly when he became excited, he thought his face was much the same. The eyes he wasn't sure of. He would stare sometimes for a long time looking into the eyes that seemed paler now as if they had lost the blue that had been in the grey and that now lit up seldom. He would stare at them and see the doubts of himself, and of where he was going and what he would be at, and slowly he would begin to depise himself and become contemptuous of his maimed body; and his eyes would grow sorrowful and hurt, and when he saw that,

he could have wept for himself, wept for the loneliness that
was creeping over him and enveloping him; a greater loneliness, perhaps, even than that he had known every time they
were about to attack and he had stood waiting among his
men but shuttered within himself, knowing that though you
walked side by side, yet you were isolated, matched with your
own hour and none other's; knowing no man could come
nigh to you or help you. It was the same now; he could not
play lawn tennis any more, nor write a letter except with extreme labour; he couldn't put on his clothes without a
struggle—and every upper garment threw his deformed
body in his face. Those empty, dangling sleeves waved before
his eyes while he struggled to sleep, and every time he passed
a mirror he looked to see whether he seemed quite as strange
and quite as different from the rest of mankind as he did in
front of the last mirror. When he was pitied he was angry;
and when his loss was ignored or taken for granted, he pitied
himself. When his sister Mary fussed over him he writhed,
and when Evelyn, who could not (he thought) possibly want
to marry him now and was (he was sure) holding to him
through loyalty—when she behaved as if he were normal, he
would sometimes begin to fumble with his cigarette-case,
waiting for her to come to the rescue, knowing he was punish-
ing her. Trotter, who had lugged him back to the trench and
had contrived a Blighty one, as the phrase had it, the next day
—Trotter always swore he lay on his back on the firestep and
waved his legs in the air to catch the machine-gun bullets—
was one of the few persons with whom he felt completely at
ease; Trotter who, with himself, or so he imagined, still
thought in terms of war, still rated people according to
whether they had "swung the lead" or not, what "shows"
they had helped to run or ruin, how many medals they had
snaffled.

They passed a Chesterford tram at the terminus, the con-

ductor standing in the middle of the road with the rope of
the trolley-pole before swinging it round, staring at them
as fixedly as though they had dropped from Mars. The car
ran now on granite setts, faintly blue, down the incline. On
each side were thick greyish-yellow stone garden walls and
wrought-iron gates. (Houghton, soon after his wound, used
to look at those gates and try to calculate how many eighteen-
pounder shells each one would provide metal for.) Behind
the walls lay a dozen yards of heavy soil, or sooty lawn with
a circular rhododendron bush in the middle—gardens to
stone semi-detached houses, from which, no matter how
often you passed, people were never seen to come forth. But,
nevertheless, the houses *were* tenanted, for not infrequently
by the door was a brass plate announcing that Miss So-and-So
gave lessons in singing or the pianoforte, adding importantly: "Pupils prepared for examinations." The number of
these musicians in Chesterford who "had letters after their
names" was astonishing. Hereabouts, too, at this top end of
Burnham Road lived builders and decorators, a stray solicitor or two and a few doctors who inhabited the corner houses
and kept a tall lamp near the gate with a circular red globe
bearing their name. All these displayed brass plates also,
from which it was possible to discern with some accuracy the
age and degree of financial prosperity of the owners; for
thousands of days' rubbing with metal polish had worn some
names almost to obliteration, while others, like that of
Miss Stephanie Vickers—who had only two violin pupils,
one of whom, a blind girl, she taught for nothing—were
green with mould. All Chesterford knew, when the brass
ceased to shine, which way the wind blew. The lower end of
Burnham Road declined in both senses. The semi-detached
property ran into unbroken rows of brick houses. The first
of them had infinitely narrow strips of garden, no more than
four feet in depth—which hardly anybody attempted to

cultivate, so that they held not much more than a stained and riven bush, old brown paper or a stray cat or bottle. The next group opened their front doors on to the very pavement, but Chesterford's housewives turned that pavement into an appendage of the houses by stoning it yellow or white as their taste dictated. Chesterford was much impressed by the manner in which that stoning was done; many a woman had things "on the slate" at the corner shop or bought more than she could afford from the travelling Scotsman (inventor of hire purchase), and still kept her name as a good wife by reason of the elbow-grease she bestowed on the flagged corporation footpath.

Where a hoarding hid a corner of waste land at the point where Mill Street runs at right angles into Burnham Road, Houghton's car turned right and shot, bumping, down the rough cobbled street, and into the factory yard at the bottom. You could, indeed, find yourself nowhere else if your car executed that dive, for Bluebell Mill Yard swallowed, as it were, the whole of Mill Street; the gates were wide as the roadway, and they were flanked by brick walls surmounted with glass-studded concrete that occupied the width of the pavements. Bluebell Mill absorbed Mill Street and those who lived therein with equal nonchalance.

Houghton ran the car almost into the mill doorway and got out. His nose was at once assailed by various smells peculiar to cotton mills—among them warm oil, cotton waste, much-used air, and sweat; and his ears were made aware of a throbbing roar, incessant, penetrating, and as impressive in its way as the roar of a heavy sea against a cliff. The roar he could endure; sometimes, indeed, it brought his tortured nerves some degree of peace; but the smells and heat he loathed—the mill half stifled and choked him. His grandfather, Thomas Houghton, who was a colonel in the Volunteers, was famed for saying: "The smell of a spinning-room or the bite of cordite—damned if I know which I like best!" and he, Philip, for all his expressed contempt for the mill, would have liked to feel at home in it. But he never did. The mill, after a fashion, overpowered him and defeated him, and, as always happened when he was defeated, he began to despise himself, and yet to flog himself into going oftener that he might be tortured. In that fashion, too, he often walked with his right shoulder a little in advance of his left, as if he were flaunting his disability before those who saw him.

He looked for a moment in passing at the blue-overalled girls packing baskets with cops behind the glass windows on his right, and then pushed back the heavily ornamented door marked MANAGER in figured glass that led towards Luke Hargreaves's room, his father's and his own. His father, he knew, was at Burnham; Hargreaves, he hoped, was in. He was. He sat at a large polished mahogany table in a corner of the room, using a brass yarn-tester—a fat Nordic man of sixty, with pouched eyes, and a grey moustache overhanging his mouth, wearing gold eyeglasses, and with an extremely flat cap that perched on his head like a pancake. (The cotton trade has produced scores of men like him, fresh-complexioned, shrewd, but lacking in guile and, in consequence, from time to time heavily defrauded by Asiatics.) Houghton put down his bowler hat and sat in his grey overcoat on the edge of the table, fingering his clipped, blond moustache.

"Well, Luke, is it strong enough to hang a man with?"

Hargreaves barely moved his eyes from the recording figures on the instrument. "Yea," he said, "I could pick a few as it 'ud do for nicely." He took three inches of pencil out of the bottom pocket of his waistcoat, moistened the lead with his tongue, and wrote some figures on a foolscap sheet of paper. "That's the best bit o' thirty-two's twist being

spun i' Chesterford to-day. Aye, or to-morrow, or next week
eyther for the matter o' that," he said.

"But I thought you could sell *anything* at present."

"Aye, so we can. But we don't, Mister Philip. You know
that. Wouldn't do. Bluebell yarn is Houghton's, an' Houghton's name is good enough for owt. If the archangels wear
cotton, you can be sure it's Houghton's. And if they have
cotton sheets at Buckingham Palace, they'll be Houghton's
too."

"Not only the best in creation but the best *for* creation,"
said Houghton drily. "I often wonder how much immorality
we've been responsible for East of Suez."

"I should doubt there was owt *we* could teach 'em," said
Luke getting up, pulling down his waistcoat which had rucked
up over his stout belly and walking over to the fire. Suddenly
he asked: "Have you applied for an allotment in the
Dacca?"

"Haven't heard of it. Is that sold too?" Houghton spoke
with light disdain.

"Rate things are goin', Houghton's'll be the only ones
that aren't soon. Yea, t' Dacca's gone to Robinson's group.
He rang me up. Offered me five hundred. Twelve and six.
They'll be fifteen shillin's by Saturday or I'm a Dutchman."

"Are you taking them?"

"Might as well. I shan't keep 'em though. Would you
like a couple o' hundred? I allus wondered what kept t'
City o' London goin'. I reckon it's this sort of a do. But
keepin' out of it won't stop it. Are yo' takin' 'em?"

Houghton thought: "Two hundred half crowns—nearly
a second lieutenant's pay for a month. Agony and bloody
sweat for it then. Now, like being asked to have a drink."
Then: "Yes, I'm on," he said.

"Miss Rolleston!" Hargreaves shouted. Hargreaves always called her. He had a bell on his desk and it was clearly

understood that two pushes on his button brought her, but somehow, he didn't care to use it; seemed too officious and pompous. So he called her. She came in, a dark, curly haired woman in her late twenties, high breasts markedly shaping her black satin frock, a large satin bow behind her waist, a faint scent about her, and a touch of rouge on her cheeks. All these things Houghton tried to ignore, together with her provocative smile, and the swing of her light step—and never succeeded in ignoring them. In a moment or two she was gone; she was to ring Robinson and say Mr. Hargreaves would take the five hundred.

Hargreaves talked again; super-tax looked like being damned heavy—they were looking round to see what improvements they could make to buildings to save paying some o' the tax—pity the factory didn't need another chimney or two. But Houghton wasn't listening to Hargreaves. He was acutely aware of the pulse near his throat that had quickened when the girl came in and he was conscious that some of the blood had left his face; it felt tight and strained.

Trotter said, sitting at the wheel as they drove away: "It don't suit you, sir; never did. It's that heat."

"Yes," said Houghton, making a great effort. His heart was still pounding. He sank back and drew his overcoat round him more tightly.

Chapter Three

THE HOUGHTONS bestrode the industrial revolution. The first Houghton who achieved importance had woven cloth on a handloom on Chesterford Edge in the days when cottages were not infrequently let with a handloom as part of the appurtenance, and pack-horses carried the woven cloth to the Severn. This Houghton, John, you may still look upon in the *History of Chesterford* in the Mechanics' Institute Library—a square-faced man with mutton-chop whiskers and a strong mouth, wearing his braided black coat every whit as importantly as Lord Salisbury ever did. John had lived in a cottage whose upper windows were thin and tall but many in number, stretching indeed, almost across the front of the bedroom; for the handloom was upstairs and weavers could afford little but the light of heaven to work by. In that cottage Humphrey was born and in that bedroom he was rocked by a rope fastened to the foot of the weaver—sometimes his father, sometimes his mother, Ann. But though his earliest recollections were of the clack-clack of the loom and of his mother sitting bent over a spinning-wheel, he never spun or wove by hand himself. For John lived up to his strong mouth and hard eyes by saving enough to become a partner in the first six steam-power looms Chesterford ever saw, distrusted, hated, and, in time, envied and copied.

That was over a hundred years before this tale begins. Humphrey it was, however, who followed him, who displayed the genius that can succeed without forfeiting goodwill. When John was lying stricken on the bed from which he never rose and Humphrey was no more than twenty-five, the Luddite rioters came—frenzied, machine-breaking bands—to Chesterford. John said they were to be fought, the doors barricaded, the militia sent for, but when they came Humphrey threw open the doors, leapt on the wall and asked them to do what they would, but first to hear him. His slight figure is protrayed in Chesterford's *History* as being tall and of extreme handsomeness, with curved lips, fine glowing brown eyes, a high noble forehead and a voice rich and of great beauty. "When he spoke," it says, "there was no doubting him," and on this day when he cried: "What shall it profit you to destroy that by which threescore of your brothers and sisters earn their livelihood and keep their children in well-being?" the crowd murmured and then grew silent. Someone threw a stone which cut his cheek and the blood ran, but he didn't move. "It is nothing," he said. "The wound will heal—that is God's gift to man—the gift of recovery, but how shall the machines recover if you smash them to pieces?" "Aye, God is in man, but t' devil's in t' machines," a voice cried. For a moment it looked as though the day was lost, but nevertheless the crowd turned and withdrew, sullenly and half-heartedly. That night they were destroying spindles and looms at Saddlebridge, but Houghton's remained secure. That speech to the rioters was perhaps the first evidence of Humphrey's being a politician. He afterwards became Whig Member of Parliament for the Chesterford Division, but there is no doubt he was well loved and that his energy and forethought in adding a spinning section to the mill secured the Houghton fortunes. His son, George, was a dreamer, built violins with his own hands and wrote hymn tunes that are still sung in All Saints' parish church. He was but little the business man; diffident when he should have been bold, stubborn when he should have bargained. People began to quote the old saying: "There's three generations from clogs to clogs." But he proved them wrong there. He avoided major disasters. He was negligent but not a fool; improvident but not a riotous liver. It is true he had too many children— eight within and one out of wedlock, and that one handsomer by far, it was said, than any of his other daughters. But large families were the rule and the love-child no greater a rarity in Chesterford than elsewhere. Then, as now, passionate lovers were likely to be looked on askance in public but admired in secret. He had money to be generous with; his adoration had been as genuine if more brief than that of his lover, the music-mistress, and no one was greatly surprised that, after the *accouchement* was over, she and the child should make their home in Chesterford or that the beautiful child, as she grew up to be, should marry Henry Brierley, the librarian, as pure a singer of Lancashire dialect verse as the county ever produced—and as ill-rewarded.

Of George's sons, Thomas, colonel in the Volunteers, and William, the image of his grandfather John, stayed in cotton; the one controlling the mills and the other the warehouse and offices in Burnham—a capital division of responsibility, for Thomas had the rough good-humour, quick tongue and sense of discipline that most workers admire in a master; and William could add up three columns of figures simultaneously, an accomplishment that won him a reputation as far as Liverpool and London.

Every one of these Houghtons was dead at the time the cotton boom of 1919–20 dazzled and blinded one half of

Lancashire: but they still lived in the minds and bodies of the Houghtons with whom our concern is: they were not to be escaped from.

Edward had something in him of Thomas, whose son he was, and perhaps even more of his grandfather, George. Edward had wanted to enter the Navy, but being the eldest and the Houghton tradition strong in his blood, he had gone into cotton. He was a good-humoured tolerably shrewd man, who could do obvious things with an air of decision and who could be relied on to see as far as most people and not an inch farther. He had a trace of devil in him: was one of the first to climb up the front of King's College Chapel, Cambridge; was a light, sturdy, fast man in the Rugby pack and rode his grey horse through the streets of Chesterford with an accustomed ease. He adopted an attitude, or, at times, took a lead not because he would have become a leader of his own volition had his origin been obscure, but because Houghtons were expected to give orders as are commanders of regiments or captains of ships. Nothing short of being a lunatic could have robbed him of a considerable measure of authority and respect in Chesterford, and had he been, indeed, mad, no doubt a part of the town would have pronounced him no more than eccentric and perhaps a genius. For the feudal spirit has never died, nor was it ever confined to the English countryside.

Edward, however, was not mad by any means. He had merely inherited a part of George's artistry. He had, for example, built himself a toy theatre in his study, and would sit there, sometimes for a whole evening, speaking Shakespeare's words, or those of Galsworthy or Barrie, moving his puppets to and fro as the play demanded, and achieving a measure of different intonation and accent; and he was always happier in the company of women than of men. He was never a handsome man, his nose was too hooked, his cheeks were too flat, and his stature was not commanding, but there was a good deal of fineness in him discernible in his eyes, his over-slender wrists and ankles and his small feet and hands. Women felt safe with him, they knew that their sense of delicacy would not be outraged, that he was no more gross than they were. They were bolder and franker with him than with other men; here was, they felt, a man who could be trusted and experimented with. And Edward knew how they regarded him and was not offended by it. Women had, to his mind, what Chesterford folk called, "the dirty end of the stick to hold." If he could make their lot more endurable, well . . . That had been his attitude for a year or two before he had, at the age of thirty-one, married Phœbe, second daughter of Rear-Admiral Wemyss Hunter, and by the time their marriage was four years old he was as ready to receive a confidence or answer the sparkle in a woman's eye with a laugh in his own as ever he had been. So they had entertained a good deal—parties, catholic in their range, generous in their hospitality, amusing and lively in themselves. For Edward was president of Chesterford Garrick Society, vice-president of the Liberal Association, senior churchwarden, chairman of the Board of Chesterford Royal Hospital and Justice of the Peace. He had been Jubilee Mayor; he had gracefully refused to become either parliamentary candidate or president of Chesterford Silver Prize Band (of brass) and as graciously accepted the chairmanship of the new Beethoven Orchestral Society. Edward knew what he liked.

On the day that his son Philip drove swiftly past Mrs. Harriet Renshaw, Edward sat at seven o'clock tying his black evening tie and regretting that he had invited Major Henderson to tell him during the evening what the figure was to which his Robinson group was now prepared to go in making an offer for the two Houghton mills. Because

he knew in his heart he had no intention of parting with
them.

He didn't know at that moment why he had discussed
the matter with Henderson at all; natural curiosity to know
what these fellows were up to, he supposed. Six hundred
and fifty thousand pounds was the sum Henderson had
named the week before and to-night he was apparently going
to increase the offer. He might jump another hundred thousand or so. Edward began to recall Henderson's father, with
his square black hat, long square-toed Glasgow shoes and
rusty tailed coat down his thin shanks. Registrar of Births
and Deaths, he was. It was said that he went about noting
in his small gilt-edged notebook the old men and women
who were looking none too well, and that in his cups this
"fause" old man would remark: "There's one or two I saw
the day as I'll be writin' down afore so long, mind ye. Aye,
they all come my way sooner-r or later-r. Aye." He was
run over by Chesterford's first motor hearse and died of
it; and there wasn't a man or woman in Chesterford who
didn't think the gods had for once a fine sense of justice.

Edward's thoughts turned to the son, Ernest Henderson—a little "fause" too, it was thought. He reflected without satisfaction that it is almost impossible to dissociate
children from their parents—and clipped the tops on to his
diamond studs. His cheeks were beginning to sag, he thought;
the jaw was broadening, getting heavier—he didn't like that,
nor the added prominence his thinning hair gave to his ears.
But he noted with pleasure that the sparkle hadn't yet gone
from his eyes, even if the skin beneath was becoming rather
like an apple kept too long, as Phœbe had chaffingly said.
He slipped into his waistcoat and jacket. His height seemed
to be decreasing—that particular something in the neighbourhood of his knees was contracting, he supposed—but

he was straight enough and he doubted if his eyes were bluer the day they opened, close on sixty years ago. He rubbed a touch of bay rum on his grey hair and deliberately refrained from washing his hands because he liked the smell to linger a while on his fingers. Then he walked into Phœbe's room and kissed the nape of her neck as she sat screwing in her emerald ear-rings. As he did so he caught the faint aroma of spirits and knew she had been drinking brandy. He wasn't surprised and he didn't dislike the smell, but he suffered that infinitesimal catch near the heart that he always experienced when Phœbe displayed one of her weaknesses to him, or when she complained of being unwell. And, feeling it, he knew that his love had grown no less and that, indeed, he loved her the more for the very disquiet she occasioned him. "Well, my sweet," he said, standing a yard away that he might admire her, and truly admiring her.

"Darling, what time's Jack coming?" she asked, turning her head and holding a hand-mirror as though she were going to her first ball. At fifty Phœbe made everyone aware not so much of the beauty that was still hers, but of the loveliness that they knew must have dwelt in her twenty years before. Her large, dark-grey eyes were now a little tired through smiling so long, and her face slightly fixed in its attempt at the old radiant welcome. She had borne no children after Edward's first four years of single-hearted devotion, but the remaining twenty-five years of marriage had been happy enough despite Edward's wide-heartedness. He had found other women attractive but had never loved them.

"Unless he's been sitting especially late, I can't imagine him keeping you in suspense much longer." He was smiling quizzically at her.

"I've always wished you were as handsome as Jack."

"As famous you mean. You're captured by the red robes and the quips. I tell him he's as proud of his Press notices as a fashionable actress."

Phœbe said: "I wish I knew as much about marriage as he does."

"Fiddlesticks," said Edward, stooping to kiss her cheek, "the wise men of the East aren't in it with these bachelors. You'd think they all kept harems."

"I often wonder," she said, "whether you'd get to know us better if, instead of living with one woman a lifetime, you lived with a good many women for a year or two each."

"A year or two *would* be a lifetime spent with most women," Edward said, screwing up his eyes and laughing out of them.

She rose and stood before the looking-glass, thinking her depth of bosom was increasing alarmingly. Did it matter any more? Would Edward care less? She looked at him and thought: "He is very sweet to me—so marvellously honest. He must know about the brandy." Then:

"Darling," she said, "what are Philip and Evelyn going to do?"

"It's their affair, my love. They're not children."

"Yes, Edward, I know. Only . . . they're both suffering. Philip's awfully on edge lately. And Evelyn . . . if we were poor, do you think it would last?"

"That's not quite fair, darling, is it? You fall in love with people as they are—knowing of their position, their brains, their achievements, their friends, their money. You can't strip people of them—see them naked, as it were, and look on them with the same eyes. My dear, if you had been a shop assistant instead of an admiral's daughter—well, I shouldn't have married you."

"Edward, what a cruel thing to say!" But she knew he was right; however, she said:

"Dearest, I'd have married you if you'd been a coal-heaver," and kissed him on the forehead. She slipped her arm through his and with linked fingers they went downstairs.

"Do you know, my sweet," he said, "this gives me as much joy as when I first knew you?" That wasn't quite true, but an infinitesimal wave of emotion still swept through his blood when her fingers were woven with his.

"You dear thing," she said, "no wonder women love you."

    .   .   .   .

Edward had asked a number of people for music at nine o'clock and before the string quartets began, they talked.

"If this boom goes on, Mister 'Oughton, we'st have to see about buildin' another factory." Luke Hargreaves cut his cigar and beamed on Edward.

"You think it's going to last then, Luke?"

"I don't see why it shouldn't. T'world's pinin' for cotton goods, isn't it?"

The boom was discussed, as men discuss an earthquake, or a royal marriage, or what will win the Derby.

"I observe," said Canon Heywood, folding his hands across his small black paunch, "that my friend the Rev. James Oldroyd has been denouncing the boom as the devil's work—says people are recklessly lighting their pipes with Bradburys and drinking champagne before breakfast."

"I don't know about champagne," said Hargreaves, "but one o' my spinners didn't turn up till after dinner to-day. He said he drank vodka last night an' his wife had to fetch the doctor to wake him. Dreamt he flew round the world in an aeroplane three times—once right through General Booth's beard. Yea, that's what he said. Beer's quite out o' fashion wi' some of 'em. Thirty-six pound five's goin' into his house every week. Rollin' in it, that's what they are."

"I was challenged to-day," said Philip, "to race by car to Southport for a hundred pounds. Mottram. A year ago he was an insurance agent. Now he lives in the American bar at the Grand."

"You refused, I suppose?" Edward's voice was urgent.

Philip's pallid cheeks flushed red near the cheek-bones. "I accepted. Somebody must deal with him. If he breaks his neck I shall deserve a medal."

"If you intend to exterminate all the undesirables in the trade, Mr. Houghton, you'll require a fleet of steam-rollers." Mr. Fred Millington, a mild-looking little man in gold spectacles who conducted the Beethoven Society went on in his high, precise, tenor voice: "A hundred and fifty men are dabbling in cotton shares every morning in the cellar of the Mechanics' Institute and there aren't a dozen who could tell whether we were playing the 'Eroica Symphony' or 'Land of Hope and Glory.'" And Mr. Millington winked his brown eyes and glanced round challengingly, having disposed of this unmusical trash.

The talk of how Chesterford was changing, went on.

Captain Brownlow, the Chief Constable, declared that applications for bastardy summonses had increased a good deal—"boom babies" apparently; and concert bars were getting artistes from Burnham and Liverpool. Canon Heywood, feeling the Church must keep its end up, asserted that a deal for £5,000 was carried through in the back pew during his sermon; he should certainly launch an appeal for a new organ. Philip said he had heard men were jumping with weights for fifty pounds a side on the cinder track, and Mr. Millington piped out again: "Jonathan Ryecroft, our first 'cello, has bought ten acres of land for rabbit shooting."

Edward looked at his watch. "Mr. Millington, are you giving us 'Borodine's D Major Quartet'?" Mr. Millington said he was and he hoped Wilfred Sherlock who had damaged his hand in the pit two days ago would be up to the mark.

"Why doesn't tha sign me on, Fred?" asked Luke, putting his hand on Mr. Millington's shoulder as they walked out. "I used to be a rare hand wi' a trombone."

"You made a great mistake when you ceased to confine your attentions to knur and spell," said Mr. Millington.

In the drawing-room the string quartet began to tune up.

.   .   .   .

"It comes to this," said Edward, who was talking to his brother, Sir John, after the second quartet. "We make over thirty times as much profit to-day on spinning a pound of yarn, as we did in 1912. Similarly with cloth. We formerly made sixpence on a piece of shirting; now we get five shillings out of it."

"How long will it continue? I see someone calls it a bubble. Last year you paid me thirty per cent."

"This year," said Edward, "it will be over forty per cent."

They were joined by Lord Henry Cope, who divided his time between the Chesterford Brewery, his wife's property and the House of Commons, a seat in which had been, as it were, bequeathed him by his father, Tory member for nine years before him.

"They tell me," said Lord Henry, "that you are going to run a horse in the Derby, Edward." He pulled his moustaches, shaped like the sound holes of a fiddle.

"You mean Phœbe has told you, Henry."

"Phœbe thinks you should have a small racing stable, a capital idea." Lord Henry had been drinking Clicquot 1909 with Phœbe and, at that moment, imagined he was somewhat in love with her. "Ah, Phœbe, I am telling Edward you are buying one of my colts."

Phœbe was flushed, her eyes, Edward thought, more brilliant and lovely than usual. "I've been asking Elizabeth Hargreaves about it," she said. "I said we must have a striking name for the horse. Elizabeth suggested 'Boxer.'"

"'Boxer?' Afraid I don't see that," said Lord Henry, exploding a moment later into a fit of laughter. "I say, that's very good. Where is Mrs. Hargreaves? I must . . ." And he went over to her to offer congratulations on her wit, and, at the same time, to admire her figure.

Philip, who was standing with Evelyn Berrye, was saying: "I've heard from Anstruther. He's keen on the hunt. Suggests Kenya."

"But, dear, how can you? . . ."

"With that light tripod stand fastened to the rifle—sort of thing we had on Lewis guns in the war—you remember the one I've had made . . ."

"I shall be anxious, Philip. You may get some fever. Isn't malaria . . ."

"I don't mind risks. Besides . . ." He didn't finish that, but looked into her eyes and narrowed his own mockingly.

She thought: "He is thinking I should be glad if he were killed or died in Kenya. He keeps throwing it in my face. One day, if this goes on, I shall say: 'Yes, I shall be glad. You had the excitement, the medals, cheers. For me, only your wounds. I should never be able to bear it when you lay with me.'"

They walked slowly towards Phœbe and Sir John. Phœbe said: "You are looking lovely, darling."

"Am I? You are sweet to say so."

Sir John took Philip aside. "About that motor-race, Philip? A bit unwise, isn't it?"

Uncomfortable under the dark unwavering brown eyes, Philip said he had accepted the challenge and there it was; wisdom didn't arise now.

"I should dislike sending you to prison for manslaughter. Every time you drive you take grave risks."

"I should expect the maximum, sir." Philip felt his heart hastening its beat as a slow anger swept up towards his head.

"You're not yourself," said Sir John curtly.

"No, sir; not since Trones Wood." But Sir John ignored that and turned to Phœbe and Evelyn again. Phœbe called "Philip, dear," as he walked towards the door, but he neither turned nor stopped. If he could carry these things off better; if his heart didn't beat so confoundedly fast; but he couldn't control it or his nerves either. He went to his own study that was in darkness, and by the light that came through the doorway, mixed a large whisky and soda. Coming out he misjudged where he was and caught his knee a sickening jab on the sharp corner of his writing-desk. In a moment his head began to swing mazily and his heart to pound as the paddle of an old steamer that is about to stop. The lighted doorway was turning over and a black void began to close him in. With a terrific effort he slid on to the edge of a chair and thrust his head down. By heavens, this was terrible. At his age—fainting. Slowly his head grew stronger but he sat there in the dark for a long time. When he felt strong enough he rose unsteadily. "At all events," he thought grimly, "this lets me out from the party." Very pale and trembling slightly, he went slowly upstairs and to his bedroom, sending a message of apology to his mother and Evelyn.

.   .   .   .

When Phœbe was in bed, Edward went in to her in his dressing-gown, sat on the bed and rubbed one foot caressingly over the other.

"Philip ridicules the idea of staying in bed to-morrow," he said.

"You must.make him, dear."

Edward shook his head gloomily. "No use, my love. I feel sometimes he's older than we are. We've got to let him go his way and . . . help him without his knowing it, if we can. When's Mary coming home?"

"Thursday, darling. You feel she's better at it than we are?"

"Mary's all you, my love—maybe just a pinch of me thrown in to make her less angelic."

"I wish she wasn't so interested in Brierley."

"Yes, I suppose so. He's able enough. It doesn't amount to anything . . . I mean, Mary's interest. She knows there's Houghton blood in him far back. I think she feels a little protective."

"A highly dangerous feeling to have, Edward. It would be disastrous."

"Would it?" Edward was smiling fondly at her and thinking: "These women are like tigers over their young." He said: "There's quality in him, and brains. Oh, mind you, I'm not advocating . . ."

"No, darling, don't. Philip's tragedy is . . . well, never mind, dear. Only we couldn't stand another, could we?"

He leaned over her and lightly pushed the hair from her forehead, and said: "No, my sweet." He was propped on one elbow looking down into her eyes that were growing a little sleepy. "You can have your Derby horse if you wish —provided you name him after me."

"Yes, darling, I told Henry I could."

"You what? Robbing me of my one delight in life—that

of making you surprise gifts?"

"Well, darling, I didn't really say anything decisive to Henry—I just said . . . at least I think I did . . . that he might put it aside for me—you know, in a small stable by itself—the Houghton stable—so that it could get used to its new colours, blue slashed with grey and a black cap. You'll adore the colours, darling."

Edward said: "If you go racing, I warn you I shall start a repertory theatre."

"Yes, darling, I know you will. That's why I thought we should have a small racing stable. I know you want your silly old theatre to play with and you've been very good putting up with the toy one for so long."

He smoothed her hair again and got up. "Shall I put out the light for you, or are you going to read a while?"

"Put it out, darling. By the way, you didn't sell the mills, did you, dear?"

"Henderson went to seven hundred and fifty thousand. I said if they were worth that to his group they must be worth at least a million to me. I'm not sure that I didn't say a *cool* million. I was feeling very Napoleonic, I know."

"I'd love to have seen you."

"Yes, I believe I was rather magnificent. Good night, my dear. Sleep well."

"Thank you, dear. I think I am going to ride Derby winners all night. Bless you, darling." She began to say something more but it became incoherent in a terrific yawn. Edward paused.

"What is it, my love?"

"Nothing, darling. I'm asleep."

He put out the light.

Chapter Four

"I WILL NOT SUFFER mine eyes to sleep, nor mine eyelids to slumber; neither the temples of my head to take any rest . . ."

Harriet didn't know which psalm these words were from but as she rocked herself in front of the kitchen fire an organ was playing in her head and the words were lulling her to sleep. She could hear the choir's voices in All Saints' Church and she knew very well the chant they were singing the words to. (She was a devout church-woman, and had been "churched" after every child.) She knew also that she must not go to sleep; she must go and fetch Sam from the Black Bull. The more she realised that, the more beautiful the singing became, the clearer the words rang out till they filled all the room, it seemed; they must, she thought drowsily, be singing the words in heaven also. "I will not suffer mine eyes to sleep, nor mine eyelids to slumber." The rocking-chair had no arms—it was a woman's chair and arms were a luxury reserved for the men—so that she sat with her arms, bursting from the print sleeves, folded across her bosom, and as she slept she slowly sagged further and further to the right till her head left the support of the wooden chair back and the jerk of her neck woke her with a fearful start. She stared uncomprehendingly for a moment at the two-and-ninepenny American alarm clock on the high

46

mantelpiece which was ticking loudly enough for one six times its size, and then, shivering a little from sleep, she sat forward and stared fixedly at the fire. Her nose wanted wiping, she felt, and she drew up a corner of her apron and wiped it, but carefully sniffed upwards before doing so that the apron might not be soiled. She felt vaguely that it was not right that she should have to go and fetch Sam. It was half-past nine and he had said he would be home by eight. "Sithee lass," he had said, "as sure as my name's Sam Renshaw I'll be whoam i' good time, and i' good fettle, too. Dunnot be surprised if I want a bit o' summat when I come, nayther. Them as makes plenty o' brass should ha' plenty o' childer, eh?" She had blushed as she poked the fire; his heavy attempts at humour she liked less than anything else about him. "Get your tea," she had said, "and let your food stop your mouth." "Why now, lass, what's t' matter wi' thee? Doesn't tha want me any moore now I'm a dam' profeshional chap makin' eawr pile? Nay, I'st not ha' that," and he had got up from his tea (he was having a fried egg on a leg chop) and walked across to her, wiping his moustache with his hand preparatory to seizing her and forcing her mouth open with his kisses. She had not really resisted or tried to resist him. But she knew he had called in the Three Jolly Carters on his way home; and almost for the first time in her life she experienced a slight repugnance to him. It had broken into her consciousness quite abruptly and had alarmed her a little. Was it the culmination of a week's tipsiness—not a coming home rolling drunk or making W's up Lavender Street, but a returning home never sober, and ponderously funny and coarsely amorous? She thought: "It's been comin' on and now it's here." And she was frightened by it. "I must love him," she thought. "I must, I must, or else what are we goin' to do? Oh, but I do wish he hadn't started brokin'." What she said, as he got on with his tea, was: "You're wearin' yoursel' out wi' this boom business, an' what good's that goin' to be to us if you mak' us a fortune and then snuff it? I'd liefer have you home wi' empty pockets than wi 'pockets full o' Bradburys at t' Black Bull."

"Ambition, lass, that's what tha wants. Thee stop a bit," he had said, and she had answered: "If it ends t' same road as it's begun, Sam, it's not goin' to do us much good. It looks to me like playin' pitch an' toss only you're usin' ten-pound notes i'stead o' pennies." But he had washed himself in the kitchen sink and gone upstairs whistling jocosely, as eager to be off as if he were going to court a woman. When, for an instant, that thought occupied her mind her heart leapt and died sickeningly within her so that the bottom of her stomach seemed to have dropped away: and she knew that Sam was nearly the whole of life to her.

She rose and loosed her apron and washed her face to take the sleep off her, and put on her black jacket with leg-of-mutton sleeves that she had had since shortly after she was married. She had said the day before, trying to stop the tremor in her voice, "I'st have to come an' see this Black Bull if tha'rt goin' to spend aw thy neets theer," and not believing she was serious he had answered: "Aye, thee do." There was a faintly ironical, bantering note in it. It was a long while since they had drunk together in a public-house; not since she was feeding young Sam on the breast and he had told her: "It's a bottle o' stout tha needs—that'll gie thee aw t' milk tha wants"—a piece of advice highly regarded and regularly accepted by those who liked stout. To get tipsy in the cause of your child—wasn't that praiseworthy? Many persuaded themselves so; but Harriet was not among them. She had drunk a bottle of stout as one may drink medicine, as she had drunk it "with the red-hot poker in it," to try to cure herself of anæmia years before.

She stole upstairs and looked at the children—two in

each bed in the small back room. "Lie as close as two spoons," she would say as she tucked them up in the tiny double-beds. Bessie was on her back, one arm flung tempestuously out and as stiff as a ramrod. Esther was a little out of bed, her shoulders on the edge and her arms drooping limply towards the floor. George was hidden up to his nose and Arthur was on his back, one knee up and breathing heavily as if he had adenoids. She stood for a moment looking at them in the candlelight, a catch at her heart. Then with dexterous hands she softly adjusted them all, turning them on to their right sides, Bessie a little at a time, Esther with a swift sudden movement like throwing a wrestler. These, by long experience, she had found the most effective methods. They squirmed and wriggled for a moment in her hands like fishes—small, jerky movements—but so soon as her touch was ended, they lay still and slept as heavily in their new postures as before. Next she went to the front room to the baby, Sam, in his cot beside the big bed. She loved him more than the others because he had always demanded more from her. He had refused to be weaned till he was fifteen months old, and he had worn her out with taking his sustenance from her and worrying her breasts with his lusty mouth. He had a strong temper and fought and cried petulantly and fiercely, and, half through love, and half through being tired out, she had given way to him. He was three now and getting too big for his cot, but there was nowhere else to go, except her and Sam's bed, and as often as not it was there he ended before the night was through, sticking his feet into her soft stomach and frequently giving her severe pains. As she watched he turned over and crashed his legs against the wooden bars that caged him, and in an instant she was petting and caressing and comforting him—but the child hadn't wakened. He could, as she knew but never could bring herself to acknowledge, make what sounded hideous contacts with the thin wooden rails of his cot without hurting himself. She tucked him up, lightly kissed his sulky mouth, and walked slowly down the creaking stairs. Ought she to go for Sam? Should she warn Mrs. Edmunds next door she was going to be absent? ("Ee, I yam sorry, y'ave to fetch Sam. It's not right, an' I yam sorry for you, but I mustn't say what *I* think, must I?") No, she couldn't let Mrs. Edmunds know. But—suppose the house caught fire, and the children—screaming, frantic—burnt? She grew sickly at the thought. Maybe she and Sam would be had up for —for murder, would it be?

She walked to the fire and examined it with the eager, frightened eyes of a mother who sees dread and danger lurking in it. She carefully poked the lumps of coal to the back to minimise the danger of their falling out. And as she did so she was comforted. She saw the danger was, in truth, small, for the grate was high, the bars no more than an inch apart, and the hearth beneath of stone (bluemoulded to a clean whiteness), and the fender was of steel, eight inches high. She put on her blue hat—she liked it being too tight, somehow, to-night; it held her together, braced her—went back to the bottom of the stairs and listened. Not a sound; only the harsh tick of the American alarm clock. She turned out the gas and was conscious for a moment of the red fire making shadows on the wall and of the chair legs, varnished brown, shining redly in the firelight.

She opened the door and stepped into Lavender Street.

She felt more free, as if she had shaken something off, so soon as she had walked a few paces down the street. For the night was brilliant. The moon was high and full, its face almost benignant in its somewhat mocking way, as it swam quickly behind thin white clouds in a green-dark sky. The street lamps burned with an unusual brightness, fan-

lights shone silver yellow and closely shuttered windows
with their red, long, sausage-like draught stoppers looked
cosy and jolly. Ryecroft's fish-and-chip shop at the corner
was throwing out the most savoury and enticing smell that
Harriet had ever encountered, making the saliva run in
her mouth and her jaws ache a little; but she resisted the
temptation. Perhaps she and Sam—on the way back. A
group of children came down the footpath singing:

"I 'ope there'll be no boggarts to-night,
I 'ope there'll be no boggarts to-night,"

and dispersed in shrill, alarmed ecstasy as two boys with
blackly smeared faces dashed out of an entry. In the light
thrown by the corner shop of Mrs. Tomlinson a second
group were playing a game of mime which started: "Three
men come a-seeking work."

"What con yo' do?"

"Anythin'."

"Set agate."

Whereupon the three in dumb show began to display their
skill, while their opponents guessed what they were at. On
a street lamp a girl with long thin legs and a pigtail was
swinging crazily round in circles, sitting in a rope tied to the
arm of the lamp. Harriet stopped.

"Isn't it time you were i' bed, Martha Ann?"

"Mi mother's gone to t' pic-chers—she said I could stop
out. I'st soon be eleven, yer know." And with this proud
declaration, of mixed defiance and explanation, Martha
Ann swung herself off her feet and whirled round the lamp
till the rope exhausted itself and brought her face to face
with the standard; a moment's halt and she pushed off
in the opposite direction and unravelled herself.

Harriet walked on, thinking: "No wonder she's like t'

scrag end of a bit o' mutton; cheek enough for forty folk
too—young beezum. Bed an' a bit o' bant to her backside,
that's what she wants, an' she should have it, too, if she
were mine." Harriet's path took her up Treadle Bank, a
fifty-foot high clay bank, worn and furrowed by streams of
rain, littered with odd pieces of old bucket and bricks, and
surmounted by Gibbs's foundry, a black low mass whose
sides supported Hogarthian shapes of lovers in strained
attitudes, wrapped in complete silence. Harriet averted her
eyes as she passed them; she didn't want to make them feel
awkward and she didn't want to feel awkward herself, and
she knew both were not unlikely, for the strangest articles,
from hair-pins to false teeth and torn underclothing were
found near Gibbs's foundry when day broke. Harriet did
not concern herself, however, with the divers ways in which
love was still being made and children begotten in the year
of Our Lord, 1920. She stumbled up the bank and crossed
the road into Pineapple Avenue. Streets ran steeply from
it to the right, short, dark, cavernous. From one she could
see a mill lodge steaming into the night, from another the
glinting boiler-hole of Chester mill where, it was said, the
firer-up had disposed of Florrie Hamer's bantling (for it
was notorious that Florrie was to bear a child and equally
known that nobody ever saw it or heard of it); from a third,
a glimpse of the canal on which she had gone for trips in a
coal-boat as a child and in the waters of which more than
one Chesterford couple, tortured by the illicit love that gave
them no quiet, sought sometimes in hope and sometimes in
despair, for that peace this world could not afford. On
Burnham Road she encountered liveliness—clanging tramway-cars shooting over points with a crash that flung
everybody sideways and brought grins to mouths or oaths
to lips; groups of scarved youths moving to the strains of
a mouth-organ or a melodeon; a miner or spinner in pointed,

fancy clogs and white neckerchief, walking his whippet in
its close-fitting jacket of dark grey, edged with red or yellow
and resembling a miniature greyhound. Enticing smells
assaulted her nose again—of black puddings, of sour beer
and sawdust and wine when heavy brass-barred public-house
doors swung momentarily open, of hot meat-pies sold in
portions from huge enamel dishes, of cough-drops, of more
fish and chips. Gaudy colours confronted her eyes at intervals in the dark grey monochrome of Chesterford—
chocolate- vermilion- or blue- or green-tiled fronts of beer-
houses, flaming posters advertising the latest adventures of
ardent lovers and provocative women on the films (the
pictures never quite, Harriet thought, lived up to the
posters), the red, green and blue carboys that occupied the
tops of chemist's shops, and the medley of coloured sweets
that the multiple shops piled, tier on tier, in dazzling
profligacy.

The Black Bull stood opposite the War Memorial which
depicted a Lancashire Fusilier—a youthful, radiant figure
on the march, his lips parted in delight, his rifle slung, his
left hand beckoning the world to follow him. That was how
a sculptor who lived in Hampstead portrayed Chesterford
going off to the war, and interpreted Chesterford's marks
of its abiding grief, and Chesterford was inclined to ponder
and say: "Well, I suppose it's all right—in a way, but there
were a bit more to it than that; aye, a bit less of a picnic
like." Harriet who had lost two brothers at "Lancashire
Landing" on Gallipoli—heavy, stolid Territorials who had
joined the Fusiliers that they might go to camp at Morecambe and found they had marched off to war instead,
would have preferred a soldier with reversed arms and thick
legs—more homely, more like their Wilfred or John—with
a small addition of her own—a shawled figure in the background bent in sorrow. However, there it was, this figure

she was sensitive enough to recognise was lovely and exquisite in its way ("gradely enough," Harriet said it was),
perpetually striding towards the Black Bull, and, looking
up that night and seeing its curly head silhouetted against
the sky she was heartened and thought: "This o' mine is
nowt to what that lad went through," and she pushed open
the ponderous swing-door bravely. Entering from the beautiful night, the place almost struck her in the face. The acrid
smell of beer and sawdust spittoons bit her throat, the
sloppy floor offended her. The small group of men and
women, talkative with liquor, who eyed her brazenly as she
passed made her feel a stranger, an outsider, and she was
glad to be that, but a little scared too. At the door of the
smoke-room she stood looking for Sam in the heavy air grey
with smoke, and had constantly to move aside to allow the
aproned barmen to come and go. "Room for one over there,
missis," they said, nudging her into the room, but she stood
there undecided. For the life of her she could see no vacant
place, nor could she see Sam. The room was full. The
crescents upholstered in dark red leather were full, the
three-legged stools were full that were clustered round the
wet, circular small tables, and the tiny stage at the far end
supported three or four men perched on the edge with gill
pots of beer at their sides. They were a remarkable assembly
—men who were enjoying a variety of liquor that Chesterford had only read about until a year before, men who
wrote with difficulty but who were now, armed with a
fountain-pen and a banking account, making more in a week
than they had earned in six months; publicans whose faces
had dropped so that their jowls hung ugly, creased and
paunched; a handful of quiet, hard-eyed side-whiskered men
in bowler hats—skilled sharebrokers; betting men with red
silk neckerchiefs protruding over their collars; young
and somewhat flashy stockbrokers' clerks, endeavouring to

be worldly and drinking Benedictine or Chartreuse; industrial insurance or club collectors who had a spurious air of efficiency gained by writing on door posts; lawyers' clerks looking very knowing as they passed soiled share forms to and fro on the moist tables; commercial travellers exchanging the latest bawdy stories and picking up the latest tips as to which mills were likely to pay most dividend; a few fresh-complexioned, thin-haired grey-suited mill managers—a little contemptuous these—who had dropped in to see the fun; a blowsy, buxom woman or two grown accustomed to look at men with a half leer and to consume stout in prodigious amounts, and one or two young women who were thin above the waist (a fact which astonished Harriet) over from Burnham, highly coloured, distressingly blonde and skilled in displaying their over-developed legs. Suddenly music smote the air. A young man with a beaked nose and long, dank, black hair parted in the middle and falling on to his forehead, a cigarette drooping from his upper lip, and his too-short, long trousers showing purple socks, sat down at the upright piano at one side of the platform that stood only a foot higher than the floor and began to play: "Follow the Tram-lines, They'll Lead You Home," with extemporaneous flourishes. A door opened near by, a head of plastered, sandy hair with a freckled, wizened, small face came round the corner and cried: "Righto, Charlie!" and Charlie, at the piano, switched off promptly into the introductory bars to: "You're My Baby." The door opened and to a flutter of clapping and cries of: " 'Ere she is," and, " 'Ere's our Trixie," a girl stepped on to the platform wearing a black silk, low-cut bodice, a frilled short black skirt above her knees and black cotton stockings, so thin and stretched that the shapely legs beneath showed dimly pale. Over one knee she wore a scarlet, rosetted garter. She stood on the edge of the platform and made a swift bow to the waist, her

arms flung outwards and backwards so that half the room
caught a tantalising glimpse of her rounded bosom; then she
minced to and fro in her excessively high-heeled shoes and
began to sing in a rather deep, husky, passionate voice:

"You're my ba-a-by, (tum)
You're a wonderful child,
I like to dance you up and down upon my knee,
I like to have you round to make a fuss over me . . ."

When she came to: "You certainly were made for me," half
the room yelled it in delirious stertorous chorus.

And the next instant Harriet saw Sam. Everyone in the
room saw him at the same moment, and if everybody in
Chesterford had seen him Sam would have been proud of it.
For Sam suddenly rose out of a group near the platform and
started to move towards Trixie, and before he could be
stopped, seized her hand and kissed it. She snatched her
hand away and he stood there swaying a little and declaring: "Trixie, tha'rt loveliest lass ["Sit down, Renshaw"] in
aw Lancashire, and tha can have owt ["Shut up"] owt tha
likes—tha damn-well likes—wi' me." He swayed forward,
backward, and sat down abruptly on the knee of a man who
had pulled his jacket; sat down with such force that they
both collapsed in slow motion on to the floor where Sam began to laugh foolishly and, for a moment or two, uncontrollably. When Sam had risen, Harriet's heart had halted
and then leapt forward and drummed as though it would
break through her breast. No longer was she aware of the
nudges of the passing barmen, of the stares of men near,
and the winked or furtive invitations of others to come and
sit down. When Sam collapsed on the floor she took a half
pace forward, or, rather, her feet moved nervously, jerkily,
as if they would carry her to him. She didn't know what to

do. Her eyes were nearly blind with tears of shame for him,
of anger at his disgracing her and degrading himself, of
pity for herself that he could let folks see how little he cared
for her. She stood there, bewildered, tragic, impotent, while
gradually it dawned on those near Sam that it was he who
belonged to her. As he was helped to his feet somebody
said: "Sithee, is that thy missis? She wants thee." Sam
turned his bemused face to her with his gaping red mouth
and muttered: "Aye," and moved, stumbling, among the
chairs towards her. She eyed him sorrowfully without speaking. "What's up, 'Arriet? Summat wrong—childer . . . eh?
Wha's want? Tha hasn't come to fotch me, by God, I'st not
ha' that." He was muttering to her, one thought chasing
another through his head.

"Oo's come for a drink, Sam," somebody said, and
laughed, and another voice took it up: "Aye, she doesn't see
why tha should ha' it aw." "Get her a bottle o' Guinness.
Here, I'll stand her one." Harriet turned and faced this
small table whence the witticisms came. She was aware of
the coarse faces staring at her, the liquor-emboldened eyes
and then, without thought, in a wild, imperious movement
of her arm she swept the contents of the table—glasses of
beer, liqueur brandy, pint pots, a jug of water—into their
laps. Vainly they tried to avoid the splash and the mess,
while near-by tables roared with laughter and besought the
barmen to bring some napkins "because these chaps have
wet theirsels." Harriet hadn't spoken; her tears were gone.
With a curt, beckoning nod to Sam she strode out, and men
made way for her to go. Outside Sam caught her up in a
shambling trot. "Tha shouldn't ha' done that, lass," he said.

"No? What should I ha' done? Kissed 'em?"

"What's up wi' thee?"

"Nowt. I like to see thee runnin' after other women."

They walked on, in great discomfort, silently, the atmosphere alive, Sam feeling somehow he had a grievance, sullen, resentful, knowing he had wronged her; Harriet, feeling her world was half in pieces, her mind occupied with a vision of this young woman with a mop of dark red hair, a mouth brilliant as a cherry, a bosom and legs, she knew, lovely enough to drive a man crazy, and enough hot life in her to hold a score of lovers. And all at once she felt old.

"Tha'rt shivering," Sam said.

.   .   .   .

The smoke-room of the Black Bull said Mrs. Renshaw "were a corker," that "it served Sam reet," that "no dam' wonder he got out of her road," that "she had all her chairs at home," and that Sam, "weren't much a pound." Then it settled down again, the men who suffered Harriet's onslaught having mopped up their trousers, and Trixie having pranced up to their table and sung, pointing to the wet clothes and floor: "Was it done by the baby? Oh, he's a wonderful child." But the men took it well enough; the liquor inside them and their sense of broad humour saw to that. As she danced back she stared into the eyes of a sallow-faced young man who was trying to look more at home than he felt, and who sat near the platform as alone as anybody in that assembly could be. She smiled at him and made a small grimace as though to say: "Can't you look pleasanter?" and his face flushed, and he looked down at his beer, which he consumed in small sips as if it were poison. He looked out of place. His face was finely drawn—a broad, squarish forehead, brown eyes so dark as to be almost black, and by turns dreamy or smouldering, an irregular nose too long, finely curved lips rather too full and sensuous, and ears slightly prominent and large. His hair was thick and unruly, his hands long and thin and like those of a fiddler. He wore a blue serge suit, and a black tie in a soft white long-pointed collar, and his ancient trilby hat perched uncertainly on his knee.

"What's browt *thee* here, Brierley? After some shares?"

"Nay, he's goin' to put us aw in t' *Burnham Guardian*, aren't tha, 'Arry? Tha'll see it next week. Tha'd best mind what tha sez."

Brierley smiled, and a light came into his eyes, so that the face which had been sardonic became almost benign. But he didn't answer. He lit a cigarette and watched the assembly. Trixie had vanished for the moment along with Charlie who "rattled the dominoes" (as the smoke-room had it), and the business of share-broking had begun. Forms stained with beer were signed on the small circular tables, men on opposite sides of the room were nodding and winking and putting up their ten fingers to one another—once, twice, thrice.

"I'm sellin' Sunrise," said a dried-up old man in a billy-cock hat and with washed-out blue eyes.

"Why, grandad, are you after some brass to buy another mill?" . . . "Yea, he buys 'em like bottles o' Benedictine." . . . "Summat up if Owd Fred's sellin' Sunrise."

"I'm asking fifteen and ninepence," said Fred Buckley, the first speaker, who was director of fourteen companies, and a "seven-figure" man.

"I'll tak' fifteen hundred, Fred," said a man in clogs with a whippet curled behind his feet. Buckley nodded and made a note in a gilt-edged book three inches square.

Brierley, sitting there watching, caught broken snatches of talk. "I'll tak' 'em wi'out the extra three-ha'pence, Jim." . . . "Nay, nay, dost want me to pay thy rent aw next year, too?" "Aye, I saw him pull out three thousand quid sittin' o'er in that corner, an' by God, next time we heard owt, he'd married Polly Holroyd, and they've taken a pub i' Southport." . . . "Yes, this boom's got summat to answer for."

. . . "Well, I applied for them as tha towd me, Tom, but I never got 'em." . . . "Tha were too late; they could ha' allotted 'em six times o'er; besides tha never greased 'im, I suppose? They're not all as innocent as babbies."

"How dost like livin' retired, Mark?" Mark Wilson, a stout florid man completely bald, eyeing the band on his Corona cigar, was understood to say it were all right but he felt like a bloody exhibit in a penny show—all Chesterford were watchin' him. "I heard this mornin' as I had sixteen pints yesterday and were takken whoam in a cab. I'm goin' to write a book about these here adventures I've never had. I'm goin' to Monte Carlo next Friday—so I were towd to-night; they've picked two lasses who're goin' wi' me, too. I believe Trixie's one of 'em."

Brierley's face and eyes leapt into eager inquiry for a second and died again when he realised Mark was joking.

The talk went on. "There's two hundred chimneys within four miles o' this pub, an' every one of 'em is belchin' brass to-day—spinnin' gold." . . . "Did t' hear o' them four spinners from Hyde who've bought a yacht at Knott End? Started out for Liverpool, but two days later were brought back on a trawler—they'd been shipwrecked on a sandbank in th'estuary. When they got off they wanted to buy t' trawler—said they wanted summat wi' engines and boilers in it next time to mak' 'em feel at home." . . . "Two bitters, Dick." . . . "I'll sell fifty Dobbold." . . . "Nay, I shall stick to my Nightstar." . . . "Aye, tha'd better." . . . "Art gooin' through wi' it, Matthew?" . . . "Course; my nod's better than some folk's signature."

There was a commotion at the door and a bow-legged little man with a fixed grin came in—his trousers far too long and his waistcoat too short so that he had hooked it down to his trouser tops with a safety-pin. His face was twisted to one side and his nose broken and marked with blue from a fall of coal.

"If I let thee in tha's got to be quiet, see?" said the barman.

"Oh, I'll be quiet, I'm allus quiet. I'll be quiet as a chap they buried at All Saints' this afternoon. I saw him, I saw him," said the little man, and his jaws went rapidly after he had ceased speaking.

"Bring t' lad a beer, Dick," said somebody. The little bow-legged man watched the barman out and then began in a high, loud voice, pouring out his words in a stream on one note and at great speed. "You're at it again, you're at it again; what did Jesus say to the money-grubbers in the Temple? He said, 'I will whip you with scorpions.' He said, 'You have made it a den . . .'" ("Put a sock in it, Sid." . . . "Does thy mother know tha'rt out, lad?" . . ." E's got 'em again; they've no business to let 'im in." . . . "It's a damn' shame—somebody ought to look after 'im.") Dick, the barman, came back, deliberately twisting the waxed ends of his thick, black moustache, and then pushed his sleeves a bit farther up. When Sid saw him his voice went a tone higher. "Why do the 'eathen so furiously rage? . . ." he began, almost shrieking but shrinking the while perceptibly down on his seat. Dick stood over him and gathered him up like a child and carried him out, the small legs moving convulsively behind as he took him out head first under his arm. The high, babbling voice was still going on.

The smoke-room was momentarily disconcerted. A spinner next to Brierley knocked out his clay pipe and said, addressing nobody in particular but so that everybody heard: "He's been like that ever sin' that explosion at Higginbottom's pit. He were th' only mon i' his level to come out livin'—an' he'd ha' bin better kilt." Everyone knew the

story but everyone felt it was right it should be mentioned—
that an explanation was needed for something that was a
little shameful. The mood was brief. Charlie was observed
going to the piano once more, and in a moment was thump-
ing:

> "*I've been out with Charley Brown,*
> *Charley Brown last night;*
> *You can trust old Charley Brown,*
> *Charlie Brown's all right . . ."*

But it was Trix they wanted; Trix to restore their humour. And Trix came and bowed, displaying that tantalising glimpse of her bosom once more, so that Brierley felt a
thrill of mingled anger and delight and jealousy, and she
began to sing: "How'd You Like to Spoon with Me?" and
to make all that ditty's coquettish and exciting inquiries as
to how they would like to have a kiss, and hold her in their
arms like this; so that Brierley began to suffer exquisite torture. As the song proceeded Trixie left the stage and went
to perch for a second or two on the knee of a fresh-faced
man of middle age, whose grey hair stood up in short
bristles, whose white broad tie held a diamond pin, who had
sat quietly drinking his whisky with plain water.

"Nah then, Mr. Blackburn, you'll have to be careful."
But Mr. Blackburn wasn't being at all careful. He hadn't
carved his way from selling fents on Chesterford market-
place to controlling the Blackburn group for nothing. He
put his arm firmly round Trix's waist, gave her a hug and
kissed her cheek with a smack. And Trix made every pre-
tence of enjoying it. She put her arm round his neck and
whispered in Mr. Blackburn's ear, and he whispered back
and they both laughed and he squeezed her again.

It was only a matter of thirty seconds all told but Henry

Brierley found it time enough to explore the very depths of misery. He was thinking: "She threatened to do it last night but I never believed she would. She said she was wanton and, by God, she'll make me believe soon that she is. She said she would stop at nothing to get what she wants. Oh, Trix, my darling, how can you do it?" He couldn't remove his eyes from her. He could see Blackburn's fat hand moving up to her arm pit and touching her breast. She leapt up then with an alarmed look, the startled look of a frightened child momentarily in her eyes until she crushed it and conjured up her hard fixed smile again. She flitted across the room and, almost dazed, Brierley found her sitting lightly—he was conscious of no weight at all—on his knee and she kissed him swiftly on the brow and rose in an instant. Back on the stage she bowed, kicked up her skirt as she went and was gone. The crowd thundered their feet and clapped and shouted for her, but she didn't come back; and Brierley sat there only dimly aware for a moment of the banter directed at him and Blackburn. "Which on yo's takkin' her whoam?" they were asked; and, "You'll ha' to mak' her a director o' some o' your mills, Mr. Blackburn."

"I've thought of sleepin' partner," said Blackburn, and chuckled deep in his throat. (All his talk came from there; you had to listen carefully when Thomas Blackburn spoke.) Brierley felt himself growing chilled with discomfort. Why did she lend herself to this, lay herself open to these insults? She knew, everybody knew, the sorts of men they were? Could he fight them *all*? Yet he was aware of a feeling that he ought to, that he couldn't sit there silent. Suddenly he said: "I shouldn't advise you to insult her, Blackburn." His voice was strained and colourless.

Blackburn turned. "Advice? Thee? Tha were havin' thy pap when I took a woman first."

"The years haven't improved you."

"Sithee," Blackburn said, "when I want thy interference I'll buy it—as I could buy thee—an' her, too. Tuppenny ha'-penny librarian." He grunted. "Tha's been readin' too many free novelettes."

There was a titter at that. Brierley was thinking: "Why did I come to this place? They know I despise them and they all hate me. I'm no match for this sort of thing." But he said; "If you mention her name again except with respect, I'll damage you," and he rose and his tall, thin body bent as he leaned forward across the small round table. Dick, the barman, who had stood listening, came forward. "Nah then, gentlemen, this is no road to be carryin' on. It were aw meant i' fun, I'm sure. Isn't that so, Mester Blackburn?"

Blackburn pulled a face and finished his whisky. "I mak' no explanations," he said, and rose. He stared across at Brierley. "I shan't forget," he said, and walked steadily and unhurriedly out of the room. One or two said, "Good neet," but he didn't answer them. He was conscious that "he could buy them up," and you didn't trouble to be courteous to folk you could buy up; not if you were Thomas Blackburn.

When he had gone, somebody said: "I'll say nowt agen him—but he'll do wi' watchin'.'"

"Tha's said it, lad. Dick, two bitters."

•   •   •   •   •   •   •   •

Brierley found Trix standing at the small bar in the passage.

But she was not alone. One of Brierley's misgivings about her and one of the causes of his heartburnings was that she was never alone; it made him at once proud and sad; he realised he must appear comparatively unexciting to her. It did not surprise him; if every man in Lancashire who had ever beheld her had been in love with her, that would not

have surprised him either. It seemed inevitable that it
should be so.

Trix was talking to Philip Houghton, who was lolling
against the bar and hiding his empty sleeve as best he could.
"Hello, Cousin Harry," Houghton said.

Brierley, not unaccustomed to this faintly ironical greeting, and a little too shaken from his encounter with Blackburn to feel he could face another, said shortly, "Hello,
Houghton. Are you ready, Trix?" She was not. She was
having a whisky and ginger ale with Houghton and was en-
grossed in Houghton's account of his father's project for
a Chesterford repertory theatre. "And," said Houghton,
"you might find yourself burgeoning forth as a new dramatist of the Manchester School, Brierley."

Trix said: "Then I might get a part in your play, Harry.
Wouldn't that be luvly?" She looked smaller in her ordinary
clothes, her navy blue coat and skirt and brown shoes. The
paint wasn't completely removed from her lips, nor the
eye-black from her lashes. She carried her small hat in her
hand and the glory of her hair in that drab, tawdry passage
was as a painting in a dark gallery. Brierley said: "I think
I might even accomplish that for you, Trix." He looked at
her, worshipping, and there was unashamed tenderness in
his voice. She flushed a little, and turned to Houghton.
"You'll promise to get me a part won't you, Mr. Houghton?
We'd have such jolly times round the back." She laughed
and smiled archly at him. "I've always thought you were
wasted here," Houghton said, and looked down and sideways at her from under his soft black hat. "You mean I
could come round to see you?"

She giggled. "Why, of course."

"If anything could induce me to use my influence with
father, that would." He drank up his brandy. "See you on
the Christmas-tree," he said, in an ineffectual attempt to be

hearty, raised his hat with something of mocking gallantry, and went. They heard his car start.

"I'd rather see his back than his face any day," Brierley said.

"I think he's nice."

"Oh, well. . . . Shall we go?"

"I don't know. Not sure I want to. Not if you're goin' to be like this. Bad-tempered thing." She pouted and looked at him with clouded, petulant eyes.

"Darling, it hasn't been very easy to-night. That fellow Renshaw and then Blackburn . . ."

"Why do you come? I don't like you to . . . not in a way. Makes me feel queer somehow—spoils my show. And they all know you're—well, after me. I have to belong to everybody when I'm doin' my part—else I don't go well. *You* know, Harry."

Yes, he knew—knew she had to make them all feel she was prepared to belong to each of them. He said: "I understand, Trix. Only you can't expect me to enjoy it. You're glad I care, aren't you?" He took her fingers in his but after a second she removed them and prinked her hair. Her drink was now finished and she examined her face in a small hand-mirror, smoothed her jacket, tried to look over her shoulder at her back, ostentatiously said good night to the barmaid at the far end of the bar and, when she could find no reason for delaying further, turned and walked towards the door. Brierley hesitated whether to accompany her but at the door she paused looking at him questioningly and holding the door ajar. He walked swiftly to her and they crossed the road past the marching Fusilier on his pedestal. Neither spoke for a while. Then she said: "A girl like I has to be careful."

"Like *me*, dear," he said gently.

"All right," she said pertly. "Needn't swank. Mighty full

of yourself. That's why people don't like you—they can see you're too up-stage for anything. Always the same; throwing your weight about—about the boom too. You're only jealous because you can't make any brass."

"I believe it's a swindle. Half of it's fictitious—the cloth's the same—one yard hasn't become ten yards because they get ten times as much for it." He rushed out the words.

She said, making no effort to follow that, and, anyway she had heard it before: "Mr. Blackburn is putting a hundred Acme's into my name when they're allotted next week."

"You won't take them." He spoke imploringly, hurt.

"Won't I just? D'you think I'm doolally?" Her voice was as hard as metal.

"Do you know what he said to-night? That he could buy you?" He knew he was plunging about uncertainly, seeking for words to turn her mind, and the next instant he was sorry he had said that. He added in extenuation: "He said he could buy me, too."

"He can't—and he knows it; but he can give me shares, if he likes." After a moment or two she added, musingly: "Them as have t' money get most things they want, don't they? Oh, don't preach at me!" as he began to speak. "You've not been brought up in a mucky slum, nor you don't live in one. I do. There's two kids to help to feed on what I get, an' a stepfather who chucks his wages away on horses every other week, and who puts the fear o' God into my mother when he gets to the end o' the street and puts his fingers in his mouth and whistles to let us know he's comin'. He's like a devil. I'll murder him one o' these nights, s'welp me, I will." Her voice rose in a sudden access of hysteria and passion and she clutched Brierley's arm. He placed his arm about her and they stopped and he held her to him near a lamp on Burnham Road as unaware of the world as if he had been in the middle of Chesterford Moor. And

when she put her head against his shoulder he felt life had
not much more to give him. "Don't distress yourself, dear,"
he said. "I'll look after you." But he was aware it wasn't
much more than a figure of speech.

"I wish you could, Harry," she said. "But"—she shook
her head—"you can't. Nobody can without they have
money. Why can't you get some money and I'll make Mr.
Blackburn allot you shares?" They were walking on again.
She began to talk with extreme quietness, almost in a child's
voice. "You see, Harry, even if you asked me to marry you,
I couldn't. You only get—what is it, four pounds a week?
Where'd we be on that? Who'd buy the furniture? Besides,
I want to be well off—have money to chuck about. Oh,
Harry, you've no idea what it is to want nice clothes and
know you could look luvly in 'em and you can't afford to
buy even one. You think I'm bad because I think about
clothes so much and about brass. P'raps I am but I can't
help it. I *could* be bad to get money to run away with from
where I live, and to take my mother with me. But she
wouldn't come any road, my mother wouldn't." He had put
his arm round her waist and, as they walked, her hips moved
against his and when he inclined his cheek towards her hair
he could smell the odour of faint perspiration mixed with
grease-paint and cheap scent. But the smell didn't offend him.
He almost liked it being unpleasant, took pride and delight
in having to love her with her faults of speech, crudities of
manner. He brushed her hair with his lips as they walked
but she took no notice; perhaps she was unconscious of what
he did, perhaps she chose to ignore it; he didn't know. They
arrived at the top of Walker Street, where she lived, and
their feet came to a slow, undecided halt. She said, suddenly,
looking up at him: "You can come into the entry for a
minute if you like." He felt his blood tingle, and his face
grow warm. He pressed her to him and they turned down

into a narrow dark entry between two high gable ends. They
had stood there before and one night a policeman had shone
his lantern on them and ordered them to come out. It had
been humiliating. He had felt it more than Trix; she had
stared at the policeman boldly, almost superciliously. Since
then Brierley had been timid and half ashamed of passers-by
mocking them or of another encounter with the police. But
there was no alternative. Trix had refused to be courted
openly or to go to his mother's house; and her own was out
of the question. They leaned against the wall and he pressed
her body to him. He sought her mouth but she gave him
only her cheek and when, after a time, she allowed him to
kiss her on the mouth, it was only for a moment. But she
held him tight as if she would never let him go. Suddenly
she relinquished him completely and he stood away from
her, trembling a little. She said, speaking quickly and hardly
louder than a whisper, though it was plain she was cool:
"It's no good loving me, Harry, without brass. Is it? You
can see what it amounts to any morning in the police-court.
Anybody can make money now if they have a bit to start
with. Look at Sam Renshaw—he's made over a thousand
quid. Why don't you use the library money—that you've got
to buy them new books with? You could pay it back in a
fortnight. *I* can get all the shares you want—it's money for
dirt, Harry." She stood closer to him, her lips parted, the
face like a pale flower in the dark, her eyes, where a fragment of light caught them, sparkling like stones. She lifted
her mouth up, and he seized her and kissed her, pressing her
mouth to his until their lips grew soft and mingled together.
She pushed him away and walked back into the street and
left him, and he leaned against the wall for a moment,
steadying himself.

Chapter Five

NUMBER 17 WALKER STREET where Trix lived was in the middle of the row. A yard to the top left of the door was a corporation lamp-bracket fastened to the wall; the lamp's light illumined the uneven flags and the doorway and window of Number 17 so that Josh Meadows, her stepfather, could read the racing tips lounging at the door till late at night, and (a circumstance which bothered Trix and her mother still more) so that no one could come or go by night or day without being observed by curious neighbours opposite. Not that people stared overmuch in Walker Street; the noise of shouts, shrill laughter, yells or screams signalled the street's happenings with remarkable efficiency; but the occasions when the street took a lively interest in your affairs alternated with those when, had you lived in Park Lane, London, W., you would not have been more rigidly left alone. Wife beating, for example, was nobody's affair but the couple's and the policeman's; and hardened constables had learnt to look on it with tolerance, for the wife could be relied on as often as not to join in and help her husband to fight the constable and to swear in court that the constable started it. Women were as kittle in Walker Street as in the Mile End Road, Shanghai or Harlem.

It was 10.45 p.m. and Walker Street was quiet. Most of the doors were shut and the front rooms in darkness, for

Walker Street earned its living by divers occupations that begin early in the morning—labouring at mills, forges, brickworks, street-sweeping, carting, and those other jobs at which men are taken on and dismissed with, sometimes, less thought concerning their welfare than was exercised on slaves, and not half the care that is properly received by both animals and machinery. And Walker Street, except on Saturdays, Sundays and public festivals, was wont to retire early.

A cat sat before Number 17 complacently washing herself. The door was open. There remained, however, a small rickety wooden gateway a yard high designed to prevent the young Meadowses from adventuring in Walker Street at untimely moments. Trix lifted it aside and walked down the lobby whose green, faded walls were hideous in the street lamp's pale yellow light (until you reached the last foot which was left in total blackness) and opened the door into the kitchen.

"Hello, mother, what are you ironin' for this time o' night?" She spoke as soon as she opened the door, and her mouth was compressed and turned down at the corners in disapproval.

"They're just a few I'm finishin'." Jane Meadows spat on the new iron taken from the fire, watched the drop of spittle form a ball and roll off on to the floor, rubbed the iron on a piece of burnt sacking and began dexterously to iron a laced pinafore.

"Is Josh in?" As she spoke Trix hung up her coat and hat on a rack in the lobby.

"No, luv."

"Been suppin' the money you're makin', as usual?"

Mrs. Meadows took a deep breath and let it go with a sigh, but she didn't answer. What was the good? Trix would have her own way, and she was probably right. Presently she said: "Does he ever come to the Black Bull?"

"Not where I am. He said he would one night; I told Dick, the barman, if he let him in, I walked off. But I don't think he came. Listen mother, will you leave him if I get some money?"

The ironing went on. Then after a while: "Nay, I can't do that." The voice was little more than breath, it was so quiet. Then, louder: "But there's no need for you to stay, luv. I've made mi bed; I mun lie on it."

Trix sat near the fire, watching this woman who had borne her, stooping over the table, her hands and forearms thin and heavily veined with work, and red with too much hot water and scrubbing. The hair, once as glorious as her own, was thin and faded, the breasts hung loose and heavy in the blue blouse, torn and pinned with a safety-pin under the arm. The face with its sandy eyelashes and blue eyes had become heavily lined and thin and the lips were grey at the edges and wrinkled for want of blood. She thought: "You know, mother, Josh'll never luv you any more. You've half killed yourself for him and the more you do it, the less he's liked you and will like you. And men bein' what they are, p'raps he couldn't help it." She got up. "Sit down, mother; I'll finish these."

"Nay, luv. You'll find your supper in th' oven. I made you and Josh a bit o' summat—a few fish-cakes."

"You're as difficult to deal with as a cart-load o' monkeys, mother."

Trix stood up and watched her mother and her mother leaned on her hands on the table and looked at her daughter. They smiled at one another. Trix knew it was no good persisting; her mother would finish when she thought she would. Her mother was thinking: "There's a lot o' me in her; they can't tak' that away from me. Aye, an' she could marry a duke if she were in t' 'right place. Well, happen she will yet. She's handsome enough." She said: "Get your supper, luv. Did yo' go well to-night? I bet you did."

"Pretty tidy." Trix took her fish-cakes from the oven where they lay warming between two plates, and cut herself some bread.

"That's your butter in that dish. No, that other's marg. They can't all have butter."

"They could if *he* fetched his wages home."

Mrs. Meadows didn't reply to that. She said, after a moment: "There's some cold milk if you want it. I took an extra gill. It's funny, Trixie, isn't it, there's so much money goin' about i' Chesterford just now and none of it comes to seventeen Walker Street?" Trix was tempted to say something about Thomas Blackburn but she didn't. Her mother went on: "I were up near t' share exchange this mornin'. A Salvation Army chap come up and started sellin' t' *War Cry* to 'em as they come out. He kept sayin': 'Count your blessin's, sir; count your blessin's.' More than one gave him a Bradbury—aye, an' seemed afe ashamed of anybody seein' 'em do it. They must be rollin' in it when they part wi' it that road. I could ha' understood it if they'd bin drunk."

"What's Josh been givin' you lately?"

"It varies." Mrs. Meadows's lips shut tighter than usual but Trix never noticed it.

"It's weeks since he gave you more'n a pound, isn't it? He must make at least two."

"They've had a bad place in t' pit—full o' stone."

"I bet they've had a sight more coal than Josh ever lets on."

"Happen they have an' happen they havena."

"You've got too much patience, mother; you'll stand anythin'."

"Well, luv, I'm gettin' a bit impatient wi' yo' if that's any consolation to yo'." A smile played about the ravaged face. Trix walked to her and put her arm round her waist and as

they stood there, a picture of weary resignation and impetu-
ous revolt, a shrill whistle penetrated to the kitchen, a
whistle that started midway up the scale and ascended and
sustained its height for a beat or two and then achieved a
dying, wailing fall akin to a factory hooter when the steam
is withdrawn. Trix felt her mother stiffen in her arms, and
her breath begin to come and go faster. She gripped her
tighter and pressed their cheeks together. "Never mind,
mother," she said. "Never mind."

"It's all right, luv. I don't suppose he'll be so bad. You'd
best go to bed; it'll be easier for me. I don't want you to
start bickerin'. I shall manage him easier by mesel'."

"I shan't leave you."

"Yea, you will. You mun. I wed him, not yo'. Go on, luv,
he's comin'."

The voices of two men and a woman could be heard near
the front door. "It'll bloody-well win, I tell thee," Josh was
saying. "Tha can put thy chemise on it, Alice—if tha wears
one. I sometimes wonder if tha does; I conna tell. . . ."
There was a scuffle and suppressed giggles and an oath. "By
God, tha'rt pins all over thee," Josh's voice said, and then
the other man, more maudlin, "Tha'rt bitten, arta? Serves
thee reet. I towd thee she were mine. Tha'rt mine for t' neet,
aren't tha, Alice? Give us a kiss—a proper 'un, an' I'll gie
thee two shares in t' Swallowtail. I will, s'elp me Bob, I
will." The two women could hear the sound of slobbering
kisses, and then Josh's voice again: "Good neet, love-birds,
I mun get in to my own owd nest"; and as he lurched up the
lobby he muttered, "Aye, bloody owd."

Mrs. Meadows pushed Trix towards the staircase that
opened into the kitchen. "Go on, Trix—to please me."

"I shan't take my things off. I shall come down if . . ."
Her mother wiped her eyes with her fingers, patted Trix's
back and turned in time to see Josh come in. That walk

down the passage had robbed him of all his liveliness. His face was, as they said in Chesterford, "like a week o' wet Sundays." He didn't look at his wife but walked to a small chair near the fire and planked himself down on it. His light cloth cap perched on the back of his head allowing his black hair—there was hardly any grey in it—to fall rumpled over his forehead. He sat forward, forearms along his knees and his muscular, thick-fingered hands lightly holding one another and staring at a spot between his fine-pointed figured clogs. His double chin rested on his plaid woollen scarf and in repose the flesh of his face, puffed with drink, sagged as though it had grown too big for its frame. His eyes were heavy with sleep and drink and he began to nod, until, slipping an inch forward on his chair he roused himself and looked up sullenly at his wife.

"What art starin' at?" he asked. She saw the disdain and indifference in his black eyes too small for his face and made diminutive by the thick, coarse brows.

"I've kept some supper for you, Josh—"

"I want no supper—whar is it? Fish-cakes agen?"

"I thowt—"

"Tha must think I'm a dam' cat wi' thy fish-cakes. Has that wench come in?"

"Trix has gone to bed."

"Tha doesn't say. Gone to bed. Aye. Anybody wi' her?" He began to sing in his thick toneless voice, "How'd Yo' Like to Spoon with Me?" simpering at the end, and grimacing.

"Hush, Josh—you've no right . . . She's as straight . . ."

"She lives i' my 'ouse, doesn't she? Showin' her legs to everybody in t' pub. No better than a tart. . . ."

"She does it to keep the childer yo' don't keep yoursel'."

Josh got up slowly, his head jutting forward, and with a sudden dive seized his wife's wrist.

"Tha bitch," he said. "Tha bitch, I'll larn thee," and he began to unfasten the leather strap from the top of his trousers.

"I'm sorry, Josh. I shouldn't ha' said that. I know you've got a bad place." The tears had filled her eyes and were welling over and down her cheeks. With her disengaged hand she tried to stem them and wipe them away.

Suddenly he let her go and pushed her from him. "We've had no peace sin' she left t' mill," he said. "Tha knows that. 'Trixie, Chesterford's wonderful wench from t' mill,' " he said, quoting the poster outside the Black Bull. "What the hell dost think men say to me—her sittin' on owd men's knees, in t' pub? Keepin' th' house, is she? Well she'd best clear out. Or, by God, I'll mak' her sleep wi' me. She's tempted me often enough."

His wife stood as if transfixed, as if some unlooked-for blow had struck her in the face.

"Tha'rt lyin'," she said. The blood had run from her face and an ethereal light shone in her face and eyes. "Tha'rt not fit to live in t' same house as a decent girl."

Josh raised the belt that hung limp in his hand and lifted it behind his head. It fell with a swish through the air and struck her across the left arm and neck. She made no effort to save herself but stood there for a moment or two as if carven, while her eyes, scornful and intimidating, taunted him to fury. A second blow fell and Mrs. Meadows now raised her arm to protect her face, and closed her eyes. She swayed and turned and collapsed in a chair, her arms spread over the ironing table and her head sunk on to the cloth. She made no sound whatever; it was as if all life had suddenly, quietly, left her body.

Josh stood leaning towards her, his hand hanging down and the belt trailing on the floor. He stood there motionless, stupid; he might, like his wife, have been turned into a waxwork. Then a sound caught his ear and he looked up. Trix was standing at the bottom of the stairs, her eyes extraordinarily wide open and shining with a vivid, preternatural light. Her face was fixed like a mask and her lips parted. She looked mad; she frightened him. She moved slowly and stealthily towards the fireplace. He was aware somehow, that she was seeking a weapon but he watched her and never moved. Neither made any sound at all. Suddenly, when two yards away from the fireplace, she leapt to the grate, seized, with her bare hand, the handle of the hot flat-iron and faced him. She was like a magnificent, outraged animal. "You devil," she said; "you filthy devil," and her breast rose and fell swiftly as she panted the word. Josh raised his belt half-heartedly and took a pace forward and as he did so she hurled the flat-iron at his head. The pointed front of it struck him above the left eye and for a second he stood poised ere he half turned and fell at her feet, his head on the floor, his shoulders and trunk arched for a moment on his head ere he rolled over sideways and lay there while the blood oozed out of the wound. Trix stood there for a moment, her face distorted with rage, fear and dismay. She raised her bruised and burnt hand to her cheek and as it touched her face she was conscious for the first time of pain in it. And the pain and the sight of blood together swept her control from her. She sprang to her mother and fell on her knees, her head in her mother's lap, and burst into wild sobs. After a moment or two Mrs. Meadows raised her head and put her arms about Trix, and the two women clung to one another, and the tears ran down the faces of both of them. Presently, when Trix had quieted, Mrs. Meadows lifted the corner of her apron and wiped her own eyes with it and Trix's also.

"There, luv," she said. "There. Don't tak' on so." She rose and looked at Josh lying there. The blood was congealing darkly round the wound and he was making a noise when he breathed as if his sleep were drunken and extremely heavy. She filled a basin with warm water and, crouching on the floor, took his head in her lap and began to bathe it. Trix's breath was leaving her lips in trembling sighs, as from a small child that cannot control itself.

After a while, when the wound was cleaned and bandaged, Mrs. Meadows said: "We'd best get him to bed."

"You'll have to sleep wi' me, mother."

Mrs. Meadows shook her head. "He might want me," she said.

Slowly, with extreme labour, half exhausted as they were, they began to pull and lift and drag Josh up the narrow stairs.

Chapter Six

BRIERLEY leaned against the wall feeling exhausted and cold and spent. Now that Trix had gone he experienced a momentary relief, an easefulness as if a strain were over; as if love were a trial that had better not be borne and women beings who were too disturbing to the spirit to be supportable for long. But he knew too, that the mood would be brief. By the morning at the latest he knew he would be occupying his mind with her, asking himself how many hours must pass before he saw her again, aching for the sight of her. He was becoming familiar with the processes through which his mind would go, as he had grown accustomed to the processes by which his body would sometimes achieve its ecstasy of love—climbing to a height, pausing there a while in a state of exaltation, flinging him thence into an abyss of tiredness and mental stagnation and beginning thenceforward to recover and slowly take him step by step up the hill once more. He was able to look on this rhythm from outside himself and regard his body with pity that it was used so ill, served him so well and was made the sport of his mind so unfeelingly.

He walked out of the entry a little uncertainly and was unfeignedly thankful to find himself walking up the street unobserved and to reach the brighter Burnham Road. His spirits rose as he walked and his pace increased. He would

try not to think too much or take life so gravely. He was
making a fool of himself over her (he told himself). She
was a superb animal, the handsomest girl in Chesterford
right enough but, after all, who was she—a mill girl whose
effrontery . . . He was smiling to himself now as he permitted his mind to run about wantonly, build this false edi-
fice and spin this fairy-tale to him. For Trix demolished all
edifices. She came, and lo! they vanished. He went on (in his
fanciful mind) : "The girl for you, my lad, is Mary Houghton—an exquisite creature—a mind akin to your own, as
fine a feeling for words, if lacking your own fire and skill
with them (he indulged in a special grin here) : sensitive,
lovely in a sombre way, adoring the theatre, and . . . and
not utterly out of your reach, despite her father's mills and
the fact that far back you share the same blood. A cousin
half a dozen times removed—something like that—far
enough, anyway, to make marriage safe. Why can't you be
sensible and fall in love with *her*?" His mind ran on, abandoned Mary and returned to Trix. He leapt over the evening's happenings, hastening past the unpleasantness, pausing when the moments had afforded him joy. How few the
moments of joy were!—hardly any till she had held him
tight in the entry—yearned to him—and spoken to him of
his making use of the library's money. That, he saw, ought
to have shocked him, affronted him, scandalised him; but
it didn't. If anybody but Trix had suggested it, perhaps it
would have done. But he couldn't be sure of that, either.
This business of money was the devil; he didn't pretend to
understand it, but he couldn't be orthodox about it. It was
as Malvolio said of greatness: some were born rich and
some had riches thrust upon them. This Thomas Blackburn,
for example, a man whose only qualities, so far as he was
able to observe them, were those of a face of brass, a will-
ingness to "chance his arm" as Chesterford said, ruthless-

ness and luck. No good railing at luck, but no good either, pretending it didn't exist. Didn't Napoleon, when choosing new marshals ask: "Is this man a lucky general?" All rot—partly rot, anyway—to say: "Luck is character." If you were born a duke's son or a millionaire's or a genius's—well, wasn't that luck? Wasn't it pure luck whether your brains were good, your character strong, your ability that of making money in a world which prizes that and gives it precedence above all but genius? Make enough money from multiple suits or a brand of lard and you could buy yourself nobility so-called to the end of time—or the end of England which was, he supposed, the same thing. Take himself, Henry Brierley. His great-grandmother, he dared swear, had been better loved and been a more gifted creature than Houghton's wife. Had she met Houghton earlier he, Brierley, would have been in Philip Houghton's shoes—well, something like it. What couldn't he have done?—nothing to do but write his plays, or travel the world looking for material for novels. He couldn't help thinking fate had dropped his bread and butter, butter side down; oh, gritty in the extreme. Of course (resuming the discussion with himself), his own luck, compared with most folk's was prodigious. What of Trix's stepbrother and sister, born of Josh, with all his coarseness and cruelty in their bones, his features stamped on their faces, the misery of their mother poisoning their home, their poverty stunting their bodies and starving their minds? A fair chance? You might as well talk of a negro having a fair chance of marrying into the English peerage. Justice? Wasn't it Shaw who said that nobody in the world had ever had it up to now? No use imagining then, that he, Brierley, would obtain it; and (with a wry grin again) happen it would be better if he didn't. It straightened things out—this thinking of the Meadowses' household—made him see he had been awarded (say) sixty per cent out of

the Almighty's hundred. And that took him back to the
money problem again. Those who had these counters, these
checks, these symbols (for that was all they were), had
merely to display them, or agree to a figurative loaning of
them to be awarded more and more and more. Talk about
usury being sinful! In this system, which, in the main, looked
on itself as Christian, half the wealthy people were nothing
but Shylocks, whatever they might call themselves. And a
good many of the others were gamblers. Brokers at Liverpool, for example, at New Orleans and at New York,
gambled in raw cotton that never existed—they bought it
and sold it, but never saw it or took delivery of it or disposed of it: they lived on their wits in the truest sense of the
term—far more so, it seemed to him, than the bogus pro-
fessors who sold you balsams to cure all ills on Chesterford
market-place, or the Jews, who, with amazing effrontery,
tricked you into buying gold watches made of brass at Blackpool. This cotton boom, too, he didn't pretend to be anything of an economist or to understand the workings of
money (he had a shrewd suspicion that very few even among
the experts did) but this 1920 Klondyke business, this get-
rich-quick hurly-burly, this declaration over-night that a
factory which was worth so much yesterday was worth five
or ten or fifteen times as much the day after—who could
make head or tail of that? It was the sort of thing you
dreamt and banished from your mind on waking. But this
wasn't to be banished, this was "fact." Since the spring of
1919 over two hundred spinning mills and nearly fifty weaving sheds had been refloated on this miraculous sea that
might (he thought) have been better named a mirage.
Lancashire was making millions, the newspapers said. And
could you gainsay it? Didn't he know Mrs. Pilkington, who
washed for his mother, who had had fifty pounds in the Dobberley mill and had now drawn five hundred pounds for the

asking?—nay, she had not even asked. This up-to-date mysterious magician that put ideas into men's minds, had persuaded somebody that the Dobberley mill, a mill that had never succeeded in paying its operatives enough to enable them to make holiday for more than one week in fifty-two, or to live in houses with baths, or to work pre-war less than fifty-five and a half hours a week, or to pay its way at all unless children toiled in it from the age of ten or so, yielding to its greedy demand half the hours that should have been spent at school ("half-time" they called that ingenious method of making children old before their time)—this magician had now made men believe that the Dobberley mill was worth fifteen times its former value; and all the Mrs. Pilkingtons had been staggered by the presentation of money out of—well, where on earth had it come from? But, indeed, the staggering had been short-lived. They soon got used to it. They read in the *Chester-ford Courier* and similar purveyors of "hard facts" that yarn that used to be worth 2s. a pound was now worth 7s., that the whole earth was crying out for cotton shirtings and calicoes and loin-cloths and damasks and sheetings and the rest of it, that nobody outside Lancashire could supply them, that sellers had buyers in the hollows of their hands, that the indubitable law of supply and demand (and who could think of questioning *that*) was working overtime, that if Lancashire had twice as many mills they would all be busy, and that since Lancashire couldn't build any more mills (at least not for months and months) those that *were* there ready built became every day of greater value, and, any-how, that the price for building one to-day was many times as much as when these were erected and, again, therefore, these existing ones were hopelessly and inadequately under-valued, and the sooner they were put on a proper economic basis the better for everybody concerned and the more

soundly business would be conducted. And if you said it all
(or thought it all) very quickly it sounded all right, didn't
it? And you couldn't blame Mrs. Pilkington for knowing
no better, could you, when most of the hard-headed, shrewd,
clear-eyed business men of Lancashire, born and bred in the
trade, whose fingers and thumbs were more scientific (so
they profoundly believed) than instruments, whose per-
spicacious nods and winks on 'Change had the authority of
written agreements, knew no better either, and among whom
a solitary voice crying out in the wilderness: "It is a South
Sea Bubble," was as little heeded as John the Baptist's two
thousand years before? No, assuredly you couldn't blame
Mrs. Pilkington. But, after all, where did the money come
from? From the capacious and rapacious pockets of Mr.
Thomas Blackburn who took a prime part in the transac-
tion? Indeed, no. Mr. Blackburn did quite well out of it.
Mr. Blackburn's syndicate bought the mill for £400,000 and
promptly refloated it with a new capital of £1 shares, 10s.
paid, that were issued at a price of 12s. 6d. and that three
days later stood at 15s. 3d. And so firm was the belief of
Mrs. Pilkington in Mr. Thomas Blackburn and his friends
that she put all her five hundred pounds back into the Dobberley mill. Because everybody said they would pay twenty
per cent dividend for at least five years—and thus you had
your money back and your capital intact and the superb
Dobberley mill still there, still spinning gold, still making
the yarns for those loin-cloths that none of the untold millions of loyal Indians could do without; for who could
conceive of their going naked, or finding they could get on
without Chesterford? And most of the Mrs. Pilkingtons—
and a great many others anxious to be in at the getting rich
fast—put their savings into Dobberley mill; and Mr.
Thomas Blackburn and his syndicate appointed themselves
directors at modest sums of £1,000 or £2,000 a year (so

that one or two of them had incomes all told—being on a score of directorates—of £900 a week), and they permitted all their friends to enter on the ground floor when shares were only at a premium of 2s. 6d. and to make their exits from an upper storey so soon as they had the wit and inclination so to do. And some—not a great many—who had more faith in the Bank of England and its Bradburys than in the Dobberley mill, did so, and live in comparative luxury to this day in Cornwall, and Sussex, or even at Lytham St. Anne's, complimenting themselves on their vision, their skill, and their decision in leaving the wreck in time, and having, no doubt, in their magnanimity, a little pity for the fools who went down, as it were, with the ship.

I do not pretend that Henry Brierley, who earned the sum of four pounds a week as assistant librarian, saw far into the future—saw the Dobberley mill in liquidation and Mrs. Pilkington penniless. He did not. But he was a sceptic: he couldn't understand where the money was coming from, and said so to his intimates; he told Mrs. Pilkington—a tenacious little woman who could drink anything but water, which, she averred, gave her indigestion—that he thought the bricks and mortar of a house of her own was as good a place to invest her money as the bricks and mortar of Dobberley mill, but that might have been, in some measure, because his opinion of Mr. Thomas Blackburn was not high. And when Mrs. Pilkington, standing on her tiptoes pegging his shirt to the line in the garden, remarked that she thought the opinions of "Themashas" were "happen more gradely than those of Themashasn't," and that, as for her, she was always one for holding that folks knew their own know best, he pursued the matter with her no further, and only said he admired her wisdom in not giving up the washing. But she was not to be mollified. It wasn't wisdom, she said: it was a question of his mother not being able to do without her; and she had taken a peg out of her mouth and stuck it determinedly on the line and thrust another one into her mouth like a gunner loading an 18-pounder—as if she were firing veritable salvoes at him. As, doubtless, in her way, she was.

By this time he was uncomfortably wet. The tramway-cars were swaying along, throwing tiny curving waves from their wheels as they rattled and lurched and clanged by him. The wet flags shone and glistened in the shop-windows' light, and an odd, occasional couple stood in a shop door-way, silent, wondering when it would stop raining, admiring (without being aware of the fact) the power and wonder and beauty of nature that could upset all their little plans so easily, and wearing the rapt expression as of profound thought that this idleness of mind commonly bestows. Brierley's trilby hat drooped in front and drops of rain began to fall on the end of his long nose and thence on to his tie, tickling him in the process. His thighs were very wet through being thrust forward, and the turning up of his narrow coat collar afforded him little more protection than if he had turned it up against shell-fire; and, anyway, it wouldn't stay up. Of course, he ought to have boarded a tram, but he was aware that people who board trams when they are as wet as he was are a nuisance to their neighbours and an object of spoken pity sometimes and of unspoken derision at others—for don't they stamp themselves as fools for having been caught so unprepared at a moment when they were so utterly without shelter, in a spot remote (and probably sacred to lovers), or without the money to ride on the tram all the way or alternatively the wherewithal to buy an overcoat or an umbrella? So he didn't board a tram and he didn't shelter; he merely walked or slipped along the pavement—for the flags were greasy and his heels were worn. The tickling drops of water falling on the end of his nose began to exasperate him. He took off his hat and swung it with a swish through the air to remove the overflow of water but the rain fell on his head so coldly and inexorably and withal so eagerly too (somehow he hadn't expected that) that he was fain to replace the hat; and in a moment the nose tickling had begun once more with scientific precision. And in like manner that constant dropping will wear away granite, even so this dropping on to Henry Brierley's nose wore away such small resolution as he had possessed that the library's money must be left intact and that he, for one, would be no party to the crazy, prevalent belief that Chesterford's other name was El Dorado. For nobody who was rich walked home in the teeming rain with water dribbling down the insides of his legs, and his nose running like a down-spout. The tyranny of wealth and the humiliation of having too little money became, in that rain-soaked walk, unendurable; and if taking a risk, and being, for a while, a borrower from public funds, and joining in the scramble after mill shares would rid him of these burdens to body and spirit, then the steps must be taken. His desire of and love for Trix, Trix's sufferings, her audacious (and to him torturing), performances in the Black Bull, his dislike of the routine work of a librarian, his hatred of Mr. Thomas Blackburn and his resentment of the slight condescensions of Philip Houghton, his true admiration of Houghton's sister, and his secret but powerful ambitions to write and use his time and his life as he would—all these impelled him towards this action. But if it had not rained that night, this first step on a new road of destiny would not have been taken; not, at all events, at that time and in that way.

· · · · · · · ·

But it must not be supposed that Brierley was one of those Napoleons among men (though one may doubt whether the Napoleons and Hannibals and Rhodeses and Bismarcks were ever so decisive in their bowels as they appeared to be) who, having made up his mind, was finished and done with it. That was only the beginning. He never bought a hat without seeing an infinitely better one for a cheaper price five minutes later. He never said, or rarely, "This is right," without immediately beginning to think it was probably wrong. He was the sort of man who commits a murder and haunts the spot till he is duly caught and hanged. So, having made up his mind to embezzle, for a limited period, two hundred pounds belonging to the Corporation of Chesterford—money that could not, so far as he could see, be missed for three months—he at once pictured himself discovered, prosecuted, sent to prison, hurled out of decent society with ignominy, bringing his mother's proud head down in sorrow to the grave, and disowned by Trix who would call him an idiot and walk off, serene, disdainful and despising, with Thomas Blackburn or any other fellow who had audacity, no nerves, no scruples and good luck. Nevertheless, he didn't weaken in his resolve. He went on. He always went on, tortured, obstinate, frightened. Of such stuff, maybe, heroes are made. But he was hard to live with during these periods; he was from time to time ill-tempered, jumpy, his sense of humour vanished, and he ceased to be generous. When he reached Number 4, The Laurels, Moorland Road, the semi-detached house his mother owned, he was nervy, and tempted, like most people who have something on their mind, to imagine every question was directed at his secret and, during the moments when he despised himself, that every look was of scorn. But he need not have exercised his mind.

His mother was not an imaginative woman. When he

let himself in with his latch-key and walked down the hall
into the middle room, exuding rain in small rivulets as he
went, she put down Well's *Outline of History,* which she was
reading in fortnightly parts (she found it fascinating but
elusive so that it departed from her head with as much
ease as it entered and left little residue), and remarked,
as she rose to survey him: "You're wet through, lad;
where've you been?" This use of the word "lad" irritated
Brierley; he heard in it admonition, an implication that
he must not imagine himself grown up, not by a long chalk.
So he answered: "In the rain," with a grim consciousness
of how unsatisfactory this reply would be. He could have
laughed, but he didn't. She stood looking at him, not aware
of his being in any way amused, and said: "You're making
a rare mess on the carpet. You'd better have a bath."

"I don't *want* a bath."

"You'll find the water hot," she went on, adding in support of her statement, "I had a bath myself to-night." She
dismissed the question of a bath, and said, as he went out,
"You'd better have some hot whisky too. I never saw anybody so wet."

"I've been as wet before many a time," he said. He felt
impelled to deny that the position was at all remarkable, and
as he went upstairs he was rather tickled by the situation.
But he didn't have a bath. He was firm on that. He changed
his clothes and put a dressing-gown on, went into the bathroom, assured himself that the water was, indeed, intensely
hot and plentiful (it burbled out of the tap sizzling and
plopping), but he only washed his hands and combed his
wet hair, and went down again. He thought for a moment
of the Chesterford worthy who bought a return ticket and
walked back to do the railway company a "thick 'un."

Mrs. Brierley—this short, deep-bosomed, imperturbable
woman with blonde, waved hair, blue-grey eyes hard and

truculent, a trim short nose and triangular face—examined him critically and sceptically. She said. "You've had a quick bath, lad."

"I haven't had a bath," he said, as offhand as he could, but feeling that he was being very honest; and he began to sip his hot whisky and lemon.

"I can't understand you," she said. "You're just like your father."

Henry thought that accounted for him quite adequately, but he contented himself with blowing on his hot whisky to cool it. Yes, he supposed, he *was* like his father—the same Celtic look, the same mixture of dreaminess and obstinacy. He often looked at his mother and wondered what part of him came from her; he couldn't think any of him did: he never felt they belonged to each other at all: the thought that he had sprung from her loins seemed fantastic. He always imagined she had married his father out of hand, as it were, she having nursed him in Chesterford Royal Hospital after he had proved that the composition of a sonnet was incompatible with riding a bicycle down Burnham Road by skidding on a tram-line and finishing up with a broken arm and slight concussion.

"I can't understand," she said, "how you got so wet. The trams haven't broken down again, have they?"

"No." ("Now we are getting to it," he thought.)

"How far did you walk?"

"From the Black Bull." He finished the whisky and put his glass down with decision. Then he added: "I might write something for the *Guardian* about it"; and at once thought: "Why did you say that, you idiot?"

Mrs. Brierley looked at the fire and said: "She's still performing there, then?" She never referred to Trix by name; it was always "she" or "her." Henry thought: "She uses the word 'performing' as though she spoke of a polar bear." He said recklessly: "She was a great success to-night."

"With you?"

This repartee astonished him. He said stubbornly: "With me and everybody else. She's—she's magnificent." And he plunged on: "There's going to be a repertory theatre and she's going to be an actress there."

But Mrs. Brierley wasn't to be either impressed or stampeded. "I shall believe it when I see it," she said. Henry swung the tassel on his dressing-gown and his mother looked at him again and compressed her lips. "I can't think," she said, "what you find at the Black Bull to write about—or anywhere else in Chesterford. Nothing happens to nice people, and the drunken, good-for-nothing louts—they're not worth writing about."

He said ironically: "The human comedy's always worth writing about, isn't it? Besides, Chesterford's making history."

"Well, don't think you're going to write it, lad," she said. "Your father wrote and it never did him a ha'porth o' good."

He thought: "She's in great trim to-night," and answered:

"If he hadn't been a poet and tumbled off his bicycle, he'd never have met you—and where should I have been then?"

"I see nothing funny in it, Henry," she said. "It was a compound fracture of the arm—quite serious."

"I know, but— Oh, well, never mind." He got up and flung up his arms and yawned. "I think I'm going to get hold of some of these mill shares," he said. "May as well be in it—have a flutter." This, he believed, was a dangerous assertion: there would be, he thought, interruptions as to where the money was coming from, and he would display his skill in evading them. But there weren't.

She rose, too, and gave him her cheek to kiss. "Time you fluttered off to bed," she said.

He thought: "Well, that's the limit." And he went upstairs, thinking: "I wonder if she'd had a glass of Madeira to-night. Um . . . having a bath, too. Damn' funny. Perhaps there is a bit of her in me, after all."

Chapter Seven

EDWARD HOUGHTON was accustomed to tell Phœbe that
their daughter Mary was ninety per cent like her mother;
but it wasn't true. And Edward knew it. It is hardly ever
true of a daughter. But he would have found it difficult to
say which he loved the more, his wife or his daughter. Nothing delighted him so much as pleasing them; and he was
wise enough to know that women adore compliments even
when they know they are undeserved or untrue. Moreover,
since his mind was as Machiavellian as most men's, his
motives were confused; he knew his wife was not deceived,
but he knew she was pleased by his thoughtfulness; he
knew Mary was not deceived either, but he was aware she
loved him for being devoted to her mother. So he proceeded
blandly on his way. He would say, in Phœbe's presence:
"Mary, my dear, you grow more like your mother every
day." And Phœbe would say: "Fie, Edward, if she had
breeches on anybody would say she was the spit and image
of you." Which was true. She had her father's rather
hooked nose, his Hebridean blue eyes—blue, purple and
green as brilliantly mixed as a peacock's tail—his wide
mouth, his sense of droll humour, his good nature, affection
and thoughtfulness, his lack of inches; she was five feet
three. She was not markedly clever; nor was he. But she
shared his love of the theatre, of music and books. And it

was natural he should turn to her when the project of a
repertory theatre took shape in his mind. He said: "You
know, Mary, we ought to encourage these northern playwrights." And Mary, instantly thinking of Brierley, said:
"Yes, I think we ought." "We ought," he said, "to foster
our northern drama and create or rather add to the dramatic
literature that already exists; do for Lancashire and Yorkshire what the Abbey Theatre has done for Ireland and
what the Scottish National Theatre is endeavouring to
do for Scotland. Do any two counties in England compare
with ours and Yorkshire for humour, for character, for salt
and flavour of life, for, in short, dramatic material, for—"

"Steady, Father," she said. "I've heard this before. You
are not at the Garrick Society."

"All right; I was wondering how long you'd let me go on.
Still . . . there it is. Lancashire is changing; dialect is
disappearing, new sorts of people are coming into cotton—
look at this boom. There's a subject for you if you like—old
types are dying out, young men with their golf, sports cars,
week-ends at Llandudno and Southport are taking their
place—or pretending to. Somebody ought to be recording
it, dramatising it—putting history on the stage, holding up
the mirror to these days, pointing out our foibles, killing
our stupidities with his ridicule, praising our qualities, helping us along, making us laugh and weep and—sometimes—
feel proud of ourselves. My heavens, I wish I could write.
No wonder Wolfe said he'd rather have written Gray's
Elegy than take Quebec. I'd rather write a fine trilogy of
Lancashire plays than be a boom millionaire."

"Well," she said, "William de Morgan was about your
age when he started. Just a moment—I'll get you a pencil
and paper."

"You'd better order the car instead," he said. "And we'll
go and look at a Methodist chapel that's for sale. There

have been a host of old chapels and churches turned into
cinemas; I see no reason why the stage shouldn't go into
one. After all, it very nearly began there."

"Not chapels, dear—churches or cathedrals."

"Don't be such a Tory, Mary," he said. "Liberalism and
Nonconformity go together and we're all good Radicals in
this family—or ought to be. Upon my soul I doubt whether
it isn't as hard for the camel to go through the needle's eye
as to bring up children who want for nothing, and then
expect them to be anything but Tories. I warn you I shall
put on all the plays by young Socialists I can find—the more
outrageous the better. Ho, won't we have a high old time
upsetting the long-bearded, fixed, priggish, narrow-headed,
humourless Methodists. I suppose, dear," he said, "this is
the wild Houghton blood coming out. Your great-grand-
father George, eh?" He was like a boy rocking himself to
and fro on his heels and talking, while Mary thought:
"Mother was terribly lucky, having him. I wonder if I shall
ever find anybody half so nice? I shall be looking for *his*
qualities all the time, his tricks of kissing mother on the
neck, and bringing her flowers from the office as if he were
coming from the country, and ignoring all her weaknesses
. . . the brandy; and being awfully patient and . . ." She
got up and walked to the door, pausing to hug him and say:
"You're a born adventurer, that's what you are, impish, disturbing people's minds, a rebel—and I think now you're
making all this money I ought to have another hundred a
year, don't you?"

Edward pulled a face and pursed his lips and rubbed his
chin and wiggled his finger in his ear. "How much do we
pay you now?" he asked, looking archly at her.

"Three hundred, sir."

"I don't see," he said, shaking his head, "how we can
make it less than five hundred, then. But I warn you"—

he added, waggling a finger at her—"I shall expect you to read all the plays submitted—and keep an eye on the box office—and not let any scandal occur among the young players—and see the tea buffet is run well—and call round at the newspapers and get on the right side of the editors—and—and do the prompting if the assistant stage-manager falls sick. You'll not have to be above working the noises off, or playing a parlourmaid's part if we get stuck—and in your spare time translating a play or two from the French or the Italian; we ought to do a really new play by Pirandello. And, darling, I think I shall advertise in the London weeklies saying we want full-blooded, sensational, truly original, tradition-smashing plays that break all the rules and all the ordinary managers' hearts. By gosh, we'll make this theatre a force to be reckoned with. . . . We'll revolutionise the theatre—create new art forms—mix the film and the stage play, do mime, play in masks, encourage poets to write verse plays again, get some lovely music written specially for plays with ballet or plays which have a music theme or motif as it were, we'll have plays in innumerable scenes, plays in five or six acts, plays in two acts, plays in one; we'll have a dramatic festival, we'll do Shakespeare. . . . What of your aged parent as Sir Toby—done in the dialect?"

They drove down to Moorgate Chapel in Whitefriars Road—and Pirandello and masks and plays with music seemed a long way off. The neighbourhood had become highly industrialised, a noisome lard works was almost next door, and a dyeworks at the back was monotonously spurting steam with a chugging hiss hiss. The building was high and square, too tall for its length; its only saving grace was a balcony round three sides. Inside it was cold, clammy and dirty; windows were broken and patched with sacking and brown paper. "No wonder the Lord deserted it," said Edward, tapping his stick up the aisle and turning to look at the cracked organ-pipes. "Do you see a renascence of northern drama being born here, Mary?"

Mary, experiencing the small feeling of awe that religion and decay and poverty always brought to her, said: "Don't be so flippant, father. The place makes me shudder. You'd far better buy the Theatre Royal as a going concern—that's the phrase, isn't it?" Her eyes were grey now and troubled until she turned and smiled at him; but the gleam was fleeting. She was grave; but Edward was keeping up his spirits.

"Drury Lane is a very nice theatre, I've heard tell."

"Don't be perverse." She shook his arm and pressed it and pinched it.

"But I thought we were going to hoist a banner in Chesterford? The Royal will be booked up months ahead with *Two Little Drummer-Boys* and *The Girl Who Took The Wrong Turning* and the latest daring Parisian revues straight from Brixton at enormous expense."

"Then you can live up to your Wellingtonian profile and unbook them. Luke Hargreaves says you can always get out of anything by paying."

"Luke is a bad influence on you."

"Luke's sweet."

"I'll let him know, dear."

"But I wish he'd stopped you making a fool of yourself by getting the art students to paint mural decorations—armadas and things—on the spinning-room walls."

"The output has gone up, Mary," Edward said mildly.

"It may have—but not due to those paintings. It makes the men smile at you behind your back and I can't bear it, and if you turn this derelict chapel into a theatre . . ."

"Yes, dear, you're very good for me, I know. But you must allow your doddering father a little of his own way sometimes. I think a stage could be built here quite well—and a small wing there for the dressing-rooms—the building is nice and lofty—and the lard factory won't be busy at night and, anyway, we can stop the odour as a nuisance. . . ."

"You're not serious. You couldn't possibly. . . . The place wouldn't hold more than five hundred."

"That's about all some of the little theatres in London hold. We should do excessively well if we got five hundred in."

"You'd never get *two* hundred in."

"Then, darling, it'll be heaps big enough."

"I shall disown you in a minute."

Mary wanted to be angry but every time she looked at her father he smiled at her and his eyes almost disappeared in the creases round his eyes and she saw only a dark, twinkling slit; and the worst of it was she knew her own eyes presented an exactly similar appearance. It was like looking into a mirror. She began to pull his arm and to drag him towards the door but he hung on to a dusty pew and they engaged in a tug-of-war till they were half doubled up with laughter. "You're absolutely impossible," she said, releasing his arm. It might have been hours since she was grave and troubled. The tugging had robbed her of all her displeasure.

"Well," he said, taking her arm walking her out, and speaking confidentially, "I don't think very much of this place, do you? I wonder if old O'Connor would sell the Theatre Royal—you know that theatre in the market-place? You must have heard of it."

"Don't be absurd, dear," she said. "They're booked up ten years ahead." They began to chink with laughter again, like two children.

Mary had driven them down in her own two-seater Vauxhall (they often went on small expeditions by themselves in this way; Edward preferred it and so did she). They

turned towards home. No question of visiting the Theatre
Royal arose—both realised other approaches must be made
first. Mary was glad of the occupation of driving, keeping
her eyes on the corners, fiddling with the gears. It gave
her excuse for silence and she was occupied suddenly with
thoughts of Brierley. She found it pleasant to think about
him and to toy with the thought that he might write plays
for their theatre. That would be fun; the reading of the
play first, her insistence that it was good (she hoped it would
be but she knew she was biased—an unjust judge); the rehearsals, the watching it take shape, the hideous disap-
pointments (she supposed there would be those) and small
triumphs; the excitement and stress of the first night—
maybe they would sit together and suffer the anxiety of
wondering how it would go. Perhaps—for it *must* be a
success, *must* be—he would, in his exaltation and fever, turn
to her, take her hands . . . She found herself blushing and
was glad to stoop to the hand-brake and pull the car up
dead at a cross-road. She experienced a revulsion of feeling;
this was absurd. She compressed her lips, thrust her bottom
one out a little. Idiot to allow herself . . . The man had
never said a word—didn't care two straws. For some time
before meeting him she had read his sketches in the *Burnham Guardian,* and being introduced to him at the Garrick
Society had congratulated him. She always remembered how
his face had glowed, like a boy's, his unaffected pleasure at
being praised, his spoken ambition to write plays. He was
her own age but she had felt, sometimes, as a mother must
(she believed) have felt, when she thought of him. Philip
had sauntered up and greeted him as "My fair Cousin," at
which Brierley had grown pale and confused and angry; and,
seeing how swiftly he was hurt, she had felt pity and a deeper,
profounder regard for him. She had found, she thought,
nobody in Chesterford so sensitively formed, so quick to

understand, so immediate in his humour, so broad and wide in his compassion. Nor so open to the world, so easy to wound. He walked abroad, she felt, with his breast bared for every spear that came along. He was far too ready with his trust and confidence; he spoke far too openly of his admiration for Trix Bishop, gloried in his infatuation, talked as if her fame and place in the London theatrical firmament were assured. Mary knew he was drawn to herself as she was to him; was conscious of the warmth—almost the flash as between two conductors of electricity—that passed between them when they met. They had come across one another in the street and paused and chatted, she had sent him an occasional book, he had posted her a cutting or two of his sketches that she had missed. Nothing more. She had rather hoped he would ask her to go with him to the Black Bull that she might see Trix Bishop. But he didn't. And to go alone was out of the question. She had thought of asking Philip to take her; but she was uncertain of his moods. He was too warped, too chiding, too likely to fly off the handle. So Trix remained only a creature of her mind. She imagined her tall, lissom, beautifully formed, passionate, lovely, domineering. She saw Brierley worshipping . . .

"Henry Brierley," Edward was saying. "I think he's one of our hopes dramatically."

Mary had been thinking so deeply about him that now, when his name was spoken, she was as awkward as if Edward had been looking into her mind. She stared ahead and then said in a colourless voice: "Oh. Do you think so? Why?"

"You've only to read his sketches to see his skill in putting a character into a few lines of dialogue. I thought you knew him rather well."

"Not particularly," she said. She felt as if she were Peter denying Christ; but she couldn't help it. Yet she wanted her father to go on, she wanted terribly to be able to talk of

Brierley easily, freely. Perhaps that would come if they talked long enough.

Edward went on: "Your mother was afraid you had some regard for him—more than she would like you to have. She'll be relieved; at least . . ." He paused there and when he resumed, it was to say: "I've formed a high opinion of his gifts."

Mary said—and she found it rather unaccountable— "He's very little money, I should say; and not much family except what he gets from us."

Edward turned to look at her but her eyes were fixed on the road ahead. "I don't know, my dear," he said, "what particular family Shakespeare had; or money. Genius and true quality have a way of breaking through. I don't know that Wells and Bennett boast of their families much. And Samuel Crompton, the maker of modern Lancashire—he sprang from nowhere remarkable and died in penury. What does the psalmist say? 'A thousand years in Thy sight are but as yesterday.' And we whose great-grandfathers were handloom weavers give ourselves airs above the poets. Don't forget, darling, that Brierley's forbears were poets. And I'm afraid I'm fool enough to put artistry and a deep insight into the hearts of men above spinning thread and successful dealing."

Mary turned radiant eyes on him. "You think he's better than we are, then?"

"I rank us high," he said proudly. "But I think his texture may be finer; I think the world may need him more, and spare him less well than some of us. Money makes Tories of most of us; it's something we've got to fight. Your mother is the most lovable creature in the world—but she's a dreadful Tory—God bless her."

Mary took her left hand from the wheel and slipped it into his and pressed his fingers.

He went on: "But she's terribly shrewd; Tories very often are. They don't see far ahead and they don't want to. But they are rooted deep in the rules of life, the accepted code of honour, the way things go. They know exactly what society will stand and what it won't; they are experts at shielding themselves and their loved ones from the jabs. They are often right. Loyalty, sticking up for one's class right or wrong—they are good at these. They may be crude, and unjust, and pig-headed and near-sighted; but as a broad, rough basis of life, their way works. They see very clearly that to marry out of your class makes for discomfort, mis-understandings, and a measure of unhappiness. They see that you have to be big to overcome those things, to brush aside criticisms, to stride over opposition, to tame the world to your way of thinking. And they realise that few of them are big enough—and they turn aside. Genius scares them; they find it unaccountable, unforeseen, upsetting; they mis-trust it; and they see that genius, when it springs from the class below, no matter how pure and serene the flame is, doesn't and cannot stand alone. It is allied to and mixed up with the family it emerges from. They might grant that if the pair were to leave the country and live in Melbourne or Vienna or Hawaii it would work well enough. But Eng-land is a small place. Tories have a horror of being called upon by people who are embarrassed by menservants, or find parlourmaids prettier than their hostesses. So if the Tories' ideas are limited, brusque, unromantic—remember they are a sort of protective colouring."

Mary was silent.

"I am trying to explain," he said gently, "a point of view—not my own, but one which I can respect."

"I know," she said. "Shall I say—I am much obleeged to you?" She flashed a quick smile at him and turned her eyes back to the road.

"While I am discoursing," he said, "let us consider money. The truly poor are not the poor, but those who have the sensibilities of the rich, their tastes, their culture, without the means to gratify them. They are half-ways, as it were. Brierley, if he isn't fortunate, may be one of them. I wonder sometimes if education isn't merely cruelty. Aren't we holding the carrot in front of the donkey's nose as we drive along? How can it be reached? If your father were a miner and you worked in the pit, too, or a cotton operative and you worked in the card-room and didn't read too much, and mixed only with your fellow work-people, you would probably be content and happy. But begin to think, to play in the orchestra alongside me, for instance, who may foolishly talk about the warmth of Nice in winter, or begin to act in a play with a lovely creature whose father brings a motor-car for her when the rehearsal is over while you are compelled to walk home in the snow—well, then the discontents begin and very often the torments. I know, of course, the newspapers and the films are doing it all the time—this holding up the contrasting mirror. The miracle is that people remain so patient. I've a good deal of sympathy with the pitman who asked the duke how he came to own all the coal. The duke said: 'My forefathers fought for it.' 'Good,' said the pitman, slipping off his jacket, 'I'll fight *thee* for it.' "

"I know," Mary said. "I've thought about that. If somebody stopped the car—a group of mill-girls, say—and asked me what right I have to the car any more than they, I suppose I should have to say, if I said what's really in my heart: 'I've no right to it at all. Take it.' "

"Well, dear, you've as *much* right, if no more. And you happen to have got it." They both laughed.

Edward said: "I don't know whether to admire more or pity more the patience and resignation and tragic nobility of our work-people. I sometimes wonder whether England would have been where she is if her people hadn't had more spirit in the past than they seem to have now. Where are our Cromwells, Raleighs, Cooks, Marlboroughs, Nelsons? Don't we breed the intransigents any more, the revolutionaries, the men prepared to die for their faith?"

"You ought really to be with the Socialists," Mary said.

"I suppose I should be if I had enough courage, and were prepared to sacrifice you all, and didn't fear hardship as much as I do. I'm a terrible coward, darling; always knowing the right thing to do—and never having the spirit to do it. I'm a little sorry sometimes I started with so much. It must be so much easier when you begin on scratch—nothing to lose, nobody to point and say, 'There goes the man who let his family down—lost the fortunes—down to the clogs again.' I'm not big enough to care nothing for the world and its tongue; I wish I were."

"It seems to me," Mary said, "you must add to those who are unhappy because they have tasted the luxuries and can't afford them except once in a blue moon, those who have them and feel they've no right to them. You're an extremely upsetting person, dear—have you ever realised that? Do you ever talk to mother like this?"

"Oh, no. She would think me a little madder than usual. Besides, I don't quite know how much I faithfully believe. I *know* there's no danger of my living up to my principles. I take a morbid delight in torturing myself sometimes, that's all. I'm the worst sort of ineffectual idiot." He said this with some small savagery and Mary again put her hand on his and pressed it.

"When you want to give away my wedding portion, you may," she said. "By that time, the Chesterford Repertory will be making pots of money and I'll be working the limes for twenty-five bob a week. And that's only a night job. Perhaps I could have four looms during the day. Do you know, dear, I believe I might be happier that way—being taken to the pictures by my young man on Fridays with a quarter of chocolates and doing a shilling hop on Saturdays. Gosh, I envy them sometimes! I feel only half alive compared with some I've seen walking like queens down Burnham Road. We waste a lot of pity on people who'd scorn it. They're just as lovely to one another as we are, you know; they sleep as sound, they eat their fill—most of them—their talk is racier, funnier, the wind and the sun and the stars and the sea are theirs just as much as they're ours, the play is the same from the pit as from the stalls, and Beethoven and Schubert bring them the identical message. . . ."

"I think, if you'll forgive me, Mary," he said, "that's largely tommy rot. They can get books from the library—provided they get soiled, germ-ridden, nasty ones and queue up for them; there's the wind on the heath, true, but how often? Once or twice a week in the daytime; other days only the night air. They see the sea usually for a week or a fortnight in the year, they travel never. They—well, they have nothing that we haven't got better, more abundantly and more pleasantly. And if we don't have a very much better time and a richer, fuller life—then we're self-condemned as a lot of worthless, irredeemable scallywags, and there is no health in us. And, upon my soul, I sometimes wonder whether people like me, yielding to their work-people a morsel more food and learning and health and leisure and delight (or trying to) than most other employers and finding complacency and satisfaction in it as if I were a benefactor—I'm not sure that we're not more contemptible than the good old Tories who have and who hold, and tell 'em to be content in the station to which it has pleased God to call 'em. Half the firms with welfare schemes—looking after their workers' bodies with food and football and their souls with folk-dancing and debating societies—only enslave them the deeper; and I'm never quite sure they don't try to. Welfare—and increased output and greater profits! Like the fat Rotarians hollering, 'Service, not self.' Service! We ought to pay our men and women as much as we can possibly afford—and let 'em go to the Devil in their own way."

"I hope you'll let me go to the Devil in *my* own way," Mary said. "I may put you to the test, you know."

"I know," Edward said. "I've had the greatest difficulty in not going to him myself—that is, if I have escaped. Though I think he has fewer habitations these days, or he has changed them. He used to occupy places that are now, if not godly, at all events not devilish. I remember him occupying every theatre and music-hall and bottle of wine and most hours after midnight, and, of course, the divorce court, and the control of the number of your children. God always wanted you to have *untold* progeny. Whether in yielding some of his fortresses the Devil has captured others, I don't know. Perhaps he's in the dance more than he used to be, and in women's painted faces and in the machines that destroy the joy of craftsmanship and in the betting that makes so many sports dirty. But I don't pretend to be an authority. Only—as we overcome one disease another usually becomes stronger; and I have a suspicion it may be the same with the Devil. Our capacity for evil remains much the same, I daresay. We don't rob men on the highway so often, but the Stock Exchange and the City are busy at it. We don't hang men for stealing sheep, but we use gases in war that burn men's lungs out. We don't hang, draw and quarter malefactors, but we drop bombs on women and children when it suits us. We don't duck witches in the village pond, but let a woman have a child out of wedlock, and being publicly soused in water will be paradise compared with what she'll be called on to endure."

Mary said: "You must be the most benevolent cynic in

Lancashire, father." But she said it fondly, and Edward replied with a thin smile:

"You can write my epitaph—'He saw the road, but wouldn't or couldn't take it." After a pause, he went on: "I hope if I see you making overtures to the Devil I shall warn you and try to dissuade you. But I won't force you or threaten you—or try to go on possessing you. We expect far too much of one another, I think. We don't allow one another to commune with the earth and the stones and the trees enough. We might wash away a good deal of the tawdriness of life, did we live alone in ourselves more. The daily round is only the machinery of living, isn't it? We're too much occupied in getting into each other's way, crossing the threads, entangling ourselves. An hour a day to disentangle yourself and ask where you, Mary Houghton, are going, and how far you've proceeded along the road to-day; one might try that. And one might ask, now and then: 'If I knew I was to die next week, what is there I should want to do more than anything? What is there I should regret more than all else having left undone?' And then, I think, one might go and do it. If, when I see you going to the Devil, you reply: 'This is something I am going to do that I should never forgive myself having not done, were I to die to-morrow'— then, my dear, I shall cry, *'En avant!'* and salute you as you go."

Mary kissed him before he got out of the car. "If I thought the Devil would be half as nice an old gentleman as you are, dear, there would be no stopping me," she said.

Chapter Eight

WHEN SAM HAD MADE five thousand pounds, they moved into The Rookery. And Sam gave up his work as a minder.

Harriet looked on the change in their fortunes and their way of life with profound misgiving. There were moments, naturally, when the clouds rolled away from her mind and she was excited and exalted by the fact that a maid called her "Mum" (the maid was Sam's idea), that the wife of the Rev. Albert Howcroft of the near-by Congregational Church called on her and invited her to tea, and that there was a bath in the house and what was described by the estate agent as "inside conveniences" which made it no longer necessary to traverse a wet and windy yard on a winter's night (though, to be sure, this new advantage caused a good deal of quarrelling among the children, who found it a fascinating place and visited it oftener and for longer periods than was natural or becoming). But fundamentally Harriet disliked The Rookery and Sam giving up his work. Women, with rare exceptions, always hate and fear their husbands giving up work, or changing one occupation for another. They are not adventurers; they fear the unknown; and unless they are sure beyond a peradventure of their men's affections, they distrust and fear a vastly increased prosperity, especially if it is quickly achieved. They know in their bones that many a man who is what is called a "good husband" on four pounds a week may become a gay Lothario on twenty or even ten, and that there is nothing like a wage that is better than penury but less than generous comfort for keeping a man law-abiding, God-fearing and faithful to them. Harriet came to the conclusion that the man who wrote the passage in the Bible about it being easier for a camel to pass through the eye of a needle than for a rich man to enter the Kingdom of Heaven knew what he was talking about. But her opposition to the new life had been ineffectual. She was torn too many ways. Lavender Street was so envious that it seemed ill-natured and captious not to support Sam by being pleased; and Lavender Street could be so malicious in its muttered, "Mugs for luck," that she was bound to stand up for Sam and turn up her nose at his traducers. As for Sam himself, he was like a two-year-old, she thought, or a dog wi' two tails. He took her for a new costume and satin dress, and insisted on her having a "bit o' fur" for her neck; he stopped her from doing the washing; he made the children wear boots every day in the week (a step which offended Lavender Street almost more than anything else—this positive flaunting of wealth as they thought it) and he ordered a supply of beer and whisky for the house. For the first time in his life he drank beer with his meals, an action which, admirable and healthy though it might be, Harriet simply could not reconcile herself to. Beer, to her, was a curse; its proper place was the public-house. The prospect of Sam sitting boozing at home (though he showed, so far, no signs of doing it) appalled and frightened her. Leaving Lavender Street had, at first, scared her, but when they became, as she phrased it to herself, a "sort of Barnum's and Bailey's" for the whole street to stare at, she was glad to go. Sam said, rather grandiloquently: "We'n risen above 'em and s'elp my Bob, they'll never forgive us for it." And he was right, Lavender Street never

forgave them; Lavender Street said: "He'll soon make a
'wakes' of it—thee wait a bit," and Tom Edmunds, with
sardonic humour told Sam heavily: "Tha'll see nowt funnier than thysel', Sam, wherever tha goes"; and the neighbours' children would come and play skipping-ropes on the
flags immediately before the door, and cry: "Pitch—patch—
pepper," and then with shrill emphasis: "Silk—satin—
muslin—*rags*," as an intimation and prophecy of what inevitably awaited stuck-up people like the Renshaws. And
Harriet grieved over it. She didn't want this change of
fortune, this envy of all her acquaintances, this being shut
out, that money was bringing. But because she was proud she
couldn't explain, or excuse, Sam to them; their attitude dried
her up inside, choked the wells of her charity and loving-
kindness and turned her for a time into what they had declared she was and what she hadn't been—a rather hard,
imperious woman who looked down on them. So that, in
some ways, going to The Rookery was finally a relief to her.

The Rookery was an old-fashioned house sitting behind a
brick wall in Halfpenny Lane, a twisty road that ran from
the main tram route as far as the Sandpit colliery, the best
part of a mile away, and there came to a dead stop. The
house had been occupied by the Misses Pennant, two old
maids who had maintained so rigid a seclusion that tales of in-
ordinate wealth had been wrapped about them. It was said
they owned fourteen rows of houses—and a cat for each
row, that they were spiritualists, misers and vegetarians, that
the elder one, Agatha, could charm warts away when she
was so minded, that they never used any light save candles,
and that curious music—some said it was unearthly, but it
proved to have been nothing but a harpsichord—could be
heard issuing from The Rookery of an evening. There was
no more truth in these pieces of gossip than is usually the
case. When Agatha died of influenza and Bridget followed

her a few days later, they lay in the house dead for five days before the antics of cats—outgrown and hideous through being rendered unable to procreate their species—drew the attention of neighbours and led to the police breaking in. Agatha had died in bed but Bridget had died in an armchair. The house was dirty, food beyond bread and milk non-existent, the four cats ravenous and savage—but neither gold nor silver was found, the oil lamp was trimmed, and the bank book showed no more than a balance of five hundred pounds. The old women were seventy-three and sixty-nine respectively, and it seemed plain that had they lived two more years they would have become paupers. Such cottages as they had once owned had been sold ten years before in part to pay off a nephew's debts, and the five hundred pounds was all that remained of the balance. Agatha and Bridget had worked out the span of their lives and died just in time.

An unsavoury air hung about the house for a time, nobody seemed to want it, the wall-encircled garden with its elms became overgrown, the grass tall and dank, and the house agent's "For Sale or To Let" board more rickety and askew. "Th' owd maids' house," as Chesterford called it, became a hunting-ground for adventurous boys, who would clamber on its window-sills and peer into the neglected rooms by day, and for dallying lovers, who hugged its shadows or lay in the grass under the elms on summer nights. Meanwhile, as its notoriety increased, its market value fell. Tom Edmunds had said to Sam: "Tha'll be buyin' property next, I reckon—one o' t' landed gentry, eh, if this goes on?" and Sam, who hadn't thought of it, said, stung by the sarcasm: "Aye, an' *tha'll* stand no chance o' gettin' one o' my houses, eyther. We'st be a bit pertikler who we have livin' i' Renshaw Street." Sam mentioned the matter of property casually to the teller at the bank, who had said: "A firm offer would

get The Rookery for next to nothing." And Sam had taken
Harriet to see it. Harriet was an enthusiast for buying
bricks and mortar, but not The Rookery. The idea of having
a roof over her head, from which nobody could eject her,
sizzled in her mind with the pleasantness of a sausage in a
frying-pan. She saw them occupying the gable-end of a short
row and her collecting the rents of the other cottages, and
adjudicating on such problems as: "Can we have a new
window-cord?"; or, "T' tap wants a new washer on, and
Bill sez, 'Will yer knock tuppence off t' rent if he fixes it
up?"; or, "T' bricks are coming out o' t' fireplace"; or,
"T' down-spout's stopped up an' it's comin' through t'
slates. Will yo' have it seen to?" Harriet felt she would be
just; she wouldn't be mean but she wouldn't be taken in,
either. She reflected, with a sudden gleam of insight and
astonishment, how swiftly, easily and naturally she would
alter her attitude from tenant to owner, from one fighting
for her rights to one giving or withholding—turned as it
were into a small god. It gave her a thrill. She thought to
herself: "I was made for that; I could do that—none better."
And then she could have flushed at the realisation of how
much vainglory there was in her. She had spoken her thoughts
on cottage property to Sam, but he had been surprisingly
firm. "I can't tie all my money up, lass, because it's what I've
got to work wi'—it's my warp an' weft, if tha sees what I
mean. What we want is a nice bit of a place wheer I can bring
my customers—if I want"—Harriet had instantaneous vi-
sions of a litter of beer bottles and a horrid premonition of
Trix Bishop standing on the table showing her legs as they
did on the pictures—"an' leave t' rest o' my brass fluid, to be
drained off here wheer there's a bit of a flood, tha knows,
an' poured in yonder wheer it's wanted." (This was a phrase
he had picked up in the Mechanics' Institute share-room.)
And he had added: "If tha wants to be different from th'

Romans tha mustn't live i' Rome." Sam, when he had said
that, was very pleased with it. "Tha's heard o' that, o'
course," he said a little pompously, but he rather hoped she
hadn't. She said: "It looks like swank—doin' it on purpose,
havin' a house wi' a name on it." "We can't help that,"
Sam said. "We didn't put it on. We shall have to put up wi'
it." But Sam was inordinately proud of that name. "Sam
Renshaw of The Rookery." Why, it was worth a quid a week
in itself, for where Sam had once thought in shillings he now
thought in pounds. Prosperity was changing Sam. He was
growing more sure of himself. After all, you can't continue to
be fortunate and hear men talk of "Renshaw's luck" without thinking you are in some measure a superior person.
Sam thought sometimes: "I'm a bit of all right, too; I can
give most on 'em a bit of a start at this job. Havin' a cut in—
usin' your head; aye, an' the more you put down the more
you pick up—same as Crown an' Anchor—same rules apply,
only they can't see it." But there was more in it than that;
Sam was exceedingly well-informed. He had started specu-
lating at a time when Thomas Blackburn was looking round
for one or two men who weren't too clever, who were, on the
contrary, men who would not be suspected of being associated
with him, whom he could employ to buy or to sell in order to
influence the market. Sam had all the qualities and for two
months had been pocketing a commission from Thomas
Blackburn and "doing very nicely for himself," as Chesterford said, on his own share deals. Apart from those who
described Sam as a "piecan" whose luck must soon turn,
there were others who declared he wasn't so green as he was
cabbage-looking; and when Sam moved and operated on the
market he began to be followed by a small coterie. "What's
best to-day, Sam?" would greet him in the Mechanics' Institute basement; or they called him "The man wi' the red-
hot hand—he's nobbut to touch shares to mak' 'em rise"—the

analogy being drawn from putting one's hand on the mercury in a thermometer; or they called him "T' miniature Midas" —Midas himself being Thomas Blackburn, or Major Henderson or Fred Buckley or any other "seven-figure man" prominent at the moment.

The taking of The Rookery by Sam was the talk of certain circles in Chesterford; it was said to be the sort of crazy thing he would do; and it was said also that no doubt he had heard there was gold buried under the hearthstone, and that if it were, he could be relied on to find it. The Rookery was certainly a bargain; he bought it freehold, with a quarter acre of garden, for eight hundred and fifty pounds, and by the time he had spent two hundred pounds more on pointing it, clearing the garden, putting in a hen run and a score of white leghorns and Rhode Island reds, and titivating up the house, Sam said it looked champion. The titivation included a pianola which Sam after three bottles of Bass (he no longer drank mild beer) played with great expression, a cabinet gramophone with fifty records selected by the shopman to Sam's instruction to "Give us lively stuff—comics, an' sentimental songs an' brass bands," so that Harriet polished her brass and scrubbed her floor to the accompaniment of whistling solos, and laughing choruses, and the Overture to *William Tell* or "Poet and Peasant," and found herself marching *staccato* up- or down-stairs inspired by Sousa or the Black Dyke Mills band. But Harriet didn't always polish the brass. Millie was brought in for the purpose but you can't alter your habits in a moment, and Harriet and Millie may be said to have accomplished a division of labour. Sam's imagination had seen early on that it would be gradely to have a servant in a white cap opening the door to his cronies—it would put 'em in their place—show 'em who was who—and the idea of a cup of tea in bed served by a rosy-cheeked wench, to get him up after a night when they had had a "do," entranced him. Harriet had said she could "manage"; Sam wouldn't hear of it. Harriet said she couldn't stand another woman knowing all her business—and when she said business she was thinking of Sam tipsy and maybe some dirty talk or Sam's coarse amours; but Sam said the wench would be kept in her place, and, any road, if she weren't, who's fault would it be? Wouldn't it be Harriet's? And then he had put his arm round her and kissed her and said he wasn't going to have her working herself to death for him and the childer and besides what was the good of it when they could afford to do some other road? And what about the gallivantings off to Blackpool or Llandudno they were going to have, and how could they go unless the childer could be left at home? And had she thought what Venice 'ud be like, or having a bit of a motorcar and runnin' down to Devon? By crikey, but they weren't half goin' to have a time! And Harriet, torn once more between wanting to be happy along with him and wanting to do as he wished when he seemed "so set on it," and knowing in her heart it wouldn't all work out like that—if *any* of it worked out like that—said: "Very well, then, Sam," and kissed him back and held him tight; and after he had gone, as he promptly *did* go, to find a Servants' Registry to ask them to send up some "samples" as he playfully called them, she cried a little. For the new world was very strange to her and she felt imprisoned in it. Sam could get out of it any time he liked; she couldn't. And she had a sensation, which her reason told her was foolish but which she could not overcome, that as Sam climbed up the ladder, she would stay where she was, or, maybe, be pushed down a rung or two. Nevertheless, she succeeded in pulling herself together. Harriet could almost always do that—as though the tide of her strength went far out and slowly began to turn and flow

back. Those who had got to the end, she supposed, the suicides, never *did* come back from that ebb towards the hori-
zon.

So that by afternoon when the first of the girls seeking
the post of maid at The Rookery arrived, she was ready for
them—wearing her new dark blue satin dress with a gold
brooch and ear-rings, having put a little oil of roses on her
dry, roughened hands, and fluffed out her dark brown hair
now turning grey over the ears. Her lips were compressed,
her heart beat too fast, there were false alarms to be overcome in the knocks of beggars, of ex-Service men selling
wretched notepaper and envelopes (she bought a good deal
of this although she saw it would never do) and of the postman delivering circulars and prospectuses. (More letters
came now in a week than had reached them in a year at
Lavender Street.) It might have been the Queen she was
awaiting instead of a serving-maid. But they came at last,
and when they came she was as calm and assured as though
she had been engaging servants all her life. She thought:
"I'm a queer 'un, if ever there was one." There was a raw
girl of seventeen, Gertie by name, gawky, clumsy, who was
too stupid for the mill and whose mother had eleven children. Gertie might have been an expert on minding them
but not much else; there was a middle-aged woman, Mrs.
Golightly, who squinted, who was a widow, and who
wanted only ten shillings a week "so long as she had a good
home"—a good home was what she was looking for; and
thirdly, Millie came. And with the advent of Millie, Sam
returned; he must have been close behind her up the twisty
Halfpenny Lane, and Harriet wondered at once if he had
been admiring Millie's figure; for Millie's figure was, she
saw, one that commanded attention. Her hips were full and
her bosom mature for a girl of her age and she carried herself with an air that she could only think of as saucy. Yet her

eyes were brown and of disarming mirthfulness. Her nose
was snub and her mouth large, her hair mousy but luxuriant
and her ankles too thick. But the whole impression was
pleasant, one of vitality and supremely confident youth and
good nature. Harriet thought: "I wonder what's amiss wi'
her that she wants to be a servant? Has she been in trouble
or summat?" They sat in the parlour, Harriet on the edge
of a chair and Millie on the edge of the sofa and Sam a little
uncertain in the doorway lolling on the edge of it and listening to the conversation with undisguised satisfaction. For
you didn't become an employer for the first time every day
in the week.

Millie turned the toes of her black strapped shoes in and
then out and then said, with more demureness than her eyes
warranted: "Mrs. Midgley sent me—the Registry."

Harriet nodded. "Have you been anywhere afore?"

"Oh, yes." But she volunteered nothing more.

"What's your name?"

"Millie Smith."

Harriet thought it a funny name (if she had known the
word she would have thought "indeterminate") for a Chesterford girl, and she asked: "Do you belong here?"

"Yes, I live in Wilberforce Street—near the Co-op."

"What does your father do?"

"He's dead."

Harriet said she was sorry and Millie said: "It's all right,
I don't mind," but whether she didn't mind him being dead or
didn't mind Harriet's blunder, Harriet couldn't be sure.

Harriet became more cautious. "Is your mother livin'?"

"Oh, yes." Millie answered that as if mothers didn't die
to the extent that fathers did, as if the answer was a foregone
conclusion. Harriet felt the conversation wasn't getting anywhere in particular so she asked: "You know, I suppose,
what you'd have to do?"

"Mrs. Midgley said you wanted a general."

"A what?" asked Sam with a sudden bark.

Harriet explained: "A general, Sam—general servant."

Sam laughed. "Oh, I see. I were goin' to say it's a private we want—not a general." He chuckled and Millie looked at him and her eyes twinkled and she laughed too. Harriet found herself not liking this exchange of laughter between Sam and the girl but she knew she was being a little unreasonable.

"Are you in a place now?"

"No," said Millie.

Harriet thought: "Why doesn't she tell me what I want to know? She knows well enough." She asked: "Why did you leave your last place—an' where was it?"

Millie said: "Mrs. Astley, the off-beer in Brazil Street. We fell out."

"What over?"

"She thought I was a steam-engine—"

"She what?" barked Sam again.

"Thought I was a steam-engine—stoke it up an' it runs for ever. But even engines want a rest, I told her—an' their bearin's oiled. An' then she ran me out o' the shop."

"She what?" asked Sam again, much to Harriet's annoyance.

"Ran me out o' the shop. Her hair was in pins an' one or two came out and her hair started comin' down like sore fingers—she did look funny, runnin' me round the lamp outside."

"Runnin' you round the lamp?" Sam asked, laughing again.

"Yes, but she never caught me, and I ran into the shop again and got behind the counter and pulled the flap down. She said if I didn't come out she'd throw a jar o' red cabbage at me. So I dared her an' she threw it an' it missed me and went through the window. An' then Mr. Snape the butcher next door came in—she's very thick with him."

Harriet thought this recital had gone on long enough. Somehow she didn't feel the conversation was on its right level; and she couldn't avoid seeing a vision of herself chasing Millie round the elms in the garden. She asked: "How much wage do you want?" and Millie, returning suddenly to her abrupt answers, said: "Twelve an' six, an' two nights off."

"You'll sleep in, o' course," said Sam, eyeing Millie intently. Harriet's heart gave a little leap and went faster while her mind told her not to be silly, that of course it had been understood all along the girl must sleep in. Millie was saying: "Yes, I suppose so," and Harriet felt she was looking at Sam with an appraising eye. Harriet asked when she could come, supposing they decided to take her, and Millie said she could come any time, and Harriet then said, well, they would let her know. But she knew Millie was coming; and to judge by Millie's confident: "Good afternoon, then, for the present," and her parting remark, without the slightest trace of self-consciousness, that she thought she had once been in the garden with her young man, Millie seemed to think so too.

When she had gone Sam hugged Harriet and gave her a kiss and said: "She's just what tha wants, lass—I reckon her's a corker, aye, a corker." Harriet thought: "A beezum —she'll want a bit o' watchin'—Sam, too—but she's got summat in her." She said: "I've forgotten to tell her she'll have to do the washin'."

Chapter Nine

It NEEDS no profundity of thought to perceive that it is well-nigh impossible to determine where the rivers that carry us away had their origin, or where the actions we are performing and the course we are steering were first determined; and it is clearly less possible still to say what effect that which we do to-day may have a century or even a year hence. We are aware that our whole human relationships, even those with men and women we make our close friends or our husbands or wives, are often decided upon by nothing more serious in the first instance than the road we live in, or the school or university to which we are sent, or the invitations to pleasant social activities we accept or we refuse. And it is certain that most of us, no matter which town in our own country (or indeed, most other countries) had been our dwelling-place, would there have duly fallen in love—or imagined it so—and married and begotten children. Those who served in the Great War are acutely conscious that their lives must have been saved or grave injury avoided a score of times by the simple fact that they volunteered or did not volunteer for this or that job, that they were liked or disliked by this sergeant or that colonel, that they went to the latrine at this or that moment, or that when they scrambled "over the top," their pace was swift or slow, and that on reaching the enemy trench they turned right or they turned left.

The Lancashire cotton boom and subsequent slump affected lives in Lancashire and turned them topsy-turvy much
as the Great War did those in wider England. Had the boom
not thrown Lancashire into turmoil, disturbed commercial
and social life to the degree it did, and left the county finally
strewn with human and financial debris and wreckage, the
Chesterford Repertory Theatre would never have been
founded, Sam and Harriet Renshaw would never have
climbed up the incredible beanstalk into a temporary fairy-
land that bewitched him and bewildered her, Henry Brierley
would never have stolen—for however brief a time—two
hundred pounds, and Josh Meadows would never have been
put to bed for a week by a blow from a flat-iron; in short,
none of the incidents so far recounted in these pages would
have happened and none of the developments that will be recorded hereafter would have occurred.

.   .   .   .

Josh Meadows did not die from the wound inflicted on
him by Trix on the night he struck her mother. Josh, when
his senses returned to him, had only the vaguest recollection
of what had happened. He had lost a good deal of blood
and he was weak. He was aware that he was lying in bed
partially undressed and with his head bandaged, and that
his wife was lying on the edge of the same bed but as far
away from him as was possible and that when he stirred or
uncovered himself she gently placed the clothes over him
again. He was accustomed to this solicitude so he neither
challenged it nor gave thanks for it; he took it for granted in
the manner that men do who are deeply loved or as deeply
feared by their womenfolk. He supposed from the bandage
that he must have fallen and cut his head open, and that he
must have been half drunk when it happened; nobody within

Josh's acquaintance ever cut his head open when he was *not* half drunk; and that condition explained everything. You were not accountable then; anything might happen at a time like that; you couldn't be blamed. Being half drunk was, to Josh's mind, the natural state of a man on two or three nights a week, and in that state of mind adventures with women, brawls, fracas or mêlées (as, he was aware, they were described by policemen in the police-court) were to be expected. Josh was disposed to be magnanimous about the affair; perhaps it was the weakness that made him like that, or some hazy recollection of having struck Mrs. Meadows. It certainly was not the fact that his wages automatically stopped and that he was dependent for his bread on his wife and Trix. That did not trouble him at all. Josh looked on that as the luck of the game—the rub of the green (for Josh played bowls sometimes). Josh was capable of dismissing money, in the sense that money was necessary to feed and house and clothe them, entirely from his mind. He had some deep-seated belief that he was entitled to be kept by somebody, somehow; and so long as he *was* kept, the way of it was no matter. Josh was as indifferent to his income, on these occasions when life laid him aside, as is, perhaps, the Duke of Westminster or the Baron de Rothschild. That Mrs. Meadows achieved the miracle of chicken broth or calves-foot jelly or new-laid eggs or an occasional glass of port wine was accepted by him quite calmly; that it was almost as miraculous as the ravens that fed Elijah did not occur to him. But it was.

It is extraordinary how much sympathy dwells in the human heart and how profound is the veneration for sterling character; how clearly, too, and how serenely integrity shines through from the inside. Every shopkeeper with whom Jane Meadows did her slender business knew that she was reliable to the last farthing; that she never "went on the slate" when she could avoid it, and that, being on the slate, she would wipe it clean so soon as hard work and unremitting toil might cleanse it. And when it was known, and it became known almost as swiftly as if wireless had whispered it to them, that Josh was "playing him" again, or had come worst off in an encounter with a close friend, or a lamp-post or the pavement (and it seemed that there were quite extensive pieces of pavement in the neighbourhood of Walker Street that had a nasty trick of jumping up and hitting you), they knew without being told that Mrs. Meadows would require "a bit o' consideration." And she got it. Nor did they marvel at her constancy and fidelity; they were used to it. It appears to be the law of God or whatever power there may be, that in the thriftless parts of this terrestrial sphere, in the regions where men tend to be despicable, shiftless, cruel and weak, there the women shall be magnificent; and it is as true of races as it is of regions. You may believe that the Almighty cannot bear to see His creatures fall so low that He will permit both men *and* women and their resultant offspring to reach the very depths; or you may believe that men and women are so made that the tawdriness of the one brings out, if only by methods of counter irritancy, the finer qualities of the other. I do not pretend to know. The shopkeepers and district nurses and sixpenny doctors and Salvation Army women who plied their trades and their professions for healing the body and the soul near Walker Street could not have told you either why this truth is the truth; they were familiar with it; they accepted it, and gave thanks for it.

Josh and his wife talked little. She tended him with gentleness, and uncomplainingly; not because she did not sorrow, but because her sorrow was too old, too much a part of her, too eaten into her being to be imparted to the world. If it had been taken away she would not have known herself or her life. She had no joy now beyond quietness, and freedom

from the brawls of drink and the insecurity of wages lost in
betting. She felt that was enough. To have Josh in bed, sober
and ill, was a measure of heaven. No dreaded whistle now,
shrilling down the street and piercing her heart; no sharing a
bed with a creature whose drunken ravings, arm wavings or
hideous and revolting physical demands humiliated and
frightened her both in themselves and in their possible conse-
quences; this illness was sanctuary; this for Jane Meadows
was now relief enough. More she could not easily have borne
—not, at least, without being ill. To have translated her back
to the days of their early married life when Josh was reckless but loving, turbulent but clean of tongue and habit would
have been as dangerous as giving a starving man a table-
d'hôte dinner at the Grand Hotel, Burnham. But there was
no fear of it. Josh could no more have retraced his steps than
she, by passing her warped fingers over her face, could have
wiped away its ravaging lines and the scars of suffering—
the map that Josh Meadows had drawn upon it.

For some days Trix watched the illness taking its course
with a strange calmness. She did not go in to see Josh. She
would inquire, in a voice of extreme quietness, how he was
and being told he was a little better, or about the same, make
no comment of any sort upon it; as though asking how he was
were of no more moment than asking: "Is it raining?" or:
"Has the cat come in?" During that first night that she had
lain awake in the room she shared with the children, she had
faced the possibility that he might die; and she be tried for
killing him. She supposed it would be murder, or at best, manslaughter. It occurred to her as she lay there how small a difference there was between being a murderer and being a normal person. If he did not die, and nothing was said about it
outside the walls of Number 17 Walker Street, and it was
not likely anything *would* be said, she would be thought to be
no different from other people; she would, she supposed,

some day, marry and have children. Yet they would be the children of a woman who might, had her aim been more vigorous, the flat-iron more pointed or Josh's skull more vulnerable, have been a convict. It all seemed curiously and indeed too much a matter of luck. Her fever and storm of suffering had been succeeded before morning by coldness and heaviness, as though she were drained of all emotion, her cup empty. In that condition she could have faced any ordeal, being at the end, with neither hope nor fear before her. She remained in that condition of mind for a few days, her body weakened, taking little nourishment and forcing herself by drinking whisky to get through her nightly performances at the Black Bull. When it became clear that Josh was not grievously hurt, that he was not probing into what had happened and that in due time he would get up from his bed and that life would go on as before, there was mingled with her sense of relief a reluctance to readjust herself to a normal life, as there may be when a person has been ill to the point of death and is then dragged slowly back to health. Her sense of the dramatic, too, was involved. She had seen herself the central figure of a notorious trial; the prospect had made her afraid but it had also excited her and attracted her. She had imagined herself splashed across the pages of the *News of the World* and the *Sunday Chronicle,* abused, no doubt, by most people but pitied too, and admired and turned into a heroine by a handful. And if she "got off"—why, then, her life story in a Sunday newspaper, engagement at fabulous sums on the music-halls . . .

This disturbance in her mind, and a dread of the ordeal of meeting Josh again as if nothing had occurred, a growing sense of the ugliness of her surroundings and a half-formed idea that her presence in the house was not truly a help to her mother—all these led to her determination to go into lodgings elsewhere. One late afternoon as Mrs. Meadows sat darning the stockings, a neat pile of Josh's grey-backed shirts beside her that she had been patching, Trix said, standing with the back of her head against the tall mantelpiece watching her mother's patient, dexterous fingers: "Josh'll soon be better now, I suppose?"

Her mother, without looking up, answered quietly: "Yea, he won't be long now."

"Mother."

"Well?"

"I'm not much good to yo' stoppin' here, am I?"

Mrs. Meadows took out the circular piece of wood over which she was working, and smoothed the darn on her knee.

"Why, luv?"

"I've been thinkin'—this wouldn't have happened but for me."

"He's hit me afore—once, when I wouldn't . . ." Her head bent lower over the fresh stocking she had begun working on. After a while she went on: "He doesn't like you—I know that—nor you don't like him—an' when it's that road, happen it's best yo' should go, if it 'ud please yo' best." She looked up then, her eyes dimming with tears and her throat aching violently with the emotion she was struggling to hide. Trix didn't see it; she was staring fixedly through the kitchen window into the high-walled yard and across to other yards and backs of houses built as closely as if it were an offence to allow sunlight to enter or as if the land were as precious as earth veined with gold. A cat walked delicately along the high wall, a sparrow perched on the top of a clothes prop, hens clucked next door where they were intensively bred in a few square yards, producing eggs as though they were machines until, worn out, they died; and as, often enough, women in that neighbourhood produced children until they, too, were worn out and died also.

She said: "I shall send you ten shillin's a week."

Mrs. Meadows had bent over her stockings again and, before she could stop it, a tear ran down her nose and fell on to her fingers. She wanted to say: "You'll do nowt o' t' sort" but she knew she couldn't do without the money; she wanted to hold Trix tight to her and draw comfort from her; she wanted to say how grateful she was. But she did nothing and said nothing—not for a while. Then she said: "Will yo' see if there's water in t' kettle, luv?"

She watched Trix striding across the kitchen to the sink; saw how beautifully shaped she was, how brave the tilt of her head, how glowing the colour of her hair, and she thought: "It's best she should go. Happen one day Josh 'ud want her that badly, he'd do her an injury through her scornin' him so."

There was a hammering on the ceiling—the knocking of a walking-stick on the bedroom floor. Josh wanted something. She put down her mending quietly and deliberately but swiftly too, and went up the narrow, curved stairs.

Josh was leaning on an elbow, his red and blue striped print shirt open at the neck, and a flimsy racing edition of an evening paper held in his massive, blue-veined hand. He had three days' growth of beard on his cheeks and his bandage had slipped rakishly over his right eye. He was in excellent humour. He lowered the paper and said: "I see Irish Vanity's at eight stone six."

Mrs. Meadows, expressing an interest she didn't feel, said: "Is that Lord Derby's horse?"

"Naw, naw, it belongs to Tim Hilditch. By God, an' it'll want some catchin' at eight stone six, I'm tellin' thee. Afe a quid on that 'ud keep us for a fortni't." And he looked up at her but she vouchsafed no sign. "Well," he said, dismissing Irish Vanity as hopeless, "I were wonderin' what I'm havin' for my tay."

"I've got a duck egg for thee."

"Is it a brown 'un?"

"No, it's green." Josh was plainly disappointed that it wasn't brown, but he took it philosophically.

"Tha couldn't do a bit o' bacon wi' it, couldta?"

"I'll see if we have a bit," she said thinking: "There'll be nothin' now for the childer's breakfast."

Josh smacked his lips. "There's nowt I like better, an' I'll tell thee summat—there's nobody can fry it better than thee, nawther. Do a bit for thysel', too." Having delivered himself of this generous speech, Josh put down his paper and stretched himself comfortably between the sheets. Already he could smell the bacon cooking. "Tha might tell Billy Jackson I want to see him; I've got an idea wheer he can get an extra quid or two for them whippet pups o' his." After a moment, he added: "It's here wheer tha wants it," and he tapped his bandaged head sagaciously. He saw himself and Billy having a great talk that night; maybe Billy would bring round a bottle of beer or two in his pocket. A sport was Billy but not much good without his, Josh's, brains at the back of him. Like a general who has made his dispositions, Josh lay down and relaxed. His wife stood regarding him, a brief smile, partly of disdain, partly of amusement at his childishness, partly despair, playing about her mouth. But Josh was unaware of it. He said graciously, "I think that's all, lass."

He might have been a king dismissing his court.

Chapter Ten

WHEN EDWARD HOUGHTON took steps towards founding
the Chesterford Repertory Theatre in the Theatre Royal, he
encountered an unexpected difficulty. It arose mainly out of
the discovery that he was not the only man in Chesterford
with a passion for the theatre, or at all events, theatrical
enterprise. He found, to his surprise, that the actual owner
of the Theatre Royal was Mr. Timothy Hilditch. Tim Hilditch was unquestionably "a card." He had started life as the
son of an Irish navvy and a Lancashire washerwoman, and
after doing various odd jobs in the way of post-office messen-
ger, solicitor's office-boy, and collector of rents, had set up in
business at eighteen years of age as a buyer and seller of job
lots of property—two or three cottages, a few square yards
of waste land. He had a sense of humour, an unquenchable
confidence in his power to do anything—"I could do it better
mesel'," was one of his favourite speeches—and a greyish
violet eye that bored into people's heads like a gimlet and
discerned most of what was there. He had a passion for buying those places where he had lived as a poor boy or had
worked. He had bought the site of Chesterford Post Office
because from there he had delivered telegrams, he had
bought the Theatre Royal because it was in the gallery there
that he had been thrilled, as a boy, by *The Grip of Iron* and
had laughed at Falstaff. The theatre genuinely fascinated

him; the spectacular was a part of his composition. Before
the boom started Tim had begun to operate in London, as
a mixture of boxing promoter—he had his own hall in the
Mile End Road where Carpentier fought—a City financier
—his solid silver inkstands and gold pens were notorious—
and as a Man from the North who could be depended on to
back a musical show provided there was some Lancashire
humour in it and the girls' legs were good. "We always have
the best legs in London," Tim said. And if the Lancashire
comedian wasn't up to Tim's mark, Tim would show how the
stuff ought to be said. Tim Hilditch was in on the cotton
boom from the start. There were those who said he *was* the
cotton boom; there was no doubt he had bought out a world-
famous Lancashire firm as early as the end of 1919, for he
had the cheque for two millions and a quarter framed in
platinum in his office in Threadneedle Street for everybody
to see. But Tim rarely operated in Lancashire. London, he
was wont to say, was plenty good enough for him to operate
in. He talked of operating as if he were a surgeon. "I put
through that operation," he would remark, "between two
puffs of a cigar. That's the way to do it, lad. Folk think too
much and take too much advice. Him as takes advice is lost—
lost afore he starts. Adam started it in t' Garden of Eden—
bewitched by a bitch. And remember this—the bigger the
twister a chap is, the straighter he'll look you in the eye. Any
detective'll tell you that." Tim had his own range of wisdom.
He had another document framed in his palatial rooms but
this he had shifted from one office to another since his early
days. It ran: "Success Stakes result: 1 : Hard Work; 2 : Intelligent Study; 3 : Keep At It. Also ran: Wish It Was Pay
Day; Can't Stop; Born Tired; Don't Care; Not My Job,
and others." Tim was a capital after-dinner speaker. He
would declare he often studied the race problem—tipping

winners; that some men were well-to-do and others hard to
do—and that he claimed to be both; and that most women
made runaway matches, catching their husbands although
they ran as hard as they could.

When Edward wrote to Hilditch, a reply came on thick
white embossed paper that Mr. Hilditch would be up in
Chesterford the following week and would be pleased to see
Mr. Houghton at the theatre. Tim paid regular visits to his
mother and sister whom he had "installed" (as he said, and
the word was right) in a large house on the town's border,
a house of which they stood in some terror; for it had his
mother's initials on the massive ornate iron gate and on the
rubber mat at the foot of the flight of steps leading to the
door. To his other poor relations he had granted pensions—
twenty-seven of them.

Tim's Rolls Royce was standing at the stage door when
Edward and Mary arrived, the liveried chauffeur reading
the *Sporting Chronicle*. They caught a glimpse of Hilditch
on the dim stage that looked to Edward—as stages by day
always looked—a cross between a dirty ship and a building
that had been on fire. Tim was saying, standing there in his
grey suit, his short-cropped iron-grey head as round as a
cannon ball, his sturdy body tight in his clothes: "I give 'em
sixty per cent and they've sent lasses who wouldn't attract
soldiers on St. Helena. Give me two afternoons and fifteen
wenches from any mill, and I'll guarantee to turn out a bevy
o' beauty—that's what they call 'em, isn't it?—to wipe the
floor with 'em. And as for the chap as painted their scenery,
why, he couldn't paint spots on dobbyhorses. That scene at
Monte Carlo looks like Belle Vue with the gasworks on fire
behind it." Tim was addressing nobody but his local manager
and a stage-hand or two, but when Tim was wound up, he
didn't mind whom he was addressing. He saw Edward and

Mary and nodded. "Be with you in a minute or two," he said brusquely but cordially. "Just go on in and make yourselves at home."

He followed in a moment. "How are you, Mr. 'Oughton? And this is your daughter, I can see." He gave Mary a wide smile, and shook hands with them both. "So you've come to buy me up, eh? Or try to? That's a new experience for me. Aye. Well?" He sat down behind his handsome mahogany desk and waited. The room was small; the walls crowded with playbills and pictures of actors in character parts or with their faces enormous and made artistic with flowing ties, large eyes and waved hair. The mixture of theatre dinginess and the prosperity associated with high finance lent it a strange air, as of an over-dressed person in a working-class cottage.

But Tim didn't mind that. He was not, indeed, aware of it.

Edward was less comfortable than Mr. Hilditch. He was acquainted with his reputation; they were on nodding terms on the rare occasions when they chanced to meet in Burnham or Chesterford—nothing more. He looked on Hilditch as an adventurer, hard, somewhat reckless. He thought himself not a snob but he couldn't but feel they were made of different stuff. He looked at Mary and thought: "Fine counts," and at Hilditch and thought: "Coarse counts, coarse but durable, extremely." He said: "We think of founding a repertory theatre, Mr. Hilditch."

"Gloomy stuff," said Tim. "Strikes—folk going mad—stuff like that, eh? No brass in it."

Edward went on unperturbed. "Not all gloom, I think. We have our north-country comedies in mind—the old Gaiety, you know—Houghton—no, no relation of mine—Brighouse, Monkhouse and so on. I want to bring out the younger men; they must be there."

"You're after appealing to their heads," said Tim. "My

experience is you have to tickle something a bit farther down
—the seat of the emotions, eh? But I'm not one to stand in
anybody's way."

Edward thought: "Yes, I know his saying: 'You catch
more flies with oil than you do with vinegar.' " He said: "Are
you prepared to sell the Royal—and how much do you
want?"

Mr. Hilditch suddenly shifted forward on to the front of
his chair and moved his Corona cigar so that it stuck out
like a gun from the middle of his lips. He puffed vigorously
two or three times, rolled it in his lips, took it out deliberately
and placed it down as though he said: "I've given you a fair
trial and now I've finished with you." He said: "Listen, Mr.
'Oughton. I never haggle, never did. Don't believe in it. I've
got ten thousand tied up here—building, freehold, scenery
and what not. I'm making five per cent on it; no more. But
money doesn't interest me, not"—he made a small gesture as
if he were deprecatingly pushing money on one side—"in
these amounts. You're an artist. Happen I'm a bit of an artist
myself. I've been going to theayters since I was seven years
old; my mother had it in her; used to take me in the gods
here. That's why I bought the place. You wouldn't believe
that, would you?" Edward conceded that he wouldn't. "But
it's true; true as God made little apples. I used to lie on my
belly on top of a cupboard in the gallery because they didn't
charge for me if I promised to go there and I used to stare
down until I was frightened to death—I could feel myself
diving down into the pit. By God, it was awful." Mr. Hilditch
ran a silk handkerchief across his forehead. "Imagination.
I always had it. I never used to go to sleep that night. I used
to be falling off the cupboard all night or else Aladdin's uncle
used to be running after me with a knife." He paused and
reflected for a moment. "I've had the cupboard taken down
—no kids can lie on it scared to death now."

"Very wise," said Edward. Hilditch shot a quick glance at him as though wondering if he were being laughed at. He sat back once more in his chair, and resumed his cigar. His glance became cold and shrewd. He said, in a voice become dry and a little slow: "I wouldn't mind coming in with you on it."

"What?" It was a sharp ejaculation and Edward felt it was.

"I wouldn't mind joining you on it," said Hilditch again. "It 'ud be a novelty—picking our own company and our own plays and giving folk what they don't want." A grin curved his mouth and vanished.

"I'm afraid we shouldn't agree," said Edward, a little stiffly.

"It takes two to disagree," said Hilditch. "Happen you know more than me; happen not. We should find that out. But I should want to be there when you were choosing the company. I know a lot about acting or, rather, them as act —specially the women." He nodded wisely when he said that, as though he were adding: "Make no mistake about that."

Mary found herself wondering instantly: "I wonder how many women he has kept?"

Edward said: "I should want to experiment. I don't expect to make profits—if the theatre paid its way I should be satisfied."

Tim said: "Nobody likes experiments more than me. Haven't I put operatives on my board—one man and one woman? Of course," he explained, with another swift curve in laughter of his thin mouth, "they're always outvoted if I want 'em to be. But it pleases 'em. Haven't I put in baths at the pit I control, though God knows nobody seems to want 'em? Amn't I giving jobs to so many Oxford and Cambridge chaps that my foreman says if I take on any more we'st be having t' boat race on Chesterford Canal? Haven't I been running a campaign for keeping clogs and shawls because they're healthier—clogs for keeping your feet warm and shawls for producing good heads of hair? Why? Because shawls are off their heads half the time and their hair is getting the wind and sun on it."

Hilditch stopped and chewed his cigar again. Edward was thinking: "No wonder he's got on. Like a steam engine. I suppose half the world's dominators are like this—Mussolini, Shaw, Napoleon, Wells, Melchett, Lloyd George, Northcliffe—all that lot. Talk you to death; you give in to make 'em shut up. The world's commercial travellers, pestering you, bullying you to buy their wares—ideas, power, whatever it may be. That navvy and that washerwoman must have been volcanoes. This mixture of Irish and Lancashire— always produces something extraordinary—good as Scotch and French."

Hilditch said: "You'd better accept. It's the best I can do. You give me five thousand and you start operations next month. I'll get rid of my contracts."

Edward said: "You will understand that this presents a new outlook."

Hilditch nodded. "Yea," he said. "Don't let me push you into doing something you don't care about. I never believe in pushing anybody." He settled his squat figure further back in his chair as though he were saying: "I should like to see anybody trying to push *me*." But Edward had that feeling, nevertheless; and he resented it. If Hilditch were part owner his vision of Mary and himself working together, creating something fine and worthy, might be destroyed. The man was shrewd enough, no doubt—might with his head for finance kindle it into a money-making concern, but that didn't, he thought, matter. That wasn't the idea; too much success would tarnish it. Quite suddenly his mind was made up.

"I'm afraid I couldn't," he said, "in any circumstances, allow anybody to share the artistic control of the theatre, the policy, choice of plays, the true intention—not whether we lost money or not." He smiled disarmingly at Hilditch and picked up his hat and gloves. He glanced at Mary whose eyes were dancing with pride and joy in him. She was thinking: "I knew you wouldn't let me down even if you *are* a bit slow in starting." She looked at Hilditch, her breast full and tight with rising emotion. She couldn't help having a sensation of having punched him on the nose, though she had never punched anybody on the nose for fourteen years.

But Hilditch didn't look at all like a man who has received a punch. He smiled back of them, saying: "I like to meet folk who know what they want; it's surprising how few of 'em there are. And you never know—you might be right—no telling." He granted that as something strange, but not to be ruled out. That anybody should be right but Tim Hilditch was not, in his world, to be looked for oftener than miracles occur. "I might agree," he said. "There's just one thing— the other night I happened to be in the Black Bull. There's a wench there ought to have her chance—she's got as much bant and go in her as I have myself. Trix Bishop—know about her?"

Mary interrupted to say: "Yes—I think you're right— my friends have spoken of her."

Edward thought: "Friends? Who?"

Hilditch was saying: "That's my only stipulation, then. We give the lass a chance, and let me have a hand in picking the funny man. I'm pretty good on *them*. Tricks don't make folk laugh, you know. You've either got it in you, or you haven't. Humour, I mean. You can tell 'em as soon as they walk on t' stage, the right 'uns."

Edward said he saw no objection to that. He would let Hilditch know. But none of them had any doubt in their

minds that it was on those lines the Chesterford Repertory
Theatre would be founded.

As they drove away, Edward said: "This Trix Bishop—I
hope Hilditch isn't going to . . .

Mary said—and her voice astonished her by its coolness
and precision—"She's half engaged already, I think. Henry
Brierley."

Edward said: "Oh!" He thought: "Ah! She doesn't mind
then. Or is she something of an actress—like her mother.
You never know them—not even those you love most dearly.
And the girl—Brierley and Hilditch. And if one writes a
play for us and the other is half proprietor. . . . Damned
nuisance. Still, may be amusing—in a way. But Mary. I shall
need all my wits."

He said: "I think we'll kick off with *Dear Brutus*."

Mary said: "I thought you were going to adventure,
dear."

"Come," he said. "We must be allowed to get off the
mark."

"I had thought of *The Trojan Women*."

They went on arguing. It might have been a holiday they
were discussing. But the catch that Mary experienced at her
heart now and then told her it wasn't.

Chapter Eleven

HENRY BRIERLEY got in on the cotton boom just in time.
Just in time, that is to say, to buy with his purloined two hundred pounds shares in the Chadwick mill that everybody said
would never be sold to a syndicate. The Chadwick family
were too proud, it was said; and too prosperous. But those
very reasons led to the sale. Their sons knew far more about
Newmarket than they did about the cotton market, and the
rise and fall of the Chinese tael and the Indian rupee were
nothing in their eyes compared with the rise of the mayfly on
the Wye or the fall of the Hodder after flood. In spirit they
had left cotton long ago; now that the mills were spinning
gold, might they not seize the moment, take the precious
metal and leave for good? At all events, this is what they did.
The Chadwicks had done their share in sapping the colour
from women's faces and the beauty and virility from men's
bodies; they had helped to turn children into machines for
producing that which enabled diamonds to be worn, champagne to be drunk, the Aegean to be sailed, the Alps to be
climbed; and now they departed. The Chesterford that had
made them they began to eye with misgiving, dreading it a
little, fearing it a little, as men do that which they don't understand. From the common mass of people they had moved
farther and farther away until they and their operatives had
looked on each other sullenly, jealously, and with no effort
at comprehension.

Blackburn's syndicate bought them out, paying £17 10s.
for the £5 shares, £3 paid, so that within a fortnight Brierley
made a profit of over £1,000. Had it not been for Trix and
Trix's friendship with Blackburn he would not have known
that it was advantageous to buy Chadwick's shares; and had
it not been for Trix's mixed love and scorn for him and her
own beauty which sent a flame through his blood, he would
never have had the wildness to become an embezzler, even
though it did involve as it proved, nothing more than delaying the payment of certain accounts for a month and using
the money in the interval as banks use that of their customers.
To his mind, with its sense of dramatic values, the affair
worked almost too simply. Old Hugh Llewellyn, the librarian, ought to have suspected his suggestion that the in-
stalment on the building of the new annexe should be paid
in cash; but he didn't. The builders ought to have questioned
the delay of a month when Brierley told them the chairman's
absence through illness had caused the meeting for passing
accounts to be postponed; Chadwick's ought to have refused
to sell, or Blackburn's syndicate ought to have gone smash at
the crucial moment. None of these things, however, came to
pass. The library's accounts were duly paid; nobody noticed
that the builders' receipt was a month late; Brierley opened
a banking account in Burnham where he was received with
the deference due to a new customer who can sign cheques
for respectable amounts; and Trix allowed him to kiss her
without closing her lips. What price she had paid to Blackburn for the piece of information by which he had profited
he didn't know. He tried to put it out of his mind but it had
a trick of returning when he was least ready to deal with it.
But in truth she was so much a part of him, so woven into his
mind and body that she was likely to emerge at any moment
—in his reading of history, in his walking on the moor—
(then, indeed, any vision of pure loveliness such as the dark,

far Pennines, or the sun glimmering on Frenton Dam, or a whippet loping across the cropped brown ridge of the hill, was enough to set his body aching for her)—in his visits to the theatre in Burnham, when, without cease, he was matching her with the actresses he saw and seeing how she would have excelled this woman or been clouded and overshadowed by that. And, when he saw her in his mind's eye—and it was always a radiant vision his melancholy soul gave to him, a vision of her with laughing, parted lips, her head tilted back a little, shaking her curls that had so much gold and the colour of autumn in them, and her dress drawn a little tightly across her firm breasts, and her hips richly curved—when he saw her thus and the thought smote him that, maybe, Blackburn's hands knew more of her lovely frame than he did, or that her mouth had given him more sweetness or her body more ecstasy, then his anguish and desire of her were almost more than he could bear. His heart was pierced as though a blade had entered it, and his stomach sank so that he could almost have been physically sick with yearning. When his adventure into high finance (it was low, rather than high, he thought, with a wry smile on his mouth) had succeeded, Trix was gay with him, rallied him on his want of courage, told him to remember how easy the game was, and didn't all the men with money do that sort of thing? He spoke little to her in reply; he was sure in his bones that he had taken such a risk for the last time. He was tempted to inquire of her with some bitterness how soon she would have deserted him had he been caught? He grew chill at the thought. Was this love worth all the anxiety and penance and torment? But for her he would never have dreamt of thieving, but for her his mind would be occupied with his writing, his body would not be sick, his food would not affront him, his eyes not be dim and, often enough, sunken in his face. Nor would his nights be half torture. The more he was tormented, the more he suffered and the more his body became less handsome, the less she liked him. He saw that plainly enough. She would say he looked like a wet week, or she would inquire when he was ordering his coffin, or tell him not to stoop so much when he walked. When that happened he flared up and told her she had better go from him. But she took those retorts with surprising calm—arched her brows and smiled quizzically at him, or would take his arm as though they had never quarrelled at all. And he could not withstand her. His heart was ready to stand still for her at any moment she chose to give him either ecstasy or despair.

On an afternoon in late May when it was certain his escapade had succeeded, and that he would not be found out, they walked on the moor together. It was a day when the sunshine was of brilliant silver, faint in its warmth. The sky was thinly blue and the light so clear that when they looked back on Chesterford the chimneys, a mile and a half away, were stark and the distances between them, one behind another, measurable by the eye. The sharp chink and bang of shunting trucks, the quick, piercing whistle of the fussy engine glinting green and brassy at Higginbottom's colliery came to them, and they saw the white plumes of smoke from the winding shed, and the slim wisps that dribbled from the factory chimneys which wore smoke protectors like policemen's helmets on their heads. From here industry looked pleasant and innocent enough; nothing to be seen of the miners deep in the earth crouched double hewing coal—nothing to be heard of the women weavers' harsh shrill voices screaming out songs against the rattle of shuttles and clackety-clack of wood and iron. Fighting, fighting; it was all fighting. And half of them—the old, grey ones—were worn out by it and the younger ones—the ones with unquiet eyes and limbs full of blood—revelled and gloried in it. No use, Brierley was thinking, pitying them too much. He knew he couldn't have endured a miner's or an operative's life, but that didn't mean that it was unendurable. He had begun to think the sum of human happiness doesn't vary much; the average man or woman achieved it whether born in one class or another, or living one sort of life or another. Maybe a pit pony in the bowels of the earth got as much pleasure out of the caress of the pony lad's hand and the unexpected handful of corn as the Dartmoor pony his race in the fresh wind across the wild moorland. You could get used to anything, they said. Happen that was right. He remembered once having toothache so long that he got used to that also. Would he get used to being tortured by Trix, to being worn out by her? For there wasn't any doubt he *was* being worn out. He could bear it more easily if he were sure of her, if she were tied to him; and when this thought came to him he began to speak of it. They were walking over the short, mossy turf that sprang beneath their shoes as though it said: "Don't imagine you can thrust me down—see, I leap up again at once." It was, indeed, a laughing day and despite his melancholy, Brierley's eyes were smiling a little and his mouth curled up at the corners. Suddenly he slipped his arm into hers and pressed it to him. He looked quickly at her and at the same moment she turned her head and smiled at him as though she were pleased. But she didn't say anything and he wasn't at all sure of her.

"Trix, you know I'm terribly in love with you, don't you?" he said.

She didn't speak for a moment. Then:

"Are you, Harry?"

"Could you be engaged to me?"

"I don't know." Her voice was dull. "I'd—I'd rather not be, I think."

He began to wish he hadn't spoken but he felt driven on. One might as well have it out, perhaps. It was hopeless, any-

way. The suffering he had undergone began to choke his mind.
"I suppose you think I haven't enough money?"

She didn't answer.

"I might become well off, you know. A fortune in cotton—
or write plays—oh, lots of possibilities." He smiled ironically. She didn't reply. "Not interested, are you?"

"Let's sit down," she said.

They had come near the ridge of the moor and to their
right was a hollow, warm in the sun. They sat down and she
leaned back and lay with her hat off, her hands behind her
head, looking up into the bright sky, her knees raised. She
was thoughtful and might have been alone for all the notice
she took of him. But he saw her bottom lip trembling a little,
as he lay on his elbow looking down into her face and suddenly, impelled by his emotion, he stooped further and softly
kissed her cheek. She turned on to her side and put her right
arm round his neck and drew him down and lifted her mouth
to his. She had never done that before and instantly he was
suffused with tenderness. In that moment all his wrath and
bitterness were gone and he found himself trembling and
feeling that his flesh and bones were molten.

"Dearest, I do love you so," he said, his mouth brushing
her lips. A small, inarticulate cry broke from her and she
pressed his head down to her.

He placed his arm round her neck and lay down beside her
and drew her close to him so that their frames were folded
to one another and they lay as still as though death had stilled
them, hardly breathing. Only their hearts, which were madly
pounding against one another, told them how violent their
emotions were. He had not meant to take his ease of her,
but as they lay and warmed each other and their lips mingled
together, the ecstasy of his passion rose until, no more than
pressing her frenziedly to him, his being gave itself to her
and he fell to frantically kissing her lips, her forehead, her

mouth, her cheek and her bosom. She lay quiescent in his arms, the colour faded from her cheek and her eyes closed.

When, presently, she sat up, she smiled faintly at him as though she said: "You see. I care also." But she only said: "I think we must go, Harry."

They went down the hill his arm about her for a space, their limbs touching as they moved, his hand beneath her breast.

He said: "Darling, we're engaged now, aren't we?" His smile was sad, his voice quite solemn.

He looked down at her. This was a new Trix who had been born. She was sad also when she looked into his face. The boldness and arrogance were gone. She spoke as if she had not much say in what happened. She said: "If you like, Harry." They stopped then and she lifted her mouth and he kissed her again.

Presently, their arms linked, he began to talk about the projected repertory theatre; how she would become the star actress and he would write a play for her; how, indeed, he had begun to do so; and they would grow famous together. He talked with enormous vivacity, knowing he was being reckless in his speech and flamboyant; and the quieter she was the more garrulous he became. And yet deep in him was a sadness and seriousness born of knowing he had given himself to her and that whatever happened in the days to come he would feel that his allegiance was pledged to her. And hers to him? Ah, he wasn't sure of that. But he took comfort from the warmth of her arm in his, her hand lightly touching his fingers, the weight of her leaning slightly on him as they walked.

Chapter Twelve

LANCASHIRE had already passed the peak of the cotton boom when the Chesterford Repertory Theatre put on *Dear Brutus*. But Lancashire didn't know it. The climb had been so steep—a veritable Mount Everest in the graphs of those few mill-owners or cotton brokers who kept charts—that a descent was no occasion for alarm. Chesterford mills still earned as much profit in a week as they had been wont to do in twenty, and though Sam Renshaw found that his stock- and share-broking occupied less time than a few months before, he was not worried. His hens and his garden knew him oftener. Harriet was inwardly puzzled. To have Sam hanging about the house wasn't right. A man ought to be working. Whether the work produced money didn't matter much. He had better be working for nothing than not working at all. Not to work wasn't right; not if you were their sort o' folk. Sam, however, complacently said it was a bit of a lull, nowt to bother about. It were a breather; soon they'd be at it agen, harder nor ever. He had at the tip of his tongue a number of glib phrases that were spoken at that time—that the world outside Lancashire simply hadn't enough spindles to make the yarn wanted, that the boom was good for another ten years or, if not a boom, then highly profitable trade; the world-hunger for Lancashire goods was not appeased. This here wages dispute—for the work-people didn't see why they shouldn't have a bit more in these fancy days of money-making—*that* was making things a bit awkward—but when it was settled, presto!—the ship 'ud move agen; share prices would rise. India, did you say? Well, everybody knew India had missed her chance—she hadn't bought when the rupee was high and would now ha' to buy when the rupee was low. (Harriet was a bit vague as to what a rupee was—it sounded like some sort of a hat—but she didn't bother to find out—she dismissed it as part of man's sporting nomenclature that was of no more consequence than "taking his middle wicket," or "getting o'er t' line wi' three chaps hangin' on to him." Men must be permitted these childish ways of speech.) Sam began to run over to Blackpool occasionally. Sales of shares by auction were taking place there. Shares you couldn't sell in Chesterford were sometimes to be got rid of in Blackpool. In Blackpool there were both those who didn't quite know what was what and those who were "buying to keep"—solid retired folk who wanted to have their money in something they knew a thing or two about; and they thought they knew about cotton. It was extraordinary how many people thought they knew about cotton. Keeping chickens or erecting jerry-built houses, or selling tea or catching shrimps—not everybody felt they had an inner knowledge about these, but cotton—this trade which embraces the whole earth, with raw material grown among negroes in the Far West and borne to Europe to be spun and woven by white folk for natives of the Far East—well, of course, *everybody* knew all about *that*. And nobody outside Lancashire *did* know. And Blackpool knew as well as anybody else. You could often obtain 3*d*. or 6*d*. more in Blackpool than in Chesterford for the same share. Sam enjoyed the excursions extremely. To be going to Blackpool on business and to stop all night at the Prince's Hotel—life hadn't much more than that to offer you, he thought. Once or twice he took Harriet with him. They journeyed on those occasions by "sharry," as Chesterford called the newly popular motor-coaches. When you got to the coast you felt you hadn't any legs left and you wobbled about a bit on your pins; but it was worth it. It was customary to call at a few public-houses *en route* and drink beer, and you rolled along the roads and narrow lanes, sometimes brushing the very hedgerows, in a condition of bemused, and rather floating tolerance. You didn't care how fast you went, or how narrowly you missed hitting anything. You had a superb belief in your destiny; you felt like a god. At least Sam did. Harriet, perfectly sober, and not mixing readily with the passengers, was not so peaceful inside. She knew they were looked on as common trippers, a vulgar spectacle, and while she resented that, she was slightly contemptuous, too, of the "sharry" and its load. But there were other occasions when Sam went alone. Then, the auction over, he would enjoy a few drinks and walk the promenade alone, or tramp the darker streets where he liked to observe the highly painted women who had that peculiar mincing gait or swaying of the hips that he learnt to recognise as the badge of the women he might buy, were he so minded. When they ogled him he had a stirring in his bowels, a fiery leap in his loins, and his heart quickened. They said: "Good-night, dear," or, "Hello, luv," to him, and he usually said, "Good-neet," in return, half-ashamedly, recognising that his stare had led them to expect from him something they were not going to get; but no sooner had he passed one than he looked expectantly for the emergence of the next. He was sorely tempted to accept their invitations; he could afford it—he jangled his money in his trouser pockets to convince himself that that was so—and what harm would it do? The lasses had to live, they couldn't all get wed, it were no different going than wanting to go and not doing, were it? (Or were it? He couldn't quite convince himself on this point.) And if he kept it to himself . . . That was the bother. Suppose Harriet got to know? He wouldn't be able to abide what she'd say and happen what she'd do. She might leave him. But worse than that, she'd look at him as if he were dirt. So more than once he put it—but reluctantly—out of his mind. And the next time he went to Blackpool, he walked round the same streets; he had got to know them well —even one or two of the women were becoming familiar. Then, one evening, when he had been drinking whisky instead of his customary beer, he half halted when he was spoken to. The woman placed her hand gently on his arm and he stopped altogether and smiled at her foolishly. His bowler was pushed back—he had bought himself a bowler now that he was a share-broker—his vivid, tartan tie stuck out a little from his stiff collar and dicky, and his brown boots were conspicuous at the end of his navy-blue trousers. "Nay, nay, lass," he said good-naturedly, as she coaxed him. She was thirty or more, he thought, her bust was prominent and her legs shapely but fat. Her mouth and eyes were very much "done up," he considered, and her hair was excessively yellow. He would have escaped her but for her scent. She smelt of something that intoxicated his hazy mind and sent a thrill through him. (It was patchouli, but Sam didn't know this.) She took his arm as they walked to her room—a bedroom in a street that might have been Chesterford. He felt shy— he didn't like the brisk, hard-faced woman who poked out her head on the ground floor as they went by and said: "Yer luck's changed, eh, Gertie?" nor Gertie's, "Yes, he loves me, don't yer, honey?" squeezing his arm. He didn't like Gertie wanting to have possession of his money before he embraced her, nor, having said when she had coaxed him in the street that he could give her just what he wanted, her haggling now and persuading him to give her another ten shillings—two pounds altogether. Was he being done? Sam suddenly found himself empty of all desire. He was affronted by her assumption that having had what he wanted, he would have refused to pay her; he was keenly aware how gross her body was compared with Harriet's firm leanness, and how gaudy and ill-fitting her artificial silk underclothing looked. She had partially divested herself and stood looking at him with a forced smile, waiting. He knew now that he was very sober and solemn and that he wished he hadn't come. "I think I'll go, lass," he said. The smile left her face and was replaced by an angry, hard, hating look. Sam was ashamed of himself —happen she would think he was frightened—and was at once sorry for her and loathed her. He shifted on his feet. "I'm sorry, lass," he said, "but it's no good. I don't want my money back." At the mention of money she moved a stride protectingly to where it lay on the dirtily frilled dressing-table. "You wouldn't get it, anyway," she said viciously. "No, I know," he said easily. "It's yours." He knew he was insulting her, but he couldn't help it. He could no more have touched her than flown. But he knew, too, that it was partly her own fault, the sordidness and commerce of it had destroyed the adventure; or wasn't he drunk enough? She never moved any more, watching him go as if he had come to harm her and was now going, carrying a murderous weapon with him. Sam opened the door quietly and clomped heavily down the stairs. The hard-faced woman poked her head out again. "Yer soon done," she said sarcastically. But Sam never looked at her. For one thing, he didn't know what on earth to say. He walked slowly to the door and let himself out. His mouth was dry. He looked at his watch. He had just time for a drink.

He walked slowly, pondering, down towards the Prince's Hotel. At the corner of Church Street another woman stood and smiled her painted mouth at him and tilted her head beckoningly. He strode on firmly. "Nay, by God," he was

muttering, "it's a mug's game. It is that." But he was possessed of a sense of disappointment. He couldn't help thinking he had been unfortunate. Some other night, happen . . .

He went into the smoke-room and ordered a glass of beer.
He rarely drank pints now. He drank it alone; there was a
time when he would have talked to whoever was there, but
not now. Money made a difference. You kept yourself to
yourself a little more. You never knew who'd be cadging. He
felt solitary, heavy-laden. He'd have been happier in the
vault with the chaps who had nowt. If he had had nowt he
wouldn't ha' gone wi' that woman. You couldn't do that if
you had nowt. Saved a lot o' bother, having nowt. He went
upstairs and sat, forlorn, on the edge of his bed, his billycock
on the back of his head, his forearms along his knees and
his hands linked. He stared down at the carpet, looking
deeply immersed in thought. But he wasn't. His mind was
practically a blank. He was just quietly doleful, as a dog
might be with nothing to do. He roused himself after a
while and mechanically began to wind up his large silver
watch and to hang it by its chain over the knob on the bed.

"Any dam' road," he thought, "I can stop i' bed as long
as I like in t' mornin'." But that thought brought into his
head a girl with golden hair wearing a red bathing-suit on a
poster at the South Shore.

He got into bed and lay tossing about, profoundly dis-
contented.

Chapter Thirteen

THE RESOLVE to speak to Philip formed itself slowly in Mary's mind, for, of course, it was not strictly her affair. Perhaps they had decided, he and Evelyn, how much freedom each must be allowed to enjoy; and that marriage was for the future. But although Mary considered these things, her mind was not eased. Philip was not normal. She thought of his wound as poisoning not only one side of his body, but warping his whole frame and his mind also; welling up and through his whole blood. And she saw clearly how Evelyn was suffering.

She, if anybody, must speak to Philip. Only three years separated them in age; before the war their friendship had been close. She looked sometimes on the old photographs of them—she a chubby child, wide-eyed, flaxen-haired; Philip taller by three or four inches, slim, dark, handsome in a cold, dominant fashion. She had been wont to let him have his way, tolerantly, lovingly; but she knew, as she thought he also knew, that in crises she was the more reliant, the more self-possessed; perhaps the more courageous. Philip, even then, was brilliant, reckless, bold by fits and starts, a magnificent player at games when he was winning; a loser who gave up too readily, not altogether from want of spirit but rather from boredom. Losing simply had no interest for him. If he were losing it meant, he thought, he was off his game; no use persevering if you were off your game. But they had been fast friends. She had borne a good deal, and he was not unaware of it. Their affection was deep. His return wounded from the war intensified it for a time, as pity will. But Mary was too fine a spirit to bear for long with equanimity the sight of him exploiting his wounded form, playing, however unconsciously at first, for sympathy, or torturing Evelyn by the display of his maimed self. She pitied him and was angry with him and ashamed for him. She had remonstrated with him on his driving his motor-car so wildly, or, indeed, at all; she had tried to dissuade him from accepting the challenge to a mad race to Southport, and had refused to congratulate him when he had won. Mary would have gone on pondering and worrying over what she should do had she not one night seen Philip emerging from the Queen's picture theatre with Luke Hargreaves's secretary, Miss Rolleston. She saw him climb into Philip's car and drive off, and it was late when she heard him enter the house.

He had constructed a miniature rifle-range in the garden and when he was shooting the following afternoon Mary walked out to him. A large X-shaped rifle rest was dug into the ground so that he could lie prone and shoot with comparative ease and certainly with skill. She watched him shoot five rounds and taking the field-glasses gave him his score— two bulls, three inners—before she spoke. He thanked her and sat cross-legged on the firing mat looking up at her quizzically. She stood staring down at him, her bottom lip quivering a little as it was wont to do when she was suffering emotional strain. But she looked at him firmly enough and asked: "Philip, do you think you will marry this year?"

He nursed his rifle on his knees, his finger playing on the trigger. Then, looking up with a faint, derisive smile on his mouth, he said: "Why? Do you want to make it a double event?"

"You know I don't." Colour was moving into her cheeks, roused by the half-veiled taunt.

"Why worry about me?"

"I'm worried about Evelyn."

"At all events you're honest." He looked up at her from beneath his lids and swiftly down again.

"Are you still in love with her, Philip?" She thought he would resent that and refuse to answer, but he replied at once: "Why not ask *her* if she's still in love with me?"

"She's loyal."

"That's not the same thing. Besides, how do you know?"

"I suppose—I suppose you know you've been seen with Miss Rolleston?"

"Ah! So that's it. Well, well." He laughed softly but more down his nose than out of his mouth, and then looked away beyond the target.

"Philip, you're being terribly reckless."

"Always was, wasn't I?"

"I don't think you know how cruel you can be."

"Oh? Perhaps I do. Life hasn't shown *me* much mercy, has it?"

"If you don't love Evelyn any more, you ought to release her."

"Love her?" He barked it out harshly, and then stopped. After a pause he said: "I could love her easily enough—any man could, I should think, with her beauty and form—" He stopped again before he added: "I think I horrify her." He placed his rifle down and leapt to his feet and paced up and down.

Mary, the colour gone from her face again, said: "I don't believe that, Philip"; but she knew he might be right.

"You say not. I *know*."

"Has she spoken of it?"

"No more than we ever speak of what is burning us out."

There was quietness between them, and then she said, knowing she couldn't leave the position there: "It's your imagination, Philip."

"Everything is, isn't it?"

She was almost defeated; the task was hopeless. But she forced herself on, wanting a decision. "If you are right, there'll be no happiness for you in marriage with her."

"Is that so unusual, then?"

"Evelyn ought to be released"—but she said it, she knew, unconvincingly.

"How do you know she wants to be released?" he demanded. "*I* may be a wreck, but the cheques are honoured—so far."

"Philip, Philip, how can you say such things?"

He turned to her, and his face was cold and a little distorted and fixed near the mouth with misery and anguish. "Do you imagine," he said, "it is nice for me to see her avoid my eyes and wince at my touch? Can you imagine our wedding night? We shall both have to drink deep."

She began to tremble at the hideousness of what he was saying, but she held her ground. "Philip, you can't—you mustn't—marry her in that state of mind. Not ever. It's wrong, wrong; you must see it is. Philip, I can't bear it." She couldn't see now for the tears in her eyes, and she stood there awkwardly, without a handkerchief, trying to brush them away with her fingers. She looked like a small child, and Philip, angry and tormented and miserable, saw her as she was when, eight years old, she had sobbed because she had slipped into the muddy stream and ruined her socks and shoes; and he put out his hand and touched her fingers and tried to smile—and felt as though his face were made of cardboard that wouldn't move.

"It's all right, Mary," he said. "Don't worry about me. I'm hopeless, anyway—just a crock. Evelyn'll have all the money she wants and I—I shall gang my ain gait; and she'll be glad enough to see me go. So that's all right, old girl, isn't it?" He pinched her arm teasingly. She didn't speak; she couldn't. Her limbs were trembling still. She longed to be comforted, to be held tight in somebody's arms and, with a sudden sense of despair, she realised nobody existed in whose arms she could be taken—no lover for her, no lover for her. She turned and hurried away without a word, the tears running down her cheeks anew. She went in short runs and walks, stumbling a little, along the gravelled path, through the window into the library and up the stairs to her room and there she sank on to her bed and curled up like a child and cried for a while unrestrainedly. And she knew now she was crying because she believed herself to be in love with somebody who cared nothing for her. And she wept because she was not a mill girl with a host of lads to pay court to her; and she wept also because she was a woman who must wait, and wait to have love made to her and be sought, and because the chill thought had struck her that she might finally die never having been loved nor wedded nor borne children. And presently, and mercifully, she dropped off to sleep.

.   .   .   .

Philip cleaned his rifle, using his pull-through with a dexterous combination of his two feet and one hand and as he drew it through the second time and the flannelette emerged with a jerk that nearly unbalanced him, he thought: "That settles it. I *will* go with Anstruther to Kenya or any other place. These women are a damned nuisance—first Evelyn, then Phyllis Rolleston and now Mary. And if I get done in— that'll save a lot of bother. Shall I ask Evelyn to be married before I go? She might come out and stay at Cairo while we go on; and" (with his thin smile) "maybe fall in love with

Anstruther on the ship going out; if she isn't in love with somebody else already—or, again, with Anstruther despite even that. Ought I to take a secretary? Phyllis doesn't wince —nothing like a little coarse blood."

He picked up his rifle and walked off in Mary's footsteps. He might as well break the news to his father.

Chapter Fourteen

EDWARD AND PHILIP were never quite at ease with one another. Their paths had diverged in some degree from the moment Philip had gone to Harrow. Edward had endeavoured to be jovial and friendly with him. He had called Philip "old man" or "old fellow" since Philip was thirteen years old, and from the days at Harrow Philip had called him "sir." Edward thought that a little stiff, but he supposed it was right enough. He had used the word to his own father, but somehow he saw himself as a little pompous when addressed in that way. It made him want to unbend even more. It made him feel as though Philip were keeping him at a distance. He knew well enough that parents are often strangers to their children. But he was never reconciled to it. He regarded that relationship as a failure; he blamed himself—never Philip. He thought: "I suppose I am by turns too fussy and then too cool—Philip doesn't know where he is with me. Why can't I be the same with him as I am with Mary? Same father and mother—born, indeed, in the same month—October, and therefore conceived in the same month; yet no likeness between them." He knew, of course, that the war had estranged him and Philip. No quarrel, no bitterness; merely that Philip had endured the worst of it and had given the best of himself and come back maimed in body and spirit. No need to talk about it. The gulf was there—not to be

crossed. Sometimes Philip would let drop a sentence about
the old men who let us in for the war, and the old codgers
who had sat in club windows in Piccadilly and said the war
must be fought to a finish, by gad! Philip was derisive about
them and their Hymns of Hate. "We shall not sheath the
sword which we have not lightly drawn, and all that bunk,"
he said, with his queer little snort. Edward didn't imagine
Philip consciously included him among the old men. But he
was vaguely aware that Philip had a grudge against everybody who didn't fight—the young, the old, the women too.
Women, Philip said, had a hell of a good time in the war;
all the emotion and thrills they wanted, suffering vicarious
wounds, finding excuses for giving themselves to men and
being wanton, as half of them had wanted to be before and
couldn't find excuses to be. They sent off their men and
thought they were tearing their hearts in pieces; but they
weren't, by God! Hadn't he twice brought home to young
wives the news of their loved one's death—and hadn't he,
before his leave was up, been invited to take them out to
dance? And been half asked to become their lover? Philip
had been a little tight when he talked thus. Edward knew
that. He had seen Philip consciously drinking himself reckless and had known his son was, as it were, challenging his
listeners to question what he said. But Edward had let him
go on. "Better let him get it out of his system," he had
thought. "The iron and the stench and the foulness has eaten
into him. Let it take its course." And when Philip was calm
and terribly quiet and self-contained Edward saw him moving about in an atmosphere—a sort of rarefied air—that
none but he and Trotter breathed. Edward had thought it
would wear off, this armour Philip had put on against those
who had not fought in the war. But it took a long time; it
might be thinner or have more chinks but it was still mightily
protective. Philip could encase himself in it, shut himself up

so that all your attempts to pierce it by a kind word or generous action glanced off it; never touched him or got near him.

.   .   .   .

Edward was playing clock golf at the time Philip was shooting; the balls were striking the back of the hole and dropping with a firm plop into the tin. He was feeling pleased with himself. His hands were warm and full of blood and he gripped the putter as though it were a fountain-pen—so easily controlled was it, so light. He was hitting the balls firmly and smiting them with the air of a conqueror. He felt full of decision—and he did not feel like that very often. So that when Philip sauntered up, carrying his rifle in the crook of his arm in the fashion of a gamekeeper, he was ready to tackle him and all the world besides. Like many gentle men Edward could, on occasion, be imperious. He wondered why it was, and put the variations down to his liver or his nerves. If he were always as fit as he was at that moment, he reflected, he might control every cotton mill in Lancashire.

Philip watched him hole a putt; he proceeded to pick up four other balls out of the hole with quiet ostentation. He popped them into his linen jacket pockets and asked Philip how the shooting had gone. Philip said it was fine; he had never shot better.

"Umph!" said Edward. And then, firmly, "I hope you've put this big-game idea out of your head."

Philip's hand tightened round the breech of his gun. "No, sir. That's what I wanted to talk to you about."

Edward stopped on the way to the house, and standing back with his weight on his heels—the way that enabled him to drive a good ball—said: "Your mother will be worried to death!" He added, feeling it was perhaps not quite fair to drag Phœbe into it so pointedly: "And so shall I." Another thought struck him. He said: "Besides, I need you in the mill. Hargreaves is good, but still not the same as your own family; no, not the same." Edward didn't like that speech much; it wasn't, perhaps, strictly true; very disconcerting, this habit of allowing somebody who wasn't truly yourself to send words out of your mouth; came of having imagination and wanting to play-act, he supposed; using those puppets on his toy stage.

Philip was saying: "And I thought of asking Evelyn to marry me and come out to Egypt for a honeymoon on the way."

This astonished Edward considerably. He had begun to fear Philip would never marry at all, that no woman held his interest for long, that his, Edward's, easily attracted nature was Philip's also and to an enhanced degree; and that a bachelor's life would suit Philip best. He had spoken thus to Phœbe when she had shown impatience at Philip's lack of decision. So now he said: "I'm sure your mother would like that—but couldn't you stay in Egypt? Evelyn wouldn't want to go to Kenya, I imagine, and you could hardly leave her in Egypt—it would be a queer honeymoon, wouldn't it?"

"We should take a fortnight or so to get to Cairo—and her brother is at the Legation, you know. She wouldn't be lonely."

"If a woman isn't lonely after being married a fortnight she never will be," said Edward drily. Married a fortnight and forsaken! He didn't like it.

Philip said: "I believe the truth is, sir, many women are glad of a respite after a fortnight."

Edward thought: "How the devil does he know that?" He said: "Isn't there a good deal of malaria in Kenya?"

On this subject Philip was extremely airy. Anstruther hadn't exactly been to Kenya but he knew the West Coast, compared with which Kenya was a health resort. And, indeed, that was what Kenya was—in the highlands white people positively thrived. Edward interrupted to say that the highlands were not free from malaria either; he, too, had looked up Kenya. But Philip fell to examining the breech of his rifle and glancing up at Edward now and then with a quizzical look as Edward spoke of the situation that would arise if Philip, married a few weeks, were unfortunate enough . . . He ended abruptly: "Of course, if your mind is set, there's not much point in asking me." They walked off then in silence, Edward angry and feeling himself growing stiff as if some hardening chemical were being poured into him; Philip unable to keep his mouth free from a hysterical, sardonic grin. There were moments, and this was one of them, when the bitterness and evil in him controlled him; he was laughing at his father's discomfiture and he couldn't stop himself. His power gave him a gleeful, wicked exultation; and at the same time part of him was horrified.

They parted at the door—Edward to the stables and Philip straight up to his room to change for dinner. Evelyn was coming early. Better go straight ahead with it now. He was almost beginning to enjoy himself.

.   .   .   .

Evelyn was playing a sarabande by Bach when Philip came down after dressing. A Spanish shawl was thrown round her shoulders and her rather long, oval face swayed slightly to and fro as her hands brought forth the rippling cascades of sound. Despite the colour of her shawl, perhaps, indeed, because of it, she looked sad. There was languor in her shoulders and her mouth drooped. When she looked up at Philip the momentary light that came into her eyes was gone swift as sheet lightning seen from afar. She played on. They had arrived at that stage in human relationship when silence is painful. Riding together, with the horses and the country-side and the road to give one's attention to, driving in Philip's car when his concentration on the road ahead gave excuse for not speaking, or the playing of games in which one took part and the other looked on—these were bearable. But walking together, meeting and parting when greetings had to be said, words exchanged—these Evelyn had grown to dread. Words had become almost unsayable. This exquisite discomfort pierced her and yet hardened her, as month succeeded month. Her natural pride and coldness were accentuated; she became a little more imperious. It was her hand or her cheek that he kissed now, not her mouth; and she could surrender them to him like a queen. It was true that when he came near to her she had an impulse to start back, and that sometimes a tremor or nervous twitch would move through her body; but it was not entirely dislike of him but also that she was so taut in spirit, so strained, that the least touch caused her to vibrate. It was months since the question of marriage had been spoken of between them. Her mind was a tempest of doubts. The need for money—her father had died leaving her mother no more than £800 a year; the conviction that were she to break the engagement it would be thought she did so because of Philip's wounded body; and the belief that nothing but happiness awaited them—these tossed her to and fro. In the surge of pity for him and pride in him and a some-what quixotic determination to do her share for England by marrying one of its heroes, she had refused to be released from the engagement when he came home and rather for-mally put the point to her. How was she to know how pitiless time is, how worn down her resolution would become, and how she would be changed as surely as time changes the leaf into mould? She did not and could not know; only the years bring knowledge such as this; only our looking back on our-

selves as we were a year or five years ago and observing what
we are become.

"Curious," said Philip when her fingers lay still in her lap,
"that a man who wrote that, wrote those fugues Millington
plays on the church organ also."

"Yes."

"John Sebastian was a melancholy bird on the whole, I
think. Seemed to set himself equations and to work them out
in music—or give himself a start and run after himself."

She murmured something, not heeding what he said. She
was thinking how marvellous it must be to be passionately
in love with somebody who loves you also; and that this was
never going to happen to her; and she thought: "I wish I
were Mary, free to choose again; free; free." But were you
ever free to choose? Didn't fate or whatever it was choose
for you? Did the moth choose to be burnt in the flame?

"Darling, I've been thinking—when are we going to get
married?" Philip had got up from his chair and was standing leaning on the piano, his chin cupped in his hand. His
armless sleeve was away from her and barely noticeable; the
hand might have been in his pocket.

She looked at him almost uncomprehending, except that
she thought his thin dark face looked handsomer than usual
with its flush of colour, and she observed how fine his hand
was that lay along his cheek.

"Marriage, Philip? Why . . . " She looked down at her
locked fingers and then up at him with her head thrown back
a little. "You haven't spoken of it for so long. I had put it
away from me."

She said this with such quietness, such freedom from irony
that he was forced to believe it, although it wasn't more than
half true. At that moment it really did seem to her that to be
wedded was a quite new thought, something that must be
considered anew.

Philip said: "But you didn't think we should go on—as we are—for ever?"

"I tried not to think of it," she said, and then quickly: "I began to think you wished to avoid it. *I* could hardly drag it into the conversation." But she wasn't bitter, as he had thought she might be.

"I know," he said, turning so that he looked away from her and leaned with his back on the piano, "that marriage with me may be—may—no longer—that you may not now wish it."

He had come downstairs ready to be cruel or wounding if the occasion demanded it; but her quietness had altered his mood. They were both speaking softly now, as people speak when illness is in the house, or when matters have reached an end. She on her part was suffering a sense of release, as though her mind were freed of its bonds.

She said: "I had wondered if we could be happy any more, that's all."

"*Is* it all?"

She thought: "If I speak the truth, we are lost. He will be inexpressibly hurt, and I . . ." She said: "It is for all of us—for me—you have given what you have given. We ought to be proud."

"*Ought* to be?" He turned his head and saw that she was looking out of the window, her body and face motionless, her eyes fixed and deep and sorrowful.

"I *am* proud." Her voice was suddenly resolute but when she turned her face to him, he saw her eyes were wet.

On an impulse he went down on a knee and placed his face in her lap. He felt the quick tremor that passed through her. She seemed very holy to him just then, as women do to those who love them. He thought: "I must love her then: and if I love her enough, perhaps she will bear with me." And again, as he still knelt there, he thought: "Why am I behaving like this? I didn't intend to do this—this is hysteria—my beastly nerves. I shall regret it, I daresay." But he didn't move and he pressed his face harder into her dress and she passed her hand lightly over the back of his head, both of them moved by memories of when first they loved one another.

Presently he said, lifting his face: "We shall be married then?"

"Yes," she said, stroking his hair and looking out of the window.

He rose to his feet and taking her hand drew her to her feet also and towards him and then kissed her. They talked of when the wedding would be and she agreed to all he had to say—the journey to Egypt and Kenya beyond. She agreed as she would have agreed to anything he suggested. The end was reached; she had made her choice; she had no true hope of happiness.

When he left her to make his way to his father and mother to tell them what was done, he found a smile that he tried to repress fluttering across his mouth, and seeing his face in a mirror as he passed, a quiver that was almost a shudder ran through him.

Chapter Fifteen

"THE SECRET," said Mr. Timothy Hilditch, pulling down his waistcoat and hitching up his tight trousers which looked as though they might split on his thighs at any moment, "is to treat 'em like any other sort o' work-folk. Why, if you didn't keep a close hand on 'em they'd be having free fights on the stage every night. They practically do it now."

He sat back on his first-class seat bound for London and put his arm through the long blue hanger that Edward had never seen anybody use before and let his fat hand dangle with the movement of the train. Mr. Hilditch believed in having his money's worth. He had a pink carnation in his buttonhole and he kept his brown bowler hat on. You might have expected Mr. Hilditch to wear a massive gold albert across his waistcoat but there you would have been wrong. He didn't live in London for nothing; he wore a chain of fine platinum and gold, an absurdly fragile-looking thing which he rolled in his sturdy finger and thumb from time to time. As he rolled it he seemed to say: "This is a bit of all right, is this."

Mr. Hilditch had encountered Edward on the platform at Burnham and since they were theatrical partners, Edward had no excuse for avoiding him. Nor was he quite sure he wanted to. Hilditch held some fascination for him. Hilditch, as Lancashire slipped into the trough of the financial and trade wave, maintained a boisterous optimism. "What's the good o' crying stinking fish?" he said. "People want a breather—only natural. People are over stocked—let 'em work off their surplus. They'll come again—they must. And where'll they come? Lancashire. There's nowhere else."

No use telling Mr. Hilditch that spinners' margins which were 43*d*. in February were now down to 21*d*. Mr. Hilditch knew that as well as anybody. But what did it signify? It signified a lull and a lull was healthy. The world wanted a breather. Mr. Hilditch himself wanted a breather. You wanted to find out just where you stood. It was healthy; it was necessary; it made for confidence. A few firms might be getting into Queer Street but what of it? They were men of straw. The sooner they were out of cotton the better. And, of course, there were others a bit panic-stricken. But what of that, either? White-livered folk were always plentiful. No. Tim Hilditch was standing firm, four-square to the whole caboodle. "Come the three corners of the world in arms, and we shall shock them," etc., as Horatio Bottomley used to print on the front of *John Bull*. Mr. Hilditch had a warm corner for Mr. Bottomley.

Firm to his policy Mr. Hilditch was spending a score of thousands of his capital in staging a lavish musical comedy at his London theatre, the Post-War; and he was now discussing with Edward how it was done. "All very well," he said, "for you and me to be putting on high-brow stuff in Chesterford where there are serious minds. But it's no good for the Post-War. Music that is catchy, some good jokes—I keep 'em up to the mark there because I keep my eyes open and cut jokes out o' the papers—and plenty o' good legs and pretty faces—that's the recipe. Cynics pretend legs are enough without faces but take it from me, they're not. The main thing is to be firm with your artistes; don't let 'em get temperamental, except when they're with you in your private office. *Then* I tell 'em: 'Now work off that temperament—get it out o' your system. Come on, be emotional; I like it.' That makes 'em as quiet as lambs. My enemies say I pay artistes to overshadow one another—take on a leading lady and pay her who is second-best ten pounds a week extra if she gets more applause. And it's true. It wakes 'em up. Northcliffe used the same tactics; he told me so. Why, do you know, the woman who is my lead in this show used to throw a fit at every dress rehearsal—did it for years before she came to me. Every show she was ever in had to be postponed. What did *I* do? I said: 'Marie, my lass, you throw a fit at this rehearsal and I'll get the firemen to put a hose on you and hang you out in Drury Lane to dry.' I did. No more bother from *her*. Butter wouldn't melt in her mouth. 'Be a good girl,' I said, 'and you shall have a drop o' brandy in that tea you drink in the second act—not much, just a tear and a drop over, as my mother used to say.' Pleased as Punch she was. And she's never passed out at a rehearsal since. Have a cigar."

Edward said he would smoke his pipe. It must be a heavy responsibility, he said, carrying a theatre like the Post-War on one's shoulders, with a pay and expenses roll of, he supposed, fifteen hundred pounds or more a week?

Mr. Hilditch nodded complacently as he cut his cigar. "It's nothing," he said. "Get used to it, you know. I was more excited over my first little boxing-booth and the first time I gave a dinner at the hydro ·at Lintock Wells. Had a floor built over the bath and during the second course it collapsed. You never saw such a mess. Pulled five of 'em out myself."

He chuckled at the remembrance. "I told 'em they mustn't always expect a bath thrown in when they came to dinner with me. 'I'll just leave that thought with you,' I said."

He fumbled in his inside pocket and produced a letter. "Here," he said, "this'll amuse you. Listen to this. Get a lot of abuse, you know. Got to expect it, a man in my position.

Written on good notepaper too. This is what he writes. 'I know you,' he says. 'I have unmasked you. The Devil has two helpers, or chiefs of staff. One is a hypocritical priest (an immortal with a human body) who could have stopped the Great War but did not intend to. Indeed, he helped it on by inflaming the Kaiser into thinking himself a god. This hypocrite is the false prophet. The other is you. You are The Beast'—capital letters, there," said Mr. Hilditch, winking—" 'you are the modern King Midas responsible for the awful state of world finance—you hope to collar all the world's gold eventually. Before the world can be saved for the second coming of our Lord you and the priest must be cast alive into the boiling lava of (say) Mount Etna. I hope I have made all this clear to you. P.S. I know you work by vibrations or radio-suggestions continually thrown out into the air. Between you, you are the direct cause of death, disease, war, crime, poverty, over-population, excess and distortion of every kind.' Well," said Mr. Hilditch, "he gives me credit for a bit o' power, doesn't he? I never believed there were so many lunatics in the world till I became famous. I could fill an asylum with my own correspondents. Fact." He placed the letter carefully back in his pocket and puffed at his cigar.

Edward began to read a play in manuscript that had been submitted to him by Brierley, and Hilditch spoke no more till they were running through the Potteries. Then: "I always think of Arnold Bennett when I go through these places," he said sagaciously. "If I'd been a writer, I should have been like Arnold Bennett." He looked solemnly out of the window. "We have a lot in common, Bennett and me. I can see it in his writings. Zest. Flavour. Tasting life. We both do it. Of course, he's not as well off as I am but he can enjoy himself. I should like to meet him. I'll ask him to dinner one night. I could tell him a thing or two. Self-made man like me, you know," he added.

"That explains it," said Edward gravely.

"You'd better come round with me to the Post-War. I've got a few jokes for 'em to work in. What do you think of these? I've been collecting 'em:

" 'There's no doubt women are displaying more backbone than men.'

"Rather neat, eh? And this one: 'Polygamy is marrying more wives than one. In Christian countries they have only one wife and that is called "monotony." ' Did you ever hear women called a 'side issue'? If the Bible's true, that's what they are, isn't it?"

"Don't you find," asked Edward, "that jokes misfire unless they fit naturally into the texture of the play?"

"Well, what do I pay 'em for?" asked Hilditch. "He's a damn' bad comedian if he can't make use of a good joke. Suppose I remind you of the husband who told his wife she was the eighth wonder of the world and she replied, 'That may be true enough but don't let me catch you with any of the other seven.' Do you mean to tell me you couldn't work in a joke like that? Why, the audience'll absolutely eat it up."

Hilditch's car was awaiting him at St. Pancras and Edward, who had an hour or two to spare, accompanied him to the Post-War, a flamboyant building of green tiles and chromium plating in Cockspur Street near Trafalgar Square. "When things go bad," said Hilditch, "I come out and look at Nelson standing up there on his Column, and I say to myself, 'Think of what he did, lad, with an eye short and an arm sawn off.' And then I go back and play hell with 'em. I put their wind up so much in the last show that the stars used to come in and ask the stage-manager, 'Is my scene in to-night, Joe?' Because if I didn't like the way they were doing it I used to cut it out. Nobody knew. You can do nearly anything in a theatre. Why, in one show I sent on tour the costumes for acts one and two didn't turn up so they played

act three first and then went on with act one afterwards. It
was a furore—and before that it had been a flop. We always
played it that way afterwards. Even the author said it was
an improvement—and *you* know how awkward they can be
about little things like that."

They went in at the stage-door and Hilditch paused a
moment to talk to Thomas the door-keeper, whose office was
crammed with letter-racks, telephones, speaking-tubes, a coke
stove and framed play-bills and signed photographs. "Letters,
sir," he said, putting on his steel pince-nez and producing a
bundle tied tightly with string. "Sort 'em out," said Hilditch,
"open all those which feel they have photographs in and
send the photographs back with that printed slip—you know,
'Mr. Hilditch regrets he cannot offer you any part at present
worthy of so lovely a lady.' Done me more good in the profession than anything, has that. Send the other letters to the
City office.

"Make 'em feel they're in your confidence," said Hilditch,
hurrying Edward off down the stone passage, "and they could
run the Bank of England for you. Thomas used to be a
sergeant at Scotland Yard. I often tell him he has an arrest-
ing personality. Not bad, eh?"

"Don't you keep a personal secretary here, then?"

"No. They get to know too much. I tried it. Every time
I had an actress up to see me, my secretary would bring in
letters for me to sign. And he always knew five times as many
intrigues among members of the company as ever existed.
Too much damned imagination, that's what was the matter
with *him*. Discovered a plot for a musical comedy I'd written
—did I tell you about that? I'll put it on one o' these days—
and he tried to sell it to me. *Me!* And after I'd fired him I
found he'd paid himself for it already. I should have had a
serious rival there, I tell you," he added, grinning.

The Lady of Liége was being rehearsed. That is to say, a

number of ladies and gentlemen scantily dressed and wearing wraps were sitting in the draped stalls, a young man in a gigantic ulster was talking from the orchestra rail to another young man in a top hat worn at an acute angle, who was standing on the edge of the stage, leaning over the orchestra, and looking as though he might fall into it at any moment; a severe-looking woman wearing horn-rimmed spectacles was sitting at the stage piano extremely bored with life and staring at the keys; nothing was on the stage save a roll of carpet, a chair and a dilapidated couch; a certain amount of hammering was proceeding, accompanied by low cries of: "Hi, Bill! sling them nails," and an occasional fleeting figure with shirt-sleeves, a bowler hat on the back of its head and an apron wound into a string round its waist, made a hurried journey across the back of the stage or past one of the wings.

Before anybody had observed him, Mr. Hilditch said with great heartiness: "Don't stop, Montague. I'm not here, see? Don't excite yourselves. Just carry on in your own sweet way. I just want to watch—shan't say a word."

Montague Schaft, the blond young man in the ulster, who was producing, said: "Why, sure, you must tell us how we're goin', sir. We'll wake it up in a minute or two. We've got talent just goin' to rot, but somehow it don't kinda fit the right holes yet—too many square pegs. But I guess we'll soon have the corners knocked off the squares." He continued his conversation with the young man in the top hat. "Now, Gus, you gotta get that dance in while she's kind of thinkin' out how she's goin' to hand it to you, see—you gotta be melancholy, a quiet dunno-where-you're-goin'-but-you'll-get-there-some-day kind of a dance—you get me? Sure you do; well, put some contemplation into it—make yer hands and feet look like they got no bones in 'em, get me? Well, then, let's see it. Let her go, Miss Bernheim."

Miss Bernheim at the piano wakened up out of her trance,

and suddenly let forth a stampede of notes, to which Gus began to move his legs and hands and feet and body as though he were, as Mr. Hilditch muttered to Edward: "a yard and a half of pump water." Presently Mr. Hilditch could stand it no longer. "What's the matter with him, Montague? Why has he come over Sissy?"

Schaft explained that he was dancing the disconsolate dance waiting for the girl's answer.

"Well, we'll cut that out," said Hilditch.

"But it's a cue dance—she comes in on that."

"She comes in," said Hilditch, "and the audience go out. It's murder. Why, I'd murder him myself if I'd paid fifteen shillings for a stall and saw that. Who's goin' to sing the *entr'acte* music?"

Montague took out a fawn silk handkerchief and wiped his head. "The *entr'acte* music ain't sung," he said.

"My *entr'acte* music is always sung," said Hilditch. "I sung a lot of it when I was a boy. You'll have to find a male-voice quartet to do it. They know nothing about singing in London, and I want to teach 'em. Why isn't the stage set?"

"The stage'll be set while we break for lunch," said Montague, sitting down resignedly.

"Well, get on with it, lad; don't let me interrupt," said Hilditch. "Have you arranged for the sun to shine in the seventh scene?"

"Sun? It's the moon," said Montague, faltering a little.

"It's the sun—I altered that last week. There's far too much moon in these shows." He turned to the row of creatures in wraps, who displayed here and there a nonchalant golden head and a pair of provocative lips and well-turned legs, and asked: "Is Miss de Keiller there?" Miss de Keiller was—a short woman of twenty-five with jet-black hair, full red lips, dark blue eyes, a plump bosom and trim legs. She was the Lady of Liége with whom, in the play, half the

British Army had fallen in love, and who returned to her hotel on all sorts of pretexts when the war was over, pursued by the wives and sweethearts of generals and gunners and sappers and sergeants.

"How do you like the new song I've had written for you?" asked Hilditch. "All right, isn't it—gets that top note in, eh?"

"I do not like eet very much," she said, coming to sit by him. "I should like a song that I sing to a violin obleegato— could you not get M'sieur Stavsky—once 'e heard me sing and 'e said I was . . ."

"Stavsky's in New York," said Hilditch shortly.

"Ah, no, 'e is in Paris, and 'e is coming to see you." She smiled entrancingly at him, and he shifted uncomfortably in his seat.

"The devil he is."

"Ah, do not be cross, Meester Eelditch. 'E would not do eet for anybody but me. It will make everything stupendous."

"It 'ud certainly make the wage bill stupendous. When's he coming?"

"To-morrow."

"To-morrow I shall be in Leeds."

"Then the next day?"

"The next day I shall be in Aberdeen."

"You are joking." She produced a lace pocket handkerchief not much bigger than a postage-stamp and dabbed the corner of her eyes.

"Of course. You too. And remember, Marie, I'm the only one in this firm who's allowed to introduce new jokes. When do you go on? Next scene? All right, come and have a glass of champagne. And forget about Stavsky. This isn't the Albert Hall, and you're not Galli-Curci—she couldn't hold a candle to you." He took her arm, and turned to Edward. "Will you come up? I'd like you to see my room." They went through the steel door into the right wing and up a short flight of stairs. The room was panelled in dark oak with slender rectangular recesses of beaten silver. Lamp brackets of silver bronze were shaped like lanthorns; the only pictures were of sailing-ships—mostly those in the grain race from Australia. The desk was of mahogany and the ink-wells were figured gold, the couch and chairs of tooled leather. "This," said Hilditch, pausing on the threshold, "is where I forget all about money-grubbing and think as an artist—or try to. I won't have a telephone in the room."

He opened an oak door in the wall and disclosed a liquor cabinet. They drank in silence, Edward wondering at the complexity of the man and Miss de Keiller pondering whether she was likely to save enough money on the play's run to buy the villa she wanted in Capri.

"You'd be astonished," said Hilditch presently, "how many actors I've shown how to do their jobs in this room. I had to have the juvenile lead up here and I took this pillow and called it 'Marie' and taught him how to make love to it. I improved him, Marie, didn't I?"

She looked at him over the rim of her glass and nodded. "Oh, very much. First 'e was a wooden block—afterwards an ape. 'Ug, 'ug, 'ug. I make 'im buy my lipstick. I tell 'im it is fair—'e get it all back again."

Hilditch unlocked another cupboard and took out three golf putters with heads of silver. He moved a small piece of carpet and showed them a golf hole. "If my pals drink too much o' my champagne," he said, "I make 'em putt me for five pounds a time. That cures 'em. I have an acute sense of justice. I'll tell you a secret, 'Oughton. You wonder why I'm rich. It's because I've always sold too soon. Another thing. Don't expect brass from your friends. My experience is they've all got their bobs nailed to the counter."

Edward said he was afraid he would have to go; he was to see Bernard Shaw to seek permission to put on *Fanny's First Play*.

"Ah," said Hilditch. "I like the story of him walking past the hurdy-gurdy man who stood with his hat out, and saying 'Press.' Well, I won't keep you, Mr. 'Oughton. Come down to my place at Epsom one week-end. Always a bit o' rat-catching, or badger-hunting or cock-fighting. I've got a new thing too—I'm teaching monkeys to kill rats by hitting 'em on the head with a hammer. They chase 'em in a concrete pit. Only so far the little devils insist on catching 'em by their tails."

Edward walked down the stairs and into the street. Buses were rolling by and newsboys crying the afternoon papers. Somehow, that struck him as a trifle odd.

Chapter Sixteen

BRIERLEY walked down to the Mechanics' Institute in deep thought. It was a fine September day with white clouds in a blue, lofty sky and a light, fresh wind to tell him that the sultriness of August—gone with a crashing thunderstorm— was past. It was eleven o'clock in the morning and Chesterford wore a sleepy look. Only children who were ailing or were too young for school were in the streets; a few women shopped, empty tram-cars swayed by. He looked at the pavement without seeing it, tapping it with his thin ash stick and carrying his soft hat in his hand. He was thinking: "Love's a strange thing—deep, abiding love seems to flourish best on happiness and contentment, but half-love—such as, I suppose, Trix's love is for me—only wells up when she's in trouble, when she wants comfort." He tried not to blame her —she had always been supremely honest about it; he saw she hadn't truly wanted to be engaged to him, and the day on the moor when she had lain so close to him and pulled his mouth down to hers—that was in some measure a reward for his recklessness in "borrowing" the library's money and again, a reaction from another stormy night at her home with Josh Meadows. So he had now concluded. Terror, excitement, fear, grief—these, he was aware, and often thunder and lightning also, and great music—caused emotional excitement in women. She might want him one day and be quite out of love the next. That, indeed, was what had been happening. Blowing hot and cold, she had tortured him, exalted him, made him wish he were dead. And he went on trying not to blame her when they were apart (although he did not always succeed) and trying to preserve a degree of independence when he was with her; and there he failed completely. He could say with Masefield now, as truly as ever he had been able to say it: "I am a coin for you, spend me as you will."

.   .   .   .

Both his own and Trix's lives had undergone great change. For two months Trix had been a member of the repertory company, living away from the Meadowses' household, achieving a tranquillity and poise and joy in herself and her work that she had never known. Mixing with players often enough of quality and always of humour, being compelled to study the writing of authors of distinction, reading about herself in the local newspapers, seeing her photograph in the *foyer,* knowing that high hopes were held of her—these things afforded her enormous delight. Not only was she accepted in prominent Chesterford circles—she had taken tea with Mary Houghton, gone with the company to the Mayor's reception of them, joined in a play reading before Burnham Playgoers' Club, and been invited to the Beethoven Society Ball—but her presence in a tram-car was noted, and people turned and stared and nudged one another as she walked down the street. "That's Trix Bishop from t' Rep," they said. "Tha should ha' seen her in *Ambrose Applejohn's Adventure*—a cabin-boy she were and dam' good, too." Or, "They say she could play a blinkin' steam engine, if she were axed to do." She was earning three pounds ten a week and it seemed a fortune. She paid twenty-five shillings a week for her board

and lodging and was treated like a princess. She was well fed
and had a neat room in a semi-detached house with a bath
(a luxury she had never known) and a name on the gate-
post. It was worth half a crown a week to see her letters coming addressed to "Miss Trix Bishop, 'Green Bank,' Burnham
Road." Where the green bank stood wasn't at all clear but
that didn't matter. She had some cards printed also from
a metal die (Brierley suggested that)—"Miss Trix Bishop,"
and in the bottom left-hand corner, "Chesterford Repertory
Theatre." The cards had gilt edges and were large and stiff.
When she went to Mason & Jones's in Burnham and ordered
a costume and gave them that card, the young ladies nearly
fell over themselves to serve her. And when she had gone
they tried to walk like she did, and wondered where she had
her hair done, and when they went home they said: "We had
an actress in this morning. They say she used to sing in a pub.
I'm fed up with serving in a shop, ma." Her own landlady,
Maud Eckersley, had taken "pro's" when The Royal Theatre
was The Royal Theatre. She could make a quartern of shin
beef go round half a dozen, she was a connoisseur of stout
and fish and chips, she knew how to let sleeping stage-folk
lie, and if you wanted to have a bit of a party after the show
on Saturday night, she wasn't the one to say you nay. And she
never came to see the show before Wednesday. She would
take no unfair advantage, wouldn't Maud Eckersley, but
after Wednesday she expected you to know it; and if you so
much as fluffed a word Maud would let you know. "Well,
how did you like us, Maud?" Trix would ask. Whereupon
if the company wasn't up to the mark Maud would fold her
arms underneath her pinafore and say: "Well, if you hadn't
asked me I shouldn't have let on I'd been. I'm not one to
hurt anybody's feelings. I'll say this—I've seen worse—but
not so much. You've not given your part much more than a
lick an' a promise this week, have yer? And as for that

woman as talked Lankyshire, I shouldn't think she ever saw a pair o' clogs till Monday night. Nor we don't say 'mysen' in Chesterford neither; that's Yorkshire, tell her. I neether laughed nor cried an' it's not much of a play as makes me do neether but I could see where I *should* ha' laughed if yer hadn't bin makin' me yawn my head off. How do yer like yer eggs boiled? Nay, I'm not jokin'. Do yer like 'em hard or soft? There's a nice photo of you in t' *Chronicle*—I saved it for yer. It's under that cushion—or it were unless t' cat's 'ad it. It's a bobby to play wi' things, that cat."

Trix's mother sometimes came to tea and that was a great occasion for Maud. Her heart went out to Mrs. Meadows. She needed no telling what those worn hands and wistful eyes had suffered. She put an extra spoonful in the teapot, she cut a plate of bread and butter so thin that it almost fell to pieces when you lifted it up, and the crumpets were so full of butter that they got all over your face and hands. "Yer mother's a lady," she'd say when Mrs. Meadows had gone. Maud would stand with her back to Trix putting the silver away and nodding her head with the hair tightly drawn over it and the tall ebony comb stuck up straight. She could let herself go better with her back to you. "Yer mother's a lady," she would say. "Don't tell me she's not. It matters nowt to me that she takes washin' in—oh, I've noticed her hands She's that gentle and quiet—never takes more than her two cups—'Ow are yer, Mrs. Eckersley?' that's always her first question. 'And 'ow's my daughter—and thank yer for lookin' after her so well.' Ee, I wish she could come and live here wi' you. *I* could look after her—*I* could get some colour into them cheeks. 'You wait till yer daughter's famous,' I told her. '*And* she will be,' I said. 'Miss Trix will be,' I said. 'I know,' I said. 'If I could look after yer both I should be as proud as Punch,' I said." And off Maud would go to the scullery, talking as she went, her voice crescendo-ing and diminuendo-ing as she pattered to and fro, her steel spectacles hiding her wall eye and her ebony comb bobbing as she went.

Trix had given Brierley beautiful imitations of Maud Eckersley before he had met her, and then, meeting her he had seen how Trix was half worshipped by her. And the higher Mrs. Eckersley's regard and the deeper the fondness the repertory company had for her, the less Trix needed him. He saw that plainly. When Nathaniel Dewsbury, the middle-aged fat character actor, put his arm round her and said, playfully: "And how's the world's sweetheart to-night, eh?" or when Gustav Davies the romantic lead, who was too good-looking by half, linked his arm with hers and lolled against the flats, Brierley saw that she enjoyed their affection just as much as his. He thought, with a wry grin: "Anybody with trousers on will do."

Two months ago he had resigned from the library. For one thing he couldn't bear the room where he had come a moral cropper. He knew he was stained by his escapade, and he wanted to run away from it. But also a fever was in his bones. There was £1,000 to play with, stuff to write and Trix to be won. He became a member of the amateur share exchange, and he began to write with fury. In four weeks he wrote a three-act play, a coal-pit tragedy, which Edward Houghton had read, spoken kindly of, and given him back for revision. *The Reaping,* it was called—a strike play wherein the manager who tried to smash the strike was killed at the coal face proving how easy it was to earn good wages. The revision was completed and he had now reached the stage when, every time the postman came, he looked for a final decision to hurtle through the letter-box. For the moment he was avoiding the theatre; he imagined they would think he was badgering them if he went. But he missed seeing the weekly play and going round the back to talk with Fos-

dyke, the producer, with Trix, with Nathaniel Dewsbury
and the rest. He was thinking of them now as he walked
along Shaw Street. Fosdyke's company especially was a loss
Fosdyke's responsibility and twenty-five years sat lightly on
him. He had acted first in the Oxford University Dramatic
Society. He looked at you from behind his spectacles with an
amusing air of innocent truculence and said caustic things
as blandly as he paid compliments. He had spent two years
with Sir Frank Benson, stage-managed for Leon M. Lion,
played in a Cochran revue, and done six months at the Liverpool Repertory Theatre. He said he had failed at everything
and that producing was the only thing left to him; and that he
only got his chance to do that when he was stage-managing a
Sunday-night show at a fee of two pounds and the producer
got German measles. The company tried to produce themselves, quarrelled incessantly and finally appealed to him on
the Friday. He went up to the gallery and, using a mega-
phone, controlled them from there to ensure they didn't
mumble, and that they could be heard. It was a serious, morbid, modern problem play and he made them act it like a
melodramatic mystery thriller, with a good deal of over-
emphasis and magniloquent gesture. When he had finished
with it, it resembled a burlesque of Chekhov, and the critics,
overjoyed not to be bored, grossly overpraised him. Everybody was surprised except Fosdyke. Edward read about him
in the *Observer,* made a point of seeing Fosdyke's next two
productions—a crook play that went like machine-gun fire
and a Cockney comedy that was dry and crisp and had a
Rabelaisian flavour. On those Edward made up his mind.
Fosdyke packed his two bags and came to Chesterford, which
he pronounced a play ready made. "I'm astonished," he told
Brierley, "that somebody hasn't been here and put gates on
the streets and called it a pageant and charged people to
come in. Let's do that, shall we? Let's make it a limited

liability company. If we could get those miners leaving the pit to sing a gloomy ditty, the Chauve-Souris wouldn't be in it. And those Tacklers' Tales—they ought to be written in blank verse and printed by the Hogarth Press. We will do them and have a limited edition on vellum—two guineas—or three guineas signed by the authors. I like the one about the owner of the hen-cote who got his pals to manhandle it to the next allotment while he sat inside carrying the perches. I think that's sweet." Brierley got on well with him. For almost the first time in his life he had encountered somebody with whom he was perfectly at ease, who spoke, as it were, the same language, who was, like himself, almost more concerned with the art of the theatre and the craft of writing than with living life itself. That was, no doubt, a weakness but he wasn't altogether ashamed of it. Then there were Mr. and Mrs. Webster, the inseparables, with whom he had formed a friendship also. Nat Beresford said Walt and Winnie Webster, although they might sound like the front and back legs of a stage horse, restored a man's faith in fidelity, but others said it was only that they were close by nature. At all events, you couldn't engage one without the other. Walt was first-rate and Winnie was what Chesterford would have called "make-weight," but Walt was so good and Winnie was so cheap—you could get her for fifty shillings a week—that they usually paired off successfully. Walt, for all his good humour, had a quiet insistence about him. They had one child—a big gawky boy who looked gormless, as Nat said, and who turned up at long intervals from either a seaside pierrot troupe (for he, too, was "on the boards") or, in the winter, from some fifth-rate touring company where he, being eighteen, played old-men's parts. Walt, who had once been a blacksmith at Sheffield, was a born actor. He could play Lob in *Dear Brutus* or Androcles in Shaw's *Androcles and the Lion* to perfection, so puckish was he, so childlike and aged and wistful all at the same time; or he could play you any North-countryman, from a back-biting Methodist as narrow as a hen between the eyes to a roystering bookmaker as broad as Market Street. But no dialect came amiss to Walt, from Devon to Highland or Irish to Somerset. He had had an exceedingly tough life, off-stage and on, and he never could have kept going but for Winnie. Winnie mollycoddled him and gloried in it. Walt's cough-lozenges and Walt's wigs and Walt's noggins of whisky in the winter and Walt's orange-juice in the summer—these were her charge.

She made herself up and then she made him up, too. She firmly believed, indeed, that Walt *couldn't* make himself up and Walt never disillusioned her. He would say to Nat: "She wanted another lad, and she's made a child o' me ever since. They've got to have their own road when they're like that." Walt could talk as if he were born in Berkeley Square but among friends he lapsed into his slow, simple speech. He was a little man going bald with a Roman nose and big horn-rimmed spectacles. In his spare time he translated plays from the German but they were usually so experimental that nobody would look at them except the Stage Society and they stopped at looking. Fosdyke christened him: "Auf Wiedersehen," and Walt never minded. He was a philosopher. "I take things as they come," he said. "I had to choose whether I'd worry myself daft or go on 'never heeding.' I've never heeded since. I find if you don't fight for your own way people are often so glad to show they're the boss that they *give* you your own way—like the lad who was put in charge of the warehouse and sent everybody home at three o'clock just to show he could order 'em about. It's surprising." That was one of Walt's sayings—"It's surprising." He would say sometimes: "The people in front are as easy to work as an engine with steam up—it's surprising," but equally he would say: "It's like putting a screw into a slab of granite to-night —it's surprising." But he made these spoken mental notes on the audience as a scientific observer and then dismissed the matter from his mind and picked up his translation. You couldn't alter folk and you'd best not try; so Walt looked at it.

Winnie was a character, too. She was one of those people whose families have been in the theatre for a generation or two, who have never thought of anything but the stage as a career, and yet who have no talent whatsoever for it, except that they have no stage nerves and can bellow out their parts with a superb self-possession and an equally superb lack of intelligence. Winnie could be relied on to know the words of any part inside three days and not to know what it meant in three years. Winnie knew the best theatrical landladies in the Number Two and Number Three towns all over the British Isles, the price of a double room to a shilling, which theatres were good dates and which were "duds," which had dressing-rooms like dungeons or refrigerators, which towns had audiences that said: "You damn' well make us laugh— what d'you think we've paid for?", which managers like booking a "joint" (man and wife), which could be relied on not to leave you stranded at Inverness or Truro, which Sunday train-journeys were pleasant and which were hell, which railway stations sold a good cup of tea, and exactly how much worth to attach to such phrases as: "World's most stupendous success!" "Millions of laughs!" "Breaking records everywhere!" or what the salary would be when Mr. Jonathan Jonathan advertised that he wanted a principal boy for his Old-Established, West-End, Number One, Specially Written, Already Fully Booked New and Original Pantomime. "That'll be worth about three pounds ten and find your own tights," she would say; "and you get your money if the mammoth takings—highest price one and six—

will stand it." But though Winnie couldn't act any more than the stage furniture, she knew an actor when she saw one; she hadn't been cradled in a dressing basket for nothing. And when she saw Walt playing the Silver King as well as ever Wilson Barrett played him, she knew her hour had struck. Walt didn't know it for some time; but Winnie did. She flattered him and mothered him, and warned off the other girl, a peroxided blonde who had increasing difficulty in persuading touring managers that she was not more than ten years older than she swore she was, and Winnie, who was herself at that time confessing to being twenty-nine but in indiscreet moments asserting that she had "been immense" in *The Face at the Window* round about 1900, gradually wore Walt down. Finally two unaccustomed bottles of stout which Walt drank at supper on the tour's last night and a measure of "Auld Lang Syne" emotion and a feeling that his lodgings off the Fulham Road were going to be lonely after this triumph, put the finishing stroke on Winnie's generalship. She had fought a great campaign and she merited her success. Walt, when he thought it out afterwards, always conceded that. And he conceded too, that he might have done much worse. For her admiration of his art was profound, she kept him warm in bed in the winter—and Walt required all the heat he could get for his lean, nervous frame—and she had the good humour that commonly goes with fatness. He wished she didn't say "nothink," and that her speech had less in it of the gutter-slang of the cheaper stage, and he would have preferred her to be less solicitous and to be acting occasionally on the west coast when he was on the east, but he kept these things to himself.

You might, were you a close observer, as Brierley was, form conclusions about these things, but no words of Walt's assisted you. Winnie wasn't sure for a while about this repertory company business, not sure, for instance, about the standing of Chesterford—Chesterford was quite definitely a Number Two if not a Number Three town, and Walt and she had worked up pretty steadily to a fair modicum of Number One engagements. And the sorts of plays, too. She thought in her inmost heart that *A Bunch of Violets* was a considerably finer play than *The Cherry Orchard,* of which she could make nothing. But no such plays as *A Bunch of Violets* were even considered. However, Chesterford, at least, stayed where it was; it didn't move a hundred and fifteen miles between Saturday night and Monday; it allowed you to make a long-standing and therefore cheaper than usual contract with your landlady, and you got to know which butcher's meat could be eaten with false teeth. But this fresh play every week or two—*that* bothered Walt who was a "slow study"; and this same or nearly the same audience every week—that had both advantages and drawbacks. Walt was soon a great favourite —every time his first entrance occurred he was clapped. But of herself she wasn't sure. These Chesterford audiences had a gift for nicknames and were given to ribald laughter, and while she rarely could make out what a solitary voice in the pit muttered, or what the catcall was from the gallery on a Saturday night, she knew what they connoted. Winnie had been in Brixton, and Chesterford thought little or nothing of her Lancashire accent, and Winnie, who had won a big hand, as she said, in *Hindle Wakes* at Southend, was grieved over it. But she stuck it out, cocked up her chin, and stared at the gallery and let them have every line fortissimo. "Aye, lass, we yerd thee !" said a gallery voice admiringly after one of her speeches. "Tha doesn't lap it up," and there was laughter and applause. Brierley had heard of this happening a fortnight ago, and curiously enough, since then, Winnie had grown more popular.

Brierley's mind ran over these new friends and a smile played round his lips and creased his eyes, and then, realising he was approaching the Mechanics' Institute, the smile vanished, the corners of his mouth, which had been curled up, began to droop, his brown eyes became sombre and deep. He disliked the Institute and its work and the men he encountered there. Was he a snob? He didn't think he was— he hoped not. Why didn't he hit it off better? True, the men for the most part talked dialect or wore the wrong things— sometimes too much jewelry, sometimes neckerchiefs instead of collars and ties; or they were ugly with their paunches or bandy legs; and he realised their coarseness and want of breeding cut him off from them to some extent. Was it that they were steeped in grabbling for money? But wasn't he grabbling just as they were? And hadn't he begun in a far worse manner, in all likelihood, than most of them? Was *that* why he was so uncomfortable among them—knowing he had been despicable and that he had brought himself down to their level? Could he win back his integrity? Could integrity ever be wholly recaptured? He didn't know—he gravely doubted it. All the same, he despised them and he knew they disliked or distrusted or hated him—a mixture of all three, no doubt. They didn't mix; they had no true points of contact. They knew he used them in his articles for the *Burnham Guardian,* that he was often ironical or mordantly humorous at their expense, and nobody likes being ridiculed although equally nobody dislikes seeing his fellows taken down a peg. It bothered him, this being unpopular and this hate for others. He was too sensitive to be able to move in a charged atmosphere with composure—he felt sometimes that currents were aimed at him. And furthermore it filled him with misgiving when he thought of his writing. A deep sympathy, a wide-flung charity, keen humour, these, he knew well enough, were essential to success. Had he got them? Were not these ill-spoken, rough-mouthed, misshapen men— and if he were fair he must grant they were not all like that

either; there were young stockbrokers, journalists, and retired magistrates mixed with the butchers, horse-dealers,
jewellers, insurance agents, and publicans—weren't they, in
a true sense, his own people? He had lived among them, done
his work among them, called them by their Christian names,
had kindnesses from them. Wasn't he a renegade to turn his
back on them or to turn away from them? And yet, had he
turned away? He thought: "Be just to yourself, lad. You
know you don't care tuppence how much money people have
or what their jobs are or who their fathers and mothers were,
so long as they have some spark, some quality in them. Otherwise you wouldn't have fallen in love with Trix, and remained in love with her when Mary Houghton . . . No,
that's too damned conceited. She probably doesn't give you a
thought. But anyhow, you know what gets on your nerves is
that these chaps just don't happen to be your sort. You can't
talk to them about anything, they think you're stuck up and
fancy your chance, and they'd liefer see your back than your
face any day in the week. So it's no good worrying." Well,
that would be all right if he could leave it at that, but he
couldn't. He wished to heaven he could ignore people and
what they said and thought and felt about him, but he
couldn't; not yet. And he doubted if he'd ever be able to. He
supposed he was, as he thought of it, "a bit of a wash-out,"
neither robust enough nor tolerant enough nor genial and
humorous enough to get on easily with folk he cared nothing
for, nor yet strong enough to thrust them out of his mind as
though they didn't exist.

He walked past one or two knots of men standing on the
kerb outside the Institute doors, and, as frequently happens
when you have made up your mind you are detested, the people you expect to look askance at you are of a sudden extremely agreeable. Two or three hailed him. "Hello, Brierley, dost want any Dawn?"; and, "There's not much doin'

inside yon." Feeling warm inside him, he made some sort of rejoinder and went downstairs.

The share exchange was a long, rather dim room in the basement, lighted by half a dozen windows and furnished with nothing more than two trestle-tables, several forms, of which two were upholstered in American cloth, a number of plain wooden chairs, and a long and narrow sloping desk arranged so that it caught light from the windows. On that table transfer-forms were being signed and cheques laboriously written out by men who twelve months ago had rarely, if ever, seen one. Few, however, of the twenty or thirty men there were doing any business. The market was in the doldrums. There were more sellers than buyers. A subdued chatter was going on, a rumble of talk of which little could be made but occasionally a voice would announce loudly for the benefit of everybody but, as it proved, the interest of nobody, that it was: "Sellin' Sparrow." This gentleman who had three chins protruding over a dirty red silk neckerchief sat immovable and apparently slightly somnolent on the upholstered form but his small grey eyes, buried in loose flesh, moved hither and thither on the groups and on newcomers. When he saw Brierley he again said loudly: "I'm sellin' Sparrow!" and Sam Renshaw turning from a group of three asked: "Doesn't tha wish tha were, Joe?" "Buy thee out yet, Renshaw," said Joe with sudden asperity, and Renshaw answered: "Bet thee ten quid tha'rt bankrupt fust." "Done," said Joe. "Here, Brierley, wilta howd t' brass? I reckon we con trust thee—*tha* doesn't rightly belong to this den o' thieves." Joe thrust his hand into his trouser pocket, leaning slowly over to the left like a heavy ship in a storm, to do it, and pulled out ten crumpled Bradbury notes. Renshaw crossed and gave Brierley ten also. No receipts were asked for. "Mind," said Joe, "t' fust chap as doesn't pay up on settlin' day loses." "I'st not have long to wait," said Renshaw with grim enjoyment. "How's thy Wiltshires goin' on, Joe?"

"Wiltshires? They're up a tanner."

"Up t' spout, tha means. They'n gone down ninepence this mornin'."

"They'll rise again, like the dead."

"Con tha afford to wait as long as that?"

The banter went on, uneasy, a little forced, like the talk of soldiers before a trench raid. Was their new livelihood coming to an end? They couldn't believe it, yet they feared it—something hidden, obscured, veiled by the future, maybe a year or two ahead, maybe months only or even weeks. They read their *Burnham Guardian* and saw that the Chinese tael had fallen from 9s. 2d. to 4s. 4d.; they heard of Burnham shippers and merchants receiving requests to cancel orders, of warehouses beginning to be choked with goods nobody was eager to buy. This basement that had been wont to see money to the tune of twenty thousand pounds change hands on a Saturday morning now was markedly cheerful if a tenth of it went from one lot of pockets to another.

"Sithee, Bill, I'm axin' thee for a job on that yacht o' thine down at Deganwy. Nay, I don't mean just swingin' t' lead. I'm dead serious."

"Yacht? Th'only boat I shall have if things don't buck up is the one we'st all be in—christened *Queer Street*."

"Here, who'll buy two hundred Pine? I paid fifteen an' six an' I'll tak' ten bob. You're not frightened, are you?"

No, they weren't frightened but nobody bought them.

"Oh, Brierley, tha'rt a knowledgeable chap they tell me—"

He turned to look into the face of Thomas Blackburn who had entered quietly and was now standing with both hands on the top of his ebony walking-stick with horn handle. He wore a grey bowler hat and his accustomed white cravat with diamond horseshoe pin. His fresh face was redder than usual and his cheeks heavy and slightly blue where they sagged.

"What art sellin', my cock-sparrow?" Blackburn asked, as he stared at him, his eyes narrowed.

"To you, nothing," said Brierley shortly, his heart quickening.

"I thowt tha'd ha' wanted all the brass tha could get for Trix—or arta relyin' on her to furnish th' house? Tha started off wi' a bit of a rush they tell me—an' tha wouldn't ha' done it but for me. That were a clever trick—Trix wheedlin' it out o' me wheer to put thy brass. It *were* thy brass, weren't it—that two hundred tha borrowed?"

There wasn't a sound in the room save the quiet shuffle of feet as the crowd gathered. Brierley was still seated on the form and Blackburn stood a yard away leaning on his stick and looking down. Brierley's heart was now pounding furiously and his face, he felt sure, must look wooden and frightened.

"What the devil do you mean?" he asked; and his voice was as far back in his throat as Blackburn's usually was. He only spoke at all with the utmost difficulty—it was like forcing words through a closed aperture. He doubted if he would be able to control his mind—it reminded him of the first moments of having gas at the dentist's. Why couldn't he be calm and possessed, as Blackburn seemed to be?

"Only what I say," said Blackburn with a sneering, insolent look in his eyes.

Brierley looked wildly round at the faces peering down at him. It was as if he were denounced. By God, he must make an effort!

He gulped in his throat, and with a swift movement leaned forward and knocked Blackburn's stick over, and as Blackburn lurched forward he smacked the face toppling towards him, moving himself to one side, and to his feet.

Blackburn was so astonished that he sprawled over the form, failed to recover himself and sagged from the seat on to the floor, a ridiculous figure. There were a few titters but no more, for Blackburn's anger was terrific. He scrambled to his feet, his face turned from red to a tinge of purple, his small eyes wide and staring. He made an ungainly rush at Brierley, who stood, white and trembling, his thin hands clenched, his breath coming fast. But the crowd rushed in on them both with inarticulate cries and confused shouts. Brierley was borne back as if he had been a lion in strength, his arms seized, an arm round his neck. "All right, all right," he said half angry now, half relieved that at all events the fisticuffs were not to go on. "Take your hands away, will you?" shaking them off. They held him less tightly, but said soothing things like, "Nah, nah, don't lose thy temper. Served 'im reet—he axed for it. No use i' feightin'. No good'll come on it," and so forth. At the other end of the basement Blackburn was fighting and struggling and swearing. Brierley could hear disjointed phrases: "By the livin' mon but I'll tear his guts out"—"Now then Mesther Blackburn, don't make a fool o' yersel' "—"Howd his arm, Wilfred"—"You'll tear your jacket off if yer don't stop writhin' "—"By Hell, I'll lame him—let me get at him."

In the middle of it the steward, Mr. Tonks, appeared in the doorway, a precise man with pointed beard and excessively debonair appearance—sleeves rolled meticulously, cap straight and circumspect as a tall hat. Mr. Tonks (he was Mr. to everybody) was a sidesman at the parish church and never forgot that; he was a sidesman in his mind every day and every hour.

"Gentlemen," said Mr. Tonks. "This mun stop. I can't allow it." (They might have been young boys he was admonishing.) There was a scuffle in Blackburn's corner. Brierley was suddenly conscious of the humiliation of the whole affair. Mr. Tonks looked from one group to the other. "If I can't have order I mun fetch the police," he said. Mr. Tonks remembered that being said at public meetings, and the quieting effect it usually had. And it was the same here. They all knew Mr. Tonks; no idle threats about this humorless man. The movements in Blackburn's corner subsided.

Somebody said to Brierley: "Come on, Harry," with the intimacy that excitement bestows, and urged him towards the doorway. He was glad to go but he moved with as much dignity as he could compass. It was little enough.

He stood outside in the sunshine, trying to capture his self-possession. He looked round at his two or three companions a little dazedly. They gave him perfunctory pats of encouragement and shuffled their feet and said awkwardly, "Tha'll be aw reet. It'll blow ovver. Forget it, lad. Nowty owd devil —always were," with a nod back towards the basement.

"Well," he said, feeling a shiver run down his back, "I think I'll be going. Thank you—thank you very much."

They opened out to let him go. He suddenly realised he had neither hat nor stick and paused. A figure darted out of the Institute door and ran towards him carrying them. "Thank you," he said, and walked off down the street. His body seemed astonishingly light and fragile; he had a sensation of walking almost without touching the pavement. He felt extremely queer.

Chapter Seventeen

HARRIET sat alone with the head-phones on fumbling patiently with the cat's whisker trying to find the miraculous spot on the crystal that vouchsafed the orchestral music. Funny; she had had it a moment ago and now—ah! there it was—a sudden swelling wave of violins came into her head —but an instant later the whisker slipped and the music was gone. She peered at the whisker and scraped it over the crystal lost in trying to fathom the miracle of it—why and how it worked. "It's a fiddle-faddling thing to be able to pick up noise out o' this quiet room," she thought. "I suppose what Sam's sayin' down in the Black Bull is in this room too, if I could only hear it, somehow." But Harriet wasn't sure whether she would want to listen to Sam or not. Oh, there it was. Now then, she could enjoy it. A voice was speaking: "This is 2ZY calling. We are now going to play you the Unfinished Symphony by Schubert—Schubert's Unfinished Symphony," and the strings began that challenging, and dominant sweep of sound which, to Harriet, seemed to say: "Listen to me before you go any further," and was followed by the quick chatter of fiddles.

At that moment the sitting-room door opened and Millie came in dressed up. Millie said, standing there and smiling with complete self-possession: "I'm off, then." As Harriet had told her half an hour before she might go out if she wished and as opening the door made it impossible to hear anything whatever in the head-phones, Harriet looked at her with impatience and didn't speak. The look said: "Can't you see I'm listening-in, and that naturally I can't speak? As if I couldn't *see* that you're off. It's a pity you're comin' back." But Millie was no mind reader or recipient of thought waves. She stood there emitting urbanity mixed with a capricious desire to plague Mrs. Renshaw and asked: "Can I get you anything while I'm out?" As it was already eight o'clock and it was early-closing day in Chesterford, this was, Harriet thought, either agreeableness run mad or mere quizzing and prying. She said, feeling she was talking right into the middle of the orchestra: "I want nowt but to be shut of yo' for a while—sling your hook," and she accompanied that dismissal with two or three flips outwards of her left hand, waving Millie out of the door. Millie smiled with the utmost good nature and forbearance as became one who was on the best of terms with her mistress's husband and mentioning: "I've got my key," she closed the door behind her and went.

The key, to which Millie referred with unconscious triumph, was her latch-key. It was sensible for her to have one and yet Harriet disliked her having one. When Harriet came to think of it, there were a power of things about Millie which you couldn't quite object to and yet which she did object to. Millie knew far too much about her and Sam's affairs, too much by half. When Sam had had a good day with his shares, he was exuberant, generous, talkative; and when he had a shockingly bad day—and there had been a good many of those lately—he was also talkative. On the first occasions his inborn good nature made him want to share his good fortune; on the second occasions he longed to be comforted. And Sam's face was a regular barometer. Millie had only to open the door (for Sam either forgot to take his key with him or fumbled so long that Millie got to the door before he

opened it—and Harriet had misgivings sometimes whether
this wasn't arranged between them but she couldn't bring
herself to admit it or mention it for fear it was true) to see in
a flash how fortune had gone. And she would say: "So you
bested 'em to-day, Mr. Renshaw"; or, "I see the market's
been playin' ducks an' drakes agen, Mr. Renshaw"; and Sam
would dawdle over hanging up his bowler and say: "Yea, lass.
Aye, but tha'rt a sharp 'un, too. There's chaps down yon
haven't afe the head on 'em tha's got. But it isn't all tha's got,
neither"—casting an admiring eye over her. One day when
he had had a drink or two and she lingered a moment he
smacked her lightly and affectionately on her shapely figure as
she turned and went; and Millie turned and laughed gaily
at him, so that the blood rushed up to his throat. Harriet
knew nothing of that incident, but she observed with a sickening feeling at her heart how Millie quickened and livened
when Sam was about, how readily she cleaned his boots,
fetched and carried for him; and how often he passed through
Millie's kitchen on his way to the garden.

The situation's difficulty was added to also by the children's
fondness for Millie, their liking for being with her in her
kitchen, the way they romped together. They called her
Millie and she called them by their Christian names, also.
She took them to buy sweets in Chesterford or to the fair
ground with its roundabouts on Saturday afternoons, and
she was as likely to spend some of her own money on them
as not. For Millie was generous. Three weeks before this, it
had been Harriet's birthday and Millie had bought her a
fireside "tidy"—brush, tongs, shovel. Harriet turned crim-
son with mortification. Millie had got up early and placed it
there in the hearth—an action in itself an impertinence, Harriet thought. But this covert suggestion that the house was
inadequately furnished, that she, Millie, realising what they
were short of was entitled to remedy the defect—all this was

unendurable. Yet Sam said it showed Millie was a gradely 'un, jannock, and that she knew a good home when she saw one, and appreciated what were done for her. And when Millie brought in the bacon and eggs and, quite demurely, said: "Many happy returns, Mrs. Renshaw," and beamed on her and didn't even, for once, look at Sam, Harriet found her words fading on her lips; until the moment was gone and she knew now she must hold her peace. But she scrupulously avoided using the "tidy"; she would have burnt her fingers first.

More than once, as the share-broking declined in activity, and Sam stayed more and more at home, tending his garden, feeding the hens, filling up football coupons and examining the racing sheets (for Sam had begun to gamble again in an effort to recoup himself for cotton losses), Harriet suggested —but with no dominance lest a rift between her and Sam should be definitely created—that it would save money if Millie were to go; and that she, Harriet, could quite easily do the housework unaided. But Sam, with a determination and an eagerness that Harriet suspected and struggled not to suspect, answered that it were comin' to summat when, at the first sign o' trouble—well, not really trouble but a bit of a slackenin' off—they should think o' sackin' somebody as were a dab hand at her job; nay, but he couldn't stomach that. Now they were employers o' labour they mun set an example, like; he wouldn't have it said as Renshaw were nowt but a slave driver as chucked folk into t' street wi'out a thought. He always went on raking up one argument on top of another till Harriet said: "All right, Sam, I were just wonderin'." Because, after all, it was Sam's money not hers and she supposed he could do as he liked with it. This money had always frightened her; she felt out of her depth, it was upsetting altogether. If the money vanished, Millie would *have* to go. But would Sam ever get his mules back at the

mill? Aye, that was a teaser, the thought that if Sam's money
vanished it would mean things were bad, and if they were
bad and factories slack, well . . .

Money had never meant anything to Harriet, not, that
is, money beyond enough to keep a comfortable working-
class home. She never envied those who had it. She wasn't
one of the meek religious folk who asked God to make her
content in the sphere in which it had pleased Him to place
her; by no means. But she imagined those well off had as
many troubles as anybody else and she had no social ambitions of any sort. There was about her a serene integrity,
a calm pride in working folk. She wasn't a lady, she would
sometimes say, and didn't pretend to be, but she said it quietly,
not truculently, and it was plain she thought no less of herself for it. She wasn't a lady and happen Millie was as good
as she was, but as long as Millie was her servant she must
do as she was told and not take too many liberties.

Harriet had noticed that Sam was getting more grey round
the temples and behind the ears and round the bottom of his
neck, and she had been glad to see it; glad to see, too, that he
was becoming a little bald where the parting of his hair began and round the crown of his head. Sam had tried one or
two quack hair-restorers advertised in the papers, stuff that
was said to grow hair on bald patches and restore its colour
but they achieved no result. Maybe he didn't persevere long
enough; Sam went at things like a bull at a gate (Harriet
always said) and then gave 'em up. Harriet was glad his attempts at rejuvenation availed him nothing. She reminded
him chaffingly of the old chap who took monkey gland and
was found next morning swinging on the chandelier. But she
was glad, not only because she regarded dyed hair and such-
like with contempt but because she was glad to see Sam looking older. Maybe he would be less attractive to young women
now; maybe his own gallantries and confidence would be

subdued by seeing how grey he was becoming. But she recognised with a sigh that there wasn't much sign of that change in him or the women either, yet.

When the music ended and a voice began to talk about the aboriginals of New Guinea, Harriet took off the headphones (which lent her a slight appearance of Mephistopheles with the tall curved rods above her ears up and down which the 'phone pieces could be slid) and went upstairs to look at the children. They lay two in a bedroom now, George and Arthur in one room at the front, Bessie and Esther at the back. There had been some argument over that but in Harriet's circle boys took precedence over girls. Harriet didn't quarrel with that idea—lads earned most brass later on and were masters in the house, or ought to be. This giving way to women, as she understood happened in well-off houses —she didn't hold wi' that. Her mother used to tell of a Chesterford saying that a chap always ought to shove his wife out o' bed the first night they were wed and if he did she'd always respect him afterwards. That was going a bit too far, Harriet thought, but women were the weaker vessel as the Bible (or was it the Prayer Book) said, and they must put up with it. They had the dirty end of the stick to hold and the sooner they learnt to hold it, the better. So Bessie and Esther went in the back room. Sam, the baby, had been promoted to a small single bed and shared her and Sam's room. The girls and the two elder boys still shared double beds. They liked that better than sleeping apart; they were warmer in winter and they liked larking about, too. The shopman at the Co-operative Stores had tried to sell Harriet suits of boy's pyjamas when he heard they were living at The Rookery but Harriet wouldn't hear of it. If that news got to Lavender Street the scorn and laughter would be profound. But Harriet made one alteration, itself almost a concession;

the boys now had night-shirts; previously they had gone to
bed in their day-shirts.

Harriet moved about the rooms quietly, folding the shirts
and trousers and jackets which lay on the floor or dangled
by their braces from the bed-knobs (The Rookery hadn't
taught them tidiness yet) and she pushed up the window a
little farther. When she went into the girls' room her heart
gave a catch and she stared at Esther without moving; for
Esther lay so utterly still, a blonde curl lying down her cheek,
her face rather pale, that she looked as though she might
have died. Harriet was imaginative enough to suppose that
one night when she came to look at them one of them *would*
have died; and she would look exactly as Esther looked now.
Harriet tiptoed over to the child and bent down and put her
mouth just over Esther's to discern the soft breathing. Yes,
Esther was living but the breaths were so gentle and slight
that her breast rose and fell imperceptibly. Both the girls
were light-haired and Harriet was sorry for that; she liked
dark-haired girls best—she thought they had more vitality;
she herself had black hair but her daughters took after Sam.
She hoped as she looked down at their handsome faces, with
rounded rosy cheeks, beautifully curved, full little mouths
and long lashes, that they would be less sensuous than Sam
when they grew up, or they would worry her life out; they
would be having to get wed at eighteen or nineteen and being
sorry for it all the rest o' their lives. Looking down at them
she didn't see how her life would ever grow easier. Another
ten years and lads would be hunting them; she could see now
how much anxiety she must have cost her own mother; those
dark ginnels, those walks on the moor, those nights in the
hayfield. And Sam wouldn't be much use as comfort when
that time came. He'd say—she could hear him saying it—
"Let 'em be. I were just t' same. Yo' can't chain 'em up—

they mun tak' their chance." And yet, whatever happened
when you were young didn't matter very much. It was when
you got older and life was short before you—then the tragedy
of it crowded on to you. The wrecks so far as she could see
among her acquaintances mostly seemed to come when forty
was reached or passed; when men like Sam wanted to have a
dash after younger and prettier women before it was too late.

She tucked up Esther and Bessie, gently putting the soft
rounded arms under the sheets. How soft they were. She
could have cried to think what those tiny arms must bear,
what toil they must encompass to work their way through
life. She walked back to the window and stared out. Her eyes
were wet but she stared and stared, conquering her tears till
they withdrew, as it were, back into her head. That was a
triumph; she didn't need to wipe her eyes, but she wiped her
nose and turned and walked firmly out of the room and into
their own to look at Sam, the baby. And to-night she was
brisk with him as she turned him from his back on to his right
side and pushed the clothes in to his back. No use being
maudlin, she was telling herself; no use crossing bridges before she came to them. She must try to be more come-a-day-
go-a-day-God-send-Sunday. Those folk seemed to get on as
well as anybody else.

She went downstairs again and seated herself in the red-
plush armchair in front of the fire, and lifted the kettle, which
was singing, into the hearth. When they had moved, she had
shifted the parlour furniture into the living-room and they
bought a suite covered with cretonne for the best room. The
red plush was warm and cosy and she liked it. She sometimes
thought this sitting quietly at night in front of the fire now
the evenings were getting chillier was one of the best things
about The Rookery and their changed circumstances. She
enjoyed having the house to herself. There was never the
same peace when Millie was in, banging the pots about and

singing. If Millie stayed much longer there wouldn't be a
pot that wasn't chipped. It wasn't the wages you paid 'em—
it was the coal and firewood they used and the china they
cracked that ran away with the brass. She couldn't get used
to that, try as she might. She couldn't abide the waste. She
had said to Millie: "You'll need ten pound a week to keep
yer house goin' if you make a 'wakes' o' things then as you
do now"; and Millie had retorted: "Happen we'st have more
than ten pound." You didn't get much change out of Millie.

Harriet picked up Dickens's *Great Expectations* and put
on her gold-rimmed spectacles. (She had these in addition
to her steel-rimmed ones now, just as she had an extra set
of artificial teeth on a gold plate kept in her bedroom drawer.
Both these extravagances were Sam's ideas but she preferred
her vulcanite teeth and only wore the others when Sam
pestered her about them. Sam was very fussy sometimes in
spending money on her; it made her wonder if he were being unfaithful.) Harriet liked *Great Expectations*. She had
read it in a shockingly printed fourpenny-ha'penny edition
as a girl and had always remembered Pip's saying: "Joe gave
me some more gravy," when Pip was in disgrace with his step-
mother. She thought that was champion. And now Sam had
bought Dickens's complete works. It was one of his passions
now, this buying things in huge lots. They had all Dickens,
all Scott, Longfellow, Tennyson, Shakespeare, Jack London, Hall Caine, Silas K. Hocking and Nat Gould. Nobody
could charge Sam with lack of catholicity. He knew the racing
stories of Nat Gould as well, he said, as here and there one,
and as for him, they would do—he wanted nowt else; but he
wasn't one to force stuff down folk's throats. If Harriet
wanted Dickens she must have him; no accounting for tastes.

So Harriet read on for a while about Pip and Joe, and
then, for the fire was warm and her eyes tired, and she had
been up since half-past six in the morning, she began to nod

and presently was fast asleep. And she dreamed they were
back in the old house in Lavender Street because Sam had
gambled all his money away and Sam wanted his mules back
and nobody would let him have any. They laughed derisively
at him when he called asking at mills, and said: "Here's t'
millionaire wantin' a pair o' mules, sithee." And next she
was asking Mrs. Edmunds if she could do a bit o' washin'
for her, for they hadn't a bite in the house. But Mrs. Edmunds grinned and said: "Why don't yer go and scrub t'
Rookery out for them new folks as has takken it?" And next
she and Sam were singing in the streets with Bessie and
Esther dragging at her skirts and Sam the baby had to be
carried in her arms and she couldn't hold him any more; he
wanted the breast and she told him he couldn't, simply
couldn't have it, because she had had no food all day and he
was too old now and too strong. She was sinking on to her
knees in the road, and she was saying: "You can't, luv, you
can't; oh, I wish you could," and tears were streaming down
her cheeks; and Sam was saying: "Nah then, nah then, Harriet, mi lass." And she awoke with a start to find she had
slipped out of her chair on to the rug, that the fire was nearly
out and that Sam had returned and was standing over her
trying half tipsily to lift her up. "Nah then, nah then, Harriet, mi lass," he was saying.

She clambered up and sat in the chair and took off her
glasses and wiped her eyes and stared at Sam, still half in the
dream which seemed far too vivid to be only a dream.

"Sam," she said, "if you don't stop gambling we'st be
ruined." Her eyes were wide and she spoke with a fixed in-
tensity.

"Ruined? Tha's bin dreamin'."

"Yes, I have; but it's true, I know it is."

Sam leaned against the mantelpiece and pushed his moist
moustache up from his mouth and blinked his eyes that were

red round the edges, and laughed good-naturedly.

"Tha'd best come up to bed and dream a bit moore," he said.

She rose and looked round her, slowly comprehending the room. "Is Millie in?" she asked.

Sam nodded, avoiding her eyes. "Yea, she come in along o' me. I met her comin' up t' road. I sent her upstairs. Wouldta like some tea?" He pointed to the kettle.

"No, I think not." So they'd come up the road together. Why was he offering to make her some tea?

She walked with tired steps to the door and there she stopped. "You'd best go first. *I'll* put out the lights," she said. Sam wiped his moustache again. "Aw reet, lass," he said. "Just as tha likes."

Chapter Eighteen

BRIERLEY'S play *The Reaping* was accepted by Edward Houghton in October for production three weeks later. Brierley thought those weeks were the happiest he had known. He told himself ironically that his was a candle whose flame would be brief, or that he was as a mayfly up for a short life; but it made no difference to his delight. A smile ran round his lips, his gaze had a liveliness that success brings, he was tolerant and far more good-natured than usual, and he carried his head high. Brierley was supremely the sort of man who needs a measure of triumph to enable him to reach his true stature. He could bear misfortune and worry with an iron doggedness often enough, but it wore him down. He might not show his wounds outwardly, but the scars were there within him. It had been the same in the war. His service abroad had been brief before dysentery flung him back to England. So he had no wound stripes to show, no medals to wear that mattered. But the petty humiliations had done their part in robbing him of spirit and resilience. He concluded that a man has only so much strength vouchsafed to him; he may husband it or he may expend it, but once it is gone it is irrevocably gone. And he had begun to suspect that it is so, too, with his creative work—that when he has written something deeply felt and emotional it is as if virtue has gone out of him.

The person who in all Chesterford was least impressed was his mother. She had had a literary husband who made next to nothing by his poetry and sketches, and she thought Henry was travelling along the wrong road. Coal and food and clothes, *they* were the things to be in; folk couldn't do without *them*. She was pouring out his morning tea when he opened the letter of acceptance and jumped up and went to stand on the hearth-rug with his heart quickened.

She didn't look up when he told her.

"Well," she said, "I suppose it's what you wanted."

"It's terrific," he said.

"Is it?" She looked at him with a quizzical smile in her grey eyes.

"Of course it is. It'll be the first new play they've done." But that didn't impress her in the least; somebody had to be first, she said. Then:

"How much will you get?"

"I don't know—five per cent, I suppose."

"What on?" (It might have been the Co-operative dividend she was talking about.)

"Oh—two hundred, perhaps."

"And how long will that play be on for?"

"A week—you know they only run plays a week, mother." Oh, yes, she knew that; that was just it.

"And how long did it take you to write it, lad?"

"But don't you see, mother, it's the—well, people don't have plays produced every day."

"If they pay you no better than that, you'll want one doing twice a week as far as I can see to make a living at it. Your father was just the same."

"But father never wrote any plays."

"It was as much as I could do to stop him."

"Stop him?"

"Yes. He was always threatening to do it."

Threatening to do it. That was good. His father might have been threatening to strangle himself, the way she talked. He said as much. She replied that he might, figuratively speaking, have strangled the pair of 'em if he'd been mad enough to give up *his* job in the library. But there was no boom to make a thousand pounds in overnight then; no, and no slump, maybe, to lose it in, after it was made. Then she asked: "Will *she* be in it?" He answered stiffly that he hoped she would; he had written a part for her. She said, then, that she supposed it was no use *her* saying anything: he would go his own way, like his father did. She added that she supposed she had never understood either of them; she was only a practical, unimaginative woman, and she couldn't expect to follow minds that went soaring. And then she stopped. And Brierley suddenly perceived that this shrewd, domineering little woman with the straight nose and sandy hair with scarcely any grey in it, and eyes that betrayed so little emotion, was on the point of tears. He went to her and put his arm round her shoulder as she stood facing the sideboard to which she had carried the sugar basin and, having placed it down, remained staring at it. He felt exceedingly strange. This was almost the first time in his life he had seen her moved like this. Presently she said: "You've never brought her to see me." So that was it. He said: "I should like to bring her. I didn't think you approved of her." She said: "I went to the Rep. to see her play that night you were over at Burnham. I thought she was—I thought she looked a beezum but I liked her." She turned and smiled at him and he saw a film of tears over her eyes. With a swift movement she picked up the small tray and walked determinedly with her short stride and her erect shoulders out of the room and down the passage to the scullery. When she returned her composure had returned also. They talked no more then about either Trix or the play. She might, he thought, be regretting her tears. But when he walked down into Chesterford it was not only the news about his play that made him feel as if all Lancashire belonged to him.

He wanted to go round to the theatre at once; but he held himself down. Was it posing *not* to go? He was exercised in his mind about it. They would think he was as a child if he went. He wrote a note saying how pleased he was; he would look in when he was passing. When he did look in, next day, Fosdyke was tilted back on the two hind legs of his chair, his waistcoat was undone, feet on his desk, tie hanging out, reading a printed play and marking it in red pencil. "Come in, Henry, my son—where've you been these months? We've not had smallpox. Don't you think farces ought to be funny? This one goes up the week before yours. This'll make 'em weep and they'll laugh like hell at your tragedy I expect. By God, you're gloomy, aren't you? But I do like the bit where the old man dies down-stage—I can see old Nathaniel toppling into the orchestra every night. We shall have to put the prices up. It'll go over big if he breaks his blasted neck. I wish to God he would." Brierley said he was afraid the play was going to be a great nuisance to stage—the scene on the pit-head during the strike, and the one at the coal-face and . . . Fosdyke said it certainly was; what the blazes did Brierley think he was writing—a play or a Hollywood film? He said the only reason he had recommended Houghton to put it on was that he, Fosdyke, might show the critic of the *Burnham Guardian* what a clever devil he, Fosdyke, was— how he could make the stage look a mile deep, and create some lighting effects that would make Drury Lane resemble a penny dip. "We'll start the pit-head meeting in the late afternoon," he said, "and keep it going while the sky turns bronze and gold and black and lanterns have to be lit. You'll probably have to write some more speeches to keep it going." Brierley said he was damned if he would and Fosdyke said with the utmost good humour that he would have to do what he was told; he would soon discover what a misbegotten, unwanted, superfluous and despised person an author was; to which Brierley said he intended to be at every rehearsal and to have a lot to say. And then, as Fosdyke looked at his watch and remembered the Green Man across the street, they went for a drink. Fosdyke over their beer asked him what possessed him to write so bitterly. Brierley said: "Why shouldn't I be bitter? Have you ever been to a pit-head at a colliery disaster and seen the women waiting—like stricken animals, so quiet? They hear there's 'summat wrong at t' pit' and they start making the beds ready. That's almost the best they hope for—that the beds'll be needed. And wha do the men get for it?—five or six or seven bob a day. The war's over for us; there's a sort of war for them that's never over. They never know that the bloke who sallies out in the winter dark with his cold tea and his bread and bacon and apple is coming back or coming back whole. I used to see them brought home in cabs with their legs or their backs broken. That was the only time they rode in a cab." He drank his beer and realised he was excited by his talk. Fosdyke on the contrary was examining his beer totally unmoved. He said: "You're an angel who troubles quiet waters. Isn't it easy to bark up the wrong tree? I don't know much about it, but don't they swop their wives, and put their quids on whippets, and feed their dogs on mutton-chops and generally have a hell of a fine life? Doesn't this danger they face put a spirit of adventure and gaiety and devil into them?"

Brierley said: "You could make out a case for war on the same grounds—bulldog breed, noble women and all that bunk. But go and look at the nameless things in wheeled chairs in the war hospitals. Do you know that coal injures as many men every year as were in our original Expeditionary Force? There's blood in the flames that leap up your chimney."

Fosdyke said: "A serene urbanity—aloofness—a godlike detachment observing with charity, irony, and of course sympathy, too—that's the attitude you want. You remember they say that Bernhardt making an exit, and acting so sorrowfully that the audience were in tears, was so unmoved herself, that with one disengaged hand she was waving to a friend in the wings?"

"Is this what they teach you at Oxford—that everything is right in the best of all possible worlds—reared on *Candide*, eh?"

"Nevertheless," said Fosdyke, "good plays are not written with bitter pens, over-charged hearts and minds with a mission; or only by geniuses."

They had many arguments in that strain. Brierley felt in his bones that Fosdyke's life had been too easy; there was always his father, the Recorder of Preston, to fall back on. His social position was assured whether his pockets were empty or not; it wasn't difficult for *him* to feel he didn't give a damn for anybody. Brierley knew that life for himself also had been comparatively smooth—a grammar-school education, a home with a fair measure of culture, plenty of food, good clothes. He had been proud sometimes and ashamed at others that two or three generations back bastard Houghton blood was in the stream. But the bastards of history were famous enough and brilliant enough, too, as a rule; not much true cause to complain of his lot. But there were others. Brierley's boyhood friends had frequently had poverty for bedfellows. "Short-time" in the mills—that almost sacrosanct Lancashire fetish for bolstering up falling prices, had taken a deep toll of wages from time to time. Too often it meant short commons. Old men still spoke with dread of the cotton famine; the "hungry 'forties" were a biting memory. The solitary penny egg that had to go round the family, a spoonful to each child—this had been common enough among those who were now living in semi-detached houses. Among Brierley's friends every penny had, with rare exceptions, to be toiled for, sweated for, wrung out of the deep earth or spun on marching spindles or woven on clattering looms in a fœtid atmosphere. No inheritance there, no certainty for *them* that the passing years were establishing a position, would ensure a safe and comfortable old age. On the contrary, grey hairs meant only that your output would probably be less, the boss more chary of employing you lest illness should overtake you, or weakened nerves or a dimming eye involve you in accident. They lived, most of them, near to the bone, every shilling measured and weighed as on a scale, the annual "wakes" holiday of seven days saved for in clubs by small sums as determinedly accumulated as ever a miser stored away his gold. This thrift achieved with gritted teeth and unswerving purpose amassed prodigious sums (or so they seemed). Chesterford quite often paid out £250,000 for the "wakes," and newspapers, both Tory and Liberal, recorded the fact with glee as evidence of a thriving working class who spent money, it was said, like dukes and duchesses during that one week, living at the rate of thousands a year— a picturesque but hollow and misleading phrase. For may not the starving and sick man live, during the moment he gulps his raw brandy, as expensively as Rockefeller? But it was true that Chesterford could both save and spend with a fine generosity, that thirty per cent of work-people owned their own cottages, and that the "wakes" savings, wrongfully thought by outsiders to be thrown away to its last sixpence on those hectic seaside resorts that a mechanical age has favoured, bought a surprising array of furniture, carpets, pictures, pianos and violins, and paid for courses of learning in music or languages or art that might otherwise have been as remote as Orion and his belt. Brierley knew his Chesterford well enough, and though he might satirise it, poke fun at those tightly closed bedroom windows, that habit of the Friday-night bath and the knife-and-fork tea and that certain cricket team composed almost entirely of one family, so that the captain would say: "Now, there's me. Any objection to me? No? Put me down. Then there's our William? Any objection to our William? No? Put him down," and so on, till "our Tom," and "our Joe" and "our Jonathan" were also firmly added; while Brierley, as I have said, could place an unerring finger on Chesterford's vulnerable places, he had for both the town and its people a considerable devotion. Had he loved it less, he might have spared it more. He was as a lover who says: "I wound you and expose you because I cannot wish you to be less than perfect. Were you but an acquaintance, your faults wouldn't matter. I should ignore them. I should, I suppose, be kinder to you. But you are not that. I love you . . . and flay you." He didn't hesitate to describe how Chesterford folk would, if the need arose, raise money on their "grave papers" if all else failed, rather than miss the Isle of Man; or leave a half-crown beneath the kitchen clock so that they wouldn't starve when they returned with empty pockets to begin once more that fifty-one weeks' saving. But he had no sort of doubt that Chesterford and its people were incomparable—the salt of the earth. And if he could place them on record in some small measure, their character, their speech, their ways, their clothes, their abiding, deep-seated worth and decency—well, that would be a magnificent job. But let nobody expect him not to be bitter about the cruelties, the stupidities, the needless tragedies, when these struck him in the face. "Fosdyke's all right" (so he thought of him) "but he knows nowt about it." He dismissed a lot of people with that mental thought, a good-humoured but contemptuous dismissal.

Chapter Nineteen

THE PLAY did not go into rehearsal until the week before production. Nobody pretended that was time enough, but the policy of a different play every week allowed no alternative. Old Nat said he had never less than three plays in his head at once—the play they were doing, the one they were rehearsing, and last week's which he couldn't forget. Fosdyke retorted that Nat never, in fact, had any of them in his head. On Monday night Nat had to come on with bits stuck in the bottom of his hat and wander, whenever he could, to the prompt side. But he never "dried up." Nat would give you the sense, if the words *did* happen to be Nat's own. Nat, they said, re-wrote the play every night till Thursday; from then onwards it was more or less stable, but remained more Nat than author.

Trix did not read the play until rehearsals began. In some respects that astonished Brierley, and in others it did not. He was learning, but with extreme slowness, not to be surprised at anything that concerned her. He was as a small dog that stumbles on untried feet exploring a new world constantly encountering chair and table legs that are not expected or seen. He banged his head, as it were, sat back, shook it, and ambled on again. If *she* had written a play in which he was to act he would have read it standing or walking, mealless, drinkless, almost breathless; he would have devoured it with

214

sighs and cheers and lamentations, his heart leaping and sinking, going to heaven and down to the depths. But then he was in love, and she? As he said to himself six times every day: "I'm damned if I know."

She had known, of course, that he had written the play but the fact did not excite her. Why, indeed, should it? Did not Fosdyke continually announce at rehearsals that most plays were the same with the names changed; did he not aver that he received a hundred plays from misguided and hopeful but in fact utterly hopeless authors every week? Did he not assert there were only two classes of people in the country, the sane and the playwrights? Did he not boast that he altered the plays as he chose, bringing the curtain down on this line or whirling it up on that if it suited him to do so, did he not assert that indeed the only thing he looked at when choosing a play was the number of characters—so many females, so many male, to see if it would suit (*a*) the company, and (*b*) Chesterford audiences, who liked to see a lot of people on the stage? And while nobody believed half Fosdyke said, some of the wit he hurled at you stuck. Besides, Trix was honest enough to know she was no sure judge of a play.

When Brierley told her he had written a part especially for her, she inquired: "How many pages have I, Harry?"— meaning how many pages of dialogues. And while that may not be a very subtle method of deciding whether it is a good part, he had to grant that it has its points; it is workmanlike, it is the attitude of the hard-worked player who has to take her part and lie on the couch with it, or sit about, or walk over the moors learning it, using one or all the tricks of mind and vision and sound that actors employ—memory of the page itself, of the cue, of the emotional content, of the rhythm. Trix, as was true of most of the repertory actresses, was a "quick study"; men, on the contrary, were apt to be slow. Old Nat relied a good deal on the young ladies of the company to help him out, and in return he gave them a lot of good advice—not to think that because they were idols in Chesterford they would earn more than tuppence ha'penny on Shaftesbury Avenue; not to be afraid of overacting: not to undervalue repose and silence: not to be ashamed of being unpopular in a week when they were playing a woman who was a bitch. "It's a pity," he said, "they've stopped chucking things at us. When they used to throw vegetables at me when I was a villain in the transpontine drama, I knew I was doing fine."

During the rehearsals Trix maintained a professional distance from Brierley. He admired her for it, but he was disappointed. Winnie Webster, who was by this time fond enough of him to pretend fright at his presence, and to say the next moment: "I'll bet you feel like a dog's dinner, don't you—seeing us mess it about?" would come and sit with him in the dark stalls. Her husband Walt, who was playing a fanatical, consumptive strike leader was silent but had done the play the honour of knowing every word before the first rehearsal and by investing it with a passion and sincerity that made Brierley remark to Winnie: "Isn't he magnificent?"—meaning in part: "Aren't my lines magnificent?" But Winnie never suspected that. She said quietly: "Walt's always good. He never lets up." Trix was the red-headed strike leader's daughter, turbulent, bitter as her father, scarifying her lover who wanted a settlement, making her own speech from the corner of the slag-heap, leading the mob who broke the pit office windows, and rivalling the viragos of the French Revolution in vituperation, recklessness and wild courage. She held more life than anybody in the play and old Nat, who liked putting his arm round her, said Duse wasn't in it with her. "She acts me right off the stage every time she comes on," he said. With a good deal of fuss and after making sure everybody knew, Nat would take her off into corners to give him what he called his dialect lesson, for Nat had been born in Cork. Brierley watched them go uneasily. He didn't care much for Nat's parade of his intention to flirt with her; he wondered if Trix encouraged middle-aged men because she thought they were safe. One day he said to her: "I see another of these bishops has married his secretary." They were standing in the wings and she turned and puckered her eyebrows at him and, knowing very well what he meant, and plunging into dialect to prevent the conversation being serious (one of her tricks) asked: "What art gettin' at, lad?" He gave it up. "Nowt," he said grinning. But there was no grin inside him. He had hoped the production of the play would have strengthened their affection for one another; he had thought her pride in him would have increased, and that their opportunity for working together would have afforded them deep content. But the content for him was small. He enjoyed being near her or watching her work, but it might have been anybody's play, judging by the manner she behaved in it. She never sought his advice and he, having by turns a shyness and strict sense of propriety (although at other moments he would interrupt the rehearsal and act as though—Fosdyke told him afterwards—he was "Jehovah arranging heaven") rarely proffered her any. He made his suggestions through Fosdyke. The truth was that never since the afternoon on the moor, when she had consented to be engaged to him, had she been as close to him either spiritually or bodily. She had never surrendered herself since; a part of her had been withheld. She had suffered his embraces, yielded him her lips, and he had told himself he must be content with that. But he wasn't content, and he knew in his bones that while he might tell himself he had enough love for both of them he was too proud to endure this half reluctant love-making for ever. He knew that it was

not possible for him to love completely and lastingly somebody who didn't love him equally, or almost equally in return.
So, at least, he was beginning to think. But he who had prided
himself on his constancy was not always himself consistent.
One day, mortified and tortured, he could feel almost cool
towards her, and the next, the sight of her and the nearness
of her stirred him to his depths. Supposing the play were a
great success? Would *that* put warmth into her? Would it
enable him to persuade her to be his mistress? For this
thought had begun to haunt his mind. He thought: "I go
on wanting her, aching for her. If she loves me as much—
then, no tawdriness can arise. But oh, hell, I don't believe
she does. She might agree—if the play is some sort of triumph, but do I want her to consent because of that?" He
didn't know. He tried to put the question higher than his
urgent need of her but there were times when he knew he
would take her on any terms. Meanwhile the rehearsals went
on: no use raising the issue yet; time enough after Chesterford had howled at it or cheered it; probably the play would
be neither a success nor a failure—some indeterminate dragging on for a week, listlessly, condemned here, pronounced
capital there. That would be hardest to bear of all, he thought.
Abuse would be better than that. What the company thought
of it wasn't easily ascertained. Old Nat said he thought it
wanted more humour. Brierley replied that it wasn't a humorous play—it was a tragedy. Nat said: "There's quite a
few laughs in it and I could get a lot more if you'd let me.
You wrote the part for me, didn't you?" Brierley confessed
he didn't. Nat said Trix had told him he did; he seemed put
out. Brierley began to be sorry he had ever said he had
written a part for anybody, or conversely that he had not said
he had written the whole play especially for this company;
but he hadn't and lying didn't come easily. Besides, he was
stiff-necked sometimes. Fosdyke said it was a good play—

but didn't Brierley think it fell off a little in the last act? Couldn't he screw up the tension a bit? Winnie said that speaking for herself she had never had a part with such meat in it—but didn't he think she might play it in Cockney? Walt vouchsafed no opinion at all and when Brierley asked him with an attempt at reckless joviality what he thought of this blasted play, Walt said the audience next Monday night would tell them whether it was any good or not. Nothing more. For half an hour Brierley's opinion of Walt declined. After that he cursed himself and decided Walt had let him off lightly. The oftener he heard certain scenes the less he liked them. Childish, banal, cheap, hysterical—he applied all these adjectives to them. He began to feel that Fosdyke was doing it deliberately, rubbing it in by repeating the worst bits. He discovered that what he had written with pride—the pieces he had read over with joy, now sounded, after innumerable repetitions, hideous. And the actors couldn't speak them with any sense. When he wrote certain lines he had heard in his mind the stress falling on a certain word; but now the stress was on another. Even Trix failed him. She had to say: "One day *I'll* lead a strike." But she said: "One day I'll lead a *strike*," and all the work of Fosdyke couldn't alter her. She was wooden, hopeless, stupid. Winnie whispered to Brierley: "It's no good—he'd better leave her alone. She's like that sometimes." Brierley thought: "By God, talk about leaving brains at the box-office; these people leave 'em at the stage door." Despair, hope, exaltation, doubt chased one another through his mind, but mostly he was in despair. The play was too long, it was too short, nobody would see the irony, everybody would laugh when Old Nat fell dead, the scene at the coal-face would be too dark, somebody would cry: "Come out o' th' coal 'ole" (he could hear them shouting it and the ribald laughter that would follow)—and he was convinced some member of the company would fall ill.

It was inconceivable that *nobody* should be ill or get run over by a tramway-car; and on the Thursday Walt did, in fact, lose his voice. He had never in his life, Winnie said, lost his voice before; but indubitably he had lost it now. And Gustav, Trix's lover in the play, on this same day knew scarcely any of his lines at all. Brierley was sure, in his misery, that Gustav had never had any intention of learning his lines. He (Gustav) loved Trix secretly (Brierley decided), and was intent on making the play a farce. Brierley, in his torment, could believe this readily; he could have believed anything. Trix declared Gustav made love like a graven image, and Brierley complained to Fosdyke about him: and Fosdyke told him not to be emotional. Not to be emotional! —Brierley could have choked, almost did choke: but went across to the Green Man and had a bottle of Worthington and came back, much better.

You will not readily imagine that in all these circumstances Brierley was enjoying himself. But he was. He was one of those of whom it is said they are never happy unless they are miserable; he preferred misery to boredom, and pain to dull content. But there was another reason—his growing friendship with Mary Houghton. And perhaps I am wrong, too, in saying he disliked being content, for it was precisely such a feeling that he had when talking with her or being silent with her. He tried to think why it was. She was not brilliantly clever: she never tried to be especially witty, though her tongue was ready enough. But he never saw her ruffled, and seldom less than radiant. When her father, or even Fosdyke, teased her, hers was the readiest laughter at her own expense; and when somebody did good work it was she who leapt forward to praise them. Brierley met her moving about the theatre, going from the box-office, on which she kept an eye, to Fosdyke as he took rehearsals, or to Mrs. Mullineux, the wardrobe-mistress. She would consult with birdlike Mr. Mill-

ington on the *entr'acte* music (Mr. Millington had accepted
the conductorship of the orchestra, and was now, said Luke
Hargreaves, on night-shift on Olympian heights of art, as
well as day-shift in Stygian depths at his coal-pit book-
keeping) ; and she would write the preliminary paragraphs
for the newspapers concerning the forthcoming play. Of *The
Reaping* she wrote that it was an uncompromising tragedy,
but lit with humour and a catholic sympathy, and with the
balance justly held. When Brierley read that, his stature may
be said to have increased perceptibly. He told Mary banter-
ingly how sorry he was she wasn't the critic for the *Burnham
Guardian;* and she answered, with an attempt at worldliness
that if they printed her paragraph before the play was performed, they would have a little difficulty, perhaps, in slating
it severely after they had seen it. But, of course, the *Burnham
Guardian* did not print her paragraph; many people felt that
it was with reluctance that this austere journal praised anything at all. Even its reporters had a godlike air; they carried
volumes under their arms and discussed at length and with
weight whether it should be a Guinness or a Bass.

As for its critics, it was said they sometimes did not con-
descend to mention the play at all; they devoted their re-
marks to the programme or the state of the upholstery. Tim
Hilditch once declared the paper was all brains but no damned
intelligence—but this was when Tim had been severely
handled for his cast-iron optimism. Mary, however, who was
an unashamed advocate of *The Reaping,* said, in a burst of
outspokenness—and gentle as she usually was, these out-
bursts occurred with regularity—that all the papers might
stay away so long as the *Guardian* came, slaughter or no
slaughter; and that she had no fears of it. No author could
hear his work so loyally upheld without being stirred; and
Brierley was not difficult to stir. He told her one morning
with some awkwardness how encouraged he was, and grate-

ful. She flushed and said it was nothing, gave him a fleeting, intimate smile from out of her eyes that narrowed to slits of deep blue when she laughed, and turned and went hurriedly. He lit a cigarette and noticed that his fingers were trembling a little. He muttered to himself that it was damned decent of her and tried to put it out of his mind. But he had no hesitation in granting to himself that she was—and he said it over in his mind several times—the nicest woman he had ever met. She was always so superbly right in what she did and what she said. He supposed it was her breeding. He made the admission with a little reluctance because he prided himself so on upholding the common people. She would make, he thought, a magnificent wife for somebody, with her sweet dignity, gentle yet firm enough. But she wasn't for him; no. Trix was a flame in his blood, burning him out. Mary would doubtless marry a duke—or ought to. Assuredly she wouldn't waste a second thought on *him*.

Walt appeared again for the dress rehearsal. His voice had returned, but now he had lumbago and some of his fire was absent. "I'll be all present and correct on the night, though," he said wrinkling his nose. Gustav was still boggling over his lines and Nat had a little sulkiness left from the day he learnt that his part wasn't specially written for him. But at least Brierley had the relief of no longer enduring, when crucial lines were being spoken, the inquiry: "There'll be a couch here, won't there—or is it the chiffonier?"—"here" being a mere emptiness marked perhaps with a chalked cross on the floor; and the doctor had now a real pair of gloves to take off instead of pulling at something invisible and non-existent. When Brierley mentioned this he was reminded by Fosdyke that he was lucky to have a dress rehearsal at all—the internal economy of running a fresh play every week didn't usually permit it. As a rule, he said, only the Almighty and himself had any idea what characters would look like until the curtain went up on Monday night; and sometimes only the Almighty knew. He broke off to watch the entry of Tim Hilditch, who lumbered down into the stalls and sat down beside Trix. Soon the pair were laughing a good deal, to Brierley's exquisite discomfort, and Fosdyke asked sharply for silence. Mary who was sitting two rows in front of Brierley turned round and smiled and he could have sworn she arched her brows in approbation, as if she said: "I was hoping somebody would shut Hilditch up." He felt warmed inside and in his nervous condition, emotion rose and filled his throat. He and Trix left together after the rehearsal was ended. Mary said as they passed her at the stage-door: "You'll take a call tonight, won't you, if they ask for you? Do. It's good for the play—and the theatre. We've never had a live author before, you know. I shall put my war-paint on." He smiled and said yes, he would if she wished him to. He was thinking how sweet she was, and as he and Trix screwed up their eyes in the early-afternoon sun he spoke what was in his mind. Trix agreed readily enough and in some queer fashion he felt Mary's goodness had brought him and Trix nearer to one another. Trix said as they parted: "You'd better rest, Harry. Get some sleep. I shall try to, also." He said: "I shan't rest till you are in my arms. You know how I want you." They stood on opposite sides of the spiked iron gate, her hand resting lightly on it to prevent it swinging to. She was looking up the road, her eyes clouded. She turned them on him rather sadly and said: "Yes, I know, Harry"; and then, quickly, "See you to-night, dear." Turning, she ran up the flagged pathway.

It was as though she were fleeing from him.

Chapter Twenty

BRIERLEY did not sleep. He could no more have slept than
have jumped over the Town Hall. He walked fast and without purpose for a while and then turned up on to the moor,
pausing now and then to look back upon Chesterford and to
calm himself by the thought of how small a matter it truly
was whether his play succeeded or not. Whatever happened
to him those houses would stand, those chimneys remain,
rearing their heads after he was dead and gone and forgotten. But this chloroforming of his mind was of fleeting dura-
tion. He found himself approaching the hollow where he
had lain with Trix and he looked down on it, the grass thin
and light brown now with the nature gone from it, and he
wondered whether her love had perished also, whether indeed it had ever lived. "The grass withereth, the flower
fadeth.". . . He was so strained, his nerves so taut that
his throat felt near to bursting. He said to himself he ought
to have been proud, proud and happy and confident. "Anybody else but you would be, you damned fool," he thought.
"At the worst you'll have a night of excitement, your words
spoken to a large audience, critics weighing your worth. At
the best, why . . ." But it didn't work. He felt physically
sick and ill, walked down to Yates's Wine Lodge and gulped
down a large glass of sherry and pulled a terrible face over
it and had much ado to keep it down. His mother had pre-

pared an enormous meal—soup, and a chop and a plum tart.
There were occasions, he felt, when women were robbed of
any small discernment they might possess. He supposed if
he were about to be tried for his life she would place a
steak-and-kidney pudding before him; in the same fashion
that Chesterford women buried relatives "with ham." "You
must eat," she said. She tried to coax him. He said he would
have an apple and brown bread and coffee. She was upset.
Thereupon he tried to eat, and swallowed the chop in large
pieces, cursing himself for a fool and her for a damnéd
nuisance. He asked himself why a man cannot have a little
peace and go his own way and starve as he wants; and
realised, as other men have done, that there is no answer to
that, and that he would always be badgered, and try to please
too many, and please nobody. He was as a dog that is ill and
wants to go away and hide himself; but he had nowhere to go.
He hung about, waiting for the time to go to the theatre;
thought of playing the gramophone, knowing how Bach's
"Sarabande" or César Franck's "Variations Symphoniques"
would soothe him, and discarded the idea. He thought then,
with a wry grin, that he was so damned miserable it would be
a pity to allow himself to be cheered up. By this time the chop
lay on him with great heaviness. He walked about like a tiger,
until he saw, with a leap at his heart, that he would now be
late, and he tore upstairs and started to dress in a fever.
Nothing was right now: his shirt was stuck together, his gold
studs were missing, his collar was too small for this shirt of
iron, and his white tie was soiled.

He almost ran down the road to the tramway-car—he had
decided against a taxi-cab as too ostentatious—and arrived
at the theatre, hot and fuming and suffering intensely from
indigestion, alternately red and pale in the face—and in very
good time indeed. Did he imagine it or was everybody exceedingly cool? He could have sworn they were all surprised to

see him. He walked about the corridor where the dressing-
rooms lay, giving sickly smiles to the players who were all
very intent on their own affairs. "Hello," they said; "Hello—
feeling all right, eh?" and dashed into their rooms. He went
into Fosdyke's room but Fosdyke wasn't there. Nobody
knew where he was. Probably he was on the stage arranging
the set. Did Brierley want him? No; oh, no, please don't
trouble him—nothing at all, he said, and went out again.
He knocked at Trix's door—a room she shared with Winnie.
"Who is it?" she cried challengingly, in a hard voice. Sorry,
he said, it was only himself, Brierley. What did he want, she
asked. She was changing; could he come back in a little while?
Oh, yes, certainly, he said; it was nothing at all, nothing
whatever. He walked away feeling a blithering idiot. Why
had he come round the back of the stage? Should he go in
front? But how do that when he would be as a figure in fancy
dress walking about, the only man in the theatre wearing evening clothes. Why on earth had he been such a fool as to put
them on? He walked, but uncertainly up the three steps to
the stage and stood watching the final touches being made
to the set. He was asked to "mind his back" as they carried
on a grandfather clock, to be careful of those ropes as he
went across the stage (they seemed to think he had never been
within a thousand miles of a stage before), and now would he
kindly stand off the carpet while they straightened it? He
stood to one side, but with enormous patience the property-
man indicated by waves of his plump, dirty hands that he
was still on it, and then shooed him off as though he were a
recalcitrant hen. He fled from the stage and went out into
the street, and stood there on the edge of the pavement,
trying to be nonchalant and to smoke a cigarette as if he did
that sort of thing—stand in evening dress in a narrow street
—every evening of his life. Suddenly the doorkeeper popped
his head out. "Mister Fosdyke wants yer," he said laconically.

Brierley almost jumped. He was delighted, he was flattered, he was overwhelmed. He was no longer the author of *The Reaping*—he was an obscure person who had been in everybody's way and whose presence was now desired by the producer, this omnipotent being whose nod was gracious, whose words in friendliness were an unspeakable delight. He hurried in. Ah! but maybe he had been summoned in mistake: doubtless it was Bryceson, the scene-shifter, they needed, and they had called him in error. But no! it was he whom Fosdyke wanted. Would he have a drink? Fosdyke took his arm and steered him down the corridor with affection. Trix popped out her head and said, radiant: "We're expecting you. Don't be long." Nat, into whom they ran, stopped and said: "A thousand-and-one nights, sir," and shook hands with great solemnity. Brierley answered, convinced now that mankind was perfect, and under a wave of deep regard for Nat, that if the play succeeded it would be due to Nat's magnificent acting. Never had he seen— But Fosdyke dragged him off, muttering: "Old scoundrel! If he dries up to-night I'll sack him. Foul old man!" They had a strong whisky, and Brierley's eyes, which had been a little moist, dried up and he felt better. He straightened his tie in the glass, and thought how excellent an idea it was to have put on his evening clothes; and he went along to Trix and Winnie, and kissed their painted cheeks with immense decision, and felt what a fine fellow he was. Fosdyke said: "We're going up in a minute. You'd better go round in front and watch the darned thing, so that when we re-write the play in the morning you can take out the bits they throw things at. Mary's kept you the end seat on the fourth row. For my part, I think the third act wants . . ." But he was grinning, and he pushed Brierley through the door into the stalls as the lights went out. And now a strange thing happened. Brierley became preternaturally calm. He sank into his seat with a lordly air, and looked about him in the dark, ignoring the stage, as if he were declaring: "I've seen this beastly thing times out of number," or, again: "Well, there it is. I created it. What do you think of it? Isn't it magnificent?" But the mood was brief. The whisky was wearing off, and he regretted once more that he had not rigorously cut and re-written *The Reaping*. He was certain now that if only he might alter these stupid speeches that sounded so forced and theatrical, the play might be saved. As it was, he had no doubt whatever that all was lost.

The applause—or lack of it—when the curtain fell at the end of Act I confirmed his belief. It was no more than a fluttering of claps. He walked, shoulders hunched a little, through the swing-doors and up the steps back on to the stage and stood in the wings. It was pleasant now to see how brisk the men were, tearing down the canvas walls, taking up the carpet, unmaking and re-making this dolls' world; he was glad to be unnoticed, glad that it didn't seem to be his play any more than another's they were busy with. He spoke to nobody and hoped nobody would speak to him. Presently, though, he turned his head, conscious of someone near by, and saw Mary. Light came into her eyes and he was aware of the humour and encouragement there.

"Pretty awful, isn't it?" he said grinning, sure that his face must be hideous as it slipped into this false attempt at cheerfulness.

She shook her head. "No, it isn't," she said. And then: "You can't expect them to be delirious over it at the end of one act, you know." She spoke gently, chiding him. He laughed with genuine delight. "No," he said. He looked down at her, and moved a pace so that he was conscious of the warmth of her. He was smiling now into her eyes and, without thinking, his hand softly took and closed on her fingers. The fingers were warm in his, they neither withheld nor returned the light pressure. But they did not resist him when he slowly raised her hand and took it to his mouth. Her eyes widened a little and then creased further in laughter. Not till she had gone did he begin to wonder if he had been fair to her.

He saw the second act from the back of the circle. It was pleasant to be further from the stage; he imagined he could appraise the work more coldly. But he was stirred by the pit-head scene, and by Trix's tempestuous flaying of her lover. Would she ever turn on him with his own words? Curious that players so rarely used for their own ends the words spoken on the stage. There was a good deal of laughter too at the two old miners who talked about their dogs and the childer the dogs had had and what had become of them— talked almost as though they had been themselves wedded to the bitches. Edward and Phœbe, who were in a box at circle level, joined him at the interval. Edward said: "Whatever anybody may say, they must grant its sincerity—there's nothing trivial there." He stood with his elbows on the red plush rim of the circle stroking his chin. He knew Brierley could not be expected to be thinking of anything more than whether the play would win through, and he spoke of it openly. Brierley liked him for it; there was a touch of true aristocracy about the way Edward and Mary went straight to their point, he thought. Edward went on: "The play makes you feel how much better man is at bottom than the petty things he often does. You see it constantly—the bickering and ill nature and beastliness of trying to best one another in commercial life and in fixing hours and wages or in the men stealing one another's output sometimes—but as soon as the true crisis occurs, and the issue becomes one of life and death, as soon as it's an explosion in the pit, or war comes, or a woman is having a baby, barriers are down, they are banded together, people rise to their true dimension."

He turned to Brierley and smiled encouragingly. "You've brought it out well," he said.

Brierley said: "I wasn't trying to do that. I only wanted to show what risks the men run, what a battle with coal they are always fighting, and how little they get for it. The other part just happened."

"You know the people and you saw straight," said Edward. "We don't always know what we're at. Maybe the Almighty has a bit of something to do with it."

Phœbe said: "The one I find entrancing is Miss Bishop. She burns like a flame—makes me feel terribly old. If I were a young man I should be scorching my wings." She smiled at Brierley and he found himself glowing with pride and with confusion too. He said, like a boy: "I wrote the part for her, you know," and looked them boldly in the face knowing he was owning his love. Phœbe placed her hand on his arm. "Come," she said, "I think we must drink to the play and Miss Bishop," and by the time they had done so, the curtain was up again. And now Brierley could not remain still. He was down in the stalls, into the wings, tiptoeing round the back of the circle, standing in the gallery. He wanted to exhaust himself. He would stare down at the stage, this lighted picture that presented him with snapshots lifted out of his mind and think how inexorably it was marching to its end, like life itself. The audience was dreadfully quiet. Was it too quiet? He hardly knew but he didn't think so. A stillness brooded over the whole house. Nat had died gloriously, toppling to the floor like some giant oak that has fulfilled its purpose and now goes down in triumph. His death had sealed the men's case, proved beyond contention the tragedy lurking behind their every day's activities; and Walt, the bitter, viperous strike leader was himself quieted. "God Himself," he had to say, "has placed His unerring finger on the truth. Who will question *Him*?" Brierley was a little disquieted by this parade of Divine action. And he was conscious too that miners don't make much of their risks, they don't think so often of it and they talk even less. But when the curtain came down the applause was without qualification. Their emotions had been stirred, and now in great relief they clapped and whistled and stamped and shouted for him. He hurried down the side of the stalls looking at nobody and hurried up the stairs on to the stage yet once more. It seemed a long while since he was there; his world had turned half over since then; the sun was shining on him now. The players were stood in a semi-circle, Trix and Walt in the middle, Nat, resurrected from the dead, towering at the far corner. They all cast sidelong looks at him as he walked in a dream on the stage; he saw they beamed on him. They made way for him, and he stood there, stooping a little, between Trix and Walt, trying to stop a laugh from curving his mouth. He didn't like showing how pleased he was. But he was nervous, too; this array of pale faces in the blue-black auditorium was mysterious. The clapping stopped; they were waiting for something. But his mind wasn't working. He stood there, bemused and smiling. Walt nudged him. "Say summat," he said. Brierley blinked and screwed up his face, and took a half pace. "Well," he said, "I don't know about you—but I'm glad it's all over. And I'm sure the company are, too. We took all the precautions we could—there wasn't a bad egg to be had in Chesterford to-day." He stumbled on. The people began to laugh. Walt, in high humour, was muttering: "By God! They'll laugh at owt, lad, winna they?" And then the curtain came down. Indeed, it came down and went up, and came down again several times, and at last it stayed down.

He didn't know when he had taken Trix's hand, but he was gripping hers very tightly and their forearms were close together. Slowly the players left the stage, but Brierley delayed, holding Trix's arm within his, waiting for the last of them to go. Now they had all gone, and the door of canvas swung to behind them. He and Trix were alone on the stage, enclosed in the flimsy walls. From behind the dropped curtain came the dull chatter of voices and shuffle of departing feet. He turned to her and took her in his arms and began to kiss her—her throat, her vermilion lips, her blued eyes. "I shall be frightfully smudged," she said; but her arms tightened round him, and she began to burn to him. "Trix darling," he said, his mouth touching her as he spoke, "I want you."

"I know."

"Let's take a car and go to—oh, Burnham would do. I could ring up the Ship."

She nodded. "I told Mrs. Eckersley I might stay with the Websters."

His heart leapt. So she had been thinking of it also!

As they entered the passage leading to the dressing-rooms they saw Mary standing there, waiting. She held out her hand frankly and said: "I'm so terribly, terribly glad. I do congratulate . . ." She shook hands with him quickly, and gave them both a smile, but it flickered and broke. She turned and went swiftly then.

He thought: "Oh, hell! what have I done now?" But since he was in love, and men in love are ruthless and have thought only for the beloved and themselves, he forgot her: for some hours she left his mind. But that vision of her had penetrated deep. As he lay with Trix sleeping quietly beside him in the Ship Hotel, Burnham, the following morning, his passion spent and a sense of fulfilment in his bones, his mind turned back to Mary, and his eyes darkened and his mouth dropped.

BOOK II

Chapter One

THOSE WHO HAVE an eye for history and the follies of man may observe with grim satisfaction that precisely two hundred years before the cottom boom laid the foundations of the partial wreck of Lancashire, the South Sea Bubble, to which the discerning had compared the boom, was dazzling men's minds, blinding their vision and reducing their intelligence to the level of believing fortunes could be won from turning sawdust into planks of woods, from importing jackasses, from making quicksilver malleable, and in one instance from carrying on an undertaking so mysterious and valuable that no one was to know what it was. Fortunes were made in 1720 as in 1920, and fortunes were lost. It was true then as two centuries later that men only grow rich from speculation in so far as others become poor. It was said that in 1720 companies with an aggregate capital of £300,000,000 were floated within a few months. It is probably true that the Lancashire boom had cost Lancashire over £200,000,000 by 1927. In 1720 men cut their throats, hanged themselves, went mad. In Lancashire they began to do that in 1920 and they have not yet ceased doing it; but they have also exercised greater ingenuity in achieving death; gas and a remarkable variety of poisons have been enlisted in their purpose.

In 1720 His Majesty's German mistresses, in addition to Walpole and the Duchess of Marlborough, successfully

feathered their nests by interest at a thousand per cent and
sums of round about £100,000. Those who made fortunes
by invading the County Palatine about 1919 and withdrawing without disorder were less famous and they go unrecorded
except in the minds of acquaintances who know that Harry
This and Tom That still keep their yachts at Deganwy and
talk in the clubs at Burnham of their skiing exploits or are
known now only by letters coming at infrequent intervals
from Bournemouth or Fowey or Cannes or Majorca.

There were syndicates of sharp-witted men from London
who saw fair game in the slow-spoken North and entered,
rifled, and departed leaving behind them mills reared on
slender, tenuous piles of figures that swiftly broke; there were
other syndicates that found Lancashire such "easy money"
that they stayed too long—so-called Napoleons of finance
who found Lancashire a veritable Moscow. But for the most
part the money that floated Lancashire cotton mills at seven
to twenty times their pre-boom worth was Lancashire money.
It came from a myriad Lancashire pockets and passed to a
comparative few; and the bulk of the few had a proud faith
in their world-wide and famous trade and handed it back
to be still further increased. And both the few and the many
saw it melt away, or rather they were duly informed that that
was what had happened to it. Some were incredulous, saying: "There's the mill and its chimney. Why isn't my brass
there?" Others said it was as though they had watched a
balloon explode before their eyes and these wondered what
had become of the gas that inflated it. But the majority took
what was happening calmly enough, as something rather outside their knowledge or control; they ranked it with the play
of lightning or belief in God. Money during the boom had
rained on them like manna, and now Providence was taking
it away. Harriet Renshaw, and hundreds like her, thought it
bore a resemblance to the war. There might be some folk

somewhere who had a say in it—though she doubted that also—but as for her and Sam they just had to grin and abide; and at grinning and abiding people like Harriet are superb. Their ignorance, patience and fortitude are at once noble and pitiable. Such as Harriet make wars possible; for they bear everything and understand nothing and their trust is great. They are not only the sport of the gods but of men and of miscreants among men. It does not occur to them that wars can be fought for nothing higher than munitions makers' profits. They would not be likely to believe that, were they told. They rank men loftier than that. They who ask nothing more than a piece of work to do and a little pleasure when it's over cannot conceive that men should by bribery, chicanery and plotting accomplish mass murder for nothing more than the ability to sail on yachts, own racehorses, enjoy many women and hobnob with kings, princes and politicians. Anybody who suggested anything so monstrous as that would be dubbed "doolally," one who has a screw loose. Haven't there always been wars and short time and cotton famines? Haven't the parsons said they were sent to try us? Why should *we* expect to be rid of the pests and burdens and Devil's work that have always dragged men down? What is it but God trying us in the fire? Once convince men and women that everything happens for the best and no evil is too outrageous for you to perpetrate upon them. The foulest acts can always be achieved not by appealing to men's basest instincts, but to their highest; for the heights to which men can rise have no limit. Tell them they are to wage a war to end wars and they will sacrifice themselves and their wives and their children; make them believe—and they are tragically ready to believe—that the gage is liberty and freedom and for that they will maim and disembowel and starve and poison those whom they have never seen or known and whom, had they known them, they would have been fond of; and in

so murdering and destroying and acting like the damned un-
loosed they will be incredibly brave and generous and charitable to their friends and, when permitted, behave with nobility
to the enemy; so that, indeed, the more desperate the throw
the greater their stature. Pile the horror thick enough and
heroes will be plentiful. But the heroes are there all the time;
horror is no more than a searchlight that illumines them;
searchlights don't create.

The slump which descended on Lancashire in 1921 was
as a ravaging army, or a plague of locusts—what you will.
It laid a heavy hand on the county, a hand that has never
been raised and will, perhaps, never be raised. It is as though
the world was marched on and Lancashire has stood almost
still, watching the vanishing hosts with incredulous eyes, the
hosts of its former buyers in the East—India and China—
who have turned in large measure elsewhere for their mer-
chandise or have found among themselves an ability to spin
and weave, if not so well as Lancashire fingers, then well
enough.

* * * * * * * *

It didn't take long for Sam Renshaw to see that he must
begin to think of earning his livelihood in a new fashion.
"Fate's played shuttlecock wi' us, lass," he said to Harriet
at a time when 176 companies' shares quoted on Chesterford
Exchange were below par and in six instances at a discount;
that is to say that Sam had to offer five shillings, and sometimes ten or twelve shillings, to persuade people to take them.
Yet only two years before, the shares of 285 mills were at a
premium, and a great many of them had stood at three times
the normal value.

"Are any more calls comin'?" asked Harriet wearily.
These "calls" by companies who found themselves in Queer

Street were for a part or the remainder of the unpaid share
capital—varying from ten shillings a share to two or three
pounds. For twelve months those calls had caused more
heartburning and heartbreaking in Chesterford than the
League position of Chesterford Wanderers, or the fortunes
of racing pigeons, or distemper among whippets, or giving
in marriage, or any other topic that made pulses beat faster
or filled stomachs with sickness.

Sam said grimly that he reckoned there'd be plenty afore
long. "Jim Harrison's payin' ten per cent interest to t' mill
on t' brass he conna find. What dost think o' that?"

"Is he the chap as mortgaged his furniture to buy 'em—
him as come to thee for advice?"

"Tha needn't rub it in—he axed me, an' I towd him as
best I could."

"I'm not blamin' thee, Sam. I don't doubt we'st suffer as
badly as anybody else. Happen we'st be more comfortable
if we do." The idea of being in financial trouble along with
the rest brought a grain of comfort to Harriet, but none to
Sam. He had taken more readily to the upward flight. Perhaps he had more imagination; certainly he had had an inward suspicion that Fate had always intended him for something better than spinning, and the thought persisted
although it was now wearing so thin that he had made tenta-
tive inquiries of one or two mill managers he knew concerning available mules. He had asked, it is true, with some
casualness, because he had for some time been meeting managers on equal terms—they had speculated together—and
he didn't relish the thought of being a workman again; so
that when they replied they couldn't find enough work for
the spinners already on their books, Sam had heard it with
relief if also with misgiving. He thought to himself: "Well,
I can't get a set o' mules any road, so it's no use botherin'."
The issue, he felt, was out of his hands. What he would have

done had he been offered a pair of mules he didn't know. "It would ha' needed a bit o' thinkin' about," he reflected. Happen things weren't so bad as folk said; a handful of shares had hardened a bit. But he knew for a fact that the Dobberley mill had sold 10,000 pounds of yarn two days ago at a net loss of fourpence a pound and that yarn salesmen had gone abroad to Holland and Germany seeking orders; and Lancashire, he thought, wasn't usually so enterprising as that. It were all a terrible mess, Sam considered. What was the good of going down to 'Change when he was pursued by folk asking did he *want* any shares, not had he got any to sell? Why, the *Burnham Guardian* reported that half the looms in Lancashire were stopped and that spinners' margins had dropped by eighty per cent—they got eightpence or ninepence now for work they were paid over three shillings for only two years ago. Already the phrase "in the hands of the banks" had begun to be used with frequency. "There's many a mill," said Sam, "as can't buy a pound o' yarn wi'out t' bank's permission. What dost think o' that?" Harriet thought little of it; technical details did not impress her. "I don't pretend to know," she said. "I only know you used to say, 'Wait till we get cheaper cotton, then we shall get a move on agen.' We got it and nowt happened. It seemed it were another tuppence off you needed. Well, that happened, too, didn't it—an' things are no different. It looks to me as if somebody's playin' ducks an' drakes wi' us." Sam, feeling it was up to him to explain these strange goings on and justify them in some degree, said it were the cotton harvest as did it—rains and a little devil called the boll weevil as got into t' cotton and ate it up. Harriet said: "It's a good job it doesn't get into corn, isn't it—or we should be payin' tuppence for a loaf one month and a shillin' the month after." Harriet had a notion that things might be different if women had a hand in them—in the same way that she thought houses ought to be different,

what wi' stairs wi' no handrails, slopstones that drained the
wrong way, taps an' door-knobs an' fenders and fire-irons
that everlastingly needed polishing, bedroom windows that
wouldn't open an' doors that wouldn't shut. But she said
nothing about that idea; no use running her head into brick
walls.

The growing lack of money strengthened her position at
home, and she found solace in that. They could no longer
afford to spend a penny where a ha'penny would do (as she
was at pains to impress on Millie, from whom, however, as
Harriet thought to herself, the information slid like water
off a duck's back) and Millie's departure, and their own removal from The Rookery could only be a question of time.
How Sam contrived to keep going at all, she didn't quite
understand, unless he was drawing steadily from the bank.
He went down to the Share Exchange with a spurious air of
brightness and of having to be there at a certain time, as
though it were a regular business. He gave her what he called
his wages on Friday dinner-time as he had always done, and
if she looked at it askance, as though he were a conjurer, he
would say. "Nah then, nah then, it's gradely stuff; nobody'll
refuse it, tha'll see. It's my job to get it and thine to make a
'wakes' on it." She couldn't complain that Sam was letting
the world get the better of his spirits, but she didn't know
whether to rejoice at that or not. Come-a-day-go-a-day-God-
send-Sunday might be right enough for one in a house, but
it wouldn't do for both. But Sam wasn't close-fisted, whatever else he might be. At this time Harriet hadn't four children but half a dozen and sometimes more. Sam's sister
Florrie sent her two along to stop for a fortnight at a time
and it never occurred to Harriet or Sam either that to share
what they had was at all extraordinary. The slump brought a
good deal of genuine communal living into Chesterford. Aunt
Harriet and Uncle Sam were aunt and uncle to a great many

children with whom they had no blood relationship; there was always a "butty" to be had at The Rookery and a drink of milk or ginger-beer. Lavender Street had been hard struck. Hungry children would beseech their mothers: "Well, can I go an' see what Aunt Harriet's got, then?" when they could find nothing in their own bread-mug.

And Harriet's own children would take to school more play-time lunch than they could possibly consume, that it might be shared. Harriet would look at her well-fed brood and think: "Happen somebody'll be good to yo' if t' time comes." She had a simple belief in the justice of God; they would manage somehow by His help. Millie was the sore point. Millie was oblivious of the slump. If she wasn't watched, she used as much coal as ever, and spread the butter as thickly. She gallivanted about in her artificial silk stockings and she danced regularly at the "Pally" (Palais de Danse) which Chesterford had built during the boom, and where you might now have an area of yards for your feet alone. She took the new film weekly and pinned the photogravure pictures of Rudolph Valentino and Douglas Fairbanks over her bed so that she got a thrill when she awoke. Her bedroom, indeed, became a sanctuary for her; she spent hours there between washing up after dinner and preparing for tea and although Harriet felt she couldn't object to it, she didn't like it. Harriet had a feeling that the wench was reading stuff she shouldn't be, and doing things she shouldn't, too. Millie began to wear a small black beauty patch to hide a tiny mole on her face, and she had the impertinence (Harriet felt it was an impertinence) to use scented bath salts, which made young George ask what that nice smell was in the bathroom. Moreover, Millie's passion for reading continued to a late hour; when Harriet went to bed she sometimes saw the glint of a light beneath Millie's door and on one occasion when Millie overslept (and, as Harriet said, she was a Bobby for oversleeping) Harriet found, on going to rouse her, that the gas was still on, at 7.30 a.m., burning like a lighthouse. Harriet took the mantle and globe off. "I'll soon put a stop to that, madam," she said. (Harriet called Millie "madam" when she was in a towering rage.)

"That wench is costin' us thirty shillin' a week, if she's costin' us a penny," she said to Sam. "An' we can't afford it— never could, an' less than ever now."

Sam wriggled in his armchair, put down the *Burnham Guardian* (he had begun to take a morning paper when they moved to The Rookery), wiped his moustache with his fingers, and put up the paper again and pretended to read. But he wasn't reading; he was wondering what was coming.

"She'll have to go—an' if you don't tell her, I will," said Harriet. This was a marked advance on anything that Harriet had said hitherto, and Sam felt he must do something. He put down his paper once more. "Nah then," he said, "nah then. Keep thy hair on."

"I'm tellin' thee," said Harriet, bustling about doing next to nothing with great energy and beginning to dust spotless chairs with her apron.

Sam tried a new attack. "I should ha' thowt," he said in an aggrieved tone, "tha would ha' appreciated havin' somebody to do thy wark."

"Aye, well, I don't," she said abruptly.

"There's no pleasin' some folk," said Sam, raising his paper again, a gesture of dismissal of the subject.

"There'll be no pleasin' me till she's out neck an' crop," said Harriet, stopping her dusting and staring fixedly at Sam's paper. Then she asked: "Why arta so keen on keepin' her?" Immediately she had asked the question her heart began to pound against her ribs.

"Keen on keepin' her?" Sam said, putting down his paper once for all. He got up and felt on the mantelpiece for his

pipe and with his back to Harriet he said: "I dunnot know as
I *am* keen." It was easier than he had thought: he was quite
calm. He turned round. "If tha's made up thy mind to sack
her, sack her. On'y don't natter at me when she's gone an'
tha gets fed up wi' washin' agen. It's thee I've been thinkin'
on. Matters nowt to me." And at that moment Sam really
felt that it didn't matter to him.

Harriet didn't believe Sam but nevertheless she was intensely relieved. Never before had she so bluntly challenged
him; only her anger now and the culmination of long irritation
and the inward knowledge that she was rapidly reaching the
end of her tether on the subject of Millie, had brought forth
the question.

It was because she didn't believe Sam that she now asked,
trying to make it as easy for him as possible: "Will yo' tell
her or shall I?" And Sam, not liking the implication, but
knowing that maybe it was wisest to accept the offer, said:
"Me? Why, I don't see. . . . Aw reet, I'll do it." After a
pause he added: "I reckon it's a man's job—a bit awkert
like." He felt more comfortable after he had said that.

Sam's opportunity came in the afternoon. The children
were at school, and Harriet had gone to see Sam's sister
Florrie, whose legs were troubling her consequent on long
standing at looms and slopstones; Harriet had offered to
finish the ironing.

Sam had been astonished at his own calm when Harriet
raised this subject of Millie. He had answered her in a bemused condition, almost convinced that there was no reason
whatever why he shouldn't dismiss Millie. He now tried
to preserve that state of mind but to his dismay he found it
slipping away. He tried to marshal his thoughts and the
words he would use. He might be bold and decisive and say:
"Millie, mi lass, you know how things are. I'm sorry but
you'll have to go. No use arguin'." Or he might be sym-

pathetic: "You know, Millie, how attached . . ." No, that wouldn't do. It was damned awkert. He was still pondering, having walked up and down, having tried standing with his back to the fire, and again having looked out at the garden and glanced round over his shoulder casually as if giving a servant notice was a thing he did every other Tuesday. He had now sat down again in his chair, still undecided, when Millie entered and knelt down at the fireplace to tidy it up. She was rather slatternly; her hair had a couple of curling pins at each side (and, Sam thought, looking at them, that he would have remained longer in love with Harriet if she had never let him see *her* in curling-pins) the calf of her leg which projected behind her wore a cotton stocking with two small holes in it, her shoes were unstrapped, and her blouse was ill fitting and coming out from the waistband. Sam noted these things with profound satisfaction. Had she been dressed for the "Pally," with art-silk stockings and blouse that showed her bust, and had she been using an Eastern-smelling scent, there was no knowing what Sam would have done; and he knew it. Her position with her back to him made it easier, too. So now, looking down at her and thinking that one untidy woman was very much like another, he said: "Millie, yo' know how awkertly fixed I am about brass . . ."

She stopped fiddling about with the small brush she herself had bought. "I'm not complainin'," she said. "I'm not one o' them sort."

"No," said Sam eagerly. "I know you're not. You've been a . . ." He hesitated, finding it difficult to describe. ". . . a good pal an' it grieves me . . ."

"But it's got to stop," she said, breaking in. "I've been wantin' to tell you." She sat up on her haunches and looked up at him, and ran the back of her hand across her itching nose.   "I've met a chap at the Pally. We're courtin'. So, you see . . ." Then she added, as if Sam were entitled to an explanation: "He's the new assistant in the butcher's at the Co-op."—and then fervently: "So he'll never be on short time, thank God."

Millie got up and stood with the brush still in her hand, looking down at him. Sam was relieved once more—two weights taken off his mind in one afternoon—but, all the same, he didn't feel as important as he would have liked. Nevertheless he said with deep sincerity: "I'm fain to hear it, Millie, reet glad." He stopped there and stood up also, that he might not be dominated. Millie said, a faint smile on her lips: "So you won't be able to come an' see me this afternoon."

Sam twitched through his whole body. "Well, I'm damned!" he thought. "But," he said, "I've never bin to see thee for long enough." He was genuinely indignant, affronted; and he found it easy to say now: "There's nowt for it, I'm afraid, but to gie thee a week's notice." After a moment he added: "T'world's in a rare mess." And then, conscious that the whole world was rather large and remote, perhaps, as applied to Millie, he said: "An' Harriet sez tha'rt costin' us thirty shillin' a week."

Millie stooped and hung up the brush, straightened herself, and said: "I'm not put out, Sam Renshaw. Don't worry yoursel'. I've had as much fun as yo'."

She turned and walked to the door, and Sam thought he had never liked her better.

There she paused. "Only," she said, turning and smiling more broadly, "I've cost you more than thirty shillin' as a rule, haven't I?"

Sam didn't like that nearly so well.

Chapter Two

As EDWARD HOUGHTON walked down Church Street on his way to the Bluebell spinning mill, he asked himself the question—and it was a question that had often been present in his mind— Do irresolute good-natured men cause more suffering in the long run, than the cruel, ruthless ones, riding rough-shod? He didn't use the word "weak" concerning the first class of men because, as usually happens when men ask themselves this question, it was of himself he was thinking, and he jibbed at the word; jibbed honestly because he didn't believe it truly applied to him. On occasion he could be decisive enough, but he was horribly afraid of hurting; and in the long run . . . Well, there it was. He wished sometimes he could be angry more easily. Just anger, he reflected, was a gift of the gods and it had not been vouchsafed to him; not, at all events, a ready enough anger. Life would have been much simpler if it had. He would have flown into rages, swiftly arisen and swiftly subsiding, and people would have said: "Look out! Here he is. Get that done at once or there'll be the devil to pay." He would, as it were, have clomped about in heavy boots and people would have heard him coming and got out of his way. But it wasn't any use; he couldn't fly into a temper, because he could see the other fellow's point of view so easily, could stand in the other man's boots as comfortably as in his own. This was the worst of being a Liberal, he supposed. He sighed.

There was this Repertory Theatre. How much longer was he going to maintain it? For he *was* maintaining it, as plainly as if it were a child. He supposed that was what it was, a child, and a very expensive child too. Two thousand a year it was costing him, because Hilditch contributed nothing and he, Houghton, hadn't the heart to ask him for his share. "You can get out of anything by paying," Luke Hargreaves was wont to say; and that was the way Edward preferred to get out of it. Perhaps Hilditch could have afforded it better; perhaps not. Timothy's (it was as Timothy he now thought of him in a half amused, half satirical fashion) financial escapades were as mysterious as his romantic ones; rumoured a millionaire one month and bankrupt the next—that might well be the way of it with Timothy. But however it was, the repertory theatre, this attempt to build up a North-country drama, was his, Houghton's idea, and he must pay for it. Because the truth was, people didn't appear to want it; or to want it in anything like sufficient numbers. Brierley's *The Reaping,* for example. There were those who liked it so well that they saw it three times in one week, but not enough saw it once. It lost money. It was a *succés d'estime*—oh, undoubtedly; but theatres couldn't live on those except by a godfather's purse. And the godfather's purse had a bottom. Did people, in fact, want to see themselves on the stage? He couldn't be sure. They ought to; *he* did, or would. Were working folk more sensitive? He believed they were. He had once offered to send an ailing card-room girl to Blackpool for a week, and her mother had refused. "What's be'ind it?" she had wanted to know. "What's Mester 'Oughton gettin' out of it?" Probably men and women who worked in mills and foundries and pits wanted to look upon dukes and duchesses busy in their drawing-rooms, or in their baths— marble baths with silver fittings; very partial to seeing people in their baths, they were, these good folks who only bathed on a Friday. Maybe that was the chief attraction of the cinema: they piled it on with a trowel, and the audience began to expect a standard. Old Nat, when he had to play a titled man, always used a monocle, unless Fosdyke prevented him. Old Nat had retorted, when a protest was made: "You and I, Mr. Fosdyke, know that they don't always wear a monocle, but the gallery know they always *do*. And you can't ignore the gallery." Edward had always argued that half the success in true comedy lay in the audience thinking "That's true. I know that—that's happened to me." But he began now to doubt it. Half Chesterford seemed to be thinking, on the contrary: "I *know* all that. I'm not going to pay money to see *that*. We have quarrels like that at home." Altogether it looked far from hopeful, this portraying the North on the North's own stage—unless one began to portray the North that was rich—and readier to laugh at itself. The dramatists, unfortunately, appeared to think they must write exclusively of people who lived in cottages or of nobody higher than the middle classes. Was it because the writers sprang from those who were not rich, or that the rich had less character than the working people, or were supposed to resemble too closely the rich of the South? Did they, in fact, closely resemble them? He thought not. If the slump continued at its present rate of progress would there be any Northern rich left at all?

He thought of that with a grim sense of humour. Where would he be, for instance? How much longer would *his* head be above water? Money was going out a great deal faster than it was coming in. Phœbe's racehorses ran away with it, with that—and nothing else. They ought to be sold. And yet . . . she got a lot of pleasure out of them, and—weren't they, as it were, a drop in the ocean? If the mills were running at a reasonable profit what the racing stable cost was as nothing. If the mills were not so running, the saving of that three or four thousand a year wouldn't prevent loss. The figures dwarfed any consideration of that sort. But again, if one continued indefinitely along that train of reasoning, wasn't ruin inevitable? Could the "Red Light," as Luke Hargreaves called it, be ignored with impunity? Tim Hilditch, on the other hand, always said: "If anybody talks to me about the Red Light, I put steam on. You miss danger oftener by going quick than slowing down and wobbling about." And Tim had been true to his word by gambling in "cotton futures"—on which way the price of raw cotton would jump. Tim said "shilling cotton," of which optimists were talking, was as likely to be seen as a moon made o' green cheese. Tim saw a break in the clouds—and cotton would rise as trade grew brisk once again.

At this point in his reflections, Edward paused. He had reached an event which he tried in his thoughts to circumnavigate, and when that could not be done, to push aside. Neither was possible. The event was this. Faced with the knowledge that the year 1921 was one of the worst in the cotton trade's history and that 1922 and 1923 were not much better, Edward had accompanied Hilditch on one of his financial expeditions in search of recoupment, as Tim called it. "Any damn' fool can make brass," said Tim, "in a boom, just as any sort of a shot can hit a sitting buffalo." (Tim said this as if shooting sitting buffaloes were an everyday occurrence with him.) "But," he went on, "to go in search o' big game, to plunge into the jungle after the man-eater, to take your aeroplane and fly through the clouds in search of the sun, to explore the icy wastes tracking down the North Pole" —when Tim got wound up he didn't mind how many or what sort of similes he used—"that's the thing. Success, prosperity, money—they're always there, just as the sun and the North Pole and the man-eating tiger are always there. They want discovering, that's all—like gold and diamonds and rubies. Now I've been a prospector all my life—adventuring. Well . . ." And Tim had tapped his thin gold and platinum watch-chain to indicate that there he was, an English, nay, a Lancashire prospector, who had prospected himself from nothing, as it were, into this remarkably substantial monument to—well, there he was at any rate. At that moment Edward had felt that to keep to the safe, well-tried, well-defined main road that he had always traversed (apart from the lapse when he took a bridle-path and founded the repertory theatre) was not praiseworthy, was, indeed, in a sense cowardly. What had he ever risked? And again, Hilditch had usually been right in his prophecies, *must* have been right, otherwise that figure that threatened to burst its trouser seams would not be there at all, would not be owning the Post-War Theatre nor "operating" so that he was a national figure. And, of course, Edward had done well in the boom—though it was equally true he had done somewhat disastrously since. But a plunge would be exciting. He was tickled by the idea of plunging, along with this supremely confident Timothy Hilditch. And now after the dive—well, now he had fifty thousand pounds less than he had before. Nobody knew this except Hilditch, and he, Houghton, disliked sharing this uncomfortable secret with him. But he disliked losing the money far more. Hilditch who had lost over one hundred thousand pounds was apparently not seriously disturbed. "What we lose on the swings," he said, "we shall pick up on the roundabouts." He had assumed Edward would continue to plunge, as he himself was continuing to play the market. But Edward had withdrawn—though whether finally he himself didn't know for certain. If Hilditch recovered his losses and more besides, he, Houghton, would feel doubly foolish. Of course there were excuses, if he wished to excuse himself, for what he had done—a desperate situation, Burnham warehouses piled up with millions of pounds' worth of unsaleable goods, Lancashire cloth lying—he thought of the bales as small mountains—in India and China and South America, ordered in hysteria and repented of with empty purses, the price of silver having fallen like a stone and the rupee and tael with it. He had miscalculated cotton but who except a magician could hope to foresee the future of a substance that pre-war was fivepence a pound, which in February 1920 was thirty-one-pence a pound and now promised to leap about as a pea on a hot plate. A yard of cloth was always thirty-six inches but judging by the price of the cotton that made it, it ought to be an inch to-day and a furlong to-morrow.

Altogether, when he thought of that fifty thousand pounds, he doubted whether he would have the heart either to close the repertory theatre or to ask Phœbe to sell her horses.

Burnham Road that morning was indicative of a town working for the most part a bare thirty-five hours a week. The air was clearer, the eye could see farther across the moors, more people were in the streets. In Burnham Road he waited for a tram. He knew and liked and understood the work-people well enough to enjoy being close to them. A small group waited at the "Stop" and he stood at the kerb, leaning a little on his stick, an amused kindly smile on his face—not of the group but not quite aloof from it. A girl in a shawl draped round her shoulders and dexterously caught round her forearms who was addressed as Sally was saying: "Mi mother an' father have gone in a sharry to Southport. Might as well be doin' nowt there as here, mi mother said. Aye, an' she went 'bout dinner yesterday to get t' last bob to pay their fares. Ee, she's a one is mi mother, she never lets on." Sally addressed the assembly with complete self-possession and impartial friendliness. She turned her bold pale face with its sharp nose and steady grey eyes from one to another.

A woman very broad in the girth whose apron strings went round her three times indenting her and then tied with a struggle, nodded her head several times in approval to temper the question she was going to ask, and then said: "But didn't yer father have shares in Nightstar? I heard he had to pay ten shillin' a week an' it 'ud take five year to . . ."

"Aye, that's right," said Sally. "But five year or fifty-five year it's all t' same, mi father sez. It'll never be paid. They've had his brass and what's he got to show for it? Nowt. A big divi one year an' then bust. Let 'em whistle for it. They've got t' factory. Let 'em sell that if they can—pawn the dam' thing." Sally dismissed the cotton trade and turned to something more weighty. "Here, have yer seen Greta Garbo in *Passion in Mexico*? Ee, God, it made me feel Pally di Dance all over." Then she noticed Edward. "How's the Rep doin', Mister 'Oughton? I'm one o' your winders. I sometimes have six-penno'th"—adding with startling honesty, "when there's nothin' special on at t' pic-chers." She smiled and almost blushed now at her own boldness, and Edward thought her rather charming. He raised his hat and said the theatre was doing as well as could be expected in times that might be better, as he hoped they soon would be.

"Is it true Mister 'Ilditch is takin' Trix Bishop to London to put her in one of his shows?"

Edward said he hadn't heard of it.

"I heard it. I believe it's true," said Sally, and Edward, pondering it for a moment, thought it might well be.

The tram came and with a jolting see-saw motion took them down towards the town. Near the War Memorial were stood knots of men in navy blue or black suits (half Chesterford's men looked as if they were in perpetual mourning) and mostly wearing scarves of artificial silk or wool round their necks, crossed or knotted in the aperture of their waistcoats and slipped round their braces beneath. They wore no collars or ties; the scarves served for both. Their caps, usually of very light-coloured cloth, rose slightly from the head in front like the prow of a boat lifting to a wave, so that you saw a little hair, tousled or curled or oiled or moistened with water as the man was something of a "masher" or a dandy or not. They stood there quietly, not talking much, stepping on or off the kerb, turning round slowly, interested in watching the trams and the passers-by, and the goings and comings at the Black Bull and the Dragon across the way. They were, in the Chesterford phrase, "playing them"—that is to say, they were standing off, on short-time, or out of work altogether. "Our Dick's bin playin' 'im a twelvemonth," a Chesterford woman will say, unmindful of that ironical description of what occurs. But these men betrayed little sign yet of the tragedy that was steadily deepening. They smoked their fags or chewed a little gum (the American habit was spreading) or whistled dolefully or it sounded doleful because it was quiet. They were indulging in that old occupation or pastime that goes on in Chesterford in good times or ill—standing at the corner of the street. The custom is begun as boys and never abandoned, just as grown men may be found playing marbles on spare bits of ground between blocks of property. There is something extraordinarily boyish about Lancashire working men in their simplicity of mind, their love of fun and pranks, and their passion for games. It is true, no doubt, of all English working men but especially true of Lancashiremen. Edward was surprised that the groups were so small but a good deal of courting—day-time courting now—was being enjoyed on the moors and in the fields (idleness led to a considerable number of hurried marriages) allotments, neglected perhaps since the war, were being tilled again, dogs were being walked, pigeons flown, whippets trained, rabbits coursed, knur and spell enjoyed, music practised, novels devoured, and scientific subjects tackled. The new leisure wasn't being all wasted by any means. Book issues from the library were up by thirty per cent.

Edward rode on top of the tram where he sat slithering gently to and fro on a seat polished by innumerable corduroy trousers till it was smooth as glass. He noted that here and there along Burnham Road a shop was to let—an uncommon sight—and that Montague Goldman the moneylender who offered you "£2 to £2,000 on note of hand alone" looked particularly busy. But then Mr. Goldman, like the pawnbrokers, had a regular clientele. There were those who, every year, borrowed from "Monty" the money for their holidays and spent the remainder of the year paying it back. Similarly there were those who pawned the family's best suits and dresses every Monday and redeemed them the following Saturday as regularly and certainly as ever a deacon went to church. Edward sometimes thought he would like to cut the unending chain of "popping" by giving them a week's money in advance, to discover how long they would remain financially straight; but he knew he would never try.

The tram pulled up with a prodigious jolt and Edward who had been pre-occupied saw it was Mill Street. The jolt had flung his knees sharply against the seat in front and knocked his bowler hat over his eyes so that he felt exceedingly foolish. He got up and straightened his hat, realising that no garment can make a man feel such an idiot as a displaced hat, and clambered precariously down the stairs, wanting to hurry before the tram started and afraid to lest he should miss his foothold. He began to think mixing with the proletariat could be overdone.

Luke Hargreaves was busy with one of his favourite occupations—testing yarn—when Edward walked in. Hargreaves looked up and half raised his cap which he rarely completely removed for he was constantly walking into the mill yard and through various departments of the mill itself. To wear a cap when working was the common thing.

"Nothing wrong with the yarn, Luke?"

"Nothin'—except t' price." Luke spoke critically. In his view the price was far too low.

"But we can't sell it, low as it is."

"There's no price low enough to beat undercuttin'," said Hargreaves beetling his brows. "Good yarn's bein' slaughtered to-day. They're tumbling o'er theirsel's to work for nowt. Ready money's more precious than rubies to some of 'em. And what does it avail 'em? Buckley's the latest."

"Bankrupt?"

"Aye. Two hundred an' twenty thousand—assets eleven hundred an' fifty. He'll make some poor folk i' Chesterford."

Buckley's deals had been put at two million pounds at the boom's height. He was chairman of three mills and a director of six or seven others.

"An' that's not all," said Luke gloomily. "There's nasty rumours goin' about concernin' t' Robinson group. I hear talk of a deficit of a million an' a half. Nor it wouldn't surprise me. He's been messin' about wi' raw cotton. It's like takin' a drug."

Edward winced at the phrase.

"Once you start," Luke went on, "you never know when to leave off." He paused and then said: "T'stuff's as good as ever it were—better if anythin'. It's been too high, we know that—but now it's too low. What's matter wi' India for instance?"

"It's my opinion," said Edward, glad of the opportunity to escape further references to cotton gambling, "that India got used to doing without us during the war when we had to leave her short. Japan filled the breach. To-day Japan sells her ten times as much or more than she used to, India makes more herself and we—we sit looking at one another."

"Aye, an' t' machinery fettlers are puttin' right second-hand stuff as fast as they can and shippin' it out to foreigners who'll use it to cut our throats."

"We can't interfere with freedom of trade, Luke." Edward spoke a little satirically.

"Can't we, by God?" Hargreaves thrust out his bottom lip. "I'd stop this sellin' below cost if I'd my road. Summat'll have to be done. More short-time I reckon—as if it isn't too short already."

"You wouldn't go back to war-time control?"

"I don't know. There's them as want it."

"You don't think much of short-time?"

"Short-time—dear cloth," said Luke. "I can't help thinkin' we did better when we started at six o'clock in t' mornin'. They don't work so hard now. Different spirit about —pictures, dancin', football coupons—let's get our overalls off and be off out—that's the idea now. Chaps back from t' war don't think they ought to work for workin's sake—some on 'em think it's an unnecessary evil. Dang it, we were *born* to work. Don't you think so?"

Edward sighed. "I think we all ought to do *some*. The question is, how much? I sometimes wonder if the war has left any single thing the same as it was before—whether the old ideas even of free trade still hold good."

"I should be sorry to see *yo'* weakenin' on that," said Hargreaves.

"I don't say I am, Luke. Only I'm perplexed. I begin to think that the notion that we can just straighten things up and continue where we left off in 1914 is a delusion. There's too many broken hearts and broken bodies." He was thinking of Philip, and of Mary without, so far as he knew, a sweetheart. Luke was silent; he knew what Edward had in mind.

Edward began pacing to and fro, sometimes pinching his chin between forefinger and thumb. Hargreaves sat with his cap pushed a trifle further back, going on now methodically with his testing of yarn. After a while he paused and looked up. "You've not thought o' leavin' the amalgamation, I suppose?" he asked but there was that in his voice that said he knew the answer. He added, as if in extenuation of his question, "There's not much we seem to agree about."

Edward said: "Yes, I've thought of it—and discarded it. If every man goes his own way—well, I don't see how that will help. Isn't that what is largely the matter, men playing their own hands?"

"It's not much use keepin' agreements other folks break," replied Hargreaves doggedly.

Edward didn't reply to that and after another pause Hargreaves rose and stretched himself. "I reckon Houghton's'll weather it, whatever it is," he said.

But Edward didn't answer that either. He would liked to have answered heartily: "Never a double of it, Luke"; indeed he turned the phrase over on his tongue, but he couldn't utter it. He paced across the floor and back, stopped, said: "Ah, well," and passed out of Hargreaves's room into his own. After a moment Luke glanced after him, and rubbed his ear reflectively.

Chapter Three

IT WAS TRUE that Timothy Hilditch had offered Trix a part in his new revue, *This Wonderful World,* which was to take London at record speed round the night-clubs, gaming-saloons, abodes of pretty women and millionaires, which are scattered about the earth's surface. "Harlem, Marseilles, Singapore, San Francisco, Constantinople, Barcelona, Buenos Aires, Berlin, Moscow, Paris and Vienna—show the pikwant side of 'em," said Timothy, "and you'll find the public stitched on to it." Hilditch wanted a girl who could play a courtesan in half a dozen countries, and Trix's flaming hair and rich beauty seemed to him perfection. He had a second idea—once she was playing such a part might not her attitude towards himself be changed? Wasn't he a better man than tuppenny ha'penny Blackburn, who thought a week-end at the Isle of Man was high life? Who was it got the wench at the repertory theatre at all? Wasn't it his (Hilditch's) doing? Hadn't he done his best to insist on her havin' good, fat parts, and stood drinks to the newspaper men while he, with an affectionate prod at their shoulders or touch on their arms, told 'em what a discovery she was and how he foresaw her toppin' the programme at the Post-War? True, that chap from the *Burnham Guardian* had listened in complete silence and had then inquired when Hilditch was going to use his influence to put on something

by Eugene O'Neill or Pirandello, and asked whether Tim
didn't think the latter's *Henry IV* was better than Shakespeare's, and Tim, feeling a damned fool, said he certainly
did, wondering whether Pirandello had ever written such a
play at all; and the next morning the *Burnham Guardian*
had declared Miss Bishop to be excellent raw material, and
had expressed the view that after a year or two's hard work
she might, etc. But then nobody ever did know which way
the *Burnham Guardian* would jump, and he (Hilditch) could
afford to smile over it.

Hilditch had progressed thus far through life without
caring too much for anything or anybody. To that he might,
without deep error, have attributed a considerable part of
his success. Certainly a good deal of his equanimity and
physical health. He had loved many women (if his tempestuous wooing and fleeting passion could be called by that
name), but he had remained a bachelor, preserving himself
from the final step, marriage, by the reflection that she
would, in all likelihood, "natter him to death." He didn't
pretend to himself that Trix's attraction for him would endure, though it would be time enough to consider that when
he had accomplished the first stage. But his presents—a gold
and enamel cigarette-case, an emerald brooch, a Chinese
bangle—chosen so that while their costliness might excite
her mind a little it should not be so marked as to cause her
to refuse them, his taking her to dine at the Adelphi, Burnham (where, with equal care, he refrained from pressing
her to take wine), his having flowers placed in her dressing-
room on occasions when her part was important—these attentions she accepted with a coquettish delight that amounted
to nothing. She received them at one time as a princess might
have done, at another as a favourite niece and had, indeed,
playfully asked him if she might call him "Uncle Tim"—
and he, after consenting, had gone away scratching his head.

Trix's own mind was in a state of perplexity. For a long period after Brierley's play had been produced she looked on herself as betrothed to him; but the play had made no more than a minor local stir—nobody beyond Lancashire ever heard of it—and from a height both of passion and momentary success they had, slowly but definitely returned to a lower level, like climbers unable to sustain the rarefied air, their exaltation diminished, their spirits reduced, their high hopes faltering. Marriage had been in both their thoughts but Brierley, although there was in his blood an impulse to risk most when the chances were smallest, to challenge complete descent, was too disconsolate to act with the needed resolution, and, as for Trix, she had a revulsion to that hardness in her that placed her career and money and success above all else. "My work comes first," she began to say, as she had said, when at the Black Bull: "Money comes first—I'll do anything to get it." No formal release was asked or given by either but Brierley was tormented by the expectation that at any moment she might announce to him her determination to marry somebody else, while she on her part was troubled by a vague sense of disappointment and frustration, and a foreboding that her life was to be cast in the shadows. She was pierced at times, too, by knowing that her body was bound to him, and at other moments by a sadness that the bond was not closer and that the completeness of their loving had not made a deeper difference to their relationship. Both of them rose and fell and moved hither and thither in their emotions but Trix's closeness to poverty throughout all her life until she joined the repertory company, and her deep realisation that without money the comforts that had grown necessary to her would vanish as if they had never existed, brought uppermost the determination to ensure her future, and encased her in the hard shell that had been hers when Brierley first met her and which he, by the warmth of his affection, had softened and, in part, removed.

It was in this frame of mind that she accepted Hilditch's presents, dined with him, and wondered how useful he might be to her, how much he would ask in return and, of far deeper import, what her answer would be when a forthright reply became imperative. That forthright reply was brought much nearer when he broached to her the question of moving to London. He had taken her again to dine at Burnham—it was a week when she was not in the cast—and she was revelling in the luxury of evening clothes, and brocade shoes and an evening cloak of green quilted satin with white fur collar and cuffs. Tim's Rolls-Royce took them over the rough sets between Chesterford and Burnham as if they were rolling over velvet turf. Trix said nothing, but a smile of delight at the sensuous pleasure she derived from luxury curved her lips. Tim sat puffing his cigar in the other corner, proud to be with her, taking pleasure in the colour of her hair and the cut of her shoes and ankles. "It's worth fighting for, is this," he thought; "worth a bit of a rough-and-tumble to be able to afford this. I shall never be able to do without it any more and, by God, I never will, either. If that ever happens, I shall have to write 'Finish.' " Suddenly he leaned over in her direction and waved his cigar. "I've got a bit of a proposition to make to-night," he said. "Not now—later on. All right. Nothing to be frightened of. Strictly business." He waved his cigar in high good humour. "Not another word now. Later on. Car's a bit of all right, isn't she? Eh?" Trix, laughing, said the car was divine. "A hundred per cent efficient," she said, "like everything you do."

"I'm glad to hear you say that," he said. "Because you're right. I agree with you. And I'm just as good a judge of actresses as I am o' cars. Isn't that right?"

"If you say so," she laughed.

"Aye, well, I do say so. That's what I want to talk to you about. But not now. Later on. Never bargain on an empty stomach—nor make love, either, eh? Doesn't do. You want something inside you." He was quiet and then: "Did I tell you I'm thinking of starting a newspaper? Well, I am. If I do I'll be dramatic critic and tell our actors and actresses at the Post-War where they get off—tell 'em where the bus stops, eh? That 'ud be good, wouldn't it? 'Tim Hilditch slates his own show.' That 'ud make London laugh, wouldn't it? Above a bit. It takes a lad from Lancashire to make London laugh. All the comedians go from up here—and the dancers, too. Did you know that? And I'm going to show 'em another star before long if I'm any judge. But not a word about that yet. Later on." He puffed his cigar and filled the car with smoke and opened the window, talking between his teeth which held the cigar and bit it deep. "About—this —here paper I was telling you about." He wound up the window again between his words. "I'll employ a posse of detectives to find out what famous men do in their spare time—where they go—who their mistresses are. That 'ud sell it, wouldn't it? 'Nowt so funny as folk.' That's a true sayin'. You watch people nudgin' one another when we walk into the Adelphi to-night. 'There's Tim Hilditch an' that clever girl from the Rep,' they'll say. And quite right, too. I get a kick out o' that. Don't you? Of course you do. Quite right, too. Don't believe it when London actresses tell you they dislike being recognised in the street or hotels. All damned humbug. Breath o' life to 'em. Do you know I could get all my actresses for nothing if I would— Society wenches, daughters of earls, dukes, lords, marquises. Give their ears to come to me. I could litter the Post-War with 'em. But they'd be dear at the price of nothing. They would. The whole lot of 'em aren't worth your little finger. But not a word about that till after dinner."

Trix was thinking how amusing he was, how pleasant it was to be with a man to whom a hundred pounds was nothing, whose bidding was obeyed by head waiters as if he were a king, who held so much power yet never tried to change his speech or be other than a bluff Lancashireman, who put on no airs and never made her feel ignorant, or a fool, as Harry Brierley so often did—Brierley who had so many gifts and so little worldly success to show for them. From her corner of this luxurious car she could at that moment almost have scorned Brierley. At that moment she would have listened with sympathy to anything Hilditch said. But the moment passed.

Hilditch drank with dinner half a pint of champagne served in a tankard—one of his mannerisms. "Half a pint is my ration," he said. "No man can afford to drink more when he's with a pretty woman. A man needs all his wits." And saying that, he pursed up his wide mouth and brought his eyebrows together and drew them down and smiled a little mockingly, as if he said: "I'm warning you. It's you who'll need all your wits. I play fair. Look out." Trix drank nothing. If business were to be talked—

But over dinner he talked of nothing but racing and of his country house at Chalfont St. Giles to which he invited her. He had had a boxing ring built there, he said, where men fought with bare fists in the old Jem Mace fashion; he himself was learning jiu-jitsu—"you never know when you may want to keep a man from your throat"—and if she cared for a bit o' cock-fighting, or whippet-coursing, or badger-hunting, if she wanted to ride a potential Derby winner, or see men going over jumps compared with which those at Aintree were hurdles, well, she must come down for a long weekend. "I'm Tim to everybody down there and half the fellows in Debrett are Jim and Bill and Harry to me. Lords are three a penny and M.P.s just makeweight. The number o' rubber stamps knocking about would surprise you—or maybe it wouldn't." And Tim looked at her from under his brows.

After dinner they danced. "This is one o' the few occasions," he said, "when a man can make a woman go the way he wants. That's the reason men like dancing and women like being danced with—though they don't always know it. Many a woman makes her own life a hell by wearing t' breeches; every wise 'un knows she's happier in petticoats." He foxtrotted with an easy precision, holding her firmly yet lightly, dancing with a decorous geniality. "I can't stand elderly gentlemen behaving like pups," he said to her, grinning and showing his teeth, as though he said: "Elderly gentlemen's rather good, isn't it?"

"Will forty pounds a week be enough?" he asked without warning, as if he had been saying: "How do you like the music?"

"What's the part?" She had narrowed her eyes and looked at him from beneath her lashes. He changed his step, holding her more closely.

"The new revue—character part—oldest profession in history. Only you're too lovely for it. You ought to play Sweet Nell of Old Drury. You shall one day, by God." His eyes had merged into dark points. She moved in his arms, protesting against the pressure, and swiftly he loosened her, so swiftly that she thought: "I believe he imagines he's in love."

"You know you can make me do what you like, don't you?" he said, looking hard into her eyes; he added quietly, "You little devil." Instantly she felt stripped, as though all his previous courtesy to her had been false, as though she were in a moment reduced from being a lady to being a common tap-room singer. Hurt and humiliated, she saw in a flash how difficult it was going to be always to preserve her

poise and dignity. When a child, boys had whistled after
her and she had turned round; and for long years afterwards
she had involuntarily half turned at a whistle although she
knew it could not be meant for her and if it were, that she
must ignore it. But that didn't prevent her from turning. She
knew now that her position as an actress of ability was estab-
lished, that a dramatist loved her, and that she could safely
be rude to Hilditch if she wished; and she knew equally well
that she would not be, that what was in her bones could not
be so easily rooted out; and she was a little ashamed.

"You're tired o' dancing," he said, quick to notice the
life go out of her. "I'm sorry I'm not better at it." He
seemed a little disconsolate and her spirits revived. "Oh no,"
she said. "You dance—nicely, but—"

"Well," he said, "I paid enough to learn. However." He
dismissed his dancing as if he were making a concession.
"We'll sit down and you shall have a—something or other.
Let's have the other half-bottle o' champagne. A glass will
revive you."

She smoked a cigarette and thought with alarm of her
inability to control her temperament better. Was she becoming soft, spoilt by a little culture and improved environ-
ment? She, who used to keep Thomas Blackburn and half
a dozen others at arm's length?

"Of course," he was saying, "I know forty pounds won't
buy you the Koh-i-Noor diamond but it's ten weeks' Chesterford salary, isn't it? And the Devil himself doesn't know
how long the Rep's going on."

"I've been wondering—does Mr. Houghton know you're
offering me this job?"

"Time enough when you've accepted," he said easily. "No
use telling anybody if you're turning it down."

Trix glanced round the square court in which they sat. A
sprinkling of Jews, Levantines and Greeks were there, a

handful of young Burnham men in shirts a little too loud, and coats a trifle too waisted, escorting women too tired and too painted.

"Not much Lancashire about this, is there?" he said. "London and water, eh? A bit paralysed about the legs." For a moment he mused. "The Germans used to be here— and the Argentines and the Dutch." He made a ring of smoke with his cigar. "They'll come back—must; as if they could help themselves." He shook the mood off. "Well? About this part in the revue." He leaned over the table and pushed everything away—glasses, ash-tray. He might have been an admiral clearing the decks for action. "You'll be on six times—and every one is enough to put you right there." He indicated with his forefinger a spot on the far side of the table. "Top notch. I know. I've been altering the script for you—making sure it's got bite. Oh, I've had you in mind all the time. Dresses, did you say?" (Trix hadn't spoken.) "Every one by a different creator—so they'll all be cutting one another's throats to make you lovelier than the others." He leaned back struck by a thought. "By God, you know, I don't know why I'm doing it, neither. You'll be besieged—hemmed in—dukes, magnates, half the Brigade o' Guards. It's like givin' your latest designs and patterns away to a competitor. However, I daresay they'll soon make you sick of 'em." And he put the dukes and the Brigade of Guards on one side.

Had Hilditch come to her with the same offer when she sang at the Black Bull she would have accepted without hesitation, too ignorant to know how small her knowledge was. Now, although she knew she would accept, had known indeed from the moment when Hilditch had first spoken of it, she was filled with doubts as well as exaltation. Her heart could turn over at the thought of what awaited her.

"You'll take it on?" he asked, re-arranging the table and

raising his finger to the waiter to order himself a brandy and soda.

"Yes." She flashed a smile at him, knowing she was doing it and thinking: "I suppose he deserves that."

Driving back to Chesterford he said: "They've a song down in the East End o' London which says: 'Liza, when are you goin' to pay me the rent for occupyin' my heart this larst month?'"

She said: "I think I shall like the people in the East End."

"I could sing that song to you, you know."

The sky was full of colour. The moon was high and full and near it the clear heavens were flaked with gold, and elsewhere the sky was dark green merging into purple. Trix was deeply aware of its beauty and leaned forward slightly on her seat. When she relaxed again she found his thick arm round her. He pulled her a little towards him but made no attempt to embrace her and, as a pendulum that has reached the extremity of its swing, she moved back to her normal position. Neither of them spoke. The Rolls-Royce sped swiftly on through the deserted streets and highways. Her heart had quickened; she sat there as a jockey might sit, riding a race, praying for speed and hoping the journey would end soon, soon. Did she appear to him to be the block of wood she was striving to be, or was he aware of her excitement? Apparently, he wasn't, for presently he took his arm away and lit another cigar. He was annoyed and angry both with himself and her. Who did she think she was? Wasn't he Hilditch, the cotton magnate and impresario? Ah well, he could wait—if his interest lasted that long. He had no use for women who weren't warm and responsive; he'd no intention of embracing a lamp-post.

When they drew up at Mrs. Eckersley's house he opened the door for her. "Good night," he said, "and thank you."

He was conscious of a little irony in his voice. He didn't get out to help her down. His courtesy wasn't deep enough for that. If she didn't like it, she could lump it. He sank back and stretched his legs and thrust his hands into his trouser pockets. Women were a damned nuisance, he reflected. Ah well! Perhaps she would be a success in London. You never knew.

Chapter Four

BRIERLEY sat in an armchair in what his mother called the parlour, writing. That is to sat, he say with a writing-pad on his knee staring past the small window table covered by a green velvet cloth hung with tassels and bearing a geranium plant. He was aimlessly running the end of his gold pencil across his lips. He saw the table and plant and he saw the roofs of the semi-detached houses across the road; but he didn't take them in. His mouth was drawn down at the corners sulkily and his face was fixed and his eyes staring. Now and then he would stop running the pencil over his lips and stroke his nose. He looked down at his pad. "The Lady of the Tides" he had written in his fine squiggly writing that his mother said she could never read. "The sea," he had written, "was beginning to push its long fingers of water up the estuary when I reached the jetty. The afternoon was wild, clouds brooding, torn and haggard, the sea grey and cold, and gulls screaming as they wheeled." Well, that sounded broken and stormy enough. Curious how much more interesting things often were on paper than in real life. You got rid of the welter of indiscriminate nothing; you charged the trivial with significance. Or tried to. If he sold this, he reflected, he would get three guineas for it— eleven hundred words, sold outright, for good and all, the idea given to the world and the immortal prose gone for ever. Three guineas. *The Reaping* had made for him the magnificent sum of twelve pounds fifteen shillings and sixpence when it was produced at the Repertory Theatre, and ten more guineas from its performance by various amateur dramatic societies since. It was said that Arnold Bennett when asked why he wrote replied that the first reason was money, and the second was money and the third was money. No doubt that was said of de Maupassant and Chekhov and Goethe also. Only by an oversight were those great journalists Matthew, Mark, Luke and John omitted. It was plain that he, Brierley, would have to find some other reason than money, for putting pen to paper. Because there simply wasn't any money in it. Not enough to buy cigarette-papers. Lamentable, but there it was. He rubbed his nose and stared at nothing and wrote some more.

The story told how, standing at the water's edge, he had seen fishermen carry a heavy white coffin on to a sailing-boat and had watched the boat sail out and work her way down into the bay, the boat dipping and the coffin strewn with spray; and how he had crunched across the shingle to Matthew Martin.

"Matt's sixty odd years," he wrote, "had given him a face rugged and brown as a contour map, eyes fathoms deep, and a voice like a church organ. 'A fine buryin' for a fine woman, queer tho' she were,' said Matt. 'To sail out into the west like that and slip into clean water.' Presently we came to his cottage and he jerked his head in invitation. 'Well, mother,' he called to his wife, 'Phœbe be gone to rest at larst.' 'It were time, poor lady,' said Martha from the scullery. She came in with the black kettle. 'She walked the shore for year after year whether the wind were high or low, as if she were expectin' him to come walkin' on the water like Our Lord at Galilee.

She never could forget seemingly.'

" ' 'Ave you an' me forgot him, missis?' asked Matt. 'Couldn't he rig a boat an' hook a salmon and ride a horse as if he'd been born wi' one leg on land and t'other on water? There ain't a woman alive as isn't taken by qualities such as them. An' Phœbe were not the sort to love for a while an' then forget.'

" 'When they were courtin',' Martha said, 'they used to come ridin' past the Three Fiddlers, her on a white horse and him on a black, laughin' into one another's eyes. They were that handsome, my eyes used to grow wet; and the horses—they seemed to know too; so proud and stately-like they walked.' 'I like to remember 'em best as they used to be on the *Flying Spume*,' said Matt; 'her at the tiller with hair blowin' and eyes clear and wide as a sky after storm, and him lyin' with his chin on his hands on the slopin' deck. "There be life in the water, Matt," he used to say. I mind once sayin' back, "There be death, too, Mister Lancelot, specially in these banks and tides and currents." "Croaker," he sez, showin' his teeth. The day he went out larst were crazy wi' wind, and the clouds were in masses with their edges red as hell. Nobody could ha' stopped him but Phœbe and she was in London seein' about her weddin' dress. He never come back nor he were never found. The *Flying Spume* come home in bits, half of her this side o' t' bay, half t'other.'

" 'She never got ovver it,' said Matt's wife. "When the tide comes up the creeks," she would say, "I hear his voice in the wind, an' his laugh in the water. When I die," she said, "I'll be buried in the water; and that will be my weddin' day. I shall meet him then." '

" 'She built that house on the edge o' the shingle there,' said Matt. "The Tides" she called it. It were almost like bein' afloat to be in the rooms. She told me one day: "I can't sleep, Matt, unless I hear the tide runnin' in and out." I suppose for seventeen year there ain't a tide come up this estuary she ain't watched by day or heard by night. Up and down the beach she would go, her face growing less lovely as sorrow bit into it and her beautiful self that waved like corn in t' wind becomin' terrible frail.'

" 'She had been ill for some months,' said Martha. 'Just before she died the tide were far out; not a ripple up the estuary, the sand banks dull gold i' the sun. She were restive; no peace. She'd lie listenin' and say: "I don't hear no sea; I want to hear him in the wind an' water again." I were up i' the house helpin'. We were rare and puzzled. Suddenly the doctor come in, pretendin' to be angry to hide the tears in his eyes. "Can't ye do the sensible thing?" he says, as if he had mentioned it many a time. "Open the door," he says, "an' turn all the taps i' the bathroom, an' carry water upstairs an' let it splash." It were almost like cheatin' the poor lovely one, but we did it, Emma and me; an' her face grew quiet an' still; an' she died so. And now she'll hear the tides till the last trump do sound.'

"Matt looked at his watch. 'She'll be in Lancelot's arms by now,' he said."

Brierley put down his pencil and got up, his fingers cramped, his mind a little tired and his spirits slightly elated. "It's too sentimental," he thought, "and everybody will say it's mad. Umph! I like the finish—that about Matt's watch. It's a good morning's work and I don't care a damn whether anybody buys it or not." That wasn't correct but he felt like blowing off steam. He stood with his feet wide apart staring out over the geranium, and he was stood thus when Mrs. Pilkington, the charwoman, came into the room, took no notice of him, went to the hearth, got down on her knees

and started tidying up after a fall of soot. After unlaying
the fire to remove the soot from firewood, paper and coal,
and laying it again, she paused and looked round at him.

"Not much use," she said, "givin' it more than a lick an'
a promise. Sure to fall again. Could do wi' sweepin'. Cheats
me why you need so many fires. Can't yer do yer writin' in
t' other room?"

"I like to find you some work to do."

"I know you do."

"It's the only thing that keeps you from worrying."

"I can work *and* worrit. Don't flatter yersel'. If I were
the worryin' sort I should be worried into my coffin by now."
And indomitable Mrs. Pilkington raised her four foot nine
inches to her feet. "An' my knees is that bad yer wouldn't
believe," she said. "I reckon nowt o' these panel doctors—
wi' their come-agen-next-week bottles." She took off her
steel spectacles, wiped them on her sacking apron and put
them on again.

"Not," she resumed, "as I dislike Dr. O'Rourke so much.
'Well, Ma,' he says, 'have yer bought one o' them mops on
t' end of a long handle as I told yer?' 'No, I haven't,' I says.
'An' if yer were a proper doctor yer wouldn't be suggestin'
new-fangled inventions. Yer'd get on wi' t' job o' curin' me.'
'Yer can't be cured,' he says. 'I can,' I says. 'Don't contradict
me,' he says. 'Talk to yersel' if yer don't want contradictin'.'
I says. 'And yer wouldn't be talkin' to me this road if I hadn't
lost all me money in t' Dobberley.' 'Sure, an' that's true,' he
says. 'I'd be bleedin' ye white till ye hadn't a panny to yer
name—an' ye'd be gettin' nothin' for it just the same. So
now ye know. Ye can't be cured an' what can't be cured must
be endured. So ye'd better buy yersel' that mop. The only
thing that 'ud cure ye would be to live like a lady at the top
of a long flight o' steps an' watch all yer enemies moppin'
em.' 'And yer'd be the first enemy I'd like to see doin' it, Dr.

O'Rourke—down on yer knees. Yer very self,' I says, 'gettin'
the same trouble that I've got in me legs.' For it's a funny
thing, Mester Brierley, but every time I talk to the doctor I
start talkin' Irish afore I've finished. And that reminds me,
have yer given my shares away yet?"

She stooped and picked up her brush and dirt-pan.

"Nobody will take them unless you give half a crown
with each of them."

"Then I'st have to keep 'em. Is there another call
comin'?"

"Shouldn't wonder."

She took a deep breath and let it out with a rush, as if it
were a challenge.

"We used to be freetened o' t' telegraph lad. Now it's
t' postman. We used to say we'd never received t' calls. Now
there's one or two mills sends 'em out registered. They make
yer sign for 'em. Like signin' for a death-warrant. Aye, an'
it's been that more nor once. But not wi' me. Nay, not wi'
me. I'll see to that."

Mrs. Pilkington was one of those admirable people who,
either by force of character or from lack of imagination or
trust in God, are not unduly oppressed by fate or what lies
ahead. If she were down on her luck she felt it to be a challenge. She had her own opinions and she stuck to them. Had
she been born to live in Belgrave Square she would no doubt
have been as considerable a character in Society as she was
on Treadle Bank. These jewels are to be found as readily in
the lower crust of mankind as the higher. You may discover
in English provincial towns and villages, men bent over
cobblers' lasts, or tubs of coal, or grocers' counters, or spin-
ning-frames, with faces that would become Ministers of
State, or divines, or leaders of industry or chief constables
or writers or any other sort of men who become well known.
The native genius or nobility in them not only breaks out

occasionally in their children who present the world with the picture of men rising as steadily as a diver to the surface, but gives the parents themselves a natural authority among their neighbours. These men and women—for the women are frequently of better metal than the men—preserve a level of integrity and industry in common life that no stupidity or chicanery in government, municipal or national, or roguery or rottenness in what are counted high places and high life, can wither.

Mrs. Pilkington had married a carter who was happy so long as he was working. He had earned a guinea a week when they were wedded, and he rose in fifteen years to twenty-five shillings, but he would have gone on working to the end for a guinea with equal contentment. He didn't consciously sit down to think that labour was good; he knew it in his bones. He worked six days a week and on the seventh he went to feed and look at his two horses; if there had been nine days to the week, so many would he have worked. "He'll addle no brass, won't Will," said Mrs. Pilkington, who was a little contemptuous of him for it, but who also, although she may not have been aware of it, loved him for it. When he died of a poisoned finger for which he refused to have a doctor till it was too late, she said: "I reckon I shall have to buckle to, now," as if she had not been buckling to all her life; and she kept herself by washing and charing, a day here and half a day there. Her charges were accounted rather high, of which she was proud. If she came for the day she wanted four shillings and sixpence together with her breakfast when she arrived and her tea before she departed. But the amount of work she did was astonishing. She could finish "a small wash" by 9.30 a.m. and a large one by early afternoon and have the scullery mopped and stoned and sanded by three o'clock.

When, four years before, she had drawn £750 for the

purchase of the £50 worth of shares she had in the Dobberley mill, she had put it back into the new company, seeing no reason why a concern which performed one miracle should not perform two. Brierley's advice to the contrary she had ignored or, rather, looked at and cast away. She had taken a holiday of four days at Morecambe and three days at Whitby, desiring not only to see the sea on both sides of England but to travel widely by train, a proceeding which thrilled her. At Whitby she bought herself a new black bonnet with satin strings, a cape trimmed with sequins, and a pair of jet ear-rings. She gave no thought to retiring, replying grimly that it would be time enough to do that when she had six brass handles round her. She, however, took the living-room carpet up to her bedroom which had never previously risen above oilcloth, and bought a bright bit of Turkey to replace the superseded threadbare Axminster. Also she made her supper cocoa a little stronger and gave the cat an additional saucer of milk until, having been presented with two litters of kittens in six months, Mrs. Pilkington, confessing to herself that there might be no significance in the matter, nevertheless discontinued the milk to be on the safe side. Apart from these matters—which were not so trifling to Mrs. Pilkington as one might suppose—her life had gone on very much as before. She had never actually handled the £750—apart from £25, with which the minor revolutions I have recorded were carried out—so that when the Dobberley mill failed not only to pay dividends but began to make demands on shareholders for further capital to support its existence, Mrs. Pilkington bore it with comparative tranquillity. She had no more capital beyond seven pounds fifteen in the Co-operative Stores (a sum she had not the slightest intention of surrendering) and her bits o' furniture, as she called them. The only thing of which she was conscious of being robbed was a strange feeling of superiority—a small inner glow—that had been hers for a brief while, to which she had never grown completely accustomed, and the loss of which left her more stable within her.

Her own heart being stout, she looked about her with curiosity. Little went on in Treadle Bank without her knowledge, and her dexterity with her work enabled her to spend some hours every day in social intercourse. The back-to-back houses of Allinson's Court and Butler's Yard that abounded near her abode may not have been all that social reformers demand, but at all events there was a communal life that permitted little boredom. A closet to three families (with a dart-board chalked on the door so that you had to claim the players' indulgence while you entered and warn them by a shout of your intended exit), and an out-of-doors water-tap to four houses, compelled close acquaintance whether you willed it or not; and Mrs. Pilkington had a tongue that throve on acquaintance.

"There's been two suicides this past fortnight," she said to Brierley, "so you can tell what things is like. We don't go in for suicides as a rule; there's not much folk hasn't got used to standin', on Treadle Bank. But it's this unemployment as does it. John Thomas Lomax was one. John Thomas had been out o' work ten month an' I knew it. Lots o' folk knew it but not his missis. What some wives don't know is past everythin'—blind as kittens t' first week they're born. John Thomas went off every mornin' as if he was goin' to his old job o' firin' up at t' brass furnace. He did it for six months, walkin' his feet off lookin' for work, goin' as far as Burnham, Stalybridge, Blackburn and I dunno where. An' if he weren't dirty enough when it were time to come home, he used to mucky his face somewhere—I found him doin' it one night on that brickcroft near Wheatley's. That's really how I got to know. 'Why don't yer face up and tell her?' I said. 'She'd break her heart,' he said. 'She's been feart o' this happenin' for long enough, me gettin' on in years an' not bein' able to shovel as well as I used to.' 'Well,' I said, 'Ow are yer doin' about yer wages?' 'Well,' 'e said, 'I have t' dole, yer know, an' I mak' that up by drawin' a bit every week out o' t' Post Office.' He started scrikin' a bit then—he said he were so sick o' walkin' about an' lyin' to his missis about what he were doin' at t' shop—an' what Jim this and Bill t' other said to him. He sad he thowt he should go out of his mind if it went on much longer. An' that's what happened to him seemin'ly. They found him floatin' in t' Rochdale cut a week sin'." Mrs. Pilkington bent down and swept up a bit of soot that wasn't there.

"The other," she said, beginning briskly, not keeping it up but still busying herself with the hearth, "was Mrs. Gibb. She'd lost all her brass i' Fred Buckley's concerns—she lived i' that gable end a cock stride from t' Bank but as far from it really as if she'd been i' Derbyshire. I did for her of a Tuesday. She allus said she had nobody an' when Buckley's went she said to me: 'I've had nobody this long while an' now I've nayther *nowt* nor nobody.' They found her hangin' o'er t' banisters last Sunday. She allus went to chapel an' when she didn't go they went seekin' 'er." Brierley could find nothing to say. After a moment or two Mrs. Pilkington added: "She'd more pluck than me. I could never do it that road. T' gas oven is as much as I should ever be able to manage."

"You've thought of it then?"

She looked at him with her straight, determined stare.

"Haven't all of us who've got owt in our heads?"

"Yes," he said, feeling he ought to add to that and not knowing what. But she didn't wait. "This is no road to earn my keep," she said, and walked straight out, and he heard her presently rattling the front door-knob as she polished the brass.

Chapter Five

IN THE EARLY AFTERNOON of the day when Mrs. Pilkington had made Brierley a little ashamed of his own discontents, he changed into flannels, slipped on a light overcoat—for it was a September day with the evenings growing sharper— and boarded a tram for Hilford Lane. Half a dozen times during the summer he had played tennis with Mary. A few days before, she had said: "If you're coming again it must be soon or—Ichabod!" "Well," he said, a laugh playing over his face, "nobody's axed me for ages." "All right," she said mimicking his use of the dialect, "I'm axing you."

The tram swayed up and down gently as though it were riding on water, and Brierley enjoyed the swaying. He was glowing with delight and was excited. He had enjoyed their previous games enormously. They had laughed at nothing, they had striven gaily to beat one another but shouted generously that balls were in when it was just possible they were out, and they had hurled badinage and raillery across the net.

She answered the door herself when he rang and came out in a short light blue coat with brass buttons, over her white dress, and they went straight down to the court.

"I suppose you're in great form?" he said, swishing his racket.

"Father says I need fitting with a dynamo. Gwen Hunter

came up yesterday and beat me six love, six two."

"Hang it all, she does nothing else but play games."

"I tell you, I can't hit a ball. Good job it's the end of the season or my reputation would be ruined."

"Don't be so confoundedly modest," he said. "It's a grave fault."

"One you don't suffer from," she said.

"All right," he said, "one to you. Only remember this—you'd better have a just estimation of your worth, or when your firm goes bust and you have to earn your living, you'll earn about three ha'pence a month—which, by the way, is about my own standard. I ought to be hawking coal instead of playing tennis with you like a plutocrat. Will you serve?"

She took the balls, and with a small, sideways twist of the mouth as she swung the racket past her head—a grimace he thought delicious—she served to him. They both played well, encouraged by each other's good humour. To see her racing across the court, her lithe body taut, to observe her stop, when she failed to reach a well-placed shot in time, break into a burst of laughter and cry, almost incoherently, her words broken by laughing, "Harry, that's too bad, making me run like that!" filled him with gladness. He seemed far removed from the tawdriness of life or the deep excitements, exaltations or despairs of sex.

"Is there any news of Trix?" she asked, when they rested.

"I haven't heard for a month," he said. At once he was uneasy and depressed but, making an effort, he added almost lightly, "The revue is still running—she's very occupied, I imagine."

Mary said: "I thought she was feeling the strain very much when father and I saw her. Don't you think she has an immense burden to carry for a first London appearance? She had her old flash and fire, but . . ." After a moment she said: "Hilditch was very much in evidence."

"I was at the first night," he said. "There was enough champagne to launch the British Fleet, and enough roses to make a flaming June. Timothy looked like six provincial Lord Mayors." His mind turned back to the party on the stage afterwards—Trix, feverish and strident, overborne by the weight of her ordeal and dazed by the adulation paid to her; himself, feeling hopelessly out of it, acutely aware of his own lack of success as a dramatist, rebellious at the lavishness and vulgarity of the display, and knowing that his coldness and contempt were earning him dislike. His heart had been sick on Trix's behalf, but when he found a chance to speak to her, he had said no more than: "This is pretty ghastly, isn't it?" And she, thinking that he was jealous of her success, had replied: "Well, if you prefer Chesterford . . ." and turned away. He was still more unhappy then—angry with Trix for being so easily won by London and with himself for being so churlish and unable to convey comfort and sympathy with her. He had stood in the wings later watching the party—Trix, flushed and excited by wine, dancing every dance, laughing too much, growing careless about her dress, the gold-leaf shoulder straps of which constantly slipped off, until finally he went, an ache devouring his vitals. Nobody had acclaimed Trix as a new star, but all spoke of her beauty and vitality. He had written congratulating her, but she had not replied for a week, and then it was a small, mis-spelt letter on Post-War Theatre notepaper.

Mary said: "You know father's going to close the Repertory Theatre?"

"No, I didn't know, but I'm not surprised." He spoke in a small voice, still disturbed by his memories of London.

"He feels it—the failure to make the dream come true."

A little bitterly he said: "I'm partly responsible—he gave me a chance and I couldn't take it."

"You *did* take it. . . ." She spoke warmly. "It was a good play—we all thought so. You'll do better, no doubt."

"Happen."

"Don't disparage yourself. You're always either near the stars or in the depths."

"Well," he said, "that's how it is—a great, barren field with a small fire burning in the middle—and the fire often lost in smoke."

"What are you writing now?" She asked as a right, and he thought: "I'm glad she asks like that, and yet—what a tartar she'd be as a wife."

"The week's work," he said, giving her *The Lady of the Tides*. "You'll never be able to read it."

"By long practice," she said, "I've got as far as knowing which is the right side up." But she read it swiftly. "You've done much worse than this."

"Aye, lass, I know." He had a trick of speaking broad Lancashire to her in a half-formed desire to remind her he had to work for his living and that she hadn't. He said: "At the rate I'm going, I shall soon have to forsake literature and idleness for cotton or bricklaying. I'm not very proud of myself. I made a thousand pounds out of the boom—buying one week and selling a few weeks later. Highway robbery. The very thing I pretend to despise. How do I know I'm not partly responsible for some of the heartbreak and suicides?"

"You only did what commercial and financial men are constantly doing."

"Once I ranked myself a bit higher than that. But I hate that attitude, too—'Lord, I am not as other men.' I daresay, in some ways, I'm worse."

"Then do something!" She spoke sharply. "Why pierce yourself if you're going to do nothing about it?"

"That's it. I want to talk to you about that. There's a

weaving shed for sale. A hundred and fifty looms. They
tried to auction it and nobody would buy it—not a bid. I've
got five hundred pounds left. If I paid that down—half
towards machinery and half for warp and weft and stuff—
I believe I could get enough credit to start it up."

"And then," she broke in, "having bought the machinery
at knock-down prices, you'll be able to undercut your rivals
and make a temporary success till you, also, tumble into
the pit?"

"I should find work for some people for a while," he said
doggedly.

"If it's a matter of conscience," she said, "there's always
the Church and the poor."

"Why are you so opposed—bitter?"

"Harry, if men in the trade all their lives don't know
which way to turn, if concerns are going down like houses
of cards, how are you, inexperienced, with no backing and
the market overrun with men ready to sell for next to nothing,
going to make a success of it?"

"Maybe," he said drily, "since all the experts are failing,
a little thinking unhampered by generations of saying, 'This
can't be done,' and, 'You can't go down that road,' might
achieve something."

"Your bankruptcy twice as fast as the others, that's all."

"There's more profit on weaving now than there was a
year ago—though I grant it's only a quarter of what it was
at the top of the boom."

"What you're thinking of is completely mad." She sat
stretched out in the canvas chair, rubbing the toes of her
shoes together, her chin sunk and her mouth drawn down.

"I daresay you are right. But what if I want to go mad
for a while? All Lancashire's mad. The world, too. Your
father was crazy when he started the Repertory Theatre.
They never do pay in the larger towns—how could one

succeed here? But do you assert he's done nothing? How do you know that in the cheap seats one night there wasn't a child whose mind was set on fire, who didn't go home trembling, to dream of when he would be Will Shakespeare or Henry Irving? How many men have died in the perfecting of X-rays, in the creation of flight? For the explorer who comes home acclaimed, how many bones lie in the wastes? How many Christs must be crucified to save the world? By God, if I were a millionaire I'd spend it all on opening Lancashire factories lying derelict, to prove to a few thousand working folk there was somebody who cared whether they walked the streets or took wages home and were tolerably happy."

He got up from his chair and walked about with long eager, nervous strides, his face pale, his eyes burning.

She didn't speak for a while. Then she said, slowly: "If you ever are, Harry, perhaps we shall have one for you to re-open."

He stopped and turned and smiled at her. "I know," he said, laughing to show he saw the joke.

"I'm not chaffing." Her eyes were wide and serious and her hands loosely clasped in her lap.

He walked about again, treading quietly and his face brooding. He waited for her to speak again.

She said: "When I appealed to father to keep on the Repertory Theatre, he tried to turn it off with banter. When I persisted he said"—she paused there a moment—"he said he couldn't, simply couldn't afford to. I still didn't believe it; I told him old Nat would be in a hole, and that the Websters were going to have a baby. . . . You didn't know that."

"No," he said. Winnie Webster a baby—seventeen years since the last! It seemed incredible.

She answered his thought, smiling. "Winnie told me it

must be because they've been in one 'shop' so long—her insides had time to settle down, she said. But not even the Webster baby moved father."

He said, speaking quietly and easily, to soothe her, "He's quite right, of course. Why *should* he throw his money away? He's given the town a chance, and the company too. If he looked on receiving so little encouragement as an affront —I don't suggest he does—it would be quite understandable. He's travelled far enough to see the outlook is dark. But I don't think you should imagine because he is withdrawing that the Houghton mills—"

"Don't, Harry. I'm not a fool. I know things are serious— so serious that father and I are about the only ones who *do* know." He stood looking down at her, proud that she should be the one to whom her father turned. She looked up quickly. "Do you think I could earn my living working the limes somewhere, and taking the money in the box-office?" She had forced herself to be merry again. She stood up and looked up into his face, her eyes narrowed in laughter.

"We'll go to the seaside and start a pierrot troupe," he said gaily. "Five hundred pounds. It's a fortune. We could run right through the summer if we never took a penny. And we couldn't help drawing half a crown sometimes when it rained or would it be when it was fine? We'd do Shakespeare. 'The Elizabethan Pierrots.' *Macbeth* for stormy days, *Twelfth Night* every other Saturday, and *Midsummer Night's Dream* for June something or other."

They walked back to the court to play. Both of them were quiet again. He said, rolling up his sleeves: "So that was why you were warning me off the weaving shed?"

"Yes. If we go bust I don't see why you should."

"I? I'm *always* broke. But you were nice to be so passionate about it."

"Was I? You'd better serve."

"Yes, you were. Look here, will you help me to manage the weaving shed? Come and do welfare work for the weavers. They'll adore you. Everybody does." Her hand was on top of the net and suddenly he placed his own on hers and held it tight for a second before releasing it.

She frowned and a hurt look came into her eyes. He began to open his mouth to say he was sorry, but somehow he couldn't. He turned and walked to the corner, hitting his leg with the racket, staring at the ground and thinking: "I dunno. Damned if I do. I thought somehow she wanted me to—to show that I . . . Oh, I don't know. I never know where I am with women. I must be a bloody fool. Yes, that must be it."

Chapter Six

MR. JOSHUA MEADOWS was on "the dole." Mr. Meadows
had, indeed, been on the dole for six months; and he showed
no sign of going off it. Josh, for the first time in his life,
was a gentleman. That was how he thought of it; a gentleman. There had been occasions before when, after a drinking bout or a rough and tumble, he had been compelled
to lie up; when, without working or by any other effort
on his part, he had received the wherewithal to sustain himself. And those occasions had taken on something of the
nature of a gentleman's life also. But not quite; not like
this. At those times, had Josh thought of it (though it must
be granted that he never did think of it), he would have
seen that he had no jot or tittle of credit for bringing into
the house the boiled ham at two shillings and fourpence a
pound (Josh was extremely partial to boiled ham) from
which he was wont to make magnificent teas. It was a miracle
into which he did not trouble to inquire. The red, twisted
fingers of his wife, the bent back, the swollen knees, the
furrowed face, the grey, thin hair, the eyes losing their
boldness and courage—these were the price of the miracle,
these and the sort of loyalty few men have ever deserved
and that has yet been vouchsafed to them and as regularly
to scoundrels as to saints. Josh never gave it a thought and
Mrs. Meadows thought but rarely of it either. She had made

her bed and she must lie herself down upon it. But about his part in earning the dole Josh was quite certain. It was paid to him for what he had contributed in the past; he was richly and justly entitled to it; he drew it in person and he spent it as he thought fit. And why not? He was a worthy citizen whom the nation recognized as such, and he was, as it were, pensioned off; he had retired. That was how Josh thought of it—retired. The amount might well have been more—twenty-seven shillings was not a fortune with four mouths to feed. He expressed himself forcibly about that. Skinny, he said it was. But as he had never reckoned to give his wife more than a pound a week when he was working full-time, and he now reduced that sum to fifteen shillings (for she couldn't expect to draw as much as she did before, could she? "Fair do's all round," was Josh's motto) he had twelve shillings a week for himself. And in 1927 you could buy a considerable amount of mild beer, and fly a goodly number of pigeons, and back a fair number of winners and even more losers with that sum, provided you operated in shillings or sixpences or, at times when the exchequer was at its lowest, in threepences, or even three-ha'pences. On one occasion Josh worked out a plan of action which began with: "Three-ha'pence each way Comet—if cash, all on Shooting Star, any to come on Man in the Moon" (devoting himself that day to horses in six successive races that were constellations before the races, if not afterwards) that would, had he succeeded, have kept him in luxuries for six months. He did not succeed, but nobody could assert he had not gambled with courage or enjoyed a run for his money. He had spent the whole morning on working it out in his shirt-sleeves with a stump of well-wetted pencil and sheets torn from young Richard's exercise-book, and he finished so fatigued that he had borrowed a shilling from Mrs. Meadows to revive himself with at the Three Jolly

Carters. For a chap deserved his 'lowance after working like that, didn't he?

Josh could never see what men on the dole had to growl about; apart, that is, from the smallness of the sum. He heard them complaining about having to queue up for it. Some of the Bolshies said it was degrading. Degrading! He didn't find it so. He usually went along with Wilf Berry and he and Wilf were always in a state of some excitement at the prospect of having money in their pockets again. They knew a lot of men in the queue, they could smoke and exchange the latest stories and gossip from the course besides Burnham United's football prospects and who had been fined for being drunk last Monday morning. They could argue about who was the best starter of a whippet, whether Young Murphy was worth backing when he jumped Butcher Redfern with weights for ten pounds, and inquire was any wrestler to-day in the same class as Hackenschmidt used to be? When they had drawn their money they naturally had to wet their whistles at the Three Jolly Carters, and Josh, becoming skittish, would indulge in a revival of the old joke at Wilf's expense, saying: "Tha needn't look so black, Berry, it's nobbut my whim, Berry, didta hear that rasp, Berry?" until the vault resounded with playful shouts: "'Owd their jackets! Let 'em get at one another," as Josh and Wilf began pushing one another about. But the cronies never fought seriously so soon after drawing the dole. Wednesday or Thursday, by which days it had all vanished, was time enough for that.

Higginbottom's pit which had employed both of them turned out little but "steam coal"—coal used in boiler fires, and half the boiler fires that had burned it, were drawn and cold. And the prospects of either of them returning to Higginbottom's looked remote. Josh had, it is true, been offered a job through the Labour Exchange as a navvy but he had refused it with scorn and also with a strange feeling in his knees. After five months as a gentleman, using a shovel—or a pick at the coal-face, either—didn't attract him at all. Still, he was a Higginbottom chap and if Higginbottom's started him again, he reckoned he'd go and draw his lamp and pick, he would an' all. Till then, he'd just go on standin' it—this bein' out o' wark. "We had to stick it in t' trenches, an' this is just t' same," he said to his wife. "An' it's up to us to mak' t' best on it. Aye. Con tha lend us a tanner?" And with that sixpence he would go, with a parting: "We mun keep us hearts up, tha knows."

When Mrs. Meadows turned it over in her mind, Josh's being on the dole worried her mainly because he was hanging about the house too much. At first he got up almost at his usual time for going to work and, with no work to go to, spent a long time over his breakfast and "made a bigger 'wakes' than usual" of what food there was. Those hours from six in the morning until nine or ten when he went out, were dreadful for her. He roamed about the house, padding about in his stockinged feet, his trousers turned over at the top, his waistcoat flapping open, his shirt-neck loose, unshaved and often without a wash. He was a vigorous man, wanting his meals and his tobacco and his wife; and since she no longer had any attraction for him, his energy found an outlet in temper and shouted songs and boisterous, ribald talk to the children, talk which made her shudder. After the first month or two he would lie long abed in the mornings, not rising till ten or eleven, knocking on the floor for her to take his breakfast to him. On mornings when she went out washing, she had to wake him and coax him to eat before she departed, or he would roll over and drowse off to sleep, leaving the tea to go stone cold and the bit of bacon to congeal. And she couldn't afford for that to happen because when it did he would start afresh in her absence and make tea again and cook whatever he could lay his hands on. That a man in his senses could be so improvident was almost past belief, but it was so. Josh honestly thought when he had handed over his fifteen shillings, that his part of the bargain was complete. Whatever food was to be had was fair game. He almost regarded her as an enemy to be despoiled. He would search the house, looking for eggs and sausages and consume them without compunction. If Wilf came in during the morning when she was out washing, Josh would say at once: "Wilt 'ave a cup o' tay, owd ship?" Wilf would shamefacedly answer: "Nay, Josh, nay, tha knows thy missis wouldn't like it." "Missis?" Josh would shout. "Here, 'oo the hell dost think's mester i' this house? Do I look as if I had t' breeches on? Missis be —— ." So her life was purgatory. Trix's success in London—for it was as if she had become Queen of England, looked at from 17 Walker Street—made life worse. "When's that dowter o' mine goin' to send us summat?" Josh would ask. At first Mrs. Meadows had said: "She's no daughter o' yore's—dunnot pretend," but he had cursed and sworn at that; hadn't she been under his roof for long enough, hadn't he put up with sneers and back chat because of her? And now—by the mon, hadn't he allus said she were a slut—and a mean 'un at that—livin' wi' Hilditch and wi'out the decency to send a bit o' brass to her father on t' dole?

His wife had grown quiet under these successive storms. She no longer replied to him. Her strength was gone. She had none for quarrelling; she had not enough to do her housework and get the children's meals (her own were often eaten standing up at the table, taking a bite with one hand and combing a head or pouring out tea with the other) and to earn the fifteen shillings a week without which they couldn't live. She had worked it all out—thirty shillings, subtract eight for rent leaves twenty-two; subtract two and six for coal and light leaves nineteen and six, put a shilling by for wakes, clubs, and insurances, and another shilling for clogs and breeches, leaves seventeen and six. Now, four people with three meals a day is eighty-four meals a week (young Richard had worked that out on his slate); seventeen and six divided by that comes to just over tuppence a meal. And not even Walker Street, with its knack of buying bacon bits and subsisting on faggots and peas, and stewing a scrag-end of mutton, could live well on twopence a meal. And Josh had to have his egg and bit of bacon and occasional sausage; and Josh could only have them if she had nothing but bread and tea. And on that, coupled with an odd meal given to her at houses where she washed or scrubbed, she lived. The endurance of the human body is amazing. She may be said to have lived on tea. Sometimes she had nine cups a day. She was a veritable Dr. Johnson. But though Josh's being about the house and swearing in front of the children frayed her nerves and seared her heart, the starving of herself and the working of herself to death she took as a matter of course.

She suffered so many pains—pains from wind and indigestion, pains at her heart, pains in her legs, pains at the bottom of her back, pains behind her eyes, that she was never at peace. She had ceased to know what peace was; she had almost forgotten what it had ever been like. But for some weeks now she had had another pain—a burning, gnawing pain at her breast, as though a mouse were inside, eating it. She didn't know why that idea came into her head, but she hated mice and the thought was the worst she could imagine; and that was right, because this was the worst pain she had ever known. One day when she was washing the clothes at Dr. O'Rourke's she fainted. That led to his examining her and ordering her to bed. She couldn't go to bed, she said.

She smiled at him. Her sort of folk didn't go bed. She was gentle with him and explained why it was impossible. She spoke to him as though he had been one of her children. He put her in his car and took her off to the Chesterford Royal Hospital and there she was X-rayed. It was as he thought. Cancer; and far gone.

Mrs. Meadows went home. When Josh arrived he was sober; for it was a Thursday and the dole wasn't drawn until Friday. She had been home but a few minutes; the fire was out. Josh was displeased. "Been out to tea, has tha?" he asked satirically. "We're comin' to summat if a chap has to come whoam to a cowd grate like this here. By Christ! Well, why doesn't shape an' get it made agen? Tha's not forgotten how, hasta?"

He stood watching her. He was thinking how ill-used he was to be wedded to her. Her lips were pale and blackened from the condition of her stomach, her hands all bone and veins, her bosom and hips almost vanished. The house was cold and he kept his cap on and his scarf round his neck and he stood motionless waiting for her to begin to make the fire. But she didn't begin. She sat at the table and suddenly, and quietly, she laid her arms across it and put her face sideways on the worn oilcloth and lay there without moving. He watched her for a minute or two; and he didn't like the look of it. Had she dropped off to sleep? She hadn't—nay, she couldn't—

He went to her and leaned over her, and his momentary fear vanished. She wasn't asleep. Her eyes were open, but they didn't blink; they were as the eyes of a painting; as still as that.

"What's the matter?" he asked. "Done up?" For the first time for a long while there was a touch of warmth in his voice. After all, he had been frightened.

"Summat's the matter wi' me, Josh. I'm that sorry." She

raised herself slowly and looked sadly at him.

"The matter wi' thee?"

She nodded.

"Tha'rt just done up—tha'll be aw reet."

She shook her head.

"I've got cancer—here." She touched her right breast timidly as if it no longer belonged to her.

"Who sez?" His voice was growing angry.

"I've been to th' hospital."

" 'Ospital? Why—what didta go theer for?"

"Dr. O'Rourke took me. I fainted."

"Cancer? I don't bloody-well believe it. They're allus wrong. I read in t' papper t'other day . . ."

"I've got it, Josh. An' I shan't get better. I know. It's no good thi carryin' on, lad." She was talking to him as she had talked to Dr. O'Rourke, with the ascendancy of those who can look already into the Gate of Death.

Josh knew it was true. And over and above his horror he was filled with fury. By the mon, but this was the rottenest bit o' luck a chap ever had. By God! but he'd been chetted —allus been chetted. Who the hell 'ud look after him and t' childer? Who'd do all th' housework? He'd never be able to afford t'ave it done. That's what a wife were for, wasn't it? And now, by God! he'd been chetted. By the mon . . .

Richard's shrill treble voice was heard outside and the clatter of his clogs. Mrs. Meadows pushed herself up from the table.

"Tha winna tell t' childer," she said. It was a command. Josh looked at her and said nothing, and turned away.

She slowly got down on her knees and began to rake out the ashes.

Chapter Seven

Mrs. Elizabeth Hargreaves put on her best bonnet and her diamond ring and put in her Sunday set of false teeth. She looked at herself in the hallstand mirror. Her eyes sparkled and her cheeks were rosy and still rounded. She thought: "Luke might ha' done worse, for all we've had no childer as lived." She drew her lips back and examined her teeth and thought there wasn't a finer set in Chesterford, not even Phœbe Houghton's. It wasn't the amount o' brass you had but how you spent it and what you got for it that counted. She wondered what Mrs. Houghton wanted to see her for. The note on that stiff ivory-coloured gold-edged little card had just said: "I should be so glad if you would come to tea one day. Would Thursday suit—four-fifteen? My love to you both, Phœbe Houghton." Mrs. Hargreaves thought those cards were admirable; a fine way of getting out of saying much. She must get some, though she didn't think she'd have them gilt-edged. No. She had told Luke to ring up from the mill and say she'd be very glad to go. She knew that would make Luke think more than once. He'd been very secretive lately, him and Mr. Edward. They'd something up their sleeves she was sure. Well, two could play at that. So she was rare and delighted, as she admitted to herself, when the invitation came. Luke had asked: "What does she want to see you for?" And she had replied: "Never thee mind. Folk know their own know best," and had twiddled his hair in her fingers and made it stand up like a cockatoo. "What were you sayin' in your sleep last night?" she asked him.

"Couldn't yo' make it out?"

"That I couldn't. You were chunnering like mad, givin' yourself away I'll be bound—and I couldn't make out a word of it. Very disappointing."

Luke had sighed. "I'll bet I were writin' champion poetry," he said. "I often do—I rhyme like one o'clock—and I can never remember a word when I wake up. Yo' really ought to listen better and get a bit o' paper and write it down."

You didn't get much out of Luke, she reflected. He was one of those who heard all and said nowt. Must be Yorkshire blood in him somewhere. She wished he had had more devil in him; they might have had another child then and it might have lived.

Phœbe Houghton didn't send for her unless there was summat up. No doubt it had to do with Mr. Edward and Luke. And the factory. There was a lot of short-time flying about—Houghton's Bluebell mill was on thirty-two hours a week, and if it were on sixteen, Luke said, they would have a job to sell the stuff. Luke had never been in favour of short-time but he could see nothing else for it now. "T' world," he said, "is standin' on its head, and wonderin' why things look so damn' funny." For her own part she wasn't worrying. Elizabeth Hargreaves had never minded a bit of excitement. She often said to Luke: "We're living in quare times, Luke, what wi' the war and that, and we must expect quare things to happen." To which Luke replied: "Tha'll not be disappointed—not by a long chalk."

As she rode in the tram she remembered she had forgotten to use her lavender-water. She liked to put some on her handkerchief and on her hair and inside her bodice.

She was a little put out. She was a particular woman and she enjoyed being at her best. A little scent gave her a feeling of well-being; she held her own better with that faint aroma rising to her nostrils. The tram conductor didn't catch what she said and she spoke sharply to him. She wouldn't have done that had she not forgotten her lavender-water.

" 'Ilford Lane," shouted the conductor, and she got up— but not hurriedly. Mrs. Hargreaves never allowed herself to be hurried. "You make nothing but mistakes in a hurry," she said. She walked up Hilford Lane, her silk dress rustling, her gold ear-rings catching the late September sun, her fine eyes, the colour of a horse chestnut, observing the leaves beginning to turn, her Roman nose enjoying the wind and the smell of earth after rain, and her body gradually becoming too warm—and she bitterly regretted the lavender-water. She experienced that slight feeling of excitement mixed with discomfort that is common with those about to plunge into a social scale which is not their own; it is akin to stage-fright and the sensation that aldermen have when about to be introduced to the King. Mrs. Hargreaves wouldn't have willingly missed it, she wouldn't have forgone the thrill although it gave her a little palpitation and sometimes moved her bowels at inopportune moments.

A smart blue and silver motor-car stood in the drive— had been at the door and drawn away waiting. She hoped nobody else had come to tea. An ordinary polite tea-table conversation after all she had been thinking about? No, she couldn't believe that. As she entered the hall, Philip and Evelyn came downstairs and went into the music-room. They were too far off to shake hands—and that was a relief because she never was quite at home with either of them. But she had no time to do more than think how pretty Evelyn was looking—although a trifle pale—and that she was even more stately than before—the added dignity and

assurance of being married, she supposed—before Phœbe
came out, radiant but a little fussed, she thought. Phœbe's
pale-gold hair was like an aureole about her head, her eyes
looked larger than ever and she was wearing a blue silk
dress that lent them a deeper colour. Elizabeth Hargreaves
looked at her searchingly, and felt no qualm in doing so.
She had come as a warm friend and the more she knew the
better her advice would be. Phœbe kissed her on the cheek
and asked her how she was with a depth in her voice as
though Phœbe's whole life depended on the answer, and
then having told Mrs. Hargreaves how well she was looking,
took her upstairs. Mrs. Hargreaves wondered whether all
the grand visitors went upstairs also, or whether it was only
because that was the custom in smaller houses and Phœbe
knew it, and wanted her to feel comfortable. However, she
appreciated it. In Phœbe's room she took her things off and
tidied her hair and breathed on her diamond ring and rubbed
it. Evelyn was playing the piano when they came down,
the music coming from behind the closed thick door, faintly
—a Brahms waltz that had a tinge of sadness under all
its bouncing gaiety—Luke had a gramophone record of
it. Somehow the tune fitted the day—an assumption that
everything was merry, and yet, that indefinable doubt and
fear. Phœbe offered her a cigarette from a silver box. "You
know Philip and Evelyn have called? They often run over
in the afternoons. She's looking so pretty. Marriage agrees
with her—she's a darling. I've grown so fond of her."
And into Phœbe's translucent eyes there shot for a second
a look which said: "I hope things are not going to be too
awful for her—or for me."

Nothing of more significance was said until Phœbe had
poured out the tea. Then: "Have you been to the theatre?"

"I thought I'd go on Saturday. The last night. There'll
be speeches, won't there?" Mrs. Hargreaves loved a speech.

"Edward says we ought to be there. I shall feel as if I were attending a funeral, though. Thespis buried once again."

Whereupon Elizabeth made a bold speech. She said, looking Phœbe in the eye: "Is the Rep's goin' like a shaft of smoke in t' wind?"

Phœbe put down her cup, and sank back in her chair. "Thank you, Elizabeth, for making it easy. I've no right to ask you and you must choose whether you tell me but—does Luke say anything about the mill? Edward used to when business was good. Lately, no. I suppose I've always taken things for granted. Edward used to chaff me with—

> *Thine not to reason why—*
> *Only to take and buy.*

He would laugh about it. He hardly ever laughs now. He's taken to spending evenings at the mill. Has Luke?"

"Yea. I told Luke they are like a pair o' lads playin' together. He says they're experimentin' wi' a new automatic loom. An' I wish it were true."

"Ah!" Phœbe breathed it with extreme gentleness and control; she might have been emitting it by a lever. She said: "What do you think they're doing?" and sat forward on the edge of her chair.

"Tryin' to make two and two into five. Lookin' for the bottom to the cotton trade. Nobody knows where it's dropped to. I think it's half way to Australia. But you're not *really* worryin', are you?" And a comfortable, cheerful smile enveloped Mrs. Hargreaves's rosy face. It did Phœbe good to see it. "A very present help in time of trouble." The line ran through her head. She leaned forward and placed her long fine hand on Elizabeth's chubby one. "You're a dear thing," she said.

"Nay, nay. Nowt o' t' sort. Only—if you've done nothin' amiss, I don't see much to be frightened of. Supposin' the worst happens—an' we lose our bit o' brass and yo' lose yore tidy bit? We'st get a livin', shanna we? I've always had an idea o' keepin' a boardin'-house at Bournemouth."

"And Edward and I?"

"I reckon you'd have to keep a swagger hotel. You'd have the Prince o' Wales stoppin' there in no time. Yo' know, there must be lots o' lovelier places than Chesterford to spend your days in. I sometimes think we're daft. Th' Almighty intended us all to keep pigs—yo' know what I mean. A ploughman's team comin' o'er t' sky-line, an' a boat on a sleepy canal, an' t' sea goin' back an' leavin' bits o' pools wi' flukes the size o' postage stamps, an' plenty o' sunshine. God very near left t' sunshine out when He made Chesterford. What I mean is, we're all missin' summat. We might lose what we've got and find a great deal more."

"You're an adventurer, Elizabeth."

"Happen I am." Mrs. Hargreaves was tickled by that. She was a trifle flushed by the way she had been letting herself go. She felt like a preacher. "After all," she said, consciously coming downstairs a few steps, "Houghton's isn't goin' to come under t' hammer. You never re-floated; your overheads are reasonable. Short o' chuckin' it away— gamblin' an' that—I don't see anythin' desperate can happen." But Phœbe said nothing. "Well, do *you*?" Mrs. Hargreaves asked because she wanted a reply. And when Phœbe got up and walked to the window and didn't answer, Elizabeth experienced a catch at her heart. She stirred her tea, although she knew it didn't need stirring, and she drank it. It was cold and nasty and she pulled a face. The outlook was suddenly depressing.

Phœbe turned. "Do you know anything about Hilditch?" she asked.

"I believe there's plenty o' young Hilditches scattered about ca'ed by other names—an' they say none of 'em are hard up. Luke ca's him a Communist on his own account. Are you scared on him?"

"What you said about gambling, that's all. Edward goes up to London a good deal. Does Luke go too?"

"No. *I* go to London when Luke goes. Men don't stop bein' men when they get married. Don't think I'm doubtin' Luke. Only—" And she smoothed her skirt on her lap. "Yo' think Mr. Edward goes wi' Hilditch?"

"I'm sure he does sometimes."

"But Hilditch was a partner in the Repertory Theatre, wasn't he? So it's natural, isn't it? Mr. Edward would never get mixed up i' Hilditch's bucket-shop companies."

Again Phœbe didn't answer and Mrs. Hargreaves hurried on, trying to thrust the doubt from her mind. "I met a young woman yesterday who said she'd seen an advertisement—'Debts purchased.' She said she was going to sell hers—if they gave her twenty per cent she'd be really well off." They both laughed but the laughter was constrained and they both stopped suddenly—and were glad to stop—when the front door opened and closed and Edward's footsteps and voice were heard in the hall. He went to the music-room and the piano-playing stopped.

Mrs. Hargreaves felt ill at ease, and she was sure Phœbe did also. Were Mr. Edward's ears burning? She and Phœbe were a pair of conspirators. She didn't know what to talk about. She had never felt more uncomfortable in her life. She asked: "Are the horses doing well?" Was that the way you asked after racehorses, she wondered? It sounded funny—as if they were a litter of pups. Phœbe said: "I sold them a month ago. I thought everybody knew." She began to speak about them rapidly—it was awkward having them at Newmarket, but a great delight to see them at the

morning gallops—to turn out when the grass was wet with
dew and see the strings of horses in their cloths parading so
delicately to the heath; and then to stand with the trainer
and watch them breasting the rise, galloping, pounding,
their hoofs cutting the turf and sending it flying and the
little men—like boys with old men's faces—sitting almost on
their necks, caps back to front, and now the trainer would
be racing after them shouting, "Ease off! Ease off!" Then
he would come back and say that Jack o' Lantern was the
best of them and he thought he might do well in the Cam-
bridgeshire; and after that you went back to breakfast,
feeling as though you owned all the world.

High voices could be heard from the music-room and
Mrs. Hargreaves would have given a great deal to be on
the tram going home. Phœbe went on: "A strange thing
is that nobody ever finds a racehorse asleep. Whenever the
stable-boy goes, the horse's eyes are open, although of course
the horse *must* sleep some time." Footsteps came heavily
across the hall and the door of the drawing-room was opened
with a jerk and Edward strode in, saw Mrs. Hargreaves
and stopped. He stared at them, and said, after a moment
that seemed necessary for him to recognise who they were:
"I beg your pardon, my dear. How d'you do, Mrs. Hargreaves?" and without waiting for a reply, turned about
and closed the door. Mrs. Hargreaves thought she had never
seen a man look more upset—his cheeks lined, his mouth
so compressed and drawn down that the corners nearly
reached to his jawbone, his eyes burning and yet unseeing.
She had risen to her feet and stood, not knowing what to
say or what to do. Both women were listening acutely—
disguise was over. They heard Edward's steps ascend the
stairs and then Philip's voice calling: "You won't make it
ten thousand, then?" And Edward's answer, bitten off and
harsh so that Phœbe thought, for the first time in her life,

it could be mistaken for that of his brother, the judge. Edward said: "Certainly not"—no more than that—but there was anguish and fury in it. Philip cried back: "I'm sorry if I'm asking more patrimony than the firm can stand"; and then Mrs. Hargreaves heard him laugh. She never wanted to hear it again. She told Luke afterwards it was like the chink of checks from the Co-operative Stores— or else bad money. Philip went back to his wife and Edward continued upstairs, and she, Elizabeth Hargreaves, turned to Phœbe. Phœbe was lying back in her chair, her head on one side, her eyes closed and tears welling from under her eyelids and rolling unheeded down her cheek and on to her silk dress. Mrs. Hargreaves knelt beside her, patting her arm and putting her own face against Phœbe's as though Phœbe had been a child that is hurt. She stayed a long while like that and when at last she let herself out she walked very quietly as if it were a stricken house she was leaving. She didn't put her feet down firmly nor breathe really deeply till she was half way down Hilford Lane.

Chapter Eight

THE LIVES OF MANY MEN do not become truly adventurous or entangled or exciting or tragic until they reach the age of forty or beyond. Sometimes it is that their contentment with their work vanishes—the work becomes odious or unsatisfying; sometimes they fall in love for the first, second or third time, welcoming the passion with a somewhat pitiable eagerness because they believe this is the last occasion in their lives (though they are often wrong there), that this tempestuous emotion will fill their bones. Sometimes they begin to look on themselves as no more than machines for earning money to keep body and soul and the bodies and souls of their families or relatives together, and against this toiling for money that runs out of their fingers almost faster than they can seize upon it, leaving them nothing with which to purchase joy now or security for the future, they revolt. Sometimes the reason is none of these; sometimes all are combined. But whatever the cause—sex, gambling, or failure in business—the life which has been running as straight as a road now becomes as a hillside path, faint or confused or lost altogether. Such a man had Edward Houghton now become; and by divers strokes of fortune, wherein the boom, the slump and Timothy Hilditch were involved. How could he trace his downfall? Must he attribute it to his love for the theatre? Would he, otherwise, have known Hilditch well enough to become a party to his financial exploits? Must he attribute his losses to his sober life heretofore that caused him to wish to live dangerously now? Or must he say: "I am the victim of a state of trade that I have done nothing to bring about—a condition of affairs that the Great War and resultant world chaos, with its over-production, ill-advised rushing for materials by those unable to pay for what they sought, a sort of over-eating by a starving man who thereby destroys himself—have of themselves inevitably created?" Must he excuse himself by asking: "Am I not one of scores? Are not bankruptcies as commonplace as mourners at a funeral? Why should I be permitted to escape?" All these thoughts chased one another through his mind—and so often that they almost assumed a regular order—but they afforded him no more satisfaction than is usually gained by a normally truthful man who cloaks his actions with lies. For there had been a time when having lost fifty thousand pounds he might have stopped; and he had not had enough purpose in him to let the money go and count himself fortunate it was no more. He had halted for a space, and then redoubled his speed, pursuing Hilditch—who rose after his every financial crash and espied a still more entrancing prize ahead.

Houghton was a lonely man; affectionate, shy and with a tendency to *hauteur* when he remembered who he was and what responsibility he bore; doubly difficult therefore to relieve of the weight that had increasingly been laid on him. He had no close friends; his brother, Sir John, was too cold and logical and far-seeing and a little contemptuous of trade; Phœbe he never regarded as having a head for troublesome matters and, besides, it was his duty to steer her clear of them; Philip since his marriage had not even professed an interest in the concern. With what sum could he take his departure from Chesterford—that was Philip's problem on which Edward had steadily turned a discouraging eye, first because he believed Philip needed work to hold him to moderation and latterly for the added reason that he dared not confess to Philip how little money could, with safety to the Houghton mills, be given him.

If Edward had ever been told that he could, month upon month and year upon year, have gone on, bearing the load of worry that was his, keeping his own counsel (except for momentary confidences with Mary to whom he had turned and in some infinitely small degree bared his doubts and unhappiness), he would have said: "No, I should break down beneath it." But he had not broken down; not yet. His sleep had been poor; he had gone to bed exhausted, so that for four or five hours he slept feveredly but without waking. Then he would rouse with a start and with a sensation of evil hanging over him, pierced by dismay and fear and, although he knew he would sleep no more, filled with a strong desire to maintain solitude and hide himself. There had been mornings lately when he had awoken and not known for a second or two where he was or who he was. At that emptiness of mind, fear had gripped him and turned him cold, his soul fainting within him until by a frenzied, powerful effort he had become himself, knowing again who he was and where he lay. He had thought of visiting his doctor but held back; to be ordered from Chesterford was out of the question; so was rest or freedom from anxiety. Throughout this period he kept Luke Hargreaves at a distance. Hargreaves knew how desperately hit the mills were but Edward replied drily, when Hargreaves spoke of it, that there were plenty in lower water. Hargreaves would say: "Why don't you attend the amalgamation meeting and speak your mind? This undercuttin'—they might as well cut our throats as our prices—it's the same thing in t' long run." And Edward had gone. He didn't enjoy it much. A large room in Burnham Exchange, pipes and cigars, baggy suits, florid faces, a good deal of looking at their sheets of blotting-paper and a good deal of prodding the table with pens, some plain talk about selling below cost (to a chorus of half-hearted "Ayes" and "Hear-hears") and a scene between the chairman and Thomas Blackburn during which Blackburn had said: "Aye, Mr. Chairman, and there's them as say some of the leading folk i' this very organisation can't be looked on like Cæsar's wife." The chairman, James Kent—sixty-odd, a mop of white hair, a black satin tie with a diamond pin, and port-wine cheeks that sagged over his stiff collar—had said sharply: "Names, Mr. Blackburn, names—I can have no vague imputations here."

Blackburn swayed to and fro a moment thinking; then he said, but he didn't look at Kent: "Are yo' prepared to support a resolution that all members' books be examined, Mr. Chairman?" There was uproar at that. Kent on his feet, his cheeks growing a deeper colour, saying: "This is an insult to everybody"—Blackburn running his tongue round his upper lip and screwing up his eyes, as he looked sideways to the top of the table, amid cries of: "Withdraw that!"—"Apologise!" and "Nay, Tom, you can't say that sort o' thing." Men whose own deals were suspect shook heads with assumed virtue and muttered that this was too thick, the darned limit, who ever heard o' such a thing? Blackburn, still on his feet, asked them if they pretended then that *nobody* had ratted from the agreements they had made not to sell below cost and would they consent to the amalgamation appointing an auditor to examine books over the past month? More uproar then, cries of: "What are we? A gang o' criminals?"—"We've summat else to do." As the tumult subsided, Edward had risen. He deprecated the insinuations but in so far as under-selling threatened to ruin them all, Mr. Blackburn was right to draw attention once more to it. Wasn't it plain that Lancashire was faced with a new set of circumstances—competitors abroad in Japan, Italy, India and elsewhere who were working mills during far longer hours, at wages a quarter and sometimes an eighth of what they themselves were paying—India both boycotting them and making her own goods to an ever-increasing degree, China ravaged by civil war, cotton goods throughout all markets being displaced to some degree on the one hand by fancier materials such as artificial silk, and on the other by coarser and cheaper ones manufactured by inferior types of labour abroad? No longer would the world come running with outstretched hands for anything they in Burnham cared to sell. He wasn't sure that there were not too many mills in Lancashire—not sure that a fire which consumed a hundred or two factories overnight would not be a blessing (shouts of, "Nay, nay!"—"Don't be so downhearted!"—"Aye, they can have mine any time!"—"Let the Jews get busy!"—"What price insurance?"). What, at all events, was beyond doubt was that the gambling in raw cotton at New Orleans and Liverpool, and the solid amalgamations with high charges on the bleaching, dyeing and finishing sides of the trade, were making the fight all the harder for individual firms of spinners and manufacturers. What did they propose to do? Put their house in order, or ask the Government to do it for them? He saw nothing for it but the closing of redundant mills and the prevention of the selling abroad at scrap prices of derelict machinery. It was happening now and hastening them along the road to bankruptcy.

The meeting heard him glumly. Men sucked their pipes and thought: "What's the use of telling us what we know? There's far too many doctors for the trade—both in Lancashire and outside it. Things'll come right—business is

bad everywhere. All very well talking about putting our
house in order—how's it goin' to be done, and who by?"
Edward went on: "I've no doubt you are more concerned
with where the hard cash for this week's wages is coming
from, than with thinking of the future. But the future comes
swiftly—and it's there that prosperity or *débâcle* lies. And
remember that wrapped up with us is the livelihood of half
a million workmen and workwomen. If we go down, they
sink also. We are thinking—some of us—of automatic
looms, or of looms that can be worked six and eight to a
weaver instead of three or four. Are we giving thought to
what is going to become of the labour displaced? We've got
a responsibility for it, as we have for the men standing at
street corners, wearing out their shoe-leather looking for
work, nothing in their pockets and not much more in their
stomachs."

Kent rose. Was it a political meeting they were holding?
Mr. Houghton was a bit of an idealist—they all knew that.
They admired him for it—but there was no room for ideals
in business—not in cotton to-day, anyhow. The best way
to consider the work-people was to think of themselves first
—if they made money the work-people got their share.
("Aye, that's right"—"That's horse sense, that is"—"Too
much damned Socialism bein' talked these days.") Kent
continued: The spinners wanted higher wages but did they
ever consider where they were to come from? They scoffed
at dividends—didn't think anybody was entitled to any.
Let the employers keep a firm hand or before they knew
where they were the trade unions would be running the
show, and a fine mess they would make of it. ("They would
an' all.")

So the meeting went on until it was time to catch trains;
and they dispersed having done nothing. A long-winded
barren statement was issued to the waiting Pressmen saying

the amalgamation had had before it matters relating to working hours, selling prices and other important subjects and had given them all its careful consideration and would resume discussion of them in a fortnight's time. Edward, leaving in a crush of flapping overcoats, and "Good nights" and "Coming my ways?" heard a reporter say satirically: "That's about as illuminating as the Town Hall clock on a foggy night, isn't it? It'll buck up our readers who're on the dole, I don't think"; and his companion: "Hush, lad. You've got to be secretive when you've got neither ideas nor loyalty." And Edward looked neither to right nor left and was relieved to enter Duke Street and gain the heavy comfort and still heavier quietness of the Liberal Club. That was the last meeting of the amalgamation he had attended. It was plain nothing was to be hoped for from there, but he didn't withdraw. When reductions of hours were recommended, those at the Houghton mills were reduced. When appeals were made to observe the fixed selling prices drawn up, Edward abided by them; to his heavy cost often enough. Despairing at the growing burden of business losses he had risked a great deal, trusted to Hilditch's fortune and *flair,* staked his judgment—or Hilditch's judgment—on cotton "futures." He had begun to visit the mills during the evening, largely to escape the soft questioning eyes of Phœbe and Mary. It was agony for him to be besought to take rest and holiday and to have them fussing round him and showing him their love. He felt he had betrayed them. As he sat in his office at nights, going over figures of costing and sales, of stock, of building and machinery, hoping to find some rich asset he had failed to note before, startled by any unwonted sound, listening to the gurgle of water in the mill lodge as it ran over the weir, hearing the watchman's footsteps padding round the corridors, walking sometimes to the boiler hole to have a word with old Sandy Craig who kept the fire going, he was never able entirely to rid his mind of the thought of how heavily the disgrace would lie on him if ever he had to part with the business. That didn't loom very near yet but if his last speculation on Hilditch's advice—the buying of oil shares which Hilditch said he would force up from five and sevenpence to over a pound—failed, he didn't know what would happen. The fact that 'Change gossip said nearly two hundred mills were in the hands of the banks didn't comfort him. The thought of it brought his own desperate position more vividly before his face.

.   .   .   .

After answering Philip's shouted question Edward had gone upstairs to his study and had closed the door and locked it. He sat down at his desk, laid his forearms along the top, his hands loosely clasped so that the touch of the fingers of one hand in those of the other might give him comfort, and laid his forehead down on them. He was trembling. His heart was beating intolerably fast; it felt too big for his chest and the shell of his ribs seemed too frail for the tumult within him. He got up and went to his deep armchair and lay back and crossed one leg over the other— to hold himself together, as it were. He was longing for the touch of another friendly human being but he must, he saw, do without it. He was Houghton, head of the Houghton Manufacturing Co. Ltd., the oldest concern in Chesterford, and one of the best-known in Lancashire. His son Philip had gone nearer to insulting him than any man had ever done, and he was as shaken as an old tree by a storm. He had thought as a young man that age would give added strength and domination and courage. That didn't seem to be true. Men were Prime Ministers and Judges at seventy

and over. Why wasn't he strong as they were? He was no
more than sixty-seven. The room was cold and he switched
on the electric fire and placed it near his chair. The warmth
penetrated him but he felt he would like to be in bed with
blankets and a hot water bottle. He smiled at that; he must
be getting extremely old—or was he only tired and feeling
sorry for himself? He held out his hands to the fire and
warmed them, and smoothed his forehead and stroked his
eyes with his fingers. He stood up, walked to the door and
unlocked it. Was he as Prospero then, that his every third
thought should be of the grave or ruin? Hanging, it was
said, was the worst use a man could be put to—and worry,
he adjudged, was a good second. What did Lear say? "The
tempest in my mind doth from my senses take all feeling
else save what beats there." The tempest in his mind—
that was well said. Edward stared about him. A shiver
ran over him again. Philip would be gone by this time;
he hoped so. That was despicable too, hesitating to go
down to his wife because he thought he might encounter
his son. "The thief doth fear each bush an officer." Edward
strode to the door and marched firmly down the stairs.
But the noise of his tread came to him as from a distance;
and suddenly his head grew very light and began to swim,
and he gripped hold of the banister and with an immense
effort lowered himself down till he sat on the stairs. Then
he bent his head between his knees and sat thus, confusedly
hoping that no one would come upon him. He sat like that
for a few minutes till the blood had run to his head and
strengthened him. Then he got up and holding a little
tremulously to the banister climbed back to the landing and
so to his room. He pressed the bell and sat down rather
heavily in his chair but by the time the bell was answered
he succeeded in asking quite firmly for a stiff whisky and
soda. Nothing amiss was noticed. He was glad of that.

Another line began to run unbidden through his head: "For you and I, our dancing days are over." He sipped his whisky. He didn't like quotations chasing, unsought, through his mind. It was disturbing.

Chapter Nine

WHEN SAM RENSHAW was treated to half a pint of mixed beer in the Black Bull he would say, making a joke of his misfortunes, that he had tumbled so far he felt as if he had a pair o' broken legs. That was when they had left The Rookery and had gone to live in a back-to-back house in Klondyke Street. Sam would laugh over that, too. Klondyke Street! Round the corner was Paradise Row and not far off, Angel Meadow. "Tha'd think comin' down in t' world took thee to Heaven, wouldn' tha?" he said to Harriet. "I've noticed afore as slums allus have names like these here. T' chaps as built these places must have bin religious." For a while it was as if he had been exalted by his "come down" as he called it. He was akin to men coming out of an anæsthetic, or those who have endured a grave wound: he couldn't feel it—not yet. Sam was gifted with imagination and he couldn't help being excited and having his mind titillated by all he had gone through. The being "sold-up" for instance. No, they hadn't had the brokers in, but it was obvious a back-to-back house wouldn't hold their red plush suite, and the piano, and gramophone, and five beds. That was how Sam put it to his cronies. But they said: "He stopped theer so long he hadn't t' price of a gill. But Renshaw allus were a dam' numbyed." There had been an auction—men coming in pasting numbers on the furniture,

315

or at least the major part of it; small placards stuck on the gate; a day "to view" with old neighbours trapesing round the house, prodding this, turning over that. Harriet had taken the three youngest children off to Florrie's for the day, much to the children's disappointment. They knew they were moving, and moving for young Sam meant having a van and horses and maybe a ride on the front high up with the driver or on the drop ledge at the back where the wringing-machine was usually tied. There was no tragedy for them in thinking of it. Not yet. They'd heard their mother say the new house they were going to had no back door and that sounded funny and enticing. Sam and Esther said to their playmates: "In our new house you always have to go in at front door. What d'you think o' that?" George, though the eldest, now sixteen and still not working (had times been good he would have been earning wages for the past two years) walked about following the auctioneer's men with resentful eyes, mortified and ashamed. George took after his mother; he had her sallow complexion and dark brown eyes, her pride and sensitiveness. He lacked the vigour and brains of the younger children but as he had grown older Harriet had turned to him and between them there was a profound bond. She would find him standing by her when she was sad, saying nothing. And when she roused herself and smiled, an answering light would dawn in his eyes and his face break into sunshine like water breaking under a shaft of light; and she would rumple his hair and pull it, chary of showing her love for him any more gently than that. "What's up, mother?" he had asked when he heard they were to leave The Rookery. "Your father's not bin doin' so well. We can't afford to stop here, but I daresay we'st be all right." "I wish I could get a job," he said. "Aye, I wish you could, lad," she would say. "But don't fret. You will. Go an' have a walk. It'll do you good."

"Can I fetch you anything back to save you goin' into t' village?" (They always called Chesterford "t' village.")

"If you see any nice kippers you can bring a couple o' pairs."

George rarely went out without doing an errand of some sort or other. After he had gone Harriet would think: "He's too nice to get on. He'll allus be put on." And she would sigh and wish he had some of Bessie's devilment in him. One incident encouraged her, though. When George had been no more than ten and Sam had been saying he thought he could do with a new overcoat, George, standing at his mother's knee, had astonished them both by saying: "The one you've got is good enough for you." The remark was born of knowledge that his father often came home tipsy. George often thought of the occurrence with a little pride afterwards, although he had been sternly rebuked by his mother and sent hurriedly to bed at the time. He thought, "There must be something in me; one of these days it'll pop out again." He was the more sure of it when he watched his mother. Nobody could have a mother like her and be just ordinary, he thought. As for his father—he thought nothing of *him*.

It was true that the family had stayed at The Rookery too long. Nobody will believe things are as bad as they may be when you live in a substantial house, especially if your normal home is a small one. Or they wish to see you demeaned and taken down a peg before they render help. Calls on shares were demanded much more rigorously and mercilessly from Sam in The Rookery than they would have been from Renshaw in Lavender Street. He was expected to pay for rounds of drinks he couldn't afford, and Harriet was pestered by beggars and ex-soldiers selling worthless stationery and by cadgers for every charity in Burnham and Chesterford. Everything costs more if your

house has a large garden, and shopkeepers look down their
noses if you buy cheap things. Harriet would say: "When I
go into t' butcher's for a couple o' savoury ducks or a pig's
foot I think his eyes'll drop out. Either that happens or he
looks straight through me and sees nothin'. I asked him
one day—I said: 'Here, have I become an invisible woman,
or what?' " But she couldn't laugh about it much. She was
like a poor swimmer out of her depth; she wanted to be
getting back where she belonged. But Klondyke Street
wasn't the place. She was staggered when Sam suggested
a back-to-back house. "A back-to-back?" she said. "Why,
I've never lived in one i' my life. We've allus had two up
and two down. Where shall *we* be—four childer—in a
back-to-back?" She couldn't get over it, but of course she
did get over it. The rent was to be six shillings and threepence,
and there was no telling, Sam said, where even that was to
come from. Thomas Blackburn had long since ceased to
put anything in Sam's way. Sam's shares were worse than
worthless; they were a liability. He couldn't get a pair of
mules for love nor money, and he was no longer a member
of the trade union. He had lapsed. He hadn't even paid up
his contributions before he was struck off. "Tha's no more
chance o' walkin' into thy old job as a spinner than a
gudgeon pulled out o' t' cut has o' walkin' into Burnham,"
they told him. He had climbed over his fellows and, besides,
had broken the union rules. Useless for him to say he hadn't
intended to do it—that it was an oversight. It *was* an oversight; Sam was too generous, too anxious to do what's
right to bilk his union; but when you suddenly become
possessed of a few thousand pounds, you're not accountable.
"I were a bit hot-headed, like," Sam said to Mark Wilson,
the assistant secretary. But Mark shook his cropped grey
head and reared his veined and stringy neck another quarter
of an inch out of his "dicky" and said: "Well, tha'll ha'

plenty o' time to cool thysel' down. If tha brings thy back
pay we'll see about puttin' thee up for election again,
but tha'll stand a better chance shovelin' muck than waitin'
for mules. Why, half o' t' little piecers (spinners' assistants)
are married men to-day." After Sam had clomped down
the stairs Mark turned to the next customer and muttered
that chaps like Renshaw gave him the belly-warch. And Sam
walked down Ogden Street and wiped his moist eyes with
the corner of his coat-sleeve and then looked round quickly
to see if he had been watched doing it. He had been to the
Bluebell mill where he had worked but Luke Hargreaves
had nothing for him. Luke had never liked him much—
Renshaw was too fond of his gill, too fond of gossiping with
the women cardroom hands, too fond of his football coupons. "It's no good, Renshaw, there's plenty come afore
you," Luke said, making no bones about it. Sam had never
thought he had a chance back at the Bluebell; he had tried
half a dozen others first. So now, desperate, he said: "I'm
worse off then a lot o' t' others. I've no dole, yo' know."
"No," said Luke shortly, "you've been your own gaffer,
haven't you?" He spat "gaffer" out of the side of his
mouth. Luke could be nasty when he liked. Sam was beginning to feel he had done something to be ashamed of. He
went and stood across the road from the Black Bull, for
want of something better to do. The wind was cold and
damp. He hadn't put his overcoat on. You didn't wear an
overcoat when you went looking for a job. An elderly man
sucking a clay pipe stood there a yard or two away and
presently he said to Sam: "It's damn' cowd 'smornin'."
   "Aye, above a bit."
   "I usually stops i' bed till dinner-time. Yer don't get so
'ungry-like theer."
   "Naw."
   Sam looked at him. The man had the patient, soft eyes of

the man who has gone a little daft with hardship and occupying an inferior position all his days.

"Do you want a match?" Sam felt in his pockets as he
asked.

"Naw. It's just summat to suck. Nowt in it." He took
the pipe out of his mouth, showed the empty bowl. "I've not
had a smook for three weeks." He said it quite gently.

"What were yo'?"

"Weaver. Missis too. We got stopped a while sin'. Don't
suppose we'st get started agen."

"Naw. I don't suppose you will."

"There's some worse off nor us. Our brids left neest long
sin'. Missis does a bit o' cleanin' at Town Hall of a Friday.
Gets us a bit o' meit." A drop of moisture gathered on the
end of his nose and he wiped it with his fingers and dried
them on his trousers. "I 'eard of a night watchman's job o'
Tuesday. I'd a rare do after it—everywhere I went it were
somewheer else—runnin' away from me if tha understands
me. Aye. There's bin sixty-five, they towd me, afore I got
theer. Not so bad, is it? Sixty-five." He spoke it wonder-
ingly, with admiration. He seemed to think Chesterford had
something to be proud of in that. "Well," he said, "I think
I'll be gettin' on a bit. Mornin'." He moved off slowly, taking his pipe out to say good-bye and putting it back so that
his sunken mouth closed round it again.

Sam watched him go and wondered whether he'd be still
out of a job himself when he was as old as that.

They removed the next day. Rain fell in clinging mist so
that it stood in beads on the grass and made the pavements
greasy. The furniture men were late coming, the van with
its one horse got stuck in the soft garden path and before
they had got the beds up at Number 11 Klondyke Street the
lamps were lit and such folk as had jobs were coming home
from them. This hour of the day always reminded Sam of

the time when, as a boy, they had had the oil lamp lit and
put on the kitchen table close by a huge brown dish of boiled
mussels or cockles in their shells. He saw himself once again
taking his saucer and scooping them up. He thought it the
best meal they ever had. Yes, this was a romantic hour and
being back in a street reminded him of it. "Summat homely
about it," he thought.

A handful of children straggled round the Klondyke
Street door commenting shrilly on the furniture carried in,
going away to play hopscotch or tiggy and running back
now and then when a treble voice yelled: "Look! They got
a gramophone"—cutting the "t" very short, and "Sithee,
they corn't get t' table in—nor t' dresser neither"—for
Harriet hadn't had the heart to part with everything Sam
had thought should go. The long kitchen dresser finally had
to be left on the pavement under the window. It rested there
all night and was sold to a second-hand dealer, Jenkins,
blind in one eye, for seven and sixpence the next day.

Harriet thought the flitting was like a funeral—the same
misery in her heart, the same sort of rain falling as on the
day when she had buried her mother. The removal men
were gruff, slapdash, good-natured and anxious to be finished, but they couldn't refrain from little jokes. "Be careful wi' that gold-plated mangle, 'Arry"; and, "Lend a 'and
wi' this grand pianner, Fred"; and they made grave inquiries
as to whether the coal-bucket was for the dining-room or the
drawing-room, and was the small bed for the nursery or the
skivvy's room? When Sam was going for the 'lowance in
a jug Harriet asked: "Shall yo' be long?" "Nay, there's an
off-licence at t' corner o' Paradise Row," he said. She
couldn't forbear to say then: "You've soon found that out,"
and her heart fluttered. Sam looked at her deeply hurt. He'd
been teetotal lately and like all men who normally run a
little crooked he was intensely aware of his keeping straight

now and he wanted to be properly appreciated for it. He
had been thinking he was a regular saint. "That's a bit thick,
that is," he said. "Tha knows not a drop's passed my lips
for weeks." But she wasn't sorry. "Chance is a fine thing,"
she said, and then, as he sulked and stood there looking at
the jug and next at her, she said: "Go on. We don't want t'
men here aw neet." He went, feeling ill-used and determined
to nurse his grievance but he was too easy-going to do even
that. Besides, there was a buxom woman in the off-beer-shop
whose bosom projected over the counter, whose fat hands
were heavily ringed and her henna'ed hair waved. She
smiled at him and said briskly: "A quart of mixed? I think
you'll like that. Mr. Renshaw, is it? I thought so"; and she
beamed very knowingly at him. Sam walked back whistling.
So she'd heard about him.

As Fred pushed his cap back and drank his beer, he said,
winking at Harry: "They'll not be short o' comp'ny in
Klondyke Street, 'Arry, will they? The fella next door took
six papers off t' walls tryin' to get at t' back of 'em, but the
little devils—and some of 'em weren't so little neither—
were still there. Good 'ealth!" It needed all Harriet's
strength of will not to cry.

There were two bedrooms. Esther and Bessie were to
share her and Sam's room. George and little Sam were to
have the other and occupy two single beds that crowded it
to such a degree that the chest of drawers couldn't be
opened more than six inches. Sam had seen no reason why
the oldest and youngest shouldn't sleep together but Harriet had seen plenty. "George is sixteen," she had said, "and
it's time you talked to him." Sam felt that was unreasonable
—you never knew what a woman would begin on. Why
drag that up just then? He pretended he didn't understand
her. "What am I to talk to him about?"

"You know what about."

"I daresay he knows all about it by this time."

"If you don't talk to him, I *will*," she said. Sam sighed. Life was becoming very bothersome. There was always something nattering him. He didn't remember his parents ever talking to *him* about it. What the hangment was he going to say, any road?

Schools were a problem, too. Bessie was going to the "Secondary" and wore blue gym slips and white blouses and long black stockings. She would have to leave. Bessie spoke hardly any broad dialect and was old enough to be deeply ashamed of Klondyke Street so soon as she beheld it. "And what about my music, mammy?" she asked, lolling up against Harriet when the furniture men had gone, and tears coming into her eyes.

"It's a shame, luv, but you'll have to stop for a while. When your father gets his mules back, happen you'll be able to start agen."

"You promised I could go in for the festival." Bessie lolled more heavily on her mother and suddenly broke into a wild cry that distorted her face. Not for several moments did the flood of tears come. Harriet comforted her for a while until, unable to bear it any longer, she pushed her away. "That'll do. Stop it—this minute. I'll smack your hands if you don't hush."

Esther and young Sam were watching a wide crack at the bottom of the skirting board, paying not the slightest heed to Bessie. "I saw it—it winked at me." "You never did." "I tell you I did, our Sam. See! Oh, mammy, look!" Harriet looked. A little mouse had emerged and was cheekily scampering across the floor. It disappeared at the back of the hearthstone. Harriet said: "Well, I don't know." Bessie stopped sobbing and asked brokenly: "Can we have a kitten, mammy? You promised—"

"Aye, an' I'm givin' over promisin'. Off you go to bed—
all of you."

But going to bed was no simple matter. Esther wanted to
go to the lavatory and the lavatory was down the street and
shared with two other families and what sort of people they
were, Harriet didn't know. She was very fearful about it.
It was still drizzling and Sam had gone out—to make a bit
more room, he had said—and George was called downstairs
from making the beds to take Esther along to the closet.
Now Bessie wanted to know where the bathroom was.
"We've got no bathroom, you little minx, you know very
well."

"Where can I do my teeth, then?"

"At the slopstone." (A sniff from Bessie.) "Who d'you
think you are, the Princess o' Teck?"

"Tap's stiff—it won't turn."

"Course it'll turn. You're spoilt, that's what you are."
Harriet flogged herself into a passion lest she should herself
break down. She ran them round and bundled them into
bed and came down and sat near the fire. Sam hadn't returned and George had gone off to see what was on at the
Empress cinema—he had no money to enter but he enjoyed
looking at the highly exaggerated posters, observing the
lights at the entrance and gaining prestige from having a
word with the doorman Patsy Bryan in his shabby, braided
cap and faded, long, blue, brass-buttoned coat.

Harriet had been preparing herself for this removal but
she had never foreseen all this. It was so much worse than
she had expected. The paper was peeling off the walls with
damp, the bedroom windows wouldn't open and such venti-
lation as there was came from broken panes, the whole
house smelled musty, the sink was in a tiny room that was
dark even by day, the front door had pieces chipped off the

bottom and the stairs had no handrail. She was sinking from fatigue and want of food. There was so much to do and she didn't know where to begin. The house was filthy, filthy to the bone; she knew it could never be cleansed. The dwellers in it had been dirty and vermin-ridden and there was an atmosphere about it akin to a common lodging-house. She had often been unhappy but never so hopelessly so as now, never so unspeakably humiliated and humbled to the gutter. That closet for three families. Suppose Bessie was there and some drunken lout went along—the papers were always having bits about little girls being assaulted. What was to become of them all? For the first time in her life she was sorry she had borne children; it wasn't fair to 'em—they'd never have a chance now. They'd have to get out of this street or she'd be going out of her mind. Sam said he had twenty pounds left. Could she believe him? He had drawn the money from Burnham and Chesterford Corporation without telling her; he had kept on paying her every Friday as if he still made profits although he had now admitted that for three or four years these sums had been taken from what remained in the bank. He had said this house in Klondyke Street was the only one he could get, that there was a list as long as your arm for Corporation houses and it meant either Klondyke Street or two rooms somewhere—and the rooms were twice as much as Klondyke Street. The Rookery he now said hadn't been theirs for a twelvemonth—the Burnham and Liverpool bank had really owned it as security for calls on shares and finally wouldn't give him a month to pay what he owed—nay, not a week. "I thought we might as well go on as long as we could and then come a cropper properly as do it in bits," he had said. "And I always hoped Tom Blackburn would turn up trumps and put me on my feet again."

She, Harriet, might go and see Mr. Blackburn. He'd

never allow somebody who had worked for him to live in a place like this surely, not if he were human. Maybe she'd take Bessie and maybe he'd take a fancy to her.

He couldn't help seeing Bessie were a little lady—happen he'd send her to school somewhere. Yes, she would go and see Mr. Blackburn. Oh, but she'd never have thought o' doing that a while back. She wouldn't have been beholden to anybody. But this horrible place—if she was frightened of it now what would she become later on? She rubbed her eyes wearily; she was fearfully tired. She sat listening to the noises of the street. It was rowdy after The Rookery. Children were still playing under the lamps, carts rumbled by, dogs barked, whistles blew, a bugle sounded afar off— some Boys' Brigade lad practising "The Last Post"—and somebody went past bawling a bar or two from a song. Once there was a scream, sudden, ear-splitting and dying away to silence followed by a shout of woman's laughter. It made Harriet shiver. You couldn't be sure whether it was a scream of terror or laughter but it was no better for that. She got up—she was stiff—and unconsciously she turned to look at the foot of the stairs up which the children lay. The bottom step projected into the room and when her eye caught it a quiver ran through her limbs, for there, crouched on the step, watching her, was a rat, lean and attentive. It sat absolutely still. For a moment she was bewitched and frightened. Then, keeping her eyes on the rat, she leaned quietly down for the poker, rose and flung it, and it fell with a terrific clatter and bounced on the flagged floor. The rat flew towards her scuttering across the floor so that it touched her shoe and a small cry broke from her. The rat didn't seem to know where to go and it stopped at the far side of the room, crouched under a chair and watched her again. And then began a pursuit, Harriet with a pair of long tongs she had seized, smiting and smiting the floor, the fender and the table and chair-legs as she hunted it. The rat flew hither and thither for a minute or two as if it were determined to remain and had a purpose. Harriet believed it might attack her and she imagined it grew savage and bared its teeth. She stood panting, her eyes wet with emotion and fear, looking about the room for it. It had vanished. She sat down, trembling, gripping the tongs. Presently she stooped and replaced them in the fender and as she did so a horrible thought entered her head. Suppose the rat had run upstairs! She picked up the tongs again, and took a candle and climbed up the narrow, rot-eaten stairs and into the room where the girls lay. She put the flame to the gas-jet which was without a mantle and flared up, six inches high, blue and hissing. She looked anxiously at the bed. Across the quilt were crawling two black beetles. But there was no sign of the rat. She picked off the beetles, dropped them and put her foot on them. The crunch nearly made her sick. She left a small light on—maybe that would keep the beetles down —and went downstairs again. She fully expected to find the rat waiting for her but it wasn't.

When Sam came home she said: "We've got rats." She said it as if she had been saying: "We've got the black death."

"I'm noan surprised," said Sam. "We'st have to get a dog. Tom Edmunds were tellin' me his Nell's i' pup. Oo's a good ratter, is t' bitch, too. We'st ha' to ha' one on 'em. I'll speak to him."

Chapter Ten

A FINE HUMAN SPIRIT is not to be easily quelled. Harriet conquered Number 11 Klondyke Street, as soldiers conquered foul trenches and explorers triumph over blizzards. She went to the Health Office and obtained vermin powder; she scrubbed with permanganate of potash till her hands were sore, she sprayed chloride of lime about the floors, she obtained plaster and filled up chinks in corners, she nailed a piece of wood across the bottom of the door, she mended windows with brown paper and she and George between them built up the back of the fireplace. What troubled her most was lack of a through draught; it was difficult to make the place smell sweet, but she burnt wood in the bedrooms and made a joke of it and said she was kippering them all. She did all these things because she had made up her mind that for a time Klondyke Street was to be their abode. She saw that, from her visit to Mr. Thomas Blackburn and she saw it from the manner in which Sam lost heart. Klondyke Street deflated Sam as surely as a puncture deflates a tyre. It wore him down, sickened him, made him suffer a sense of degradation and frustration. Before they had lived there a week it was Harriet who was comforting and sustaining him; not Sam who was cheering up Harriet. That hadn't lasted much more than twenty-four hours. Klondyke Street turned the tables on them. Sam had been forced to go to the relieving-officer, since he had no source of income and he was not entitled to the dole. "That'll make us paupers," Sam had said. "That's it," said Harriet. "By Christopher," he said, "I dunnot like that." She didn't speak. "Does *tha*?" he asked, hoping she'd say— No, they couldn't descend to that. But Harriet was too practical. She said: "The childer have got to eat if we don't. Pocket thy pride, lad." Sam had had to wait his turn at the Poor Law Office and answer a lot of probing questions from a red-headed man twenty years younger than himself who wanted to know if he were the same Renshaw of whom tales used to be told concerning "Renshaw's luck." Surely Sam had saved a bit out of what the young man called "the fire"? Sam, honest, and anyway glad to say he wasn't without a penny said— Yes, he had twenty pounds put by; it made him look less of a fool, that twenty pounds. "Then," said the sharp young man, "I'm afraid you'll have to spend it before you get anything from the guardians. We only help the destitute." He spoke as if he had caught Sam out and he looked very pleased with himself. Sam felt he had been trapped. "If I'd spun thee a yarn I suppose tha'd ha' gan me summat," Sam said, leaning across the counter. The relieving-officer retreated a few inches. "We have means of finding out, you know. We could prosecute for wrong information." "Prosecute be —— ," said Sam and walked out.

The same afternoon Harriet visited Thomas Blackburn. She went to his house, a large bay-windowed stone house in Farthinghall Lane. An Airedale plunged at the end of a chain at the house corner, barking ferociously at her. Blackburn was part owner of the whippet-racing track, a director of Chesterford Wanderers football club—he had many sources of income besides cotton mills. He owned half the slums in Chesterford—but nobody except his lawyer knew that.

He sat in a leather armchair in an enormous, over-heated drawing-room. The oval mahogany table was littered with documents. The mantelpiece was filled with bronze ornaments, cabinets and chairs crowded the room, long thick curtains shrouded the window, and the heavy plush table-cloth reached almost to the floor. The room stifled you. Blackburn sat, red in the face, his bristly, white upright hair matching his stiff linen tie with its great knot. He didn't get up. Harriet was glowing from the walk and the warmth of the room made her face rosy. She had put on her neat black costume with a fur necklet, and her body, grown stouter from seven years at The Rookery, was shapely and a little plump. Blackburn eyed her with pleasure. She was, at second-hand, almost a creation of his, he thought, for where would Renshaw have been but for him?

"Well?" he asked. "What is it?" He dropped his chin into his collar and spoke as if he had acute asthma.

"I'm Mrs. Renshaw . . ."

"I know that." He looked searchingly at the end of his cigar.

"Can't yo' do somethin' for Sam?"

He still looked at his cigar. "Why should I?" he inquired slowly and then left his mouth open, his jaw dropped as though he would absorb the answer through his mouth as well as his ears.

Harriet sat on the extreme edge of her chair. When she had entered Farthinghall Lane and had begun to examine the forbidding houses for Broadacre she had wondered at her foolhardiness. She was glad she hadn't brought Bessie. She had mentioned the projected visit to Bessie and Bessie had asked: "What are you going for, mammy? Are you invited?" Extraordinary how a child's questions could strip a proceeding of its plausibility. Harriet thought: "Aye, she'll be teachin' me my manners, next, let alone history an' geography."

"I'm goin' to buy some crutches for lame ducks," she said, "an' as you're so smart you can stop at home an' get t' tea ready in case I'm late back." Yes, it was a mercy Bessie wasn't there to see how fruitless the visit was going to be, for she had no doubt about that when Blackburn sat with his mouth open, waiting for her answers. Sarcastic, she thought it looked, that mouth. So she said: "He was very useful to you, wasn't he, when you were floatin' companies?"

"What makes yo' think that?"

She couldn't abide this attitude. She said: "You paid him well, didn't you? You aren't in th' habit o' payin' for nowt, are you?" She had intended talking fine, but when she got angry, it was no good—she couldn't do it.

"Aye, I paid him well. I owe him nothin'. What d'yo' think I ought to do—tak' him into partnership?"

That pleased her better; for all his sneering, she didn't care how angry he was if he'd talk to her and not to an imaginary bit o' dirt.

"It cost me summat to come here. You know that, don't you? I wouldn't come within a thousand miles of yo' if I could see any other road. But I can't. We're in a mess. We're livin' in Klondyke Street. Do you know where that is?" She rapped it out as if Klondyke Street were the uttermost hell, as, indeed, to Harriet it was.

As Mr. Blackburn owned Klondyke Street he knew very well indeed. But he only raised his brows, drew at his cigar and stared at the end again.

"Yo' could find Sam a job again if yo' would. He's a good spinner. Three days a week 'ud be enough."

Mr. Blackburn was amused at her.

"I can't sack somebody to find your husband a place. *Yo'*

know that. If he'd as much guts as yo', he wouldn't be where he is." But if he imagined that piece of flattery would please Harriet he was mistaken. She retorted quickly:

"You can leave my husband an' his guts alone." And then she became red in the face with mortification at the silliness of that reply.

Blackburn got up and stood with his back to the hearth and she got up also and faced him.

"Didn't you use to be a weaver?" He was an inch or so less than her height and he looked up into her eyes and raised his thick brows. She saw how loose the skin of his cheeks and jaws was and how his eyes burned.

"What if I did?" she asked, with her blood quickening.

"Because I might find you some looms if I'd a mind." He put his strong square-ended fingers round her forearm, squeezed and let go, and as he did so she gave him a push in his protuberant waistcoat which sent him back half a step.

"Nay," she said contemptuously, "I've not come to that."

She made a sound down her nose half a sniff and half a grunt. She turned and walked towards the door with the air of a conqueror. "Here, come here," he said, but she never looked round. She marched down the hall and jerked back the catch and slammed the door behind her. When she got into Burnham Road she stopped at a milliner's window that possessed a dark background and made a good looking-glass. There she took a long look at herself. She hadn't made up her mind till then about it. Now her eyes were sparkling and the corners of her wide shapely mouth were turned up. She could have laughed at herself. She thought: "I ought to be insulted, but I don't think I am. In fact, I know I'm not." However, the pleasant feeling of being a bit wicked soon wore off. The thought of Klondyke Street washed the smile from her face.

After a week or two Sam didn't know how to put his time in. No garden to work in, nothing to do, Harriet glad to get him out of the house. He thought to himself: "I haven't even the dole to queue up for." He tramped about till he was weary, looking for a job. He hated being asked how he was and what had happened to him to put him in Klondyke Street. He had handed the twenty pounds over to Harriet and she allowed him a shilling a week spending money. On a shilling a week Sam's father had managed to get drunk and to buy a set or two of clog-irons as well; but that was a long time ago. He bought an ounce of thick twist and two packets of woodbines. He learnt to smoke a cigarette in four smokes, dousing it after three or four draws. If you didn't roll the twist very well, it kept going out: that was an advantage, too, in one way. After the night of removal he didn't drink at all unless he was treated. And treating soon stopped. There's no conviviality over ale bought by one pocket. Sam was sheepish. He soon learnt to walk without seeing folk he knew, and grew expert at crossing the road before he came to them.

Sam tried the Highways and Cleansing Departments of the Corporation. He might have fared better there had he been a Socialist, for both the chairmen of those committees were Labour men. But Sam had never been anything particular. (He had once been asked by a Tory canvasser: "Do you want your barber's shop nationalised?" and that had settled it for Sam. Nationalised hair-cuts eh? Nay. Trams were bad enough. They ran in threes and fours wi' gaps five-miles long in between. He was a Tory working man, was Sam.) For want of something better to do, he walked to the pits, Higginbottom's and the Radcliffe. But he might as well have tried for a job at the Town Clerk's Office or the Empress cinema. He walked about Chesterford and learned more of it than ever before. He contemplated from street corners

the various forty empty factories. The tall chimneys were
cold chimneys now. "Brick monuments to man's inability to
bridge the gulf between manufacturer and consumer," he
had read in the *Chesterford Courier*. "I suppose that's what
they are," he thought. "Spinnin' gowd a few year sin', too."
The last time he had been in the Three Jolly Carters, Tom
Edmunds had been saying they were going to take the old
machinery out and make mills into hen-cotes—the rooms
split up into sections. "On th' intensive system," Tom had
said. "Th' electric light'll make 'em lay like mad. An' they're
goin' to fix up telephones so th' hens can notify when they've
laid a whopper."

Sam trudged on. It was a beautifully mild day, soft as
spring for all it was the end of October; a day made to enjoy yourself. He kept going over what people said to him.
At the Highways Department the clerk said: "We don't
take on anybody if he's heavier than his shovel—if you know
what I mean." Sam said: "That's a new 'un to me—but I
con understond." Heavier than your shovel, eh? That were
a good 'un. It reminded him of something else he had heard
—there was a woman next door but one had been going to
have a baby and she'd started being sick. There was nowt
strange in that but she went on and on. She vomited herself
to death the doctor said (aye, they'd buried her the day
before) and he said she wouldn't have done it but she'd had
nowt proper to eat for such a long time. It were a rum
carry-on, thought Sam. Even this walking about had to be
watched. For one thing it made you so hungry, and for another shoe-leather didn't last for ever. You couldn't stir
without running into chaps out o' work. People said it were
like the cotton famine over again, but he didn't see how they
could know that—they weren't as old as all that.

He had passed the Empress cinema when he saw a figure
he recognised coming towards him. She wore a light check

coat and flesh-coloured stockings and carried one of those short, chubby umbrellas. She began to smile at him. It was Millie. She stopped without any hesitation. "Hello," she said. "Hello, Millie," said Sam, in the manner of one who greets a former employée. He appreciated her not calling him "Sam," as she might have done now she no longer worked for him. But Millie never *had* called him anything at all; not "Sam" nor "Mr." nor "sir"; none had seemed right. But she felt very comfortable with Sam, as Sam did with her.

"Where are yo' off to?" she asked cheerfully.

"Gettin' my walkin' about done," he said, pulling his moustache and his red mouth curling.

"How'd you like to come and see *Downhill* with me?"

"See what?"

"*Downhill*—Ivor Novello at the Empress. Have yo' seen him?"

"Never heard of him," said Sam.

"You've missed somethin'. Yo' have really. *I* think he's better than Rudolph Valentino. You've seen *him,* I suppose?"

"Nay, I don't remember t' men somehow. Women now, I remember one or two o' them." And he laughed and winked at her, and she thought: "He's as big a rascal as ever, I'll bet."

"Come on," she said. "I'll treat yer. It's warm inside, an' it'll buck yer up. Come on. It's on'y threepence—special shows for them as is out o' work."

Sam pushed back his cap half an inch, and scratched the back of his head. He didn't know what to say. It were nice of Millie—she meant nowt wrong, he was sure but somehow—well, he felt awkert—she'd bin their skivvy and he'd —well, theer it were, like; but she looked very tidy this afternoon, he wouldn't ha' minded treatin' *her* if times had been different; still, he'd nothin' to do, and it 'ud be better than moapsin' about.

"It'll keep yo' out o' mischief," Millie said, smiling all over her face.

"Aw reet," he said. "But remember—I'st owe it yo'."

"All right," she said, "yer can buy me a weddin' present.' She walked briskly up the imitation marble steps and from a pace behind her he asked: "Yo're still courtin' then?"

"Yes, rather."

"Same chap?"

"Well," she said, "it's been off but it's on agen now. He didn't like me goin' to the Pally so much but it's all right now. He sees now a girl must have her reelaxation."

"Two back seats, please," she said firmly to the girl with a prodigious bow on her hair who flashed a torch at the torn half of the tickets, waved a beam of light across their waists and turned without a word, expecting to be followed. She took no notice whatever of Millie's remark but marched down the gangway.

"Spiteful little devil," said Millie under her breath, hesitating, but Sam, who couldn't see that it mattered where they sat, started off and cannoned into her. The electric light was winking and flashing at them half-way down the dungeon-like gangway and Sam, with masculine dislike for being conspicuous, gave Millie an encouraging push with his hand. "We'd best go," he said. He was a little surprised to find what a thrill he got when he touched her, but any rising of his spirits was overwhelmed by a voice which muttered, "Hullo, Renshaw," as they started off. Sam looked towards the voice but said nothing. He couldn't make out who the chap was. It were the devil being well known, he reflected.

The seats were at the far end of the row and Millie sat next to the wall. She snuggled down like a kitten, and wriggled with delight. The picture had just begun and Mr. Novello's classic profile was making over three hundred fe-

male breasts palpitate and causing over three hundred
imaginations to invest their companions, wearing dark suits
and silver chains and "dickies" or mufflers, with some of his
qualities. Mr. Novello was responsible for scores of hot
hands, voluptuous sighs, hugs and whispered protestations
of devotion that October afternoon, and for many a risk
taken boldly that evening. Sam didn't enjoy himself very
much. Millie, he thought, might have had a flea judging by
the way she bounced about. It reminded him of when he
had slept between Esther and Bessie when both had chicken-
pox and he had lain rubbing the heat-spots of first one and
then the other. Millie leaned up against the wall, she leaned
towards Sam, she sat up, she sat back, she crossed her legs,
she put her foot on his, she pushed his arm off the rest between them, she thrust her arm through his, she asked him
for a match which he hadn't got, she smoked a cigarette
which constantly went out, she giggled, she sighed languorously, she drew his attention to couples in front who were
making open love to one another, and she cast sidelong
glances at him. Indeed, Sam suffered all the disquiet and
discomfort of the male who is being tempted by a female he
is determined to withstand. In part it was the memory of
Harriet and in part it was the fact that Millie had paid for
the seats that was responsible for his resolve. It wouldn't
have been so bad, he thought at first, if he hadn't been fond
of her and wanting to take hold of her. But as time went on
she annoyed him so much that he had no desire to touch her
—and then it was worse than before. To be tempted by a
woman who leaves a man cold is purgatory; he is affronted;
he is aware that his chivalry is involved and he knows he
can do nothing about it. He didn't care for the picture,
either. Mr. Novello was nothing in his line; he was far too
good-looking. Sam preferred *Tarzan of the Apes* or the
acrobatics of Douglas Fairbanks or the old-time humours of

Fatty Arbuckle. Where had *he* got to, he wondered vaguely.
Millie's conversation irritated him, too. She spoke in cap-
tions. If a light went up she would murmur: "Came the
dawn." "Eh?" Sam would ask, thinking she was saying
something needing a reply. It took him a considerable time
to discover that her sentences were really the expression of
an overcharged soul. She was quite happy murmuring such
words as: "When night's shadows descended on the lovers,"
or, "Into the starry west their boat went sailing," or, "And
so we leave them, united at last."

The picture appeared to Sam to last fully twenty-four
hours. It wouldn't have been the least use telling him that
these cheap matinées for a few coppers were keeping men
and women sane, transporting them to lands of romance
and so "taking them out of themselves" and putting up a
barrier between them and complete despair. Sam hadn't
been out of work long enough, or rather, hadn't been in
Queer Street long enough, to recognise that. The end of
the picture represented, for him, a release. The way he shot
up on to his feet when the lights went up, was as though
he had come through a trap-door. Millie looked up at him
with displeasure. She was disgusted and bitterly disappointed. Sam was acutely aware of it. When they got outside
Sam said with great vigour: "It were a champion picture—
a gradely do, Millie." "I'm glad you've enjoyed it," she said
coldly, holding out the tips of her fingers as she had seen
frigid duchesses do on the films. Sam took her hand and enveloped it in his and shook it heartily. "Aye," he said, "he
kept gettin' into trouble, didn't he? I mun say he's a good
actor is yon." He talked on garrulously, pumping her hand.
"Well, you'll have to be gettin' along I reckon an' so shall
I." He was terrified she would ask him how Harriet and
George and Bessie were and he was eager to be off but he
didn't want to look as if he was. But she didn't ask him any-

thing. Millie's interest in him had evaporated. To take a
fellow to the pictures and him not— Nay, it was past everything. "Well ta-ra," she said, turned the other way, and
went. Sam stood watching her for a moment and then turned
towards Klondyke Street. He was feeling comfortably
pleased with his behaviour. He was inclined to moralise a
bit. Easier for a camel to pass through a needle's eye than
for a rich man . . . Kingdom of Heaven. Aye, there were
a lot in that. You couldn't go so damn' far wrong when you'd
no brass in your pocket. It put a tidy brake on, aye, it did
that. He thought about Millie. That perfume she used—not
a patch on th' one she used to have. "Aye," he thought,
"she's not t' lass she used to be. She's gone off. Aye. Gone
off." He thought he'd be safe there in future. He'd always
wondered what would happen when he met her again. He'd
got over it all right. There was that moment when he first
touched her in t' gangway. Ah, well. It were all finished wi'
now.

.   .   .   .

When he got home he found Harriet rocking herself.
Her nose was red and shiny with constant wiping and now
and then she took the corner of her apron to her eye.

Sam was feeling somewhat masterful after his encounter
with Millie, so he said: "Nah then, lass, tha'rt not frettin'
about T' Rookery, arta?"

Harriet shook her head and another tear welled up into
her eye.

"Well, then . . ."

Sam dismissed everything else as of no consequence. The
Rookery and all that it implied . . . there could be nowt
else.

"George has gone," she said.

"What dost mean—George gone?"

"He's gone—left home."

Sam gave a short laugh, to hide his queer feeling inside.

"He'll come back. I were just t' same at his age."

"He winna come back." She said it so quietly that he didn't now question it.

"Why's he gone, any road?" He had to bluster a bit.

"He sez we can't afford to keep him—he sez he's not goin' to live on what I earn by washin'. So—so he's gone—half an hour since. I'm sorry you missed him."

"Art tha tellin' me he's gone off wi'out"—Sam swallowed something—"wi'out a word to me—his feyther?"

"There were a lorry goin' to Burnham. Somebody he knowed said he could have a lift. He said he'd bin thinkin' about it ever sin' we left—left t'other place."

Sam was profoundly disgusted and profoundly moved.

"So he'd rayther catch a lorry than wait for me, would he?"

"I wanted him to wait—but he said he didn't want to make any more upset."

"Has he ta'en owt wi' him?"

"I made him tak' his overcoat an' a bit of a bundle. An' I gan him ten shillin'. He wouldn't have any moore. He sez happen he'll get odd jobs. An' he sez he can allus get a night's lodgin's for nowt."

"Wheer?"

"In t' work'ouse."

"Work'ouse?" Sam invested the word with all the loathing and fear with which respectable working people regard it. He picked up his cap. "Dunnot thee worry thysel'," he said. "I'll work'ouse him."

"If tha thinks he'll come back—even if tha finds him—tha'rt mista'en."

"We'st see about that."

"It's no good, Sam." Sam's hand was on the door.

She went on. "If he wouldn't stop for me, he winna come back for thee. I towd him he were breakin' my heart. But his mind were made up. I wouldn't ha' minded if he'd been two or three year older. He's nobbut a babby." She didn't weep any more but she sat looking into the fire, her face pitiful to behold.

Sam stood with his cap pushed back, his elbow on the mantelpiece, his foot on the fender, looking down into the fire also.

"It's this bloody slump," he said.

Chapter Eleven

On the 15th November, 1927, Edward wrote to Phœbe as follows, from the Carlton Hotel, S.W.1:

My darling,—Before this reaches you, you will, I am afraid, have read that Hilditch has committed suicide. I am not long back from Chalfont St. Giles and I must stay over for another day in case I am wanted for the inquest. It is a terrible shock. I wish I could talk to you. Hilditch has crashed, and I am ashamed to say that in some degree I have gone down with him. How far I don't quite know. You will have read how he was found—dead from some poison. Smethurst, his man, called me at eight this morning. Hilditch was lying in his evening clothes, his head hanging off the bed. I won't go into it, but he must have died in distressing agony. There was a note for the doctor:

"Go gently with me, old man. I'm dead from prussic acid. Don't spoil my looks with that knife of yours."

Smethurst says he never heard a sound. Hilditch had forced up the Golden Gate oil shares from as low as 5s. 7d. to 24s. 3d. It is almost more than I can bear to have to tell you that I also gambled on those shares. They were 11s. 9d. when he invited me in—and in the past three days they've fallen to 7s. 10d. I told you how often he talked of the

342

"golden gusher" and "the millionaire's mile"—the river of oil he believed existed below ground—or conjured himself into believing. A good many are involved.

Forgive this letter if it is long and rambling. It will ease my mind to tell you—the nearest approach to talking to you. It's been an extraordinary week-end—Lord Meadow-croft, who made a fortune out of shipping during the war, was there; Nicholas Jones, part author of the revue; Joe Cragwell, the rider; Murphy, editor of the *Sunday Comet;* Isaac Goldberg, who makes films, and Oliver Brass, who wrote that novel in verse about the East End. Marie de Keiller, the French girl who starred in *The Lady of Liége,* and Trix Bishop were there also. Hilditch was said to have gone back to de Keiller—but I don't know.

I drove down with him on Friday night, rather late. He looked worn and tired and for the first time I thought he seemed really shaky. He talked about his early days—how he had walked from Burnham to London in 1902, how he once paid a 'bus driver five pounds to take him to St. John's Wood, how he went out pheasant-shooting in Hampshire and threw the guns in a ditch, how he won fifty thousand one year on the Cesarewitch and gave ten thousand pounds to the Salvation Army. I can't recall all he said. It was as though he were trying to stimulate his belief in his capacity for doing strange things. Then he would say suddenly: "A bit of codology goes a long way but it's no use with the Almighty." He said that two or three times. He wouldn't talk about oil, beyond saying that he had an ace or two in his pocket. Once, after a long silence, he said: "Who was it said she'd have Calais written on her heart? I shall have a tape-machine engraved on mine."

Most of the others arrived Saturday morning—Trix was resting from the revue for a night. For Saturday afternoon Hilditch had arranged a cock-fight—and there was the

nauseating sport—which I didn't see—in the concrete pit
with the monkeys he had tried to teach to hit rats on the
head with a hammer. Hilditch seemed better. Two of his
stable-men turned out, stripped, and fought eight rounds
with bare fists, Hilditch acting as second to one of them.
Afterwards he himself wanted to box a round or two with
Murphy, who refused. Hilditch seemed to lose his head for
a few minutes then—wanted to jump Cragwell with weights,
or swim us for ten pounds in the pool although it was a
rather bitter day with a touch of frost.

Before dinner he began talking theology, said you can't
go against God and wondered whether God knew about the
trials and temptations of to-day—mass production, men
ousted by machines, tractors ploughing His land instead of
horses and did the Almighty approve of aeroplanes flying
the Atlantic? Roulette was played and Hilditch, who insisted on our acting as croupier in turn, gambled heavily
and lost heavily. He wrote elaborate notes of hand payable
this morning at ten o'clock. My own was for four hundred
pounds. I think I had almost made up my mind then that
he was deranged. Trix Bishop shared my misgiving. It may
be we had more genuine feeling for the man. As she and I
walked together before dressing for dinner—the sky was
fresh and swift-moving and the countryside strangely clean
and lovely after the fret of indoors—we were both anxious
for the week-end to be over that we might get away from
the house. We talked of Chesterford and the theatre—she
was eager to know what had become of old Nat and the
Websters. She said, a little bitterly and sadly: "People fall
in love with you in London but they don't become your
friends." She said she didn't know why Hilditch had asked
her down—she had seen nothing of him for some time. I
thought she was trying as gently as she could to tell me she
no longer was his mistress.

Am I wearying you? I am trying to keep this record of what happened in some sort of chronological order. Over dinner Hilditch and I found ourselves ranged, as it were, against the other men. They were ridiculing Lancashire— her inability to put her house in order at a time when cotton has fallen to 6½d. a pound—the cheapest for ten years— and at a time when despite what we call the slump, she is receiving fifty to a hundred million pounds a year more for her exports than she did in 1913 and for one-third less cloth and yarn sold. Hilditch was now very quiet and restrained —a new mood. Murphy observed the change and referred to "Lord Hilditch": but Hilditch let it go. Looking back now I feel sure his mind, failing some new stroke of fortune, was made up. Whenever the telephone rang—we could hear it faintly—his face took on an intent look. Towards the end of dinner, Meadowcroft said abruptly: "Look here, Tim, but how *do* we stand over this Phœnix Mine? I don't mind telling you, I'm extremely anxious. We don't question your ingenuity and courage but can you possibly meet this attack?"

"Meet it—and smash it," Hilditch answered. Hilditch went up to his study. Downstairs, bridge was played and billiards. We were all a little on edge, as if expecting something to happen. Nothing did, and most of them went to bed fairly early. Hilditch sent word asking me to look in on my way up. He lay on a couch in a dressing-gown. He grinned and said: "What do they say? Happy is the host when he gets away from his guests?" He was almost enjoying himself in a grim sort of way.

"I wouldn't tell them, but I'll tell you now," he said, "I'm at the end—broke, finished." He said he was extremely sorry he'd dragged me into it—and so on. I said what is true —that it is my own doing: one makes mistakes. I asked him what he was going to do. He said quickly: "There's only one thing for a chap like me to do." I asked him then what he meant, but he would say no more.

"You're surely not thinking of suicide," I said. He countered that with: "Do I look like a man who commits suicide?" And added, "That needs pluck," and laughed queerly. I didn't like it.

He invited me to have a glass of brandy. With his old boastfulness, he said: "There's not a hotel in London with anything so good. You can keep a head clear as daylight on it," adding he had been drinking it for two hours.

I was horribly perplexed. I said again that I supposed I could dismiss suicide from my mind. He waved a hand lightly, looking the while at his brandy. What, I asked, did he propose to do about the oil shares? He said sardonically there would be no need for him to do anything—his enemies would see to that. He would default—have no alternative— again adding how sorry he would be for me—my name would be remembered a long time, as would, he thought, his own. "When a rocket has reached its height, it begins to die. It is the tops o' the chimneys the lightning strikes."

I had nothing much to say: nothing seemed worth saying. When I got up he held out his hand. "I won't get up," he said, "I might fall over. Tell Smethurst what time you want calling. I may not be down." We shook hands. I went to my room, sat there a while, decided sleep was out of the question and went out for a walk. The heavens were peculiarly beautiful—I stood in the garden watching the moon sail behind the square chimney-stacks and I walked down the road where a faint bluish light was diffused. I could almost have read a book there. It wasn't yet midnight and from time to time a motor-car drove by. I was impressed by the closeness of one's affairs and that whatever happened to Hilditch or me was of not the slightest moment to these people. And as I walked, I was calmed, comforted by the loveliness of the night and the splendour and immensity of the heavens. I hated going back to the house. In my room I felt much less certain that Hilditch would not kill himself. The house was quiet. I wished now that I had spoken to somebody. What does one do, I asked myself, when one suspects a suicide intention? Ring up the police? Do they come and make an arrest—or stay to see the threat isn't carried out? But how foolish I should look if I rang up and they came and Hilditch told them I was a fool. I was uneasy, tormented, assuring myself these were night fears, that the morning would disprove them. I went to bed but not to sleep except in brief half-hours and then to wake up, listening. I think it was a shot I listened for. It never occurred to me that his way out would be poison. And in the deep silence I lay in acute misery: more frightened, I believe, than I have ever been in my life. I heard all the hours and half-hours strike until half-past five, and after that nothing till Smethurst came in to summon me. It was eight o'clock.

The doctor came and the police. I said what I knew. It was all very ponderous and unpleasant. I'm afraid I'm certain to be wanted to give evidence. I shall know later this afternoon. I travelled back to Town with Trix. We sat in opposite corners—nobody else was in the compartment. Again I was struck, seeing the rumbling carts, cows moving into the fields, fishermen casting their lines, by the manner in which the world's business was going on undisturbed. I was possessed then by an intense desire to live somewhere a long way from cities or factories. I still feel like that. I told Trix I hoped she wouldn't hesitate to come to me for help or advice if she wanted it, that many of us in Chesterford thought very warmly of her and of her work. She said there had been a trying scene between her and Hilditch last night. He had made love to her and she had repulsed him. He had said it would be the last time she would have the opportunity of making him happy. I felt inexpressibly sorry for her. She asked if I thought her refusal had caused him to do it. I replied that I was certain that it had not—that his mind had been made up all the time, that neither she nor I nor anybody on earth could have stopped him. She spoke of Brierley, asked how he was, and said, rather wistfully, she hadn't seen him or heard from him for a long time. It occurs to me, darling, that if you see Brierley you should tell him. I doubt if the revue will go on. Hilditch had told me it had not been paying for some time.

About my own affairs, I don't quite know. Hilditch's oil speculation, had it succeeded, would have meant a hundred thousand pounds to me. As it is—the overdrafts are heavy. If the banks insist, the mills will have to go, but there should be enough left to keep us quietly but comfortably. I put it at its worst; I don't want to extenuate anything. My heart is very full and I grieve for the stupidities I have been guilty of, for the uneasiness and wretchedness I have caused you, for the fear that maybe Houghton's will cease to exist. I see there are things worse than death: it is a bitter moment in a man's life when he realises that. But at all events, I can send you my dearest love—if you will accept it. It has never wavered among other things that have broken. Give my deep love to Mary also. It will be hard to face Philip. I shall wire you so soon as I know when I may come, and I shall come at the earliest moment. Till then, my darling, good-bye.

Your loving,

EDWARD.

Chapter Twelve

PHŒBE received Edward's letter in bed. The blue envelope lay on the tray with her morning tea, the shapely and rather ornamented writing with a dash in the capitals as recognisable by her as Edward's face or voice, and equally loved. She took it up with a beating heart and read the letter at once and then lay back on the pillows, and tears, soft as a welling spring, rose in her eyes. They were sweet, healing tears, tears of sorrow for Edward, tears of relief at Hilditch's death, tears of joy at what Edward said about their love. She did not try to stop them nor for a moment did she dry them, not until they ran on to her cheek and produced a tickling sensation. She lay there, a fond smile playing about her lips as she thought how foolish he was to imagine the money mattered so much. That he should think so almost made a boy of him, reduced him far below her in wisdom and knowledge of what was of true account. But she loved him all the more for it. She thought, lying there, that she never loved him so deeply as when he betrayed his masculine lack of perception and gave her an opportunity to support him with her profounder insight and strength. It was peaceful now to lie there and let her mind run easily over their life together, and on their sorrows shared. For she didn't think just then of their moments of great happiness. She dwelt on the day that Philip went to France and the trenches for the

first time, the day the news came that he was seriously
wounded, the times when they had talked over his and
Mary's future and seen little in the sky but darkness. She
could look back on their troubles tranquilly and she could
face this new trouble tranquilly also. Edward had made
everything so easily bearable. She blessed him for that. She
had never known him angry with her not when she had flirted
in her younger days with Sir John, or in her older ones with
Lord Henry Hope, not when she had drunk too much brandy
and talked to their guests a trifle garrulously, or spent or
betted too extravagantly at Newmarket. She saw that Edward had had far more to bear with than she had. But she
didn't begin to weigh his faults against hers and add to them
this new catastrophe. There was a song in her heart, for she
knew she had foreseen this even before the day Elizabeth
Hargreaves had come to see her and Edward and Philip had
quarrelled, that she had dreaded it and that now it had come,
it was as nothing. It might overwhelm her a little later on, as
she saw, but not now. She lay there quietly, her tea neglected,
her other letters unopened, while she wondered what to say
in a telegram. She decided on: "Thanks for letter, darling.
Don't worry the least bit. Take great care of yourself. Much
love. Phœbe." She dictated it with great firmness and precision over the telephone as she lay in bed and then got up
feeling like a conqueror. She thought to herself that Hannibal must have had a similar sensation when he crossed the
Alps, if it *were* Hannibal and it *was* the Alps. She hummed
a bar or two from

> *And when I told them how beautiful you are,*
> *They wouldn't believe me . . .*

(the best tune, in her opinion, she heard during the war) and
was down to breakfast half an hour earlier than usual. She

had rarely felt so exhilarated for years. Mary, who was eating toast behind the *Burnham Guardian,* said: "Hello,
darling. Who pushed you out?"

Phœbe, who hadn't known till that moment she was going
to say this, said: "How would you like to come to London
to-day?" She knew immediately she had spoken that they
must go. Why hadn't she thought of it before?

"Love to. What's up?"

"We're ruined, dear. And I think I'll have an egg with my
bacon." She felt a little drunk with recklessness. She handed
Edward's letter to Mary and walked to the bell. Mary read
in silence, her mouth growing heavy with sadness. She folded
the pages and put them down very quietly as though they
were sacred. "Poor old darling," she said. "We'd better wire
him."

"I've done that, dear."

Mary looked up, a smile transfiguring her face. "No wonder he adores you. I say, what train shall we catch? Shall
we tell him we're coming? Let's not—let's just walk in on
him. Are we extravagant? We've a right to be if we're
ruined, haven't we?" The fact that her mother had already
wired lifted up her heart.

They kept up their spirits while they packed a bag, drove
to Burnham, read their magazines and books during the
journey, and until the train lunch was served. They found,
then, that neither of them could eat and, in their hearts,
neither was surprised.

"You must eat something, darling," Mary said as they
looked at their mutton described as lamb, having left the
soup and rejected the fish.

"Yes, dear, I know. But—I feel as though I don't know
what to do with it. I was just the same the first time I was
given a golf driver." She took up her knife and fork and
contemplated them quizzically and put them down again. "I

think I should like a brandy and soda."

Mary said: "I suppose we're both worried to death that father won't be glad to see us. Prying."

Phœbe nodded. "The wheels have been going—*Hough*ton's sold, *Hough*ton's sold, *Hough*ton's sold—and then, as they go faster—Houghton's sold *up,* Houghton's sold *up,* Houghton's sold *up.* This morning I was exactly as I was when I came out of the anæsthetic—light-headed and lofty —and now I've flopped. I think I *will* have the brandy."

When they returned to their compartment, Mary asked: "Do you think Lancashire is finished, darling?"

The question astonished Phœbe. Phœbe had never thought of it. She had thought of Houghton's as an unrelated concern. Edward was in business. Whether it was shipbuilding or coalmining or bootmaking was no matter. But she said, loyally: "If Houghton's can't pay, dear, I don't see how any other firms can. Do you?"

Mary pondered. "They won't all go smash," she said. "At least I can't believe they will. It's like the war. I was talking to Henry Brierley—"

"Who?" Phœbe asked the question coldly, although she had heard perfectly well.

"Henry Brierley," repeated Mary steadily. "He's very shrewd. He likened it to a bombardment—shells pounded trenches until the barrage obliterated them—you wouldn't have believed a single living thing could exist there. And yet, so soon as the bombardment stopped and troops moved forward, there began the firing of machine guns and the shooting of rifles. Men were living there after all. Lancashire's like that, he said. As soon as the worst of the depression is over—and indeed while it is on—some firms will make money, and new life will go on springing up." She paused a moment before adding: "He's bought a small weaving shed. You remember that man Renshaw—the 'Renshaw's luck man'—his wife has become a weaver there."

Phœbe said: "Well, dear, I don't see what this has got to
do with us." She was irritated that Mary spoke so quietly
and with such assurance about Brierley. She had never ceased
to fear that Mary would fall in love with him. And now the
old fears were re-awakened. She said: "I daresay he won't
last long. He's a writer. Writers are always unpractical. If
a business man like Edward—" She left it at that and Mary
left it there also. It gave her pleasure to talk of Brierley even
though she knew how unwelcome his name was. What he
had said to her was right; she felt it in her bones. Counties
were not snuffed out. A weaving-shed starting without any of
the appallingly heavy overhead charges that swamped so
many of them had a reasonable chance, he said. He had got
a manager who knew his job—there were men and to spare
to be had. He could afford to sell his shirtings at slightly less
than most people. Undercutting? If you overweighted a ship
till it was below the Plimsoll line it was bound to be out-
sailed by one loaded lighter. Mary, looking on the adventure with biased eyes, found it easy to agree. How long did
idealism last unless it paid its way? Where was the Repertory
Theatre? Where was Houghton's, holding fast by the
amalgamation?

Edward was out when they arrived and nobody at the
hotel knew when he would return. Phœbe, grown suddenly
tired, decided to rest in her room but Mary went out to walk
—up the Haymarket, and along Piccadilly. "Tim Hilditch
—Inquest—Full Report," cried the posters. So that was
where father would be. She bought an *Evening Standard* but
the full report had barely begun. In a way, she was glad.
She dreaded reading it. The sky was leaden, and bluish-grey
mist blurred every outline two hundred yards away. Already
the shops were lighted. She shivered in the dry wind, and
fastened her fur necklet a little tighter round her throat.

She was wearing a dark-grey worsted costume, silk stockings and black shoes. One or two curious men sauntering, warmly clad, eyeing every solitary woman with appraising eyes, looked at this small grave-faced woman with mouth turned heavy by her thoughts and swiftly looked away again. Mary saw the looks, disliked the curiosity and hated more the quick aversion of eyes. "I suppose," she thought, "I look like a small sparrow alongside London's cockatoos." At that, her mouth curled up at the corners and she could have laughed. "I feel terribly Lancashire here," she thought. "I shall have to come to London oftener. No use pretending I'm not a country girl." Her shoes were stoutly soled—that is to say they were about half the thickness of a man's instead of a quarter the thickness—but her knees were cold. She hurried on under the portico of the Ritz Hotel and turned into the Green Park. She paused a moment wondering which way to go and half a dozen sparrows—surprisingly chubby for November, she thought—leapt on a low rail in a row and cocked their heads at her apparently waiting to be fed. Those sparrows cheered her up. "I'm so sorry," she said to them. She strode off quickly towards the Mall, and presently began to enjoy the walk, for her face began to tingle and her blood grew warmer. She had come out to think and so far she hadn't thought at all. What was she going to do about Trix? Phœbe had, so far as she could tell, completely forgotten Edward's suggestion that Brierley should be told. There had not really been an opportunity to tell him. And she, Mary, had been glad of that. Brierley was a creature of generous impulses; if he knew Trix were thinking of him. . . . Was it *her* duty? Couldn't Trix write to him if she wanted him? She *was* capable of writing, wasn't she? Mary flushed then as surely as if she had been observed. It was contemptible. She walked on, looking at the ground. Across the Mall she strode, down towards the lake, dark and cold and bitter, on which a solitary drake swam noiselessly, crossed the stone bridge and turned towards the Horse Guards Parade. Life was dissolving like snow in her hands, she thought. If Houghton's were sold and they left Chesterford; if Trix became Brierley's love again and she saw him no more; what would life hold for her then? Had she not a right to fight for his love? Oh, but she was tired of being cast in the rôle of a sweet, charitable lady who bore everything uncomplainingly and had no passions, no excesses, no torments, no spleen to vent! She walked on partially blinded by the tears that now filled her eyes and ran down her cheeks, and her breast rose and fell swiftly from the tempest within her. She walked down Whitehall and stopped opposite the Cenotaph for a moment. Weren't they fortunate, these men who died and became honoured for ever? Weren't all men fortunate whose lot was doing and not waiting, asking and not waiting to be asked, taking in marriage and not merely being taken? How long yet must she wait for a man's firm mouth to be laid on hers, for a man's loving hands to caress her breasts, and for a man's strength to support her? Was *she* to be one with the wasted years, the generation that was denied its lovers? Did life hold anything so beautiful and magnificent as two people living as happily together as her mother and father? And why should she, who felt within her an inexhaustible spring of affection, be starved of what was all women's due? Her thoughts turned to Philip and Evelyn. They seemed tolerably happy; there was a bond between them. Evelyn had attained a new dignity and serenity despite Philip's sombre moods and his bitterness, his feeling that life had cheated him of its laughter. Evelyn, she thought, must at all events feel she had something to fight for, some charge, some purpose to make her hold on. Besides, she might have a child; and a child was one's own no matter how tortured sometimes might be the home into which it came. A child, she was sure, must bring fulfilment, some depth of satisfaction that was akin to being at one with the trees and the rocks and the earth. And she knew how deep within her was that kinship. She could understand full well those women who desired a child even if, achieving it, they had to lose the world and take that fragment of themselves into a seclusion that approached hiding. She crossed Parliament Street and walked towards Westminster Bridge and turned along the Embankment towards Charing Cross. A pavement artist still crouched hopefully beside his crayon drawings in the gathering dark and one or two creatures that were an offence to civilisation huddled, a heap of foul, motionless rags, on the Embankment forms. She turned her face to the river that was a dirty bronze, whipped and choppy, and watched a heavy deep-laden brown-sailed barge going towards Greenwich with the wind and a tug coming upstream pulling three lighters high out of the water. And she grew calmer. The width of the river and the lights reflected in it, its comparative remoteness from mankind, the fact that it was older than the mind could easily imagine, soothed her. How would Philip take their ruin, if they were, indeed, ruined? She had heard of former millowners glad enough now to hawk round quarter-pound packets of tea, wealthy men who now owed corner shops for a year's tobacco and newspapers. But it had all been difficult to believe, remote from Houghton's—remote at least until the past year or two had cast their shadows.

Philip had been more casual in his work since his marriage. Visits to agents in London, Glasgow, Liverpool, Nottingham—these had been as much as he had accomplished. He had turned towards politics, following upon a toast he had proposed at his battalion dinner and compliments that ensued. But he was no Liberal. He declared the country needed more discipline—a dictator; England for the English and

keep out the shoddy stuff from Japan and Poland and
Czecho-Slovakia; that was his line. Cement the bonds of
Empire; knit the fellowship between the lads who came from
Australia, Canada, India and South Africa to fight for the
Motherland. Let peace finish what war had begun. And let
his father capitalise what he might regard as his (Philip's)
just due from Houghton's and let him leave Lancashire and
live in a decently civilised place in the South and go into
Parliament. Edward had been dry about it. Dictatorships
were un-English and barbarian—precisely what Englishmen
had thrown off with the sword—or the axe—half a dozen
centuries ago. The Empire was all right—but the Empire
was going its own way so far as tariffs and commercial
treaties went. And Philip's place was in Houghton's; there
was none other to take over the job; was it to be said that
the Houghton metal had rung false at last, was a name
known over the world to die out or the flag be borne by another family? Mary had heard them argue time and time
again, her own blood stirred, her heart crying: "Oh, that I
had been a man! How proudly I'd have done it." She had
thought sometimes: "Why shouldn't I do it, anyhow? Aren't
women in business? Didn't Lady Rhondda take over coal-
mines and the rest of it?" But so far she had held her tongue.
Speaking might strengthen Philip's case, and all her heart
was with her father. And *now* where were they to be?

It was turned five o'clock when Edward walked into the
private sitting-room where Mary and her mother had taken
tea. He came in as he had entered from the street, his silk
scarf hanging down, his overcoat loosened, his soft black
hat in his hand. The hat he dropped on to a chair and went
straight to Phœbe, who had risen to hold out her hands to
him. Nobody spoke. Edward put his arms about her and
buried his face in her hair while the tears ran unchecked
down the side of his nose and trickled into the hair that hid

her ears. Mary he seemed not to see. It was as though he had reached home after a long journey. "My dear one," he was saying, "my dear one. You shouldn't have bothered to come."

Phœbe laughed with a catch in her throat. "We wanted a jaunt, you know. Just an excuse. Didn't we, Mary?" Mary had turned away to pull the curtain aside and study the Haymarket. "Yes, darling," she said, looking out. She had spoken with an enormous effort and her voice was very loud and clear and a little hard. It startled her.

Chapter Thirteen

THAT NIGHT Mary took a taxi-cab to the Post-War Theatre to see Trix. She could do no less, she had decided. No performance would be given, Edward said. Notices were up; the revue was finished. Edward's drawn face and sunken eyes into which a hurt look crept now and then that made her more sorrowful than anything she had ever witnessed, had affected her profoundly. She saw then that whenever she was confronted with suffering that might be assuaged by her at the cost of her own pleasure or future, she would sacrifice herself. But she didn't count it to herself for virtue. Were she removed from the suffering she might do nothing. She thought: "I suppose I am weak." She wasn't clear in her mind what she would say to Trix except to inquire if there were anything she or her father could do; and to promise to bear any message to Brierley that Trix cared to send. If those two were to become lovers again, it had better be done quickly. From her own selfish point of view, it would be easier so; better than suspense. As she stood before her mirror, putting on her fur coat, she smiled sadly at her reflection and wondered whether she wasn't, perhaps, taking too much for granted. What evidence had she that Brierley in any event had thought of her as she had thought of him? None beyond a kissed hand, a turning to her with his small pieces of work for her criticism, a flash between them from

time to time as of a current between two perfectly attuned
instruments. She thought then of how her father and mother
had moved towards each other earlier that day, achieving
a complete unity. She had felt an intruder and had hurried
from the room with a full heart. Later Edward had sought
her, put his hand on her shoulder and smoothed her hair.
She could remember nothing they said; perhaps they had
said nothing. There had been no need.

"The show's off, miss," the wizened taxi-driver said when
she asked him to go to the Post-War. All London knew,
then. All London had read her father's evidence also, seen
his photograph as he entered Hilditch's house where the inquest was held. She hated that. A crowd was outside the
theatre as though they were awaiting arrivals on a first night.
A sprinkling of people in evening clothes moved in and out
of the glass doors—the *foyer* was crowded—and a photog-
rapher or two were taking pictures with flashlights. Women
in brocaded cloaks, women in furs, women in green velvet,
women with lorgnettes, women wearing monocles through
which they stared very fiercely, women using very long
cigarette-holders in jade and ivory, women reclining against
corners and staircases until they promised to fall over at any
moment, women painted and scented until they were not to
be distinguished from expensive courtesans, women bored,
expectant, excited, delighted at the crash, supercilious, insolent and grieved that their free tickets were now useless,
talked loudly of how Tim had told them this or that, of how
inevitable it was, of who his latest mistress had been, of how
much he paid de Keiller, of how many hundreds a week he
had been losing on the revue, of how many contracts would
now be broken, of how he had uplifted or degraded the theatrical profession, of stars he had made and stars he had
failed to make, or how good-natured and ignorant and impossible and generous he was; until, having exhausted all

the thrill they could capture, they drifted slowly or languorously or pettishly or angrily away accompanied by sallow-faced men and red-faced men wearing silk hats and red carnations who were anxious to be off. Out of this atmosphere of fever and instability Mary walked, filled with a vague fury, and went round to the stage-door. She stood aside there to allow a skip to be pushed by. "Blimey!" said a stage-hand leaning against the wall, "*he's* soon out, ain't he? You'd think there was a bleedin' fire." " 'Old yer row, Ernie, there's a lidy there." Ernie hunched his shoulders and walked down the passage.

Thomas the doorkeeper, with his peaked cap on the back of his head and his steel pince-nez on, leaned over his counter and asked Mary what she wanted.

In the midst of this ebb and flow of theatrical fortune, Thomas was as fixed as a lightship.

"She's took it well, Miss Bishop 'as," he said. "Red 'eads for pluck. You in the profession, miss? Didn't think you was. Everythink or nothink, that's what it is. Don't s'pose she'll be long. There's a gent from the *Mornin' Herald* up with 'er." As Mary waited, a thin stream came in and out, some going up the stairs two at a time without a word, chorus girls coming down in twos and threes, the laughter and chatter fading as they reached the bottom, and they bade Thomas "Good night" and "Good luck." One said: "Send my letters on to the Savoy, will you, please?" and Thomas said: "You oughter go an' see the Winter Garden show—some *real* girls up there."

A middle-aged man with a comedian's broad moon face, curled grey hair and bowler hat slightly on one side came down and handed Thomas a key. His heavy-lidded eyes were sombre and his wide mouth was mobile as indiarubber. He spoke in a low voice. "I'll have the stuff sent for to-morrow, Thomas. Don't let 'em touch my room."

"You'll feel a bit lorst, sir, to-night."

"I'm going to have a pint of beer, and then I'm going to the Palladium to watch people trying to make *me* laugh. And I'm going to pay for my seat. That'll make it harder for 'em." He shook hands. "I expect we'll work together again before long." Work together! That was a compliment. Thomas beamed.

Beyond a sentence or two—"Pity abaht Mister Hilditch," or, "He was a card and no mistake, wasn't he?—good sort, though"—Mary barely heard the tragedy mentioned. Not a word of lamentation or complaint as to what would become of them. They had the cheerfulness and fatalism of common soldiers. " 'Night, Thomas, see you on the Christmas-tree"; " 'Night, Thomas, the Green Room'll find me"; " 'Night, Thomas, don't forget to put the cat out."

"An' a lot of 'em," said Thomas, "will be thankin' Gawd for provincial pantomimes." He thrust his head back with a jerk to indicate what a fall he thought *that* was.

Mary was thinking: "They're all alike, they were just the same at the Repertory's last night. I suppose uncertainty gives a zest to life. 'Take no thought for the morrow.' Didn't Christ say that? Perhaps it isn't what happens but how you take it that counts. Winnie Webster—saying they'd been so happy that the baby's middle name, whether it was a boy or a girl, was to be Chesterford; and they didn't know where the next job was coming from." Thomas had given her a chair behind his counter and she sat there in great content, glad to feel herself on the edge of this community.

Trix turned round from her dressing-table where she was packing her paints box when Mary walked in; and at once Mary's heart was stabbed. For Trix, she saw, was very beautiful. The months in London had given a new depth to her eyes—they seemed larger from the infinitely small amount of make-up that Trix used—her darkly red hair rose in a thick luxuriant wave on her forehead, her cheek-bones appeared to be rather higher than of old, and her cheeks slightly sunken, giving her face a melancholy note that made her brilliant vitality the more lovely; and she was inches taller than Mary and exquisitely shaped in her body. Mary thought: "No man could help loving her."

They shook hands and Mary kissed Trix on the cheek, and Trix whose pale cheeks flushed lightly, said: "It's nice of you to come. I didn't know you were in London. Mr. Houghton was—I don't know what I should have done without him. I should have thought you all—" She turned to her paints and re-arranged the tubes again. Mary didn't speak and Trix went on: "There was no pretending about Mr. Hilditch at any rate," she said. "He was never worse than his word—not with me, anyhow."

Mary said: "Father liked him—in many ways. After all, there aren't many people who're likeable all through, are there?"

Trix turned and sat facing Mary, her hands in her lap, and spoke a little sadly.

"Do you know what I want to do more than anything? —go back to Chesterford. Not for ever, but while I try to settle down a bit. You get so sick of the fuss everybody makes in London. They're more up-stage on ten pounds a week than your father with two mills." There was a knock at the door and a young man with pointed shoes and extremely wide trousers came in and stopped on the threshold. He had a large belted coat with the collar half up and hair that fell over his forehead. It was a rather noble face, with a mouth as well formed as a woman's. "I'm so sorry," he said, and then to Trix: "Can I do anything, darling, or shall I just wait?"

"I don't think I can come, John."

"Darling, you must. It'll do you good. You can clear off

whenever you like. You'll be safe there—the Press won't find you."

"I shall be half an hour at least."

"I'll wait"—and he went. Mary thought: "They'd produce a child like a god."

Trix said: "John Lawford, that was—he's giving what he calls a 'heartbreak party.' I'd much rather go to bed but the telephone and the door-bell keep going. Half the time it's newspapers."

"Like ghouls," Mary said.

"Yes, but when you know the men—and they've given you publicity before. Doesn't seem fair now to— The *Sunday Courier* has been worrying me—wants me to write. Write! Takes me all my time to write a picture post-card. I should have to get Harry Brierley to do it."

Mary controlled herself and said: "Yes, I expect he'd be glad to," and thought: "So it's come at last."

"How is he?"

"Gone into business—taken a small weaving-shed."

"Must be mad. Always was a bit mad, though."

"Like most nice people."

"Yes, he is nice, isn't he? You find things out—afterwards."

Mary, strung up as if she were about to take a high dive, said: "Why not come back with us to-morrow? If that paper still wants the article . . ."

"I *ought* to come. My mother's gone into hospital. Cancer. It's simply wicked the way she's suffered all her life. If my step-father had had it, that would have been . . . I don't know what God's thinking about. Do you believe in Him?"

"I do my best."

"I pray but— I never feel sure it's getting anywhere. I expect I don't pray the right way. I broadcast once and thought what a sell it would be if nobody happened to be listening. Praying usually seems like that to me. But I only pray when I want something—when I've wanted Tim Hilditch to forget about me—or wanted to be sure I didn't dry up—or wanted my mother not to suffer so cruelly—or wanted Josh, my mother's husband, to be teetotal for a spell. God must have thought I was asking for a lot when I mentioned Josh."

Mary thought: "She still thinks like a Chesterford girl."

"How's Harry Brierley managing to run a weaving-shed? He knows nothing about it, does he?"

"He's got a manager to see to the weaving. Most of the buying and selling he does himself."

"The last letter I had from my mother she said half Chesterford was on the dole, kids being fed at school, and that. No wonder the Rep went."

"Yes."

"What's happened to them all? I do hope the Websters are all right—and old Nat? I heard he'd gone to Northampton. Fosdyke wrote to me. He's doing a show at the 'Q.' Said he'd come round to see me but he hasn't been."

Mary thought: "Is Fosdyke an admirer too?" She said: "The town's dead-alive. I've lost my job now the theatre's gone, you know. I think I shall have to go to the mill—except that soon, perhaps, there won't be any mills left to go to."

"You could always get a job with Harry Brierley. I was mighty jealous of you when we were engaged." For the first time there was laughter in Trix's eyes, and it hurt Mary more than antagonism; as if the idea of her being a rival was absurd. But she managed to laugh and say: "All the more reason why you should come back to Chesterford."

Trix said: "I ought to have gone before." She stood up and ran her fingers through her thick hair and shook it back and stood with her long hands on her hips. "I'll go—not to-morrow, but the day after. May I come and see you?"

Trix was then filled with extraordinary activity, as if that decision had released a spring in her. She shut her paints box, flung down the lid of her dressing-basket, locked it, ran to the door, yelled: "In one minute, John," pulled on her hat, seized her coat and stood smiling before Mary.

"Come to the heartbreak party!"

But Mary excused herself. She wanted to go back to the hotel and be quiet. As she drove back, she thought: "Working does something for you. I can't go on without a job." She heard imaginary Chesterford voices saying: "Has tha heard t' latest? That wench o' Houghton's is running t' mills. She is, by gow, an' she's not so dusty, nayther." She was still smiling when she walked into the Carlton.

She hadn't shirked anything.

Chapter Fourteen

MRS. MEADOWS occupied the far corner bed in the Houghton Ward in Chesterford Royal Hospital. She had come in for her second operation. Nobody had expected her to recover from the first, for the breast had been almost entirely removed; but such was her desire to live a while longer to look after her children, that she had defeated death and returned to Number 17 Walker Street and appeared before Josh's eyes like a living skeleton. After three more days in bed at home she had begun to move about the house getting the children's and Josh's meals. There were odd moments when her pain vanished and she thought, in the inexpressible comfort of that relief, that she was cured. But there were times also, and these recurred more and more often, when the gnawing, scalding pain reduced her to feeble impotency. Her pallor was ghastly, her eyes large but sunken, her hands almost bereft of flesh. Josh thought to himself: "She gives me the bloody creeps." She had for him all the horror that those who die so dreadfully have for the base, the unloving and the ignorant. He was glad when she went back to hospital. Perhaps Jane Meadows was glad also. When they put her back into her old bed she uttered a quavering sigh. To feel those strong but gentle hands tending her, not allowing her to do anything for herself, to glance down the spotless ward with its scarlet quilts and see the sisters and nurses with their

367

starched large bows and fresh cheeks—there was a bit of comfort for her there. She whispered to Nurse Halloran: "It allus looks like Christmas here," and Nurse Halloran said: "Sure and 'tis so, and there's a kiss for you, mistletoe or no. And the docthor'll have ye fixed up as right as a trivet in next to no time. I've missed you. Ye'd no right to be goin' away from us so soon at all. I niver approved of it."

There were one or two women in the ward who remembered her, having been there all the time she was back in Walker Street, and who sent her by the nurse or in low shouts their wishes for good luck and an easy time. One woman, Mrs. Roberts, who lay next to her, had undergone five operations, from the last of which she was now recovering. "The Almighty got all His bits an' pieces mucked up when He was makin' me," she said, "He must ha' knocked off for His dinner afore He'd finished—and ever since, th' doctors have been tryin' to straighten 'em out. There's some on 'em missin' awtogether now." An astonishing slice of vitality was Mrs. Roberts and she and the other suffering women helped Jane Meadows to bear her lot. Nothing seemed quite so bad when others were going through it, she thought. "They've stopped this hurdy-gurdy as used to come outside and play opposite t' Brown Cow," said Mrs. Roberts. "Not afore time neither. Have you t'ave another one? I'm that sorry. But you've a long way to go till you catch me up. I tell 'em I'm nobbut a bit o' butcher's meat." Jane Meadows liked to hear Mrs. Roberts talk; she wasn't aware of half she said but it was companionable to hear her going on about them drawing the dole as had no right to it, and them being refused as needed it badly, and how she'd won £5 in the Otley Sweep, and how their young Albert could copy Charlie Chaplin a treat, and who made the best black puddings, and how Ramsbottom, the butcher, had made his brass out o' turnin' his odd bits an' scrag-ends into pies, and what the night nurse did when she wasn't in the ward (very scandalous and racy this was), and what the Sister with the sandy hair said about it in her hearing. Oh, there was no stopping Mrs. Roberts once she got going. Nurse Halloran confided to Jane Meadows, as she made her bed and lifted Jane about as though she were a bag of feathers, that the surgeons had popped a gramophone into Mrs. Roberts during her last operation.

Jane Meadows lay there, breathing small short breaths straight in and out, her body as still as if it lay in its coffin, and her mind going round in small circles. Would Trixie come afore Thursday when she was to go to the theatre again? (And what a funny name to call it—theayter. But, when she came to think of it, afore the new Theatre Royal was built they used to call it "T' Blood Tub." So happen . . . not as there could be much blood left in *her,* she thought with a thin shudder.) If Trixie came and saw her afore Thursday she thought she could be content. She didn't see how she could get over it this time. Did she want to? Oh, God, it were hard to make up her mind about that; tears ran down her cheeks as the question fluttered to and fro in her mind. She turned her head sideways and shut her eyes so that the wetness just fell on to the pillow and sank in and made it damp. Her thoughts wouldn't be still. There was Josh—she'd be glad to get away from Josh now. He'd been too cruel since she was bad. He couldn't bear to come near her, she could see that; and since she'd been took so ill, it was as if all her nerves had had fresh, sensitive edges put on 'em, and she couldn't bear ugliness and foul talk and ill temper or childer scriking. And Josh and the childer had provided all these. She'd shouted at the two childer a good deal during that month or two at home—and when the pain had gone she'd had them at her knee, huddling them to her and telling 'em to tak' no notice of her. Happen they'd

ha' scriked less if they'd had more to eat. Josh's dole wasn't
nearly enough to go round. Calves-foot jelly and Benger's
food the doctor had said she must have, and a raw egg now
and then. He might as well have ordered her to Bournemouth, aye, or Buckingham Palace. The childer got a meal
at school now, thank God—that put 'em on till tea-time.
There'd be more for *them* now she'd come back to hospital.
She didn't think they'd miss her much. They were both
young, Sarah twelve and Richard ten. Childer soon forgot.
They'd made a great "to do" over her when she came
home, but in half an hour they were out playin' 'em again;
and they told her what fun they'd had wi' Owd Mother
Cheetham from the top o' the street and Mrs. Morris, the
Jewess, next door, who, between them, had been looking
after 'em. Mrs. Morris was a widow, who kept herself by
her sewing-machine; fat, and a slattern with a house that
smelt always of rancid oil but a heart as wide as Walker
Street. She'd made the childer bread with caraway-seeds in
it, and large round, flat, fatty cakes and they'd watched her
for hours, in their early years, standing near by as she
treadled her sewing-machine, and sang: "Go to sleep, my
little pickaninny"—while the yards of calico or sateen went
through her machine with that bright shiny leg and the needle
shooting up and down. Jane Meadows had been hurt to see
how much they thought of the novelty of having Mrs.
Morris and Mrs. Cheetham making two fresh homes for
them, but she was glad now. It was funny what a difference
being ill made, how soon you felt nothing mattered so much.
She'd fought and fought to get better last time because the
childer had haunted her, Richard with his legs that were a
bit bandy through rickets and Sarah who was always wanting to dance and say bits of recitations and was too fond by
half of showing off and talking about her Auntie Trixie who
was a lady now. Jane Meadows wouldn't have believed the

house could have gone on a day without her—but it had. Josh had even sobered up a bit; he was a better man when she was away than when she was at home. Happen when she'd gone for good he'd pull hisself together again. Happen he'd takken a fancy to Mrs. Morris—or that woman Alice she had once heard him kissin' at t' street door . . . the night Trixie had thrown the flat-iron at him. Aye, maybe they'd be better off awtogether when she'd gone. An ailin' woman weren't much good to a chap as was on t' dole, an' childer soon forgot, aye, soon forgot. The tears welled up in her eyes again. She was crying for Jane Meadows now, and she couldn't stop. Convulsive sobs shook her, long shuddering sobs that wracked her poor body and brought Nurse Halloran hurrying to her to dry her eyes and smooth her hair and pat her back and treat her just the same as she herself had treated so often her Sarah and her Richard. And she didn't mind being treated so. She was twenty years older than Nurse Halloran but sometimes now she felt so old and worn out and weary that she was like a child again.

Josh came to see her on the Tuesday afternoon. He came in a rusty black suit with a red neckerchief twisted and tied in a small knot at the side of his throat. He was looking better, his eyes were sharper now he had less drink in him, and his flesh seemed firmer on his face. But he was very glum, glummer than when drink loosened his tongue. He came up the ward trying to walk quietly on his toes, his knees bent, his long arms dangling by his sides so that he looked ape-like. He sat on a cane chair by the bed and put his cap on his knee and looked at her and she looked steadily back at him. She'd no fear of him now. She was beyond him.

She asked: " 'Ow are they?"

He said: "Aw reet, I think."

She nodded. "Is Mrs. Morris doin' for yo'?"

"Aye, she comes in most days. Childer want to know if

they can come and see thee."

She turned her head away. "Better not, I think," she said. "I dunnot want 'em to think on me like this."

"Just as tha likes," he said indifferently. He sat there and stared about him a bit, glancing up and down the ward and shifting his cap from one knee to the other. "Dost know yet when it's to be?"

"O' Thursday," she said. " 'Afe past ten."

" 'Afe past ten." He repeated it for something to say. And then, sheepishly, for he didn't believe it: "Mebbe they'll set thee up proper this time."

"I dunnot think so." It wasn't much more than a whisper.

"Tha never knows," Josh said, doing the best he was capable of.

He was a little over-awed by the cleanliness and stiffness of this hospital. He felt they knew about him; he felt he was in some mysterious fashion the cause of his wife's cancer and that they knew that and were accusing him every time they looked at him, and every time a hoity-toity sister would say to him: "Come this way, Meadows," in a voice like acid. All spinsters, thought Josh. Never had a man and at war with him. They'd all takken the side of his missis against him. Weren't it bad for him, too? Didn't he look like being left wi' a couple o' young uns and there weren't many women as wanted to tackle a chap burdened that road. He would have liked to let fly at 'em.

As he sat there Nurse Halloran came to shake up the pillows.

"Well, Meadows, and how are you kapin'?"

"Aw reet," said Josh being pushed on one side as she came round the bed. He had to lean back to avoid his face impinging on the back of her skirt.

"Is it on the dole, ye still are? Too bad, indade. But there now, ye've got the greyhound racing and the whippets too,

and it'll be the fine time ye're having at the pictures in the
afthernoon." She chaffed him, but there was depth in it.
She went round the other side and suddenly stopped with
her hands down on the pillow like a woman baking bread
and looked at him. "I wonder now," she said, "pwhy ye
don't be after takin' a bit of a field an' growin' some spuds
an' kapin' a pig or two. 'Twould be better than puttin' your
dole on the two-thirty ivery day, wouldn't it now, Mrs.
Meadows?" And then she went on with her titivating of the
bed.

Josh gulped and wriggled on his chair and tried to say
something. By God, these women—a pig or two—talk about
sense—and tongues as—as long as Ogden Street. Aye. "Yer
must 'ave a tongue-stretchin' shop 'ere, I reckon," he muttered, and glowered at her with his face stuck out. He went
on muttering something to his waistcoat about being able
to tell when women weren't wed. She waited till he'd done
and then, her Irish blood rising: "That's a thrue word,"
she said. "There's more than one got her marriage lines
written on her poor face. An' most o' ye's got an ugly hand,
I'm thinkin'." And with that and her hand smoothing a wisp
of thin hair from Jane Meadows's brow, she was gone.

"She's a bitch, is yon," commented Josh. He sat a while
longer.

"Tap wants a new washer on," Jane Meadows said. "I
forgot to tell thee."

"Aw reet."

It occurred to her that she was probably looking on him
for the last time, on this man who was the father of her two
youngest children. And that she had practically nothing to
say to him.

"Tha'll look after 'em," she said, and then, feeling that
was too much to ask, added "as well as tha con, winna tha?"

Josh was still ruffled. "They'll ta' no harm if they han

to rough it. A dam' pity afe-time were ever stopped" (the practice of children working half-time in Lancashire mills).

"Nay, Josh, giv' 'em a chance." She spoke patiently, and very low.

"Did thee an' me ever have a chance?"

"Times are different."

"A seet wuss. Why—" But he didn't go on. It was too gigantic to be talked about.

She said again, after a long pause: "Richard ought to ha'. sunlight treatment."

"Wheer? Italy or somewheer?" He wiped his nose with his finger and thumb and rubbed them on his trousers, and his mouth twisted in a sardonic grin.

"They were tellin' me here about it—it's at t' clinic."

"Tha can see to it when th'art better," he said. He implied he didn't believe it and he couldn't be bothered and it were a fancy idea and if she wanted fancy ideas carrying out she'd better get better and attend to them herself.

So there was no more to say. She lay on her back with her head turned away from him towards the broad high window through which she could hear the rattle of horses' hoofs jigging past in milk-floats, the heavy clomp! clomp! of the drays, and the hum and singing and grinding of brakes and tinkling and buzzing of bells on the trams. There was a stop outside the hospital—just as there was a dyeworks behind it and a church, St. Mark's, that chimed the quarters all night long, next door. Patients who wanted rest and quiet never got it; maybe that was too much to expect—quietness by folk who paid nothing for their treatment. But Jane Meadows liked the noises; she came to know drivers who jumped on their gongs, some once, some twice, before they released the brake with a rattle of the cogs and went off down the slight hill; the first trams at half past five in the morning were pleasant to hear after a night of racking pain

and burning mouth—and then the gradual stirring of life—
clatter of boots, whistling of boys, ringing of bicycle bells—
and she felt less alone. Josh saw the head turned away, felt
the quietness descend on them like a curtain being drawn,
and knew his time was up. He was glad. This sort o' business
was no cop. It weren't as if you could do any good, eyther.
He scraped the chair back and stood up.

"I'd best be gooin'," he said.

Her head turned slowly in his direction and her lips made
the word "Aye." She looked steadily at him and he didn't
feel comfortable.

"Happen I'll come agen to-morrow, if they'll let me . . ."

She shook her head slightly. "Nay, I shouldn't bother,
Josh." She turned her eyes away from him once more, which
made it easier for him to say: "After Thursday, then—
when th'art fit to see anybody—" The words trailed away
to nothing.

She looked back at him and a decision formed in her
mind. "Under"—Josh moved a foot nearer and bent his
head—"under t' newspaper as lines t' top drawer in t' bedroom—there's a post-office book—two pound five in. If owt
'appens—it'll buy 'em a bit o' black."

"I've ne'er seen it."

"Naw." A smile so faint as to be hardly discernible, broke
across her lips and was gone.

"Aw reet," Josh said abruptly.

Two pound five, eh? Saved out of his wages and he hadn't
known. It didn't occur to him she had saved it out of her
washing money. He had badly wanted something to restore
his sense of grievance, and lo! here it was. Heh, but he was
pleased!

He hesitated a moment longer but she had turned her
head back towards the window. He moved the chair to indicate he was going. She took no notice. He started off

down the ward, gladly, putting his heels down now. Two pound five! He didn't care a tuppenny damn for any of 'em. Every stride he took made him more cheerful. It was as though weights had been taken from his feet. He went down the stone stairs two at a time in a shambling run. He felt in his trouser-pocket. Aye, a sixpence and two pennies. Two pound five, eh? He walked straight across to the Three Jolly Carters.

Chapter Fifteen

TRIX HAD WRITTEN to Maud Eckersley saying she was coming, and it was to Green Bank that she proceeded from Chesterford station. Some quality of excitement had been present in her throughout the journey, for was she not going home? She left Euston at half past eleven, travelling first class—she had saved more than half of her forty pounds a week at the Post War Theatre and the sable coat Hilditch had given to her and her jewel-case of blue leather would have looked odd third class, she thought. At first she couldn't avoid feeling rather triumphant. But she was sorely perplexed about her mother, and the closer she got to Lancashire, and the more sidings of coal trucks she saw, with miners on railway platforms standing in the cold wind with jackets buttoned up to the neck looking exactly like Josh with their red-rimmed eyes—the more the feeling of triumph diminished. She had reached a different land, where money was hardly come by, where what she had on her back would keep a family for a year, perhaps two years, and what she and Hilditch had spent on a dinner maintain a family on the dole for a month. True, she had at first sent money to her mother but her mother had returned nearly all of it, saying that if Josh were kept in real comfort on it work would never enter his head again; she added they were "managing" and, anyhow, she and the children couldn't have

377

anything different to Josh—not without ructions—but, someday, happen, if things got different. . . . Thinking over it, Trix felt she ought to have insisted. But she would make it up richly now. Mrs. Meadows hadn't told Trix about the first operation until it was over and she was back at 17 Walker Street—she couldn't have Trix risking her work by running up to see her, she said. This time, however, she had written, buying for the purpose a packet of violet-coloured notepaper in order that Trix might not be ashamed of it and writing:

"DEAR TRIXIE,—I have to go into hospitle again because my trouble is not quite better as the doctors had hopes of, and as I feel rarther bad I should like to see you if quite convenient but I shall quite understand if it should not be. So with much love from your loving Mother. P.S. The operation will most likely be in a few days. I am not frightened. x x x."

Trix half expected Brierley to be at Chesterford station but he wasn't. How could he know? And yet, if he had asked Maud Eckersley . . .

She had to lift her bags out of the train herself—only one porter near the engine and him semaphoring the train off almost before she had them out. What a filthy station it was; and so quiet; only the clatter on the other platform of a milk churn. Nobody else had alighted.

"Do yo' want 'em carryin' up? Aye, that's right."

The porter brought them up but paused half way on the steps, his arms bulging, to talk to a man descending.

"Workin'?"

"Workin'? Me?" The man spat. "They smashed up my looms wi' a sledge-hammer last week. I watched 'em at it; fifteen shillin' they fotched for scrap. An' t' chap as smashed

'em did it for threepence ha'penny an hour. Threepence
ha'penny! By the mon." That was the *ultima Thule*, to be
broken up at that low rate of pay. "The factory's goin' to
be a motor garage."

"A what?"

"A motor garage—though who the hell is goin' to be able
to ride in a motor-car if this 'ere goes on, I dunno."

"Happen it's a motor-hearse garage."

They both laughed at that. "That's not so bad, isn't
that," said the weaver, going down grinning. The young
porter came up smiling broadly at his success. "Things is in
a mucky shape," he said cheerfully. "Yo' don't belong 'ere,
do you?"

Trix, tickled by his friendliness, said: "I do an' I don't,
like," and enjoyed watching the smile come off his face. But
he didn't recognise her; her face conveyed nothing to him.
She was a little disappointed.

"Anybody meetin' yo'?"

"No."

He put his fingers in his mouth and blew a whistle and
looked up the street. Nothing happened. "Must be out," he
said, after a third whistle was unavailing. He pondered. "I
could bring 'em up on t' tram when I have my tea," he said.

"The cloak-room then?"

"Nay, it's no good wastin' money that road. I'll put 'em
wheer they winna run away." He resolutely picked them up
and turned. "About 'afe-past four," he said.

She walked up Vincent Street. The Sunset weaving-shed
which used to hum like a spinning-top was so still that you
could have heard the tick of your watch at the gate. Opposite
was a corner shop flying that white flag of distress: "To
Let." What she had heard was true, then. The tram stop
was opposite the Black Bull but she didn't wait there; she
had grown over-conscious of the splendour of her fur coat.

She would be glad to get into Maud Eckersley's sitting-room. Chesterford was dirtier than she had thought, more grim, less . . . less warm in its welcome. People in the tram stared frankly and openly at her. A child whose nose needed wiping lolled against its mother's knee opposite to her and looked up at her fixedly. Trix smiled at it but the child never relaxed its face. Trix was apparently something it didn't comprehend; it looked sullen and resentful. Trix felt a little abashed, and angry too.

Maud Eckersley was shy, and her shyness restored Trix's good humour. When she kissed Maud's cheek, Maud blushed like a child. A bright fire burned in the gloomy sitting-room glinting on the cruet and glass that decorated the sideboard but the air was stuffy and close, and so soon as Maud went out Trix opened the window a foot so that a draught of chill, clammy air flowed in; a situation at which Maud stared with disapproval but in silence when she returned to lay the tea-cloth. Maud didn't inquire if Trix wanted tea; she began to prepare it and as she darted to and fro between the sitting-room and the kitchen she conversed, a running commentary. "Life's movin' fast," she said; "yo' can't keep up with it. First the Repertory an' then no Repertory; one minute t' town boomin' and the next slumpin'." Trix interrupted to say that it was more than a minute. "Yes, I know—but yer know what I mean. Up to-day and down to-morrow, clogs to clogs, dust to dust." Maud shook her head and the tall ebony comb bobbed in her hair. "You'd think the Lord was preparin' 'em all for heaven the way He's takkin' their riches away from 'em. Talk about puttin' folk on their feet, them as had horses and pairs—"

"And how are *you* getting on with no theatrical companies?"

But Maud didn't answer that. She disappeared into the

kitchen; she was an expert at that when the question was awkward. She brought the tea and hot toast and two boiled eggs. Maud had recovered from her shyness and was giving Trix what she thought she ought to have. "This'll put yer on till yer have a proper meal," she said.

"I asked how *you* are getting on," said Trix with a mouthful of toast and recovering with her tongue the butter oozing from the corner of her mouth. She was home again.

Maud went out for the tea-cosy and came back and said she mustn't grumble; there were plenty worse off than her; she wasn't like them as hadn't sense to come in when it rained. She'd a bit put by, like. But Maud didn't like this personal discussion. Had Trix decided when she would go and see her mother? She'd heard Dr. Ainsworth who did the cancer operations was very clever. Oh, and Mr. Brierley —he had called and left word he would come round after his weaving-shed closed.

Trix's heart leapt and she lifted her cup and drank. When she put it down she asked, calmly: "When did he call?"

" 'Smornin'. Miss Houghton had told him, he said."

"What time will his mill close?"

"Half past five, most likely."

"Could I go to the hospital to-night, do you think?"

"Yea, I fixed that up, because—because they've put the operation forrard a day."

"Maud, why didn't you say so before?"

"It's all right, Miss Trix. I didn't want to fluster you. When I got your letter, knowin' how anxious you'd be to see your mother, I called at t' hospital and saw t' matron and told her who yer was. It's all right. Yer can go any time to-night up to eight o'clock. I told 'em they must tell your mother so she wouldn't be frettin'. Did I do right?" Maud stood there motionless, her hands hanging down, and her small face with its wall eye very solemn. Trix leaned over and took her hand and pressed it. "All right, luv," she said. "You've done champion."

"Get yer tea," said Maud. "Yer want plenty inside yer for—for this cold weather."

It was nearly six o'clock when Brierley came. Maud had prepared his tea also. "You've plenty to do and plenty to talk about, I daresay," she said.

"Hello, my dear," he said when Maud had gone. He took Trix's hand and held it.

"Hello, Harry," she said. She had changed into a green corded velvet frock with a white frilled collar and cuffs. Her eyes were large and brilliant with excitement and her breath came fast.

"You've been working too hard," she said. His face was thin-cheeked, his lips too pale, his hands long and white-looking.

"I'm all right." He tried to smile but his face was stiff and went back to its solemnity except that creases near his eyes remained and brought benignity to them. He didn't tell her that he had tossed all night in his bed because he knew she was coming or that her face had been walking ahead of him through the alleys between the looms and looking up at him from the letters he had written. But she was lovelier than he had imagined her. Her cheeks were less rounded now, her brows more arched; suffering had refined her face and deft and delicate fingers had taught the manner of beauty that can be created. But how much was of God and how much of man he didn't pause to think, and would not have cared had he done so. It was enough that she was before him, turning his bones to water as she had done in the past, and making the old fire leap in him.

"Darling," he said, "you are beautiful." He caught his breath sharply, as though he might almost break into a cry.

She saw his eyes regarding her with adoration and wonder.

Brierley did not think of her as one who had lain in his arms and with whom he had fulfilled himself; that was past; she had gone away from him. She must be won again, if she were to be won at all.

As they stood near to one another at the mantelpiece, both of them a little on fire, Maud came in with his tea and toast and Trix said: "Don't be long, Harry. I'm going to the hospital. You'll come with me, won't you?" He looked at her and smiled and nodded but didn't speak and went and sat down and Maud, before going out, poured out his tea and put his sugar and milk in it. Trix said: "I'll put my things on," but as she came past him he put out his hand and took hers and as she stopped he put his arm round her waist and drew her to him and rested his head against her bosom. She stood looking down at him and passed her hand over his hair. Neither of them spoke. He kissed the velvet of her dress near her breast and released her and she went out and he ate his toast and drank his hot tea, consuming it fast and ravenously. When Trix returned he was standing waiting. "You've not had enough," she said.

"Yes, I have." He was amused and delighted by her thought for him.

He put out his hand to her and she took it and pressed it swiftly and as swiftly released it and said briskly: "I think we ought to go, Harry."

"Yes," he said with some energy. He saw that she didn't want to have love made to her.

She stopped at the doorway to call to Mrs. Eckersley and turned to consult him. "Shall we have dinner here, or—"

"Don't you know," he said, "that I'm one of those who have high tea? None of your five-course—"

"What about fish and chips and trotters?" Her eyes sparkled. "I've not had any for months."

"That'll be reight up to t' mark," he said, putting on his dialect.

"Maud," she shouted, "fish and chips and trotters—half past eight. Trotters first—*hors d'œuvre*—plenty of vinegar, mind."

"Yo' don't alter none," said Maud emerging from the kitchen. "Remember me to yer mother; she's always welcome here, tell her."

They were more at ease with one another as they walked along.

"How's your factory going?"

"Not bad."

"Got a job for me?"

"Happen. But not that sort of a job." He looked at her, his lips curled in a laugh, but she turned her head towards the shops.

"You'll lose all your money, I expect."

"You never know. I'll have to write a modern Nell Gwynn story for you. You might easily marry into some Mid-European royal house."

"The butler, more like." After a while she said: "You don't think I'm hard—not talking about mother?"

"No."

"I'm a bit frightened."

"I know."

"Harry, if—when—if it isn't too bad—you'll see if I want to be alone with her, won't you?"

"Of course you'll want to be alone with her. I can stay in the waiting-room."

"No, I want you to come—only—"

"Yes, dear, all right. I'll try and be intelligent."

"Do you think people ought to be allowed to be killed—if they want to be?"

"Yes, I think so. Insisting on people living on in agony

is monstrous. Like doctors refusing to give women twilight sleep. Might as well saw legs off without an anæsthetic."

When they entered the ward they saw Mrs. Meadows at once. She had raised herself up on one elbow and was watching the door. She stayed thus until Trix was within a yard or two of her and then she sank down with a contented sigh lifting up her arms to put them round Trix's neck. Nurse Halloran got Brierley a chair but he didn't sit down; he stood waiting till the greeting was ended. When Trix raised her head from her mother's pillow, she still gazed down at her and held her hand, and kept touching her mother's face and neck with her other fingers. "Hello, mother," she kept saying and Mrs. Meadows said: "Hello, luv," murmured several times. Then she said: "I'm glad you could come. T' last hour or two seemed a long while." She smiled and the pale grey eyes and furrowed sallow face lighted up with a faint gleam.

Trix turned. "Harry." Brierley came to the bedside, embarrassed and unhappy at what, he felt, Mrs. Meadows must regard as an intrusion. But he was wrong there. She looked up at him, noting the creases near his eyes, the sensitive mouth, the triangular face.

"This is Harry Brierley, mother."

Mrs. Meadows nodded and again the thin gleam of pleasure crossed her face and faded. "It was nice of yo' to come," she said. Brierley put his hand into hers for a moment and then sat down, hoping that mother and daughter would exclude him from their conversation.

Perhaps Mrs. Meadows knew that. She wasn't shy or awkward as she would have been had she been well. If the King had called upon her now, she would not have been disturbed. The tall stature that the world has bestowed on riches and high birth was shrivelled by pain and the proximity of death.

The screen that Nurse Halloran had thoughtfully placed round the bed made them private.

"Yo' know it's to-morrow?" Mrs. Meadows asked, addressing Trix.

"Yes, mother. I suppose there's no other way. It seems so soon—after the last time."

"I daresay they know best."

"You're brave."

"Nay, nay. It'll be a rest—while I'm under. Yo' don't know anythin'. No pain." After a long pause she added: "An' happen I shan't come—back."

These words spoken so quietly and with such longing for peace in them filled Brierley's throat and brought a rush of tears to Trix's eyes. Her mother looked at her sadly and almost as if she were surprised at her breaking down.

"Dunnot tak' on so," she said. "It 'ud be best that road. When a woman like me canna do her work, oo's better—"

"No, no. I could look after you. Take you away."

"I dunnot want it, luv. I dunnot want to be takken away. Nuthin' but a new body"—she touched her breast—"is any use an' they can't do that wi' aw their wonders."

"They wouldn't be going to operate again if there wasn't any hope," said Trix desperately.

"Happen not." Mrs. Meadows moved her hand towards Trix and Trix took it in both hers. "This is what I've been wantin' above everythin'. It's better than aw their physic." No sooner had she spoken than her eyes opened wider in a paroxysm of horrifying pain and a low moan escaped her and her lips twisted back from her teeth in her agony. Trix rose to her feet and looked wildly round the screen for Nurse Halloran, and her mother, in fear of causing a commotion, whispered, a few moments later as if she had run a long race, "Better in a minute or two." After awhile she lay back, her eyes closed and her body exhausted.

Trix looked across at Brierley and murmured "Harry" and he walked on tiptoe round the foot of the bed and placed his hand on Trix's shoulder. They were thus when Mrs. Meadows opened her eyes.

"It's gone," she said. She turned her head, the more easily to regard them and nodded as if what she saw was what she wished to see.

Brierley had felt constrained and moved from the moment he arrived and now, seeing Mrs. Meadows close her eyes again, he whispered to Trix that he would wait for her outside and quietly withdrew. Trix sat on, and, on an impulse, leaned forward and tried to kiss her mother's hair without disturbing her, but immediately a smile crossed her mother's lips and a hand was raised to touch Trix's face.

"Are yo' goin' to wed him?"

"Would you like me to?"

"He looks nice—his eyes are kind. Dunnot be freetened because o' me and Josh."

"I'm not."

"There's good men as well as t'other sort. Yer father were wild—but he never lifted a finger to me."

Her mother went on: "There's times when yo'll be rare an' lonely wi'out yer wed. It's a bad do often enough but women aren't content any other road. I should be more satisfied if yo' were settled."

Trix said: "You've no right to be thinking about me. It's you that matter."

"Nay it's not. My candle's gettin' down to t' wick." She rested a few moments and then said again: "If he wants thee, I'd like to know tha were goin' to tak' him."

"Mother, don't keep on talking as if you weren't goin' to . . ."

"I've done."

She lay relaxed, a contented look on her face, her eyes

fixed lovingly on her daughter's.

"I brought you some grapes and eggs and things."

"Thank yo', luv."

"I gave them to Nurse Halloran."

"That's right." After a while she said: "They'll be wantin' to tidy me up for t' night, luv."

"Do you want me to go?"

"No—only they're good, an' I don't want to be any bother."

"Does anybody come to see you?"

"There were Miss 'Oughton yesterday. Oo brought me them carnations. Oo's nice. This is th' 'Oughton Ward. Oo comes sometimes. You'll know her, happen."

"Yes."

"I thowt so. I didn't let on who I were." The remembrance of this small subterfuge sent another film of light across her eyes. "I've never axed yo' how you've been gettin' on or told yo' how grand yo' look. I've been proud. I kept aw t' bits yo' sent me from t' papers. I've got 'em here." She smiled as though she were displaying a weakness. "A lot o' folks begun to pretend to know yo' as didn't."

Nurse Halloran put her head round the screen and said briskly: " 'Tis nearly time, my dear," and withdrew again.

For a moment a look of distress came into Mrs. Meadows's eyes but she forced it out.

"You'd best go, luv." As if in extenuation of that, she added: "They've been very good."

"Why shouldn't they be?" asked Trix, tormented.

Mrs. Meadows put out her hand again and drew Trix to her. "Come an' kiss me," she said. Trix put her arms round her mother's neck and raised her body, so light now, and strained her to her breast as though her mother had been a child. Her own rich mouth with lips warm and soft and full, lay on her mother's, parched and dried like leaves, as if she would pour life into them. "Oh, mother," she said, "why is it like this?" Mrs. Meadows's thin arms held her tight and it was the mother now who did the comforting, saying: "Theer, theer," and patting Trix's back.

At length Trix raised herself. "It's only good-bye till to-morrow," she said, trying by the force within her to persuade her mother she would recover. Mrs. Meadows smiled at her and nodded, but with such a look of resignation and farewell that Trix's lips quivered again.

"Good-bye, mother, till to-morrow, then."

"Good-bye, luv, good-bye. It's been too nice."

Nurse Halloran moved the screen swiftly so that Mrs. Meadows could watch Trix go down the ward. The tired eyes rested for a moment or two on the door through which she had gone; then closed. There was nothing more she wanted.

Chapter Sixteen

WHEN HENRY BRIERLEY bought a weaving shed with what remained of his profits won in the cotton boom, he had no thought of creating a domestic revolution in the household of Sam and Harriet Renshaw. Yet that is what occurred. Of course in one sense it was not Brierley who did it, so much as, perhaps, Mr. Gandhi and other brown gentlemen of the East who evolved in India the boycott of Lancashire; or again not so much Mr. Gandhi as Timothy Hilditch and Thomas Blackburn and all the rest who turned the county into a gambling den in which mill shares were the counters. But it is incontrovertible that the slump which drew a rising curve from 1923 onwards turned thousands of the world's finest male cotton operatives into housemaids; for it happened that when only half or less than half the shuttles flew, mill managers and tacklers and overlookers had a general preference for allotting such looms as were throbbing with life to women rather than to men. There were several reasons: often enough the women's skill was greater, their fingers more deft, their cloth freer from faults; they were more amenable, easier to manage, and readier to sweep round the machinery or fold cloth in their own time; and— they were women. Many a man meeting a tackler in the street and asking: "When arta goin' to send for *me*?" was answered: "*Tha* doesn't wear skirts, doesta?" It is easy to exaggerate that factor; it would be foolish and inaccurate to ignore it.

Sam Renshaw was not a weaver; he spun. That bare-footed tramp up and down the oily polished floor after the marching spindles had never yet fallen to women. But Harriet had been a four-loom weaver and when she heard that Stone End shed was re-opening she applied for looms; and after an interview with Brierley, who was impressed by her vitality and frankness (she admitted she hadn't woven for seventeen years and was in a fix), obtained them.

"Do you want to invest any money in the mill?" Brierley had asked her. "No," she said. "I don't want to do. Have I to do?" Brierley had laughed. "No. Some weavers have been coming and offering to put in twenty pounds in the hope of getting a job." "Well," Harriet had said, "I dare-say there's been many a twenty pound spent worse. But we'n lost enough i' cotton already." Brierley had enquired then if she were Sam Renshaw's wife. "I am that," Harriet said pursing her lips and looking straight at him, as though to add, "An' yo' can mak' what yo' like on it." But Brierley had merely asked: "Can you weave jacquards?" and Harriet said she reckoned she could, unless looms were made different now. "Mine," Brierley said briefly, "were built about the time I was born."

So it was settled. Harriet found it very tiring at first and a little exciting. The first day or two she could barely touch her dinner after that long morning standing on her feet in the warm fœtid air amid the roar and clackety-clack of the looms. She felt more like being sick than eating, and her back was well-nigh breaking by eleven o'clock. She had bought a new pair of clogs and they chafed her ankles, and her fingers were all thumbs. Nor did she like getting up so early. It was all very well rising early to do an extra wash, or to go off in prosperous times with Sam to Southport, or for whatever else, she, as mistress of a household, decided. But this rising at 6.30 a.m. because she must, to get ready for that summoning blast on a siren—she didn't like it at all. The bed was warm and Sam's back was warm and—she realised she was getting older. The bed pulled so strongly that for the first week or two she had time for no more than a cup of tea and a piece of bread and butter; that is to say after the first morning. Then, she was so anxious not to be late that she and Sam were up at six o'clock and prepared an elaborate meal they couldn't afford of bacon and eggs; only to find she couldn't eat it because she was so excited. (Sam looked at it ruefully when she was there but he polished it off in no time after she had gone.)

But at first Sam disliked the arrangement altogether. It offended his supremacy as a male. Wasn't he an aristocrat among cotton operatives, a spinner? Hadn't he earned his six and seven and eight pounds a week sometimes? It wasn't so bad for weavers who were accustomed to having their wives weaving also (and often earning more than they did) but between them they never earned more than five pounds a week and rarely more than three. Sam was never convinced that weaving *was* a man's job at all. But for a spinner's wife to work while *he* stayed at home—that were a corker, that were. He said to Tom Edmunds: "By the mon, Tom, but I ne'er thowt this 'ud happen to me," in the manner of a man whose fate is finally sealed.

"Is her puttin' on airs?" asked Tom.

"Nay, I'll say that for her. Oo doesn't say much. Oo eits what I get for her—at least about enough to keep a sparrow when it's moultin'. But I find her washin' t' pots o'er agen sometimes—just quiet-like, sayin' nowt an' hopin' I'm not lookin'."

"What dost do then?"

"I do nowt. I haven't made up my mind whether it's a

good idea to pretend to be a bit of a numbyed so's she winna expect me to do so much and so's she'll happen get fed wi' th' arrangement or whether to be ratty at her doin' agen what I've already done. It's a gradely mess, is this. Whichever road I look at it, it's no better. It's not natural. An' how much better off are we than bein' on t' parish? Nobbut a two-three bob a wi'k. An' that'll be gone i' rent when we get i' that council house."

"You're surely not goin' in a council house! They'll hear aw yo' say next door. However, it's better than goin' to t' pictures, they say—th' entertainments yo' overhear. Talk about listenin' in! But I thowt they'd a waitin' list as long as Ogden Street."

"Aye, so they have. But Harriet's managed it. Her boss knows Miss Houghton an' her feyther—wheels within wheels, tha knows. We're movin' next week."

"I thowt tha said her didn't put on airs. Her seems to do as her likes."

Sam reflected that the ability of Tom Edmunds to put his finger on a sore place was that of the Devil. He came rooting round, soft-soaping you until he found what he wanted and then—by God, it were worse than goin' to the dentist, wi' him poking about on a tender tooth.

"Dunnot imagine oo wears t' breeches," said Sam. "Th' house'll be i' my name."

"But her'll pay t' rent," said Edmunds roaring with laughter. "Tha corn't tak' me in. Tha'rt hen-pecked—allus were, Sam."

There was enough truth in this to make Sam livid. "Tha'll buy thy own ale i' future," he said. "That'll be a change for thee." This was grandiloquent, because Sam had had no money for ale for sometime, but it was true in essence; Edmunds was a fumbler. It took a lot to upset Sam, but the truth could do it. This all came o' bein' out o' work he thought as he walked away—and it weren't a chap's fault, eyther. Nobody wanted work more than he did. He didn't grumble at havin' to leave T' Rookery—they'd flown high and they'd come a cropper. That were aw reet. A chap could stand that. But everybody ought to be able to work as were willin'—aye, and at the job he'd served his time too an' all. What were England comin' to? More important, what were Lancashire an' Chesterford comin' to? One mill were a dog-biscuit factory, another full o' bricks and tiles, another a cotton-waste business; it didn't seem five minutes sin' they were worth anythin' from a quarter to half a million. There were plenty o' folk not gettin' enough t' eat. Yo' only had to look at 'em—pasty as skirtin' boards a lot of 'em were, an' no heavier than jockeys by t' look on 'em. "If I get much thinner, I'll be able to ride a whippet let alone a racehorse," some of 'em said. You couldn't quell their humour. It were like t' war over agen. T' worse it got, the more some of 'em joked. An' their George. Harriet were frettin' her heart out over him. He were down i' Dorset stoppin' at a Home of St. Francis recoverin' fro' a bout o' influenza got through gettin' wet and sleepin' in "spikes," which George had explained were workhouses. Spikes. Sam had never heard tell of the word afore. George were no better than a tramp, and that a lad of his should be a tramp got Sam's goat.

"Why doesn't he come whoam?" he asked Harriet, as if Harriet knew all the secret workings of George's heart. And Harriet, as if she did, in truth know, said: "Because he's got plenty o' bant about him."

"He'll get locked up nex' thing."

"Well?"

"That'll be a fine thing, winnat it?"

"Depends what he gets locked up for," Harriet said, her voice hardening.

Sam blundered on. "They dunnot lock chaps up for nowt."

"Tha'll say next they don't kill folks for nowt eyther."

"Nawther do they."

"Didta ever hear o' Christ crucified?"

That finished Sam.

"Let me tell thee," Harriet added, "that if our George were as soft as some I know, he'd ha' been whoam long sin' scrikin'. He's not goin' to be kept by me, George isn't."

"Hah," said Sam with dreadful calm, "I wondered how long it 'ud be afore tha threw it i' my face."

He stood with the pot towel in his hand, washing up after their tea while Harriet rested herself for a while. So long as Harriet worked and he didn't Sam had vowed he'd do all the housework, duly assisted by the children who, however, did precious little; and there were rare times when Sam valiantly tried to keep the vow.

Sam stood with a cup suspended in one hand and the wet towel limp in the other. He felt grieved and downcast and miserable.

"I wasn't throwing it i' thy face," said Harriet wearily.

"I'm not as dense as that." He was relieved by what she said, but he couldn't relinquish his ground all at once.

"I've never blamed thee and I'm not blamin' thee now." She rose and went across to him. "Gie me that towel."

"What for?"

"Go and sit thee down and have a smoke. This is my job. I never like to see thee at it." Sam after a half-hearted attempt to continue wiping the pots, surrendered the towel and sat down.

"I brought thee an evenin' paper," Harriet said. "Tha'll find it in t' shoppin' basket."

But Sam's housekeeping didn't always lead to unpleasantness, especially after they were settled in the council house on the Ormrod Estate. There were jobs he grew to like. Harriet's spirits rose; she felt clean and dignified again; she could hold her head up; the children no longer ran risks of contamination from dirty closets and the unbridled tongues of men and women. She had to rise earlier and she could not always get home to her midday meal, but those drawbacks were as nothing. She earned thirty-two shillings a week on an average and the rent was ten shillings but she achieved the miracle of making ends meet. If you went to Shawcross Market at five minutes to nine on Saturday night —it closed at nine—you could buy enough meat for a shilling to last all the following week. The butchers almost threw it at you. One day she bought a conger-eel a yard long for threepence. Bessie wouldn't touch it because she had seen it before it was cooked; she swore it was a young sea serpent. There was plenty of cocoa and oatmeal and tea that had no name on the packet, but which would do, to be had at half the price of the well-advertised stuff. Harriet said you paid for the advertisements; she simply wouldn't believe that folk could take whole pages in newspapers and put up winking electric signs without you paying through the nose for it. "I'm a scavenger," Harriet said, and she said it almost with pride. She would walk a mile to save a penny. How much shoe-leather she might expend in saving the penny she didn't pause to think. Harriet had a school of economics of her own. She rummaged old fent shops for ends of cloth to make the children's dresses and after she had rested a while at night, she would begin to treadle her sewing-machine. Harriet lived with a vengeance up to the North-country working-class saying: "It's all bed and work."

Sometimes in the evening Sam would bake while she sewed. Sam enjoyed that. You couldn't go far wrong in baking bread provided you had a nose for the smell of it; and what a gorgeous smell it was. Baking night! "It makes your chops slaver," he said, when the whole house was redolent with new crusty bread. Sam had a secret belief that baking bread came as natural to a man as digging up the garden. But he didn't say so. No, that wouldn't quite have done. But to arrange the bread mug, beautifully smooth inside and empty the flour into it so that it puffed up in a small cloud, to make a hole in the middle and pour in the yeast and water so that it bubbled in a small lake and then to plunge his arms in and begin to mix it—he hadn't enjoyed anything more since he made sand-pies as a boy at Morecambe. When he had kneaded it dry he would pour more water round the edges.

"Is that enough?" He would carry the water-jug to Harriet as she sewed. She would cock an expert eye at it.

"Nay, yo'll drown it. Half that'll be plenty."

"That's what I thowt, only I know tha likes to be axed."

He would knead again, making his moist fingers, dipped in the water-jug, plop like a bullock's hoof coming out of mud, as they went in and out of the sucking flour.

"Here," he would say, "come an' wipe my nose."

That had followed his craning his neck to wipe his nose on the shoulder of his shirt, since he couldn't get to his handkerchief with his hands covered with dough.

"Tell *me* when tha wants thy nose wipin'," Harriet had said.

"Nay, it's not wipin' exactly; only it itches like mad."

"Now then, don't tell me that tale," she had said, going to wipe it.

"Give us a kiss while tha'art here."

"Of aw the daft—" But she had kissed him.

So now when Sam kneaded the bread on Tuesday evenings, he always declared his nose wanted wiping, and Harriet knew when he said that, that he wanted to be kissed. And it didn't displease her, although this making her go to him caused her to feel as shy as a girl.

She would give him his orders. "To-morrow tha mun

clean t' gas-stove an' t' top shelves. Thursday we'll have t'
cupboards done, Friday tha con do a bit o' black-leadin'."
Sam knew that he didn't mind. The council house had so
restored Harriet's serenity after what they had gone
through that, as he told Tom Edmunds: "She's i' rare fettle."

On a particular Saturday morning he had given the steel
fender and fire-irons an extra polish and had put them away
under the sofa with a newspaper over them until, after dinner, when Harriet was home, he brought them forth with
pride.

"What dost think o' them?"

Harriet cast an appraising eye at them.

"They'll do."

"Do? I should just think they would. There's a shillings-
worth o' elbow-grease on them. Here, dost know what?"

"Nay, how *should* I know?"

"We'n formed a trade union, me an' two-three chaps
round here who're aw skivvies now. We want our wages
raisin'. Aye, we want another ounce o' bacca a week and
fourpence for t' pictures. An' when art gooin' to tak' me to
Burnham? Dost know we hanna' been for six months or
more? Here, what art cryin' for?" For Harriet had unac-
countably turned her face to the mantelpiece and was wiping
her eyes with the corner of her apron.

"Nowt."

"Nay, I'st not ha' that. Tha doesn't cry for nowt. Is it
George?"

She shook her head. Sam put his arm round her waist and
turned her round and unresistingly she leaned her head on
him.

"Nah then, nah then, tell me."

"I'm freetened we're gooin' t'ave another child, Sam."

Sam stroked his nose.

"Nay, surely not."

"I'm a fortni't over my time."

"Well, lass, tha's been longer than that monny a time."

"Yea, I know, but I've felt funny. I suppose I've got catched because we've been happier t' last month or two sin' we come here."

"Well, I'st ha' to learn how to weave and happen Mester Brierley'll gie me thy looms." Sam tried to joke it off but it was a serious matter. After a moment or two he asked: "Dost think tha'd better tak' summat?"

"I have been doin'. That's what's made me feel so queer sometimes."

"It's aw my fault." Sam felt very contrite.

She put her hand over his mouth. "Don't say that."

"Well," he said, "don't worrit thysel'. We'se manage some road. Tha remembers what t' poet says:

> *Tha'rt welcome, bonnie brid.*
> *Tha shouldn't ha' come just when tha did—*
> *Times are hard.*

Folk'n gone through it afore."

It wasn't so much that Sam was a philosopher as that he was incapable of worrying for long together.

On the Sunday Harriet walked to Burnham and back to exhaust herself in an endeavour to achieve her purpose; and at midnight she awoke Sam and told him it was all right.

"What's aw reet? Eh? Oh, aye—aye. I towd thee tha were worryin' too soon. But tha'rt a gradely lass."

He patted her posterior affectionately and rolled over and went to sleep again.

Chapter Seventeen

TRIX HAD BORNE Hilditch's death with comparative equanimity. The shock had been akin to that of physical violence; no more than that—as though she had been involved in a street accident. No true affection was concerned. But her mother's approaching death was, when she allowed herself to dwell on it, almost unendurable. For she had no doubt now that her mother would die. Death, rather than the suffering she was undergoing, might, her reason told her, be the kinder way. Yet that knowledge reconciled her very little. She had no spiritual faith or poise to uphold her. She was as completely without religion as an Englishwoman can be who has had nothing but scraps of Bible or Prayer Book teaching at a secular school, has never attended church, and has found life such a harsh fight that it has never seemed possible that a Loving Saviour can have intended her to be tried in that way.

Brierley's sea was scarcely chartered either. Orthodox Christianity he had thrown aside as incredible after reaching the age of eighteen, consequent on reading something of other faiths, learning that the Cross was a religious symbol long before Christ and that Buddha, Confucius and Mohammed had preached doctrines embodying both profound wisdom and saintliness. The war had finally destroyed his membership of the Church of England as it had of countless others. Slaughter blessed by the ministers of Christ was outside his comprehension as were also the wide discrepancies in pay among the clergy, some rich, some hideously poor; and as was the position of those people of wealth who professed to worship the Carpenter but who, with rare exceptions, were of such social pride that no sawyer of wood would have been allowed to break bread with them. Individual life after death he found difficult to believe in too. He could never understand where all the dead could be, and such messages as purported to come from them were so childish and vague when they described the life beyond the Styx, that his reason pronounced them unconvincing. And yet, did the dead live, he found it easy to suppose that some of them would have the power of communication; and some of the living, power to receive messages. Assuredly life after death couldn't be counted on, and perhaps that was just as well, if the powers who ordered this life on earth were responsible for the second life also.

"I'm sorry, Maud, we can't eat," Trix said after they had both failed at the supper-table.

"Happen you'll have a cup o' coffee later on."

"Happen so," said Trix, trying to smile.

Maud cleared the table swiftly and Brierley sat fiddling with a cigarette. When they were alone and sitting on opposite sides of the fireplace, their approach to life knocked out of time by what they had seen, Trix said, feeling the silence heavy: "How do you like being a millowner?"

"You should see the mill," he said drily. "Ought to have the old-age pension."

"Is it paying?"

"I'd never have believed it, but it is."

"Must be the old Houghton blood in you coming out." Her eyes were smiling now.

"Just luck; I daresay. But I had the sense to take on the

old manager. He knows his job. And then the play helped—
this way. The papers wrote bits about me becoming a millowner. When I went on 'Change at Burnham men who were
curious—some of them had seen the play—talked to me and
gave me orders. We can weave cloth a bit lower in price than
most; we've got as much work as we want."

After a moment he said: "But that's enough about me.
What's . . ."

"No, it isn't, Harry. I don't know anything about you.
If you thought it wouldn't pay, why did you take it?"

"Do you really want to know?"

"Yes." She leaned forward, her face cupped in her hands,
and he leaned forward also so that their faces were only two
feet apart. But the tension was too great. He leaned back
again.

"I thought it was my job to try and provide some work."
He spoke slowly, explaining. "There's nobody I could say
this to but you. Having that money has worried me to death
—the whole boom was crazy of course. We've been paying
for it ever since—that and other things. And the workpeople
have suffered most, as they usually do. Well, if I lost what bit
I had in giving somebody a job—" His eyes were bright and
fixed on hers.

She laughed a little uneasily. "And you can't get rid of
it."

"No. It's funny. I pay them I suppose a shilling or two a
week on the average more than most weavers get, but that
seems to be profitable, too. Those old looms fairly shout a
song of labour—smashing and clattering along till you'd
think they'd tumble in pieces. You've no idea what people
these weavers are. I'm not fit to clean their boots. I've had
men and women coming to me offering to buy the chance to
work—because that's what it amounts to—offering to buy
shares in the factory—ten pounds, fifteen pounds, twenty

deserved it. I've never been sorry for it. But if I'd killed him, I shouldn't be sitting here, should I? You wouldn't have loved me then—a convict, I suppose."

"Nonsense."

"But you wouldn't, Harry." She added, without thinking it out: "You'd have married Mary Houghton, perhaps."

"Perhaps fiddlesticks," he said flushing. But she didn't notice it. She was looking in the fire.

"Have you worked life out, Harry, rules and that?"

"I'm all fits and starts. I've a rough belief that you pay on earth for what you do amiss. I've a notion that a lot of people ought to be jumped on with both feet and that most of us are too cowardly to do it. I'm on the side of the 'have-nowts' against the 'haves'—being one of the 'have-nowts' myself. I hope I shan't change if I ever grow well-off but I can't be sure. I've got a troublesome knack of thinking of Housman's poem where he says:

> *The laws of God, the laws of man;*
> *He may keep that will and can;*
> *Not I;*

I'll bet he's a lot to answer for."

"I should have thought you were enough of a rebel."

"Not half enough." He sighed. "If you want to believe, you'll believe, and if you don't want to . . . The religious would say, no doubt, that God is within us all—that still, small voice of conscience—and why look on the outside for it? And why should you and I expect to solve the riddle that man has been worrying his head over since soon after he took breath? A Cornish mining engineer once told me that in a native compound in North-West Australia—a place where no Christian missionary had ever penetrated—the natives had carved on shells the story of the Garden of Eden.

pounds. Aye, they've told me they'd pawn their furniture to do it. Some mills have taken the money too; made it a condition of giving 'em a job. With shares worth not tuppence. And the wages they've earned have often enough been less than the dole. But they'd rather work for less than the dole, some of 'em, than not work at all." He stood there impassioned, glaring at Trix as though she had been challenging him. "The right to work," he said; "I've never known what it meant till lately. I've seen it on banners. It's right though. It's something worth fighting for. There's an apotheosis of work now. Men'll fall down and worship it. It wouldn't surprise me if men set up models of factories and ships and ploughshares and coal-pits and blast-furnaces and fell down and worshipped them, as men once worshipped the Golden Calf."

"Harry, you shouldn't get so excited." Trix didn't like it. It reminded her of Hyde Park Corner.

"It's time somebody got excited."

"There's always been poor people," she said. "Look at mother." They were both quiet again. She said, with the eternal conservatism of women, fighting for their own, "If you give all you've got, it'll make no difference. There's plenty like Josh too. They're not all saints because they work in pits and factories."

"I know that, but—"

"Hush, luv," she said, just as her mother might have done. Brierley sank down on the rug and took her hand and pressed it to his cheek and kissed it. Holding it, he said: "You've not told me what your next part is going to be."

"Perhaps there's not going to be one," she said.

"Rot. I expect half the managers in London are after you."

"They've a funny way of going about it if they are. Do you know, Harry, I've not had a single job offered to me?"

"You will have—lots." He could never understand why everybody didn't love and seek those he loved.

"I don't mind—not just now. I thought I should have had fits. P'raps I shall later on, if nothing crops up. Maybe I shall need that play you talked of. You've not stopped writing, have you?"

He nodded, as he crouched staring into the fire.

"Why?"

"I got fed up. I found I was so busy living the lives of other people I'd no time to live my own."

"Was it my fault you stopped?"

But he disappointed her.

"I don't think so." He looked up at her and saw she didn't like that and then added: "I daresay it was, though."

"You're just buttering me up."

"No, I'm not."

"Yes, you are. But go on. I like it."

"Well," he said, no longer strained and feeling content, "I think you're the loveliest woman I've ever seen. Will that do?"

"Not bad," she said. "You can go on."

He knelt upright and put his arms about her so that his hard chest felt her softly moving against him, and kissed her.

"When are you going to marry me?" he asked, his lips lightly brushing hers after the kiss was ended.

She pushed her head back and looked downwards at him from beneath her lashes.

"Whenever that's said to me I always reply, 'I've not been axed yet.'"

"I'm asking you, you beezum," he said.

She didn't answer.

He shook her gently. "You belong to me. Don't you know that?"

Suddenly he saw that the dark line of eye he was glistening. "Darling, what is it?" And though women—talk about changing as fast as the weath

She said: "You don't know about London, and I

"I don't want to know."

She kissed him on the cheek and pushed him gen She said—and again he was astonished at her w "We're both excited and overwrought, with not se another for so long and through my mother being as

"Those things don't affect me," he said; but ev he said it, he knew he was wrong.

"Harry."

"Yes?"

"Go and sit over there. I want to talk to you—and talk quietly with you—with you so near to me."

Pleased, he went and sat in his chair again.

"Do you believe in God?"

"I don't know. Do you?"

"I should like to—with mother as she is."

"I know. But it isn't any use—not like that—it off."

"Do we live after death?"

"Some part of us maybe. Our thoughts. I don't k I'm very vague about it. I don't think you and I live a and I, but there are places—I found it in Cambridge on there seemed such repose and serenity in some of the co grounds; and if buildings can hold an atmosphere like I think sometimes there must be something in immortali

"It's hard to know what sin is if you don't believ God."

"Yes."

"I've often wondered—when I was in London I mean suppose parsons know. I once nearly killed Josh. I never t you. He hit mother—and I threw the flat-iron at him. I

There was the apple-tree and its fruit and there was the serpent. This story was the reason, they said, why there were not gods any more. You and I may say that proves the Old Testament is no loftier than fairy-tales told by savages, but others may reply on the contrary that it proves that God has made Himself felt in all races and at all times." He turned to Trix. "But what matters to me, darling, is that I am in the same boat as you—I should like to be a devout Christian believing everything blindly. 'Lay thy burden upon the Lord and He will sustain thee.' It would make life so much easier. But I can't achieve that. Yet people a vast deal more intelligent than we are, have achieved it."

Trix said: "If I were a Salvation Army captain, I believe I could convert you."

"If God enlisted missionaries as beautiful as you, there's no telling what might happen. He must be disappointed sometimes to see how plain His servants are." He stopped and smiled. "Don't you think I've been good long enough?" He held out his hand for hers and when she gave it to him, he kissed her fingers.

"But we haven't reached anywhere," she said.

"This far," he said. "We don't know what's to become of us—either on earth or in heaven. There's only one thing to do, adventure together."

"The blind leading—"

He stopped her with a kiss.

"If I married," she said, "I think I should like quiet and peace."

"I promise," he said. He took her hands and she rose and they stood together. He put his arms about her and looked down at her with deep pride.

"What is it Congreve says—let us be as strange as if we had been married a long time, and as well-bred as if we had never been married at all."

"Will you put me on four looms?" she asked, laughing into his eyes (this being a talked-of Lancashire reward for a woman who is loved by her overlooker).

"The whole bag o' tricks," he said fervently, feeling that life's purpose was not, after all, so obscure as he had thought.

· · · · · · · ·

At about this time Nurse Halloran was giving Mrs. Meadows morphia.

Chapter Eighteen

THE SALE of the Houghton Mills was the greatest sensation Chesterford had known; and Chesterford was becoming
inured to sensations. For Houghton's was none of your
flibberty-gibberty affairs. If Houghton's went, the Bank of
England might go. Sam Renshaw found in the news a
justification for his own downfall. "Tha sees, Harriet, mi
lass," he said, "tha sees." Sam didn't enlighten her on what
it was she saw but she had a vague notion that it was meant
to include a reason for having sojourned in Klondyke Street
and for George wandering the roads of England, and herself
rising at 6.30 every morning and Sam having cooked the
dinner for so long.

Harriet said: "We shouldn't be i' this house if it weren't
for Mr. Houghton. Tha forgets that. Tha ought to be
sorry."

"Who sez I'm noan sorry?"

"Tha doesn't sound so sorry," Harriet said.

Sam reflected that some folk seemed to have no natural
feelings at all; no humour. Weren't it natural to feel a funny
stirring inside you, a bit of elation, when you saw somebody
else come a cropper? This coming down a peg—there'd be
monny a pint drunk on t' strength of it.

The Bluebell spinning-mill and the Daffodil weaving-shed
shut down on a Saturday forenoon and Chesterford dis-

cussed the matter inside out that week-end. Houghton's was broke; Houghton's was sold to Thomas Blackburn for the price of a set of dobbyhorses; Houghton's would shortly re-open but folk would find automatic looms installed, and if anybody fancied they'd get their old four looms back they were mistaken; Houghton's was shut for an extraordinary stocktaking before launching out on new enterprises; Houghton's was shut because Miss Mary was "going into every-thing" preparatory to taking over the management; Houghton's was shut because Mr. Edward had had a nervous breakdown and wouldn't get better; Houghton's was in the hands of those accursed banks who owned half Lancashire and, rather than let it run and work itself round to a good position again, the banks were going to sell it up; Houghton's was shut because Mr. Edward and Mr. Philip had had a ter-rific quarrel and Mr. Edward had ordered Mr. Philip out of the house and said rather than allow him to succeed to the business, he would part with it first. In church and chapel porches, in smoke-rooms and vaults, in tram-cars and at street corners, in back-to-back houses on Treadle Bank and in square-fronted houses that sat down like battleships on Chesterford Edge, these various tales and rumours were told, contested, discounted, ridiculed and believed.

There were those who said Houghton's were the best employers Chesterford had ever had, that you always knew where you were with them, that Chesterford would never be the same again, that the secret instances of Mr. Edward's charity were legion but, Chesterford having an edge to its tongue, there were those also who asserted that Mr. Edward ought to consider himself lucky to have been *in a position* to send people to the seaside for the good of their health; and that far from being grateful to Houghton's, wasn't it they who had made Houghton's, and enabled them to be what they were? And wasn't it plain now that Houghton's weren't "much a pound" after all? And furthermore, who was it who was going to get it in the neck now more than anybody else? Wasn't it the workpeople, on successive generations of whose backs Houghton's had climbed to fame and fortune? Nevertheless, mightily articulate as the latter group were, they were outnumbered ten to one by the former.

The *Chesterford Courier* pointed out to Mr. Edward Houghton that its readers were agitatedly awaiting news of what was going to happen (managing to infer that all Houghton's workpeople read its pages), and asked him to inform them through its columns. Mr. Houghton replied in confidence that he had nothing to say at the moment and would communicate it when he had. Meanwhile seven hundred people went on the dole, and England took over the burden that Edward Houghton had been bearing too long. The afternoon cinemas did better business, a burst of painting and decorating began in quite half of the newly workless houses, dogs were washed, pigeons flown to a greater extent than hitherto, clog-irons and shoe-leather worn off in tramping the moors, and soon there wasn't a tap-washer wanting replacement in more than half a dozen out of all the houses that Houghton's former workpeople inhabited. And for seven hundred more people began that slow progress towards degradation and a wasting of body and spirit that became common throughout England in the next six or seven years. So much had world chaos, assisted by the late Mr. Timothy Hilditch, done for them.

It would have been more than difficult for Edward to tell the *Chesterford Courier* what was going to happen; for at that time he truly did not know. While the Liverpool and Burnham bank, and the St. Paul's Bank who, between them, may be said to have now become the firm of Houghton's were making up their minds what was best for them to do (not, naturally, in the interests of Houghton's or of the

workpeople of Houghton's, but of their own shareholders),
the factories were closed. This was three months after Hilditch's death.

Three months' respite had been granted to Time or Fate
or Mr. Gandhi or the controllers of the rupee and tael to
show whether Houghton's dared hope. But there had been
singularly little sign that they dared. The assertion made in
Lancashire with great conviction over many decades by those
prospering that there was "no longer any money in rags"
was indubitably true at last. Those three months cost the
banks several thousands of pounds and Edward a lot of sleep.

It was a morning in March, gusty and with a high wind
and wild broken sky, on which the sale began. Sam was there
early, but not, as scores of his former workmates were, for
entirely sentimental reasons. Sam had got work. Sam was
now, and had been for a month, a roast potato man. From
nine in the morning until eleven at night (and midnight on
Saturdays) Sam peregrinated Chesterford and neighbour-
ing grey towns such as Saddlebridge and, on occasion, the
magnificent Burnham itself, with his mobile contraption
drawn by Judith the black and tan pony. The contraption
christened "King of the Road" was of black ornamented
with brass which set off its high chimney (you might have
mistaken it at first sight for a model of Puffing Billy). Sam's
wages were twenty-four shillings a week and for an aristo-
cratic spinner who once took home eight pounds it was a
come-down and no mistake, but contrasted with being on the
parish or being kept by Harriet, it was living in Buckingham
Palace. "King of the Road" Sam felt was not an unfitting
name.

Posters of the sale which had disfigured the mill walls
and had been tucked away on obscure hoardings and stable
doors, so that you would have thought the very poor were
expected to be bidders, announced that the sale would begin

at 10.30 o'clock, that the mills would be offered as a going concern and that failing a satisfactory sale would then be disposed of in separate lots. Sam, who had read one of them, was tickled by the phrase "going concern."

"That's a bit good is that," he said to Harriet. "Goin' concern. Aye. Gone, I call it."

"I suppose tha'll be theer," she said coldly, as she "sided" the evening meal, while Judith and the "King of the Road" waited for Sam outside.

"I shall that. Trade'll be good. Aw t' women as han forgotten to cook t' dinner'll want their two pennorths."

"Aw t' men, tha means. I don't think tha ought to go, gloatin'."

"Gloatin'?"

"That's what I said."

"Nowt o' t' sort. It'll be a sort of entertainment—like whippet-racin' or t' pictures. Folk'll want to chew summat."

Esther bounced in and lolled up against him. "Can I have a prato?"

"She's not had her tea five minutes sin'," said Harriet. "Get up off your father."

"Only a ha'porth," wheedled Esther.

"I dunnot sell ha'porths," said Sam twiddling her plaits.

"Oh, what a story! You sold a ha'porth to Tilly Bradshaw last Sat'dy."

"Heh, these women," said Sam, simulating a groan and getting up and wagging his head and going off to the cart. "Dost want any salt wi' it?"

"Course. A big 'un," she cried, coming to the door to watch him.

After Esther had bounced off, leaping like a young colt, Harriet said: "A lot o' use me tryin' to do owt, an' thee spoilin' 'em aw t' time," and Sam as he walked Judith off down the rutted unpaved road thought: "If oo doesn't get better tempered soon, we'st ha' to ha' another child. Oo's ne'er reet unless oo's carryin' one. A pity she weren't catched, after aw."

Sam recalled that thought as he trundled off to the Bluebell mill on the morning of the sale, for she had been "at him" again. It was a strange thing how, now that he was behaving himself, Harriet should be "pots for rags" so often. Happen this weaving was too much for her. Happen they were both getting on a bit. His own hair was getting dry and grey and he could glance at a pretty wench now without turning round or thinking much about her.

"Hi, Sam, off to t' funeral-like?"

"Funeral?"

"Aye, Houghton's."

Tom Edmunds crossed Ogden Street and walked along with Sam. "Art 'avin' a front seat, like? Or art i' charge o' t' bar?"

Sam didn't answer that. "Wheer's tha left t' babby?" he asked. "Nay, don't pretend tha doesn't know. It's thy reg'lar job, isn't it, to tak' it out every mornin' while thy missis goes to t' cardroom?" For Tom, to Sam's secret joy, was now out of work also and was one of the "pram-wheeling brigade." Sam was acquiring skill in banter since he had become a salesman. "I do everythin'," he was wont to say, "buyer, manufacturer, salesman. No middle mon about this job."

The mill gates were open and Sam, after a moment's hesitation, drove Judith inside. The old watchman, Michael Kane, was crossing the yard.

"Aw reet comin' in, Michael?"

"Phwats's that ye've got there? Is it an incinerator ye've brought for the ragtag and bobtail I see comin' in at the gate? By the Holy Mother o' God, ye'd think 'twas the 'wakes' we was havin' here. Coffee an' cakes an' tripe an' the like o' that. Is it stoppin' outside ye are?"

"This dam' machine winna go *in*side, will it?" asked Sam
ironically. "An' talkin' about a 'wakes,' that's what you call
'em i' Dublin, isn't it—buryin's? How long's it goin' on?"

Michael put up his three fingers.

"Three hours?"

"Days," cried Michael staring wildly at the incoming
crowd, "three days to mortify my sinful soul, unless 'tis
bought outright. And there's as much chance o' that as
there is o' Michael Kane flyin' sthraight to the bosom o'
the Virgin Mary." Michael crossed the yard with his stiff,
rapid walk, eyeing the incomers as though they'd been car-
rion.

"A pretty tidy turn-up," said Sam judicially, serving a
stout woman, who wore two underskirts, with a pennyworth
on her way in. "How are yo' doin', missis?"

"Heh," she said, "it's a feast at week-end an' a famine at
after, like a lot more."

As Sam said, it was a pretty tidy turn-up. He had shouted
"How do?" to a score or more—folk who had worked at
Houghton's anything from two to forty years; he had
nodded to Luke Hargreaves and his wife who, however,
hadn't seen him, he had picked out Henry Brierley and Trix
and thought: "By gow, but he's a lucky chap," he had raised
his hat with a strange feeling in his throat to Mr. Edward
and Miss Mary and noticed how pale and fixed Mr. Edward's face was and how Miss Mary looked neither to right
nor left, and he had said to Judith, as he stood and stroked
her, that: "T' lads han put their Sunday best on for t' job,"
for there were spinners and beamers there wearing bowler
hats and stiff collars and raincoats so that they were hardly
to be distinguished from metal-brokers and buyers of machinery from concerns up and down Lancashire. By the time
the crowd had entered the mill, over a dozen motor-cars

were parked in the yard, from a Rolls-Royce and a Bentley down to Jowetts and Austin Sevens; and by them were a higgledy-piggledy array of bassinettes and go-carts; for the precocious young of Chesterford are introduced to life everywhere, from the vaults of the Three Jolly Carters to lectures on manures for allotments at the Free Library, and are in the streets from early morning until All Saints Church shows on its dirty yellow dial an hour approaching midnight.

The yard being now deserted and Judith, under her leather apron, disposed to resume her meditations with her muzzle a foot from the ground, Sam, admonishing her not to indule in any funny tricks while he was away, tied the reins to a drain-water pipe, and went inside.

·   ·   ·   ·   ·   ·   ·   ·

Mary and her father went to the sale of Houghton's mills, as to a challenge flung at their honour. They knew their presence would serve no useful purpose, that the scene would hurt them intolerably, that its memory would never leave their minds. But it did not occur to them to evade it. Edward, indeed, went almost gladly, as a man to his just punishment. He had an inchoate belief that this height of suffering would assuage the pain that was deep within him, that what came after would be easier to bear. As for Mary, she seemed to endure as much pain as her father. Phœbe did not; Philip did not. Phœbe's sadness was relieved by the prospect of dwelling in the more gracious south; Philip's by the fact that the issue between him and his father of his part in Houghton's was now disposed of inexorably—nobody could raise it again; no slur could be cast on him. But for Mary it was as if she were in very truth part of her father's flesh bearing all he bore. Perhaps she was attuned to him the more by her own secret suffering of which none knew—her knowledge that Brierley and Trix would soon be married. She had felt in her bones that it would come to this, she told herself that, had she wished to marry him, Edward and Phœbe would have been distressed immeasurably, she reminded herself that her people were not his people nor her habits and outlook his, but she knew now, when it became certain that she could never belong to him, or turn to him with her sorrows and her triumphs, or comfort him in his moments when the world proved too much for him and overbore him, that she loved him. Now that he was lost she could make that admission to herself. She saw him now as a cord that had stretched between her and the life she hoped for, almost as a cord that is between a newly born child and its mother, and she wondered how she would live now it was severed.

.   .   .   .

Edward and Mary arrived at the mill a few minutes before half past ten and made their way to Edward's private office. He walked slowly, as a man who is recovering from illness. He had dressed himself with care—a dark-grey overcoat, stiff white collar, black bowler hat, black boots polished like enamel. His nose, Mary thought, was rapidly growing sharper, his nostrils still more fine. His hair was longer than usual and it curled over his ears as that of sick men often does, and his blue eyes were filmed with thought. Mary walked with him, her arm through his, putting her feet down firmly, noticing with a disturbing emotion that Edward was inclined to shuffle a little. From the day they had returned from London he had grown more quiet; the whole house brooded. Edward had flogged himself into an energetic mood to meet his bankers or lawyers from time to time, only to relapse swiftly as soon as the ordeal was over. Once or twice he rode with Mary on the moor, striving, she could see, to capture his old joy in the sharp wind, the cry of peewits, the whirr of a startled grouse, but his untroubled moments were as fleeting as December sunlight.

He had spoken in some detail to Philip. Philip and Evelyn had driven over to dinner and afterwards Edward had taken Philip into his study. The meeting was trying, Philip at first resentful, convinced that life had now cheated him not only by inflicting his wounds on him but by robbing him of the better part of his social position and security, and yet finding in the situation a twisted, malicious satisfaction in the knowledge that he wasn't alone in shortcomings and that the firm of Houghton's, that had been alien to him and, as it were, subjugated him, was now toppling. To his father's statement, half explanation, half apology, he didn't know what to say. He wished Edward had been unrelenting, had thrown responsibility for what had happened on to the world situation, as he did and as others such as Luke and Elizabeth Hargreaves did. (Elizabeth picturesquely said it all came o' treatin' niggers like spoiled childer—lettin' 'em have all their own road when they didn't know what was good for 'em. Might as well let a child please itself whether it took spring medicine or not. If they didn't buy the goods they needed from us, they ought to be made to. She went on to say that Liberalism was soft and the British Empire hadn't been built up on it. We'd made these niggers' lives worth livin' and now they were turnin' their backs on us and puttin' us in t' workhouse.)

Philip had only one question—how much would be saved from the crash, if anything? Edward said he doubted if anything would. Phœbe had her own income from her marriage settlement and what he had invested in her name in the good trade years since; Mary had her £500 a year secured to her also.

"I've spoken to your mother. We shall live quietly some-where on a good deal less than there'll be. We shall allow you and Evelyn four hundred and with your pension and what you'll earn, I hope you'll manage."

Philip said: "I won't take it unless I must." He stood leaning on the mantelpiece, looking down at the fire and chewing the side of his bottom lip. He had prepared himself for something far worse than this. "I expect I'll have to take the money for a bit. You know, father, I believe at bottom it's largely my fault. If I'd buckled to in the firm, you wouldn't have taken those chances—not anyhow to such a degree. . . ."

Edward managed to say: "Don't reproach yourself."

Philip went on: "Met two of the battalion chaps to-day —Jones and Parkinson—cardroom men, if you remember. They seemed to be much more upset about us than them-selves. 'Oh, we're getting the dole,' they said. 'We shall manage.' Then Jack Parkinson said: 'I reckon it's the war really. We've never got over it.' "

Edward, deeply moved, had said, trying to hide it: "A cynic might say—'If the son hadn't lost his arm and his father hadn't lost his head . . .' "

Philip had felt his father's hand on his shoulder. The grip was very tight.

.   .   .   .

Edward sat down slowly in his leather armchair at his desk and laid his hat on the table and wiped his forehead. It was a cold day but his forehead was moist. His hands were moist also. "Anxiety complex," the doctor had called it. "Funk," Edward had answered more shortly. He, no more than his work-people, had a use for wrapping things up.

Edward looked up at Mary and smiled at her and she

smiled back. Never had their faces looked more alike, the same creased dark blue eyes gazing fondly at one another, the same troubled expression in them when the glance was turned elsewhere. Before she had met Brierley she had thought she could never fall in love unless by a miracle her father was duplicated. "Are we wise to come, darling?" she asked.

He shook his head. "Not wise, dear; but we'll look it in the face. I shall be more content." After a moment he said: "Has it occurred to you we never staged at the Repertory a more dramatic thing than this? Though no doubt," he added, "It'll be drab enough. It's these writing fellows who make things exciting and coloured. I daresay King Lear never suspected what a figure of tragedy he was."

Mary looked out through a side window towards the gate. "There's nobody coming in now. The man with the roasted potatoes is tying up his pony."

The mahogany clock on the mantelpiece chimed the half-hour musically. Edward looked round at it. "Your mother gave me that; insisted on the office being civilised. Flowers, too. Different from my father's day. Softer, folks would say. Come, my dear."

There was a momentary hush when they walked arm in arm into the cloth warehouse where the auction was to begin. A handful of Windsor chairs had been placed on the left of the auctioneer's portable dais. To these Edward moved, nodding his head in a series of jerks to the greetings that fell about them from all sides: "Mornin', sir"; "Mornin', Mr. 'Oughton"; "Mornin', Miss Mary." "Keep yer hearts up, sir," and, " 'Oughton's is noan finished yet," were called out from the rear.

Luke and Elizabeth Hargreaves hurried forward.

"Glad to see you, Elizabeth," said Edward, shaking hands. "How are you, Luke?"

"Not so bad," said Luke glaring round at the crowd, taking his cap off its precarious perch on his head and putting it on again no more securely. "I notice t' vultures have honoured us," he said grimly.

"We've got to expect it," said Edward seating himself and holding his bowler on his knee. "Ah, Brierley, I hope you'll find a bargain." He beckoned him nearer. "If somebody must run my looms I'd liefer you than most."

"I don't know that I came to buy, sir." Brierley was not enjoying the eyes on him. "I'm here hoping to see the place taken over as a whole." Edward shook hands with Trix. "I was very sorry to hear from Mary about your mother," he said, thinking how handsome Trix looked in mourning. Mary smiled at her and motioned her to a chair. On the other side sat Elizabeth Hargreaves.

Mary, knowing the effort her father was making, pressed his arm proudly and secretly and smiled sidelong at him, and Edward smiled back.

Mr. Ernest Baxendale, the auctioneer, stepped down from his dais, where he was arranging papers, and approached Edward.

"Do you think we might begin, sir?" Mary noted his waved iron-grey hair, his horn-rimmed pince-nez, his spats, and thought: "We're to be polished off efficiently, then," having caught a little of her father's acted nonchalance.

Edward said with a grave smile: "I'm only a spectator, Mr. Baxendale. It's as you wish." His eyes left Baxendale and moved among the crowd. Thomas Blackburn was there, his stubbly grey hair standing up in spikes, his florid face sunk deep in his horsy collar; Major Henderson had come, immaculate, to see the mills that he had failed to buy go under the hammer; there were shabby men in red-silk neckerchiefs, scores of operatives whose faces were familiar to Edward from long years of service in his spinning-rooms and weaving-sheds, tacklers whose adventures with women operatives had caused him anxiety sometimes, spinners he had admonished for dealing in football coupons, Miss Rolleston, Luke's secretary, with whom he had heard Philip was too friendly, there in the forefront furtively taking a lace pocket-handkerchief to her eyes.

Baxendale was on his dais, rapping sharply with his hammer for silence. Silence fell. Michael Kane came through the swing-door at the rear and stood there glowering while the swing-door rocketed to and fro before it became still.

"Ladies and gentlemen," Baxendale began. Then he paused. He had stayed up late the previous night preparing this speech. This was the most important sale he had undertaken. This was his opportunity. "Ladies and gentlemen," he said, once more. "This is for all of us a melancholy occasion."

Elizabeth Hargreaves said under her breath: "Liar to start with."

Baxendale passed his hand over his waved hair and resumed:

"Never in my long experience has it fallen to my lot to officiate at a more important, a more historic, a more tragical sale than this." He paused and the reporter from the *Chesterford Courier,* who could go much faster than this, looked up expectantly.

"You all know, ladies and gentlemen, what a proud name is that of Houghton, not only in Chesterford but in Lancashire and, indeed, throughout the world."

"We do an' all," said a voice from the back.

Thus encouraged, Mr. Baxendale took off and put on his pince-nez and went on: "Cotton spun and woven in this historic mill has carried the fame of England to the wide-flung—er—Empire" (" 'Ear, 'ear.").

Miss Rolleston dabbed her eyes and the reporter from the

Courner observing her, made a note: "TEARS," and under-
lined it; and Sam Renshaw at the back, feeling the silence
was long added, "Aye, that's reet."

"Every one of us must be profoundly grieved at this new
evidence of Lancashire's unavailing struggle against economic forces too strong for her" ("Except thee," said Elizabeth Hargreaves, not quite as completely under her breath
as before).

Edward glanced sideways at Mary and heaved a deep
sigh. This was worse than he had looked for.

"Get on, mister," said a buxom woman, her hands folded
beneath her apron.

"How can we," asked Baxendale, with immense energy,
"make this occasion less sorrowful for Chesterford than it
is bound otherwise to be?" He looked round expectantly.
"I imagine you know what I am going to say. Ladies and
gentlemen, it is by one of you coming forward boldly and
buying this famous concern of Houghton's outright." There
wasn't a sound.

"That is what I propose first of all to do—to offer the
mills and machinery in one lot—forty-two thousand spindles
and sixteen hundred looms in grand condition in premises
conveniently situated, as you are all well aware, and in buildings thoroughly up to date. You have seen the catalogue of
sale, gentlemen. I will ask you for your bids." And Mr.
Baxendale leaned forward on his dais and allowed his rov-
ing eye to wander over the mixed assembly before him.

There was no response and Edward uncrossed his legs and
crossed them again. Edward had not expected there would
be an offer, but he had lived in hopes. Some dignity at all
events would be saved if the premises and machinery did not
fall piecemeal.

"I do not need to tell you," Baxendale resumed when this
first appeal failed, "that there were seven hundred people

employed in these mills, that their livelihood depends on work being resumed. If anybody is hesitating whether or not to come forward and re-start a business that must, I venture to say, succeed when Lancashire takes, as I hope she soon will, her rightful place once more as the leading industrial county of England, and therefore of the world, let him remember these seven hundred fellow townsmen and women deprived through no fault of their own of the work they did so well." Edward winced at this unconscious thrust of Mr. Baxendale's and Thomas Blackburn took snuff audibly.

"I await your bids, gentlemen."

The crowd shifted uneasily, feeling somebody really ought to do something. Men looked at one another.

"I hope, gentlemen, you are not going to force me to record that Houghton's didn't receive a solitary bid. Come, gentlemen, come!"

Edward who felt that he was himself being humiliated and scorned turned to Mary and whispered partly to her and partly to himself: "For Heaven's sake, let him shut up."

"It's a shame," said a voice at the back and a woman, more shrill answered: "It is for sure." But shame or not, it was a fact. There wasn't a bid for the firm whose name was as well known in Calcutta and Hong Kong as in Burnham.

"Then," said Mr. Baxendale, his oratorical flights at an end, "I am compelled by the conditions of sale to proceed lot by lot. The first lot, gentlemen"—he no longer bothered to add the ladies as possible buyers—"is the furniture of the private office—the handsome mahogany table inlaid with leather, and including bronze ink-well—"

Edward rose. This was the first of seventeen hundred lots in the spinning-mill alone. There was no more to be done. The sale would occupy several days. Luke and Elizabeth Hargreaves lingered on. Luke had risen when Edward did but Elizabeth pulled him back into his seat. "They'll not want us botherin' 'em," she said.

The merely curious began to drift out at the back and Sam returned to Judith. "Roast p'ratoes, all hot," he called. A handful of people gathered round. Sam listened to the conversation as he doled out pennyworths:

"I see t' smashers-up are yon," said Tom Edmunds. "Happen we'st get a job wi' t' sledge-hammers . . .

"I remember t' time when t' *Courier* had two full pages o' jobs in India advertised. Tha could go an' be a fettler out i' Bombay—aye an' ha' as many piccaninnies as tha liked . . .

"Aye, there's better looms bein' smashed up than some o' them as is runnin'. What about ours—fifty year owd if they're a day . . ."

"Our Willie? He's proper poorly t' lad is. But any road it saves his boots. I were plagued to death to know how I were goin' to get 'em mended. . . ."

"I see 'em goin' i' their fur coats to draw t' dole an' they're off to Blackpool every 'oliday . . ."

"Blackpool be jiggered. Why, dost know what *I* live on? I buys a peck o' p'ratoes and a dozen o' oatmeal an' that's aw I get. I'm freetened to death I'st slip down t' rat-holes. Cat's had me on t' doormat twice this week . . ."

"Aye, an' when things gets better, he said, it'll be automatic looms for our firm, he said. I said: 'That's no bloody good to us.' 'Naw,' he said, 'I know it isn't . . .' "

.   .   .   .

As Mary's two-seater Vauxhall climbed Hilford Lane she turned momentarily to her father and then, looking ahead again, pressed his hand.

"What are you thinking, darling?"

"I was thinking," he said, "that it's a legal offence to strand a theatrical company."

"Don't, darling."

Hilford Lane suddenly became blurred.

Chapter Nineteen

ON THE DAY when it was decided that they should leave Chesterford on the morrow Mary was filled with a great restlessness. She wandered from room to room. She stood looking out over the moors that rose greyly behind the house, and down at Chesterford with its tall chimneys piled in tiers, in groups, in ones and twos, scattered as though a careless hand had dribbled them out. Fifty or more would never again fly that pennant of trade, a curl of drifting smoke. The factories were idle or derelict, their machinery taken out and either smashed up or sold abroad and the buildings given over to minor and various trades which were no more indigenous to Chesterford than to London or Glasgow. She thought of that with a sorrowful heart.

After dinner she went to her room and stood looking down at the spangled lights of the town and on an impulse put on her fur coat and brown close-fitting hat, changed her shoes and took a stick and, telling her father she was going for a short walk, set out. This was her good-bye.

The night was crisp with a late spring frost and the earthen path in Hilford Lane crunched a little beneath her feet. Below her Chesterford was picked out with lights that were dimmed by smoke and by the grim masses of buildings —enormous hulks of brick and stone where no lights shone and above which the chimneys rose as black lines drawn up-

wards towards the stars. Nobody was moving in the lane
and the sounds of the town rose to her vividly—the sharp
clang of Werewood Forge on the way to Burnham and the
upward shoot of a tongue of flame from its squat stack; a
train coughed out of the station towards the Yorkshire
border at Bridgeworth; a roundabout on Barfields fairground was grinding out a skirling tune on its steam pipe
organ with high emphasis from cymbals and drum. But there
were spaces of quiet too, and into them a dog would bark
from the dairy farm on her left or a whistle, like a police
whistle, would shrill out from those dark streets she was now
approaching. In that hideous mass below lived scores of people she knew but now they all seemed remote from her and
mysterious. Chesterford was as a slumbering ugly giant,
sinister, primeval and imponderable. She drew her coat
tighter about her, and walked faster. Once into the lighted
thoroughfares, she grew more cheerful. It was curious how
ordinary life seemed, how everybody was knocking about
normally, how busy they were. Lancashire might be as a
clock that was running down but it would take a long time.
There was one street corner she passed, Myrtle Street,
whence you could throw a stone, it was said, into five of the
derelict fifty mills—but a hundred and thirty mills, she was
aware, were still working even if the hours were short, and
yarn and cloth being manufactured often at a loss and wages
so poor that half the weavers would have been better off
queueing up for the dole. Uncle John had asked ironically
how long it would be ere the county became mainly agricul-
tural again and Edward had been wondering whether three
or four acres to farm in Hampshire (where Phœbe's people
came from) would not afford him the occupation he would
need.

  She could see only one solution for herself also—that of

work. She saw plainly that her joy and zest in the Repertory Theatre had existed not simply because she loved the stage but because she was busy there, using her mind and hands, rubbing shoulders with people hurrying to and fro with an end in view and driven by ambition or need of money or joy in their craft. Her mind went back to the days when she had envied the mill girls and their lads who took them on the moor and to the cinema. The need for labour, she now saw, was stirring in her then. Labour and love. They were the two great things in life. The one she had possessed and lost; the other she had and must now strive to renounce. For she was too proud and to resilient to lay herself aside. The ache, perhaps, would ease. Who was it said the normal person had three loves in her life? And this was her first and, unconsummated by so much as a kiss, was it a love at all? In an instant she was pierced again as her mind flew to Trix in Brierley's arms. But she must conquer it, conquer it. Yes, she knew in her bones she would do that. She thought of those Houghtons who looked down from the walls of the Council Chamber of the Town Hall, John, square-jawed, side-whiskered with Roman nose; Humphrey, light, dashing with the eye and brow of a poet; and the arrogance that rarely moved in her, began to stir. She welcomed it; family counted, blood told. There was something there to lean upon. In that moment she had a vision that it was from her womb that Houghton's would rise again and make their name lofty in men's sight. Not in Chesterford, maybe, but in the more gracious south. But she did not truly want that. She would leave Chesterford but she would return again. Houghton's was Chesterford and Chesterford was Houghton's. Yes, that was arrogant enough, but wasn't it true?

A small light was burning above the Wayside Pulpit in Ogden Street. She read:

Let nothing disturb thee,
Nothing affright thee,
Everything passes,
God is unchanging,
He who has patience,
Everything comes to him;
He who has God,
He lacks for nothing—
God, only, suffices.

Everything passes. Oh, but she didn't want everything
to pass, she wanted to keep it and hide it and bury it within
her; this love, this lover she had been denied. She was
trembling a little. How swiftly she was stirred again. She
must be firmer, firmer. She walked on and on, past the stalls
on the market-place where vendors of pots and second-hand
clothes and sweets and fruit were doing a desultory trade.
She saw the roast-potato man who had been at the sale and
she watched him for a moment leaning against the shaft
and pulling gently at his pony's mane. A woman in a black
jacket and an old blue velvet hat that looked a trifle too
small brought him a thermos flask of tea and stood talking to him. After a moment she recognised her as Mrs.
Renshaw. Mary stood a little further off but she could still
hear.

"It's t' best cup o 'tay i' Chesterford, is this," he said,
blowing on it in its metal cup.

"How are yo' doin', Sam?"

"Reight up to t' mark, lass, to-neet," he said, putting his
arm round her shoulder and giving her a hug that dislodged
the blue hat a little so that she had to straighten it.

"Stop thy foolin', lad," she said, but Mary could see
she was smiling.

"I've been thinkin' like," he said.

"Oh?"

"Aye—that letter from George this mornin', sayin' he's comin' whoam. Well—I've never towd thee but owd Isaac as owns this here"—he indicated the "King of the Road"—"he's gettin' on an' I think he'd sell. He's getten two."

"Well?" she said.

"Well, if I had one and George had t' other we should be set up, shouldn't we?"

"If pigs had wings," she said.

"Aye, but listen here. I've an idea wheer I can get t' brass. Tom Blackburn coom past this mornin' an' . . ."

Mary thought it was time she was going; it was almost eavesdropping. She liked the look of Mrs. Renshaw—a lively sort of dignity about her, a fine long nose. Mary walked on, pausing to look at the flaring vermilion and yellow hoardings outside the Theatre Royal that was now a picture palace, having her eyes captured by gable ends advertising patent medicines and startling fiction in penny periodicals, and her nose by fish-and-chip saloons. And as she walked and heard snatches of the homely, racy speech and was spoken to by here and there a man who had worked at Houghton's and who, rather shyly, lifted the neb of his cap half an inch as he said, "Good neet, miss," and pulled it then still further on as though regretting this ostentation, or by a woman who had been a patient in the Houghton ward at the Royal Hospital and remembered her visits and smiled gratefully at her in the lamplight, or by somebody who had regularly gone to the Repertory Theatre and shared her joy in a good play—as this warm tide of humanity flowed about her, her heart was lifted up.

It was ten o'clock. She turned towards Chesterford Edge again and saw the string of lights rising before her as though the heavens had laid a crooked line of stars there; and as she walked up the rising ground she was as one who has passed through tumult and gained a measure of peace.

February 19th, 1933—January 18th, 1934.

A NOTE ON THE TYPE IN
WHICH THIS BOOK IS SET

This book is set on the linotype in Caslon, so called after William Caslon (1692–1766), the first of a famous English family of type-designers and founders. He was originally an apprentice to an engraver of gun-locks and gun-barrels in London. In 1716 he opened his own shop, for silver-chasing and making bookbinders' stamps. The printers John Watts and William Bowyer, admirers of his skill in cutting ornaments and letters, advanced him money to equip himself for type-founding, which he began in 1720. The fonts he cut in 1722 for Bowyer's sumptuous folio edition of John Selden, published in 1726, excited great interest. A specimen sheet of type faces, issued in 1734, made Caslon's superiority to all other letter-cutters of the time, English or Dutch, quickly recognized, and soon his types, or types modelled on his style, were being used by most English printers, supplanting the Dutch types that had formerly prevailed. In style Caslon was a reversion to earlier type styles. Its characteristics are remarkable regularity and symmetry, as well as beauty in the shape and proportion of the letters; its general effect is clear and open, but not weak or delicate. For uniformity, clearness, and readability it has perhaps never been surpassed. After Caslon's death his eldest son, also named William (1720–78), carried on the business successfully. Then followed a period of neglect of nearly fifty years. In 1843 Caslon type was revived by the then firm of Caslon for William Pickering and has since been one of the most widely used of all type designs in English and American printing.

THIS BOOK WAS COMPOSED, PRINTED, AND BOUND BY VAIL-BALLOU PRESS, INC., BINGHAMTON, N. Y. THE PAPER WAS MADE BY S. D. WARREN CO., BOSTON.

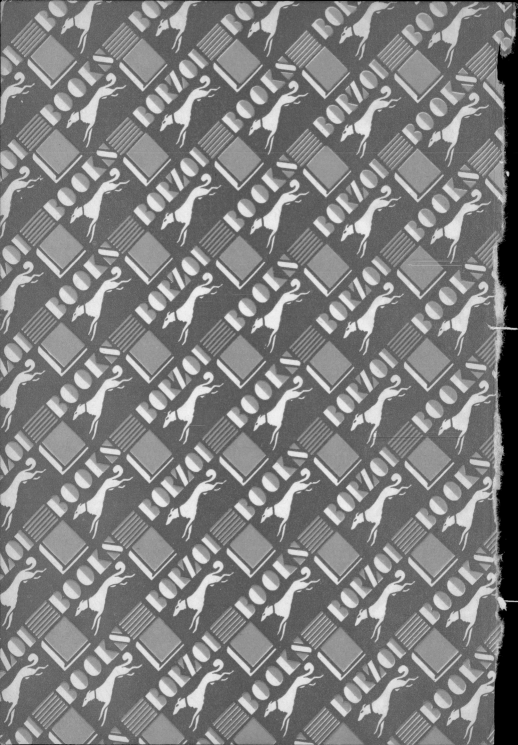